BETWEEN YOU ME and US

Other Books By Kate Smith

The Hamilton Series

Everything we Lost, **The Hamilton Series #1**
Everything for Love, **The Hamilton Series #2**
Never let you Fall, **The Hamilton Series #3**
Everything left Unsaid, **The Hamilton Series #4**
Everything we Dream, **The Hamilton Series #5**
Everything we Promised, **The Hamilton Series #6**

You Me & Us

Between You Me & Us, You Me & Us #1
Before You Me & Us, You Me & Us #2

BETWEEN YOU ME and US

KATE SMITH

PROLOGUE

Every day since my trip to Toronto to attend the Celebration of Happiness, my life had grown infinitely more complicated. I'd descended deep into this new sum total of my existence. Evading phone calls. Burying myself in busyness. Avoiding the embarrassment of justifications. I couldn't explain. Not to anyone; least of all myself.

Disappearing. Becoming the invisible woman. *Enticing.* If only I could accomplish complete anonymity. *Fade to black.*

Perspiration trickled down my back as I arched into the next pose, planting each foot with purpose, absorbing the faint burble of the diffuser and the light aroma of some supposedly uplifting and calming yoga blend.

What better way to escape responsibility and confrontation in the middle of the afternoon on a Thursday besides a yoga class? Except this room, packed with perspiring bodies wrapped in colourful spandex, made me feel even more exposed, rather than providing adequate cover.

Most of the city's residents should be locked in corporate battle or slaving for that all-important pay cheque. So why were all these yoga devotees crammed into this tiny room when all I craved was peace and a chance to replenish my reserves?

Get back to work, slackers.

The resident yogi frowned at my smothered giggle.

I bit my lip. Hard. It wasn't even funny. Don't even know how that snicker sneaked out. *Must be losing it.*

"Breathe, everyone. Slowly. Deeply," the yogi said. "In for five ..."

I took her advice and focussed on the gurgling diffuser with its light orange and patchouli scented mist. *In ... one ... two ...* Maybe that observation was directed at myself, anyway. Work was where I should be, and would be, if I hadn't begged for one of my rare personal days.

No argument came from the head pharmacist at the hospital. "Have a relaxing day, Amara. You deserve the break," she said, her soft words accompanied by a gentle smile. "After everything."

Huh. Everything. My lips twisted even as I pressed my flattened palms together, forming a rock-steady tree with the sole of my foot tucked inward against my leg. My distress over seeing Jake must be showing. Or the pain over my separation from Kyle. Or that looming fear of remaining forever alone at the ripe old age of nearing-thirty. Or maybe it was the relentless *tick-tock* as my biological clock revved, fuelled by a wedding and a pointless discussion about kids. Or my overall sense of doom. *My full smorgasbord of angst options served up for everyone's entertainment.*

On cue, I moved into mountain pose, pushing out the tiny bosom that accompanied my touch-too-thin athletic frame.

Perhaps I wasn't as level as I hoped, even when focussed on being the consummate professional. It seemed impossible to maintain that calm and collected external sereneness on the busiest and most stressful of days. Was I inadvertently projecting my turmoil far and wide? Maybe my colleagues rolled their eyes in the background as I mired myself in a funk.

"Lengthen those backs." Our yogi's gentle voice cut into my thoughts. "Breathe."

I opened my eyes, cringing at the intensity of her stare under arched eyebrows.

Ah. *In ... one ... two ...*

"And gently into warrior."

Jake. His refusal to cut this off. Reeling me in, begging forgiveness, apologizing, texting daily, imploring me to call him. Then he'd sent a heart-rending missive tucked inside the ridiculous kiss-up display of stargazer lilies. Lucky for him, I hadn't dumped the whole works into the nearest trash bin.

Ha. Never. The vibrant mass of delicate blossoms tugged the slender strings of my heart, transporting me to that long-ago night. Me, bending to Jake's emotional and masterful twist, sucked in by a bunch of stupid flowers.

"Loosen up." A soft tap on my wrist pulled me into the present. "Relax. Breathe."

I uncurled my fists one finger at a time and shook out my hands before stretching into the next pose. *In … one … two …*

Kyle. Sending me asinine, cryptic texts. No explanation. No I'm sorry. No nothing. Well, except for that "call me, we need to talk" nonsense.

Wiggling my jaw to ease the ache, I bowed into the next pose, all the while my gaze flitting left to right, right to left. *Could anyone hear my teeth grinding?*

"Focus," the yogi murmured as she sidled past.

Right. *In … one … two …*

Kyle, my not-so-lovely soon-to-be-ex-husband and his bold, "Why haven't you been to the lawyer yet?" A stellar question from a brilliant mind. It wasn't that I held any delusions. My marriage was kaput. Totalled. Irretrievably over. A fact I accepted. Welcomed, even. Yet my heart begged for rescue from underneath the crushing defeat, remaining raw, battered, and bruised.

"Clear your mind," came the whisper as the slim figure stole through our contorted bodies, all manifesting various renditions of an extended triangle. The gentle reminder could be for the whole class, but realistically, this was directed at me, as was her benevolent expression.

Right. *In … one … two …* Clear the energy. Reframe the thoughts. So many good intentions, but the unforgotten, unforgiven men from my former life skulked through my reflections, clouding me in a dense fog. Faithless men whose volley of strategic and crippling body punches sent me reeling.

I sucked for breath, searching for my sacred mantra, but finding only a dull echo. Never enough. Unlovable and unloved. Unappreciated. Irretrievably broken and bent. Beyond redemption. Or worse; over-analytical hot mess.

The counters to these floated into my mind. Okay as I am. Loved. Strong and independent. Living my best life, daily. *Believe. Believe.* Damn. *In … one … two …*

Mantras supposedly grounded and soothed, ending that enduring ache. Perhaps they did, if one believed in that sort of thing. *Out ... one ... two ... three ...*

Why drag this out? No reason. None at all. There were no second chances. Not with Kyle. Never with Jake. Only the delusional might believe any of this was fixable. *In ... one ... two ... three ...* Right. Time to call and make that appointment. I closed my eyes, my head shaking of its own accord. *Signing those papers turned my abject failure into certain reality.*

Envisioning a future with Jake in my current state of being was ludicrous. A monumental mistake, shredding me, surfacing every bleak and vulnerable moment of my past. The wedding.

If only I'd had the sense to stay home.

CHAPTER 1

Here I was—completely committed, yet totally miserable. Why? Why subject myself to this? It wasn't like I had untold wealth to pay for two fabulous new outfits, or a direct flight from Vancouver to Toronto, or even the overpriced five-star hotel. My credit card protested the top-tier gift from the couple's wedding registry, bought during a moment of guilt-induced weakness. *Ah, guilt.* The age-old inconvenient lure to do things you shouldn't.

I smoothed the scarlet dress over my hips and squared my shoulders, grateful for the tiny boost of confidence. Time to resign myself to a fate of awkward reunions and false levity, but at least I didn't have to walk down the aisle in a froth of blue chiffon, only to stand mere metres away from blissful best man, Jake, while his lovely wife looked on.

Taking one wobbly step forward, then two side-steps to dodge the partiers milling about inside, became its own feat of courage. I plastered on a smile and scanned the room, searching the crowd for familiar faces. *Wait.* I'd spotted it. *Nirvana.* Or at least close enough for tonight. Situated toward the back of the dim room, the gleaming, strobe-lit bar beckoned. Yup, a drink would loosen me up. Or maybe it would take two. Whatever. Nobody would keep track, especially not me. As long as I avoided the dreaded drunken striptease, getting a little tipsy was no big deal.

"Amara." Vivienne, the maid of honour and a close friend from university, popped out of the crowd. "About time you got here."

"Viv!" I threw my arms around her.

"So glad you came." She curved an arm around my waist and drew me onto the dance floor. "Missed you," she mouthed, pressing her hip to mine.

As we swayed to the music, thoughts niggled at me. *Why had I cut myself off? Why had I even run in the first place?* No. Absolutely no. Reminiscing and pining were rock-solid off-limits for tonight. Celebrating my amazing friend at this swanky bachelorette party took first priority. "Where is the bride, anyhow?"

"Dara's dancing," Vivienne said, fluttering her fingers toward the packed floor. "You look amazing." She caught a strand of my dark curly hair, fluffing it slightly. "Love that you grew this out and left it natural. Gorgeous."

Viv released me, returning to her solitary moves, and my eyes drifted closed. I lifted my arms and lost myself in the steady thump. Song after song blended, real life fading into the background.

Too soon, Vivienne's light touch on my arm dragged me back to reality. She fanned herself and pointed to a table half-surrounded by party guests. "I'm parched."

A server descended the second we reached the table, dropping off several drinks before taking our order and hurrying toward the bar.

Vivienne leaned in close. "Next round, make it two so you can catch up."

My thoughts exactly. Liquid courage may be the only thing that got me through this weekend.

"Wish you could have joined us for the shower," Vivienne said.

"Sorry I missed it." I pasted on a fresh smile. No matter how much I adored my friend, I couldn't have faced the madness of a bridal shower. People would ask too many questions about my defunct marriage at a time when my friend was launching into her happy new life. "How was that?" I asked, accepting my extra-dry martini from the server.

"Ohhh! The guys will be here soon." A woman on my left craned her neck, peering toward the door.

"The guys?" I gulped several mouthfuls of my drink and glanced toward the entrance while trying to place her vaguely familiar face. Brief flashes connected in my mind. The woman had hovered on the periphery of our group at Dalhousie University before Jake and I became an item. Kara? Carmen?

"The men from the bachelor party. I hear there will be several eligible hotties." She performed a small jig, wiggling her hips, her breasts quivering under her low-cut top. "Got my eye on a doctor."

"Do you remember Celia?" Vivienne whispered in my ear. "She's a bridesmaid. It should have been you Dara asked, not her."

Right. Celia. Yes, yes. I wrinkled my nose as I pictured that long-ago night at one of our regular Halifax haunts, and the woman's blatant passes at pretty much anything male that moved. Her constant ogling of Jake irked me, though that had been before he and I became an us. "It's fine, Viv. I'm happier being a guest. Imagine how strange it would be to—"

Celia's shrill squeal drowned out everything but the thud of the bass and she, along with several of the other ladies, abandoned the table. The decibel level rose as the fresh batch of men flooded into the room. Fortunately, Jake didn't seem to be among the new arrivals, so I drained my drink and shook out my tense muscles.

"Now the real partying begins, just like old times." Vivienne sucked back the last of her cocktail and rose from her seat in one lithe move, tugging on my arm and dragging me into the crush on the dance floor.

❧

Hours later, I finally made it to the bar and claimed a stool, fanning myself as I took a load off my aching feet. "Water, please."

The bartender nodded and winked as he served up a tumbler of ice water. Those blue eyes and his sexy scruff sent my heart racing, though he was a touch young. Early twenties, if I was lucky, while I was fast approaching the big three-zero.

He placed a flute in front of me, and I returned his smile, tracing a finger along the rim and admiring the artfully curled lemon peel. "Champagne?"

"Close. It's a French 75." Flirty bartender winked. "An elegant drink for a beautiful lady. On the house." He wiggled his brows before turning to the next person in line.

I took an experimental sip, detecting hints of gin and lemon, the tingly champagne bubbles tickling my tongue. *Delicious.* After a slight nod and smile at the bartender, I turned to observe the continuing action, Celia's teal dress catching my eye. Yup, she'd caught her first victim, hauling the poor soul toward the crowded patch of floor in the centre of the room.

Wait. Was that …? I squinted at the figure in the well-cut suit. He was thinner than I remembered. A touch scruffier, too, with his hair curling over his collar, the shadow of a beard darkening his jawline. Hmmm. This rough and tumble yet thoroughly hot and sexy look suited Jake. Married looked mighty fine on the man, even if I hated that another woman had brought him the happiness I'd only dreamed of.

Jake's amber eyes paired with his dark, silky hair and broad shoulders always had an immediate effect on women, throwing their libido into overdrive. In the early days of our relationship, I'm sure I'd worn an expression similar to the one Celia wore now, many, many times. I'd often wondered why he'd picked me when he could have chosen one of the model-perfect blondes who continually flirted with him whenever we ventured into public. On those occasions, he'd been polite but never returned their blatant interest.

It seemed nothing had changed. Politeness ruled as he performed his obligatory best man duties, including dancing with the flirty bridesmaid. Though if he were my husband, I'd be stepping in and telling that particular pushy woman shaking her assets in his face to shove off. Where was his wife, anyhow?

I sighed. None of my business, that's where. More unwelcome news greeted me as I turned, searching for the adorable bartender, but a slender blonde with a pixie cut had replaced him. *Damn.* Now I had nothing to do but stare into my half-empty drink, avoiding the sight of my ex-boyfriend cutting those moves on the floor. I downed the remainder, nodding as the new bartender motioned to my empty glass, then I chanced a look over my shoulder. Time to leave, or should I risk my ex-love catching me ogling him with pathetic longing? Maybe I should hang out until his wife made an appearance and satisfy my curiosity about Mrs. Cavallaro.

"Hi." A blond man leaned on the bar beside me, his chin tipped down. "Care to dance?"

This cutie represented a risky distraction bound to drop me into the line of fire. The minute I hit the floor, Jake would spot me, and nothing would make me happier than buckling into my seat for the return flight to Vancouver without engaging in a single awkward conversation with my ex-boyfriend.

I tilted my head as he smiled, and his gaze travelled upward, revealing startling blue eyes. *That's right, dude. Eyes go up here, not down there.* I tugged at my dress and shook my head.

He shrugged and moved on to the woman three seats away, checking out her ass as they headed toward the floor.

I settled in with my drink, peering through the crowd and keeping tabs as Celia kept Jake on the floor for a second and third song.

When the strains of a slow melody floated through the air, Jake leaned in, saying something to the woman before breaking away and heading toward the far side of the club.

Celia scouted his progress, a pout forming as she approached the bar and flagged down the bartender. She arched one over-plucked brow as she waited for her cosmopolitan. "Why are you sitting here … alone?"

I shrugged. "I'm recuperating."

"How will you find a man if you don't join the fun? Weddings are for hot drunken romps between the sheets. You should get out there." She scooped up her glass, sucking down the drink in seconds, still scanning the dance floor. Her eyes lit up. "My good doctor is back. Maybe later he'll give me a physical." She fluttered her fingers and trotted away with tiny, mincing steps.

"He's married," I said, even though Celia was half-way across the floor. "Anyway, he's not that kind of doctor." But if the woman didn't care about the wife, why would she care that Jakob Miguel Cavallaro was a marine biologist who'd never given a physical in his life? Not an official one, anyhow.

I waved a trembling hand at the bartender and motioned to the empty flute, amazed at Celia's progress in her tottery heels as she bore down on the group of men Jake had joined.

Jake's eyes narrowed in the direction of the advancing bridesmaid, then he ducked into the crowd, reappearing moments later, weaving toward the bar. The familiar dimple creased his right cheek. "Well, well. Imagine running into you here." He leaned on the bar and flagged down the bartender, the gold ring on his left hand flashing. "Whiskey, please, and another drink for Amara here. Make mine a double." When our drinks arrived, he said, "Can you charge these to room 3412? Thanks." He promptly downed a good portion of his whiskey. "Where's your other half? I was looking forward to meeting the man who finally won you over."

"Haven't you heard?" A wiggle of my fingers drew his attention to my missing ring.

"Oh, Mar." Jake frowned and leaned closer, his woodsy masculine scent combining with the slightly sweet smell of whiskey, creating a heady combination that sent a shiver racing through me. "I'm so sorry," he said, rubbing my back.

I lifted one shoulder and sipped my fresh drink, sitting a little straighter as he withdrew his hand. Now my secret was out, and everyone would know I was a total relationship failure. No surprise to this man, I was sure, since I'd failed him too. "Jake." I grimaced at the sight of Celia bearing down on us, a determined glint in her eye. "Don't look now, but your friend is on her way."

Jake glanced over his shoulder and hunched, his knuckles whitening as he clenched his glass. "What'll it cost for immediate rescue through phone-a-friend?" His words slurred, rounded at the edges.

"Hmmm." I tapped a fingertip against my pursed lips before sipping my drink. "Who says I can be bought? Anyway, isn't that your wife's job? When do I get to meet Mrs. Cavallaro?"

His head dropped further, the curve of his back becoming more pronounced as he pinched the bridge of his nose.

"Jake?" I rested my hand on his shoulder. "What's—"

"I love this song!" Celia said, shoving in between us and practically gluing herself to Jake's side. "Dance with me." She pawed his arm.

He shook his head, his pained look bringing tears to my eyes. Without a word, he drained his glass and pushed it away, barely sparing me a glance before bolting for the door.

"Great. You chased him away." The woman glowered. "That one's mine, so mitts off." Her lip curled as she scanned me from head to toe. "Like he'd want some stick woman in a sleazy red dress, anyway."

"I'm not trying to pick him up." I glared at the woman. "Unlike you, I don't hit on married men."

"Are you crazy?" She rolled her eyes. "His wife is long gone."

"You're the crazy one. How about that wedding ring?"

"That's for show. It's been months, and he's up for grabs. Back off, bitch. I'm warning you." Celia flipped her hair over her shoulder and strutted away, leaving me white-knuckled and clinging to the edge of the bar, suddenly stone cold sober.

Gone? Jake's wife had left him? I cupped my hands over my face, blinking hard against the burn.

"Are you okay, Amara?" Flirty bartender stood in front of me. "Do you need another drink?"

"Thanks, but no." Another drink would definitely not fix what ailed me.

Vivienne. She would know what happened.

ʠ

After several minutes of searching, I located Vivienne at one of the high tables scattered throughout the club.

"Hey, Viv." I slid onto the seat next to her.

"There you are! Having fun?" She looped an arm around my waist. "You're a touch pale. Okay?"

I shook my head. "I ran into Jake at the bar."

"Ouch." She wrinkled her nose. "How'd that go?"

"Terrible." Time to get it over with. "What happened with Jake and his wife?"

Vivienne's eyes widened. "Didn't you hear? Alysa d—" The cheer of the crowd blended with the shouts of the DJ and the thump of the music drowned out her words.

Cupping my ear, I leaned in closer. "What?"

"His wife died. About six months ago," she said. "They were married for less than three years. Devastating."

I clapped my palm over my mouth, shaking my head, picturing Jake hunched and defeated, looking as if he'd rather be anywhere but here. Oh, Jake, my poor love. I cursed stupid Celia for interrupting and cursed myself for that idiotic comment. He had reached out to me. Or was the reaching idea wishful thinking? "How did it happen?"

"I don't know the details. Anyway," she said, patting my hand, "it's not my place. Talk to Jake. I bet he'd like that. He needs his friends."

Me? Viv thought I could make a difference for Jake? "Did you know her?"

"Not so well. Dara and Dean hung out with them quite often, doing couple's things. Dara took it pretty hard when Alysa died."

I looked toward the parquet floor where Dara danced with abandon, her skirt fluttering as Dean twirled her out and back into his arms. Happiness radiated from her. And so it should. No way would I be the one to bring her down on the night before her wedding by delving into her dear friend's death.

My worries about attending this wedding without a date now seemed stupid and petty. Marital breakdown often involved awful, excruciating tussles over everything, and mine was no exception, yet my estranged husband was alive and well. Jake's wife had just … died. Ended. Hopefully, it was quick, not long and painful.

"Thanks, Viv. Today's been interminable, so I'm heading out." I hugged her, saddened that I'd lost touch with this wonderful woman and vowing to do better in the future. "See you tomorrow."

"Night, sweets. Sleep well."

The moment I stepped into the lobby, I slipped off my stilettos, the coolness of the marble soothing my aching feet as I padded to the bank of elevators. Once I was inside, I hit the button for my floor and slumped against the side of the car. My ears rang from the hours inside the club, and my energy level sank below zero.

I stared as the numbers lit up, each floor passing … twenty-two … twenty-three … I smothered a yawn, finally feeling the past week of anxious and sleepless nights. The door slid open at twenty-five—my floor—but instead of exiting, I hovered my finger over the button then pressed thirty-four, barely breathing as the upward journey continued.

At times like this, I needed the advice of my best friend and confidante. That was Beth, the woman who'd forced me onto the SeaBus and then onto the Canada Line to the airport, not leaving my side until I joined the security queue, my finger devoid of the four-carat cushion-cut security blanket. *"What are you wearing that thing for?"* Beth had squinted and grabbed my hand, tugging my wedding ring free and tucking it into her pocket. *"Head high, Amara. Feel no shame. You're the perfect trifecta—successful, single, and sexy. All those eligible men at the wedding need to know you're likewise unattached. Live a little. I'll be expecting a full report of uninhibited shenanigans when you get back."* Yes, she would know if I was doing the right thing, but it was beyond late on the West Coast, so I was on my own.

When the elevator opened, I stepped out, scanning the numbers until I found myself in front of his hotel room, fingertips resting on the gleaming wood, struggling for that perfect opening line. Simple was best. I'd apologize for my careless remark, relay my condolences, then return to my room. That would be that.

I tapped on the door and stepped back. Maybe he was asleep already. Maybe this would disturb him. Maybe he was angry. *Maybe he wasn't even in his room.* I glanced at my watch, squinting at the hands. Was it really three in the morning? Had I lingered at the bar that long?

"Amara?" He leaned in the doorway, staring at me through bleary, red-rimmed eyes, adorably dishevelled in his unbuttoned shirt and wrinkled dress pants.

"Jake. I just wanted to … sorry. It's late."

He stepped aside and beckoned. "Come in."

I closed my eyes for a moment before shuffling inside, taking in the low hum of the late-night talk show and the rumpled bed with its indented pillow. The true tell was the empty tumbler on the side table with the open bottle of Crown Royal beside it. "Not sleeping?"

He shrugged. "Drink?" Without waiting for my answer, he retrieved a glass from beside the coffee maker, poured a generous fifth, and pushed it into my hand. He refilled his own with a double shot.

"About before—"

"No need." Jake shook his head. "To old friends." He lifted his whiskey. "Cheers."

By the time I'd taken a ginger sip, he'd drained his own and poured another. "I'm so sorry. I didn't know about your wife."

He sank onto the side of the bed, massaging his temples with one hand, the other dangling loosely between his knees, glass suspended from his fingertips.

"Are you okay?" I rescued his whiskey and set it aside, then sat beside him. After a moment, I slid my arm around him. *Yet another stupid question*. Obviously, he wasn't handling his wife's death well, but I was still his friend, wasn't I?

Wordlessly, he turned, wrapping me in his arms and tucking his face against my neck, entwining his hand in my hair. "I can't believe you came," he whispered.

My heart practically broke as I hugged him tighter, closing my eyes and enjoying his closeness. The heat of his body. The wonderful earthy tang of him. *Ahh, Jake*. I turned my head and kissed his cheek, sighed, and then kissed him again, wanting him to understand I felt his pain. The third time I met tender lips, my knees trembling as warmth crept from my toes, his enticing scent invading my nostrils. A soft moan escaped low in my throat when he nibbled at that tender spot on my neck. His silky hair curled around my fingertips as I savoured the gentle sweep of his touch against my back and the sweet taste of orange on his tongue.

As one, we shifted, him rising above me, settling me deep into the bedding. I wrapped one arm around his neck and slid the other hand across his shoulders, then down to squeeze his tight ass, our kiss growing longer as he slid the strap of my dress aside and cupped my breast.

Jake stroked my inner thigh, working my dress over my head and tossing it aside, soon sending his shirt with it. "My beautiful *Mare*."

Mah-ray. The deepness of his voice and the rolling wave of the *r* attached to this delightful Italian word brought on a shiver. I sighed against his lips. Mm-mm, this man's kisses were delectable, riling me up as always. I loved stroking the smoothness of his bare back. Ah, feeling the hotness of our flesh melding …

Buzz … Buzz … Buzz …

The vibration on the bedside table dug into my consciousness, but just as quickly, the sound subsided.

He removed my bra, his lips grazing my neck, the light scruff on his jaw tickling my tender skin as he skimmed downward, brushing his fingers over my navel.

Buzz … Buzz … Buzz …

"Jake … phone."

His pause lasted only for a second before he tangled his fingers in my hair.

Buzz … Buzz … Buzz …

"Ignore," he mumbled. "Message."

No problem. My only concern was his pants and how soon they were leaving his body. I ached for this fine man, longed for his naked …

Ding.

"Shit, they're persistent." He groaned, tucking his head against the crook of my neck before he released me. "I have to check."

I remained motionless, struggling to control my breathing, missing the gentleness of his touch and the weight of him as he reached toward the bedside table. Kneading my palms against the sheets, I closed my eyes to stop the world from spinning, desperate to hide the inconvenient sight of the gold band on his finger.

"Sorry. It's important." He rubbed my arm and pecked my lips, the mattress quivering as he moved to the edge.

What the hell was I even doing here, sprawled across my ex's bed while he dealt with his oh-so-important text? Who wanted to be the widower's rebound girl, to be his drunken wedding shag? Clearly, the loss of his wife had sent him reeling and clouded his judgment if he thought an ex-girlfriend was the ideal candidate. He might even be seeing someone, and I was simply a convenient diversion. A wander along some distant memory lane.

"… what's happening?"

That damn wedding ring, still on his finger. The one another woman had given him when he'd pledged to love her forever. Alysa. Alysa Cavallaro; the woman who'd replaced me.

What were the rules here? Were there any? Maybe rule number one should be to heed the fluttering red flag. To end this particularly trippy out-of-body experience. To protect my ravaged heart.

"How high?" A latch clicked, and his voice grew muffled.

I stared at the closed bathroom door for several seconds before scuttling from his bed, hauling on my dress, and scrambling for my shoes. The low rumble of his voice accompanied my rush across the carpet and my slight pause as I inched the door open and slipped into the hall, stilettos dangling from my fingertips. The door swooshed shut, and I trotted toward the illuminated exit sign, plunging into the gloom of the stairwell. The rush of cool air raised goosebumps on my bare skin, my unshod feet slapping the steps as I descended, zigzagging downward until I reached my floor.

What a fool for imagining I could visit my ex-boyfriend's hotel room in the wee hours and expect nothing, besides my simple apology, to happen.

Being Jake's one-night stand would be embarrassing. Unbearable. Our story had ended four years ago. No good could come of revisiting it. Now to get through the rest of the weekend.

CHAPTER 2

The following afternoon, after hours of tossing and turning and fretting about even being in the same room as Jake, I strolled into the church, keeping my head held high as the usher led me to a middle pew. I settled into my seat, admiring the massive bouquets of blush and cream roses and the multitude of flickering gold candles.

My own dream wedding might have looked something like this, but reality hadn't measured up. The initial excitement at Kyle's proposal and the amazing diamond sparkler faded at his words not long afterward. *"Let's get 'er done."*

Scarcely two weeks later we had, though why I'd agreed to forgo the froth of satin and tulle I'd dreamed of and settled for a simple cream evening gown, I'd never figured out. Within minutes, our no-frills, no-fuss ceremony, attended only by one of Kyle's closest friends and my best friend Beth as our reluctant witnesses, was over.

Now I understood Beth's hesitation during the hasty planning phase. My marriage to high-financier Kyle Weston had fizzled before our second anniversary, our divorce now wreaking havoc on both my sanity and my pay cheques, which were in meagre supply, at least compared to Kyle's.

"Amara! I'm so glad to see you."

The familiar voice brought me to my feet. "Luciana." I drew the young woman into my arms, squeezing her tiny frame in a hug, her soft floral scent surrounding me. "It's so good to see you."

"Urgh. Not so tight." A giggle escaped as she wiggled from my grasp. "Nice to see you too."

"Sorry." I grabbed her hand. "Why are you here?"

"Jake couldn't face this wedding alone. Where's your guy? I heard you were married."

I shook my head, lifting my empty hand for the obligatory wiggle. "That's over."

"Oh, I'm sorry to hear that."

I bit my lip as Luci glanced at me, her lips twitching. *Ha. Sure, you are. Bring on the comment. Three … two … one …*

"Have you seen my big brother yet? He'll be joining me in a minute."

I clasped my hands in my lap to stop their trembling. "He's not the best man?"

"It's a surprise he even came." Luciana tilted her head. "He told you about Alysa?"

"Viv did."

"Then you understand why he declined best man duties, but being so close with Dean and Dara, he insisted on coming."

"Sounds like Jake." That same obligation led me to be here for Dara, but I didn't have a Luciana to spare me the agony of a solo attendance.

"Losing someone you love is awful. In those circumstances … I can't even imagine," Luciana said. "He's talking to Tía Marisol but should be in soon. She's babysitting, so he wanted to check in."

My mouth grew dry, and I squirmed as her words sunk into my over-tired, sluggish brain. "Babysitting who?"

Luciana gripped my hand. "Didn't anyone tell you?"

I dug my nails into my palm and shook my head.

"He has a daughter. Sarina's the sweetest little thing."

A slow burn crept up my neck. "Jake's a dad?"

The man under discussion slid into the pew beside his sister, his faint smile accompanied by a terse nod in my direction. "Amara."

"Isn't it great she's here?" Luciana squeezed my hand.

Jake shrugged, keeping his head bowed.

Luciana heaved a sigh, her lips flattening into a thin line. "Somehow, I thought you'd be happier," she muttered. "How's Sarina?"

"She still has a fever, though it's gone down some since this morning." He scrubbed a hand through his hair. "Two days is too long to be away."

"It's the teething." Luciana squeezed her brother's hand. "Tía will take excellent care of Sari." She peeked my way, widening her eyes and tilting her head slightly toward her big brother. "Excuse me. I have to use the ladies' room."

Jake's mouth set in a grim line as Luciana scooted past his knees and hurried down the aisle.

"Jake. About last night." I glanced around the rapidly filling church, lowering my voice to a bare whisper. "Let me explain."

One eyebrow rose. "Explain what? Your mastery of extreme sprinting?"

"I'm sorry." I slid closer, resting my hand on his arm. "That wasn't supposed to happen. I only wanted to say—"

He looked at the row of people to his left, then back at me. "This is not the time or place."

Those words yanked me back four years in time. Jake's favourite phrase, always uttered at the worst moment. The last time I'd heard it from his lips, I'd bolted, packing my bag and boarding the first flight headed to Vancouver, which conveniently, was located on the opposite side of the country from Halifax. Maybe he wouldn't forgive me for running this time, either. Why would he? "Pretty name, Sarina. How old is she?"

"One," he said. "Dara didn't tell you about my daughter?"

"No. I've been out of touch. Congratulations."

"Excuse me. Pardon." Luciana shuffled past the guests who'd filled our row, eyeing us before she manoeuvred around me. "Scooch over." She wiggled into the tiny space on my right, forcing me closer to Jake.

As the warmth of his thigh pressed against mine, I wrapped my arms around myself, squeezing my legs together and attempting to become as small as possible.

"Sorry." Jake shifted, creating a sliver of room between us.

The music changed and heads turned as Dean, his best man, and his three groomsmen strolled up the aisle to take their places. Once they were lined up at the altar, the music flowed into the next piece, punctuated by *oohs* and *aahs* as the adorable ring bearer in his dark suit crept up the aisle balancing a white satin pillow.

A girl of about three followed the sombre toddler. She skipped down the row, flinging handfuls of blush and cream rose petals from her basket, her dark ringlets flying as she hurtled toward the altar, coaxing a few indulgent smiles and light laughter from the onlookers.

"She's adorable!" Luci whispered.

A familiar classical tune I couldn't place accompanied the bridesmaids as they marched down the aisle. I peeked at my ex-boyfriend, doing my best to keep that teeny space between us. *Jake the dad. Sarina's dad. The single dad. Sexy single dad. We'd almost had sex. Another thirty seconds on his bed …* Nope. He's just Jake, the ex-boyfriend I'd run from—more than once. The one beside me, ignoring me, when all I wanted to do was …

Luciana nudged my shoulder.

Crap. Lusting after the man while his little sister sat right beside me? I swept the back of my finger across my lips, searching for any signs of drool.

Luci's eyes widened, and her chin jutted toward the aisle as the melancholy opening notes of Pachelbel "Canon in D" flowed from the string quartet.

The bride, the actual reason we were squished together on this narrow wooden bench, was now gliding toward the altar, flanked by her beaming parents. Spots danced in my eyes as I wobbled to my feet to join the forest of people craning their heads. I swallowed hard to quell my nausea, clutching at the pew in front of me. An arm snaked around my waist, steadying me.

"Okay?" Jake's low voice sent a shiver through me and goosebumps popped up on my arms. "You need water?"

My vision cleared as I shook my head, and he moved his arm to his side. I swayed toward him, then straightened. Leaning into him wasn't allowed. Not now. Especially not after last night. I angled toward the aisle and focussed on Dara, who was now stepping up to join Dean. Today, living her dream, a picture of joyful perfection in her embellished princess-style wedding gown.

We all sat as the ceremony began, the minister's voice soaring above the guests.

I sneaked another look at the man beside me, shifting and tensing my thigh. *Dangerous Jake. Jake, the daddy.* Rule number one; don't expose your ravaged heart. Rule number two; don't mess with the widower, especially the elusive single dad version. "Ouch," I mumbled, rubbing my ribs, which now ached from the sharp jab from Luci's elbow.

She leaned in and whispered, "Quit fidgeting." Her pointed look and motion toward the altar tuned me in to Dean's deep tones as he recited his vows.

"Dara, my sun, my moon, my life ..."

I pressed a hand to my chest, blinking hard and sniffling. It took a strong man to stand in front of three hundred wedding guests and, with no hint of embarrassment or irony, tell the entire world exactly how he felt about the wonderful woman sharing the altar.

Dara's adamance that she'd never marry a man who didn't have the words to express his love was paying off. *"I want a man who tells me he loves me, a man who isn't scared to share his feelings, with me, with our family, or with his friends."* My dear friend had found her ultimate treasure by marrying Dean.

The small movements to the left caught my eye.

Jake sat with his head bowed, rubbing his hands against his thighs, that damn ring on his finger taunting me. His eyes were closed, the wrinkle in his brow the tell-tale sign.

Without a second thought, I reached out and rested my hand on top of his, entwining our fingers and squeezing, a memory flitting into my mind of a tiny dock not far from Peggy's Cove. We'd spent the day paddling in Prospect Bay—the first of one of our numerous kayaking adventures—afterward dangling our feet in the water, my nose wrinkling at the salty, slightly fishy tang lingering on the late fall breeze.

That day, as he told me about his family and how his father left when he was thirteen, his sister barely eight, a similar look had appeared, only clearing when he spoke of his mom. The courageous woman had made the best of their situation, working full-time, yet still doting on her two children, taking them on long adventures exploring the wild Maritime coastlines. They'd hiked, explored tidal pools, and she'd fostered a love of the ocean, especially in her young son. It was no surprise he chose to study marine biology and spend most of his time on the ocean.

That same love of everything to do with water had given birth to my nickname. *"Mah-ray," he'd said. "My sea. Every bit as intriguing and wholly unpredictable, beautiful, and full of wonders yet to explore."*

It could have been the worst pick up line ever, but something about the look in his eyes spun a spell, turning me into putty. That night we'd spent together, forming our inseparable bond.

Jake twitched, but he didn't pull away from me, so we remained with our hands linked until the string quartet took up the strains of "A Sky Full of Stars."

Then he stood, pulling away and flexing his fingers as the wedding party exited amid a flurry of snapping camera shutters and bright flashes, the eager guests capturing the happy couple in their newly wedded bliss.

Did Jake remember our first night together? Did he even care?

✿

"The reception doesn't start until six," Luciana said as we emerged from the church, trailing close behind Jake. "We should grab a coffee and catch up. Coming, big brother?"

"You two go ahead. I should check with Tía and make sure Sari is okay." Jake waved and strode in the direction of the hotel.

"He worries too much, but it's natural, I suppose. It's the first time he's left my darling niece for more than a single day." His sister sighed. "How about you? Are you ditching me too?"

"No. I'd love to catch up, but I need more than coffee."

As we turned in the opposite direction from Jake, she asked, "What was that in the church?"

"Nothing, it was—"

"You were about to pass out."

Oh. That. "Late night. Too much to drink. No appetite for breakfast." I shrugged. "Sorry. I chased Jake off."

"It's not you. He's just moody these days," she said with a sad smile, "but you noticed that."

I wrinkled my nose. "So, tell me about you. Last I heard, you were finishing undergrad at Dalhousie. Did you do it?"

"Medical school?" Luci grinned. "I sure did. Guess where I'm doing my residency."

"Here in Toronto?"

"No! North Vancouver. We're neighbours."

"That's amazing. I'm proud of you." I beamed, slinging an arm around her shoulders as we walked, even as a little pang hit me. Luci must have started residency last July, and she hadn't called. "Now you're on the West Coast, you probably don't see Jake much."

"Not as often as I'd like, but you know Jake. Even after he lost Alysa, he insisted I stay in Vancouver. I offered to come home and help with Sari, but he refused," she said. "I love my brother, but he's stubborn."

"That's a serious understatement," I said, wrinkling my nose, "but you have to respect his decision. He'd never hold you back."

Jake remained the same man I'd loved so hard. That he'd encouraged Luci to succeed even as his life disintegrated into shambles told me that much.

"I've missed you, Amara." She slipped an arm around my waist. Her amber eyes, so like her brother's, turned my way. "You didn't even say goodbye."

"I'm sorry," I said, looping my arm around her. "It wasn't about you."

"What did Jake do? Can't you forgive him, whatever it was?"

"I haven't been there in ages," I said, pointing at the small family owned restaurant two doors down. "I should eat before I pass out. Tell me. Is there anyone special in your life?"

Luci narrowed her eyes. "One day, I'll get the truth out of you."

"You've heard all I have to say. Anyway, I'm excellent at keeping secrets."

"Meaning you never told him?"

"About what?"

"You know," she said with a grimace, "about me."

"Jake doesn't know? Does Marisol?"

Luciana shook her head. "My family is traditional. Especially Tía. They'll freak."

"Jake would accept it. Trust me."

"No. Maybe someday, but not now."

I slung an arm around her shoulders and squeezed. "If you ever want to talk about it …" This was what having a little sister felt like, and I missed it. Maybe now, with her living in North Vancouver, we could regain some of our connection.

❧

When Luciana and I arrived in the small reception hall outside the hotel ballroom, guests were already milling about, sipping the couple's signature cocktail and nibbling appetizers.

"There's my brother." Luciana waved at Jake, who chatted with a waif-thin blonde.

The woman scowled in our direction, seeming to send an unspoken warning to stay far, far away.

I snagged one of the cocktails from the server's tray. *Don't you worry.* Spending an entire evening with Jake was on my list of events to avoid. Where he was concerned, I couldn't trust myself to make rational decisions. Our fortuitously interrupted make-out session was proof positive.

Luciana grabbed a drink before she looped her arm through mine, eyeing Jake and the blonde. "Cougar alert." She rolled her eyes and steered me toward the corner.

"Be nice!" I hoped my stern look would shut her down.

"She's probably fifteen years older than him. That's a cougar."

"So what? They're both adults." I sucked up the last of my cocktail, eyeing the two who seemed immersed in deep conversation, oblivious to my inspection. Setting my glass aside, I flagged down the server, retrieving a second. "These are good. Wonder what's in them?"

"Lots of tequila." Luci giggled, motioning toward the double doors that were now open. "Let's find our seats."

We joined the rest of the guests filtering inside, roaming in search of their tables. The fine linens and china, centrepieces loaded with cream and blush roses, soft drapery, and tall, elegant candleholders were everything I pictured for Dara's wedding. "This is over the top. Good thing they have great jobs."

"Her parents are footing the bill." Luci nudged me and pointed at the wedding cake.

"That thing is taller than Dara." I stared at the eight-tier extravaganza, shaking my head at the elaborate gold detailing and the delicate sugar roses cascading down the side. "Look at all those rosebuds. Must have taken hours."

"Some friend of the family baked it." Luci pulled me along as she checked place tags. "Yay." She clapped her hands and pointed. "You're sitting beside Jake."

Welcome to the seventh level of hell. I shot a look around the room, but most of the guests were already claiming their seats.

Luci grinned. "Oh no, you don't." She pressed on my shoulders, forcing me into my chair. "You're with us."

There were only two people to thank for this debacle. If Dara and Dean were unfortunate enough to be anywhere nearby, I'd throttle them with the satin ribbons on her bridal bouquet, but the cowards were lounging in some posh antechamber awaiting their grand entrance. How could they ever think seating me beside Jake was a good idea?

"Oh, what are these?" Luciana picked up the silver bell and rang it before reading the card that sat underneath. *"This bell will make us kiss, but be warned; one too many rings, and we'll open the kissing jar."* She giggled and wrinkled her nose. "What fun. Too bad I'm here with my brother."

"Get that thing far away from me." I jabbed the bell by my plate, shooing it across the linen cloth with my fingertip until it rested in the shadow of the centrepiece. "Count yourself lucky you don't have to put on a kissy-face sideshow. Who comes up with this stuff? All those lovey-dovey couples, that's who."

"You mean, all those smoochy, nauseating ones?" Luci snickered. "I'll never forget my brother's guilty look and attempted diversion while you scrambled into your blouse when I dropped by unannounced. Back then, you two were all over each other, constantly."

Nope, nope. Not having this conversation, especially after last night. Most definitely not with Jake's little sister. When

Jake planted himself beside me moments later, I almost hugged him for saving me from more of Luci's embarrassing anecdotes.

He narrowed his eyes and pinched the bell beside his plate between two fingers, then tossed it beside the one I'd discarded. After he scanned the card, it met the same fate.

"I had nothing to do with the seating," I said under my breath.

"Well, you're stuck with me now." He swigged the remainder of his drink and glanced around. "Where's the damn bar?"

"There's wine." I leaned forward and reached for the bottle, even though I agreed with Jake. Another two or three of the fruity vodka concoctions might make this bearable and would be far superior to the Merlot on our table.

Jake scooped up the bottle and peered at the label. "Merlot?" His lip curled as he focussed on the dregs in the tall glass clutched between my fingers, and then he stalked across the room and out the double doors.

Luciana widened her eyes as she craned her neck, squinting in the direction her brother had disappeared. "Should I send a search party? He keeps running away."

I lifted one hand and waved. "That's my fault. Maybe I should make myself scarce."

"Don't be silly." She leaned across his chair. "Don't let Mister Grouchy Pants scare you off. He's even impatient with me sometimes since Alysa died." In a low voice, she said, "Thank you for comforting him at the ceremony. He's struggling."

I blinked hard, noting the shimmer in her eyes. "What happened to her?"

Luci's eyes grew even shinier. "It was all so awful. I can't ..." She sniffled and turned her head away, dashing the back of her hand across her eyes.

A flash of movement made me look up.

Jake stood only inches away holding two cocktails, a bottle of wine tucked under one arm. He stared at his sister with a grim look, then closed his eyes for a moment before he placed one of the glasses in front of me, setting the other along with the new wine bottle at his spot.

"Thanks, Jake." I wrapped my fingers around the cocktail, spinning it to occupy myself. What could I say to make this better?

Without a word, he drained his drink and opened the bottle of wine. The silence was only broken by the rich red liquid glugging into his glass, followed by the thump of the bottle against the table.

Before I could even try to talk to him, the other guests joined us, their cheerful chatter a merciful respite.

❧

Between Luci's rambles, Jake's moody silence, and the constant ringing, dinner was almost unendurable. The newly married couple barely took their seats after one round of kissing when tinkling bells had them rising to their feet again.

"Enough. Enough. We warned you." Dean wagged a finger as the main instigators, situated to his right, started in again. He stood, opened the crystal jar, and held it out to his bride.

With a flourish, Dara pulled out a tiny vellum card and extended it to her new husband.

"Brian and Gina." Dean scanned the room and pointed at a table to his left. "On your feet. Make it a good one."

A couple rose, the man I supposed to be Brian pecking Gina on the lips before they sat.

A guy behind us let out a loud groan. "Dude, you can do better than that!"

I looked around, searching for the source of the unfamiliar voice before turning back to my maple-glazed salmon. "Better them than me," I said as several guests clapped and whistled, but mercifully, everyone soon returned to their dinner.

Only a few minutes later, the bells rang again.

I refilled my glass, sucking down half of my wine while Dean and Dara repeated the kissing jar process with another couple.

By the time the kissing-couple count reached seven, I was wishing for a hasty end to this torture, but the servers were delivering more bottles of wine, encouraging the guests to linger over their entrées. Corks popped and liquid sloshed into glasses, the buzz of conversation rising, the incessant ringing adding to the din.

Dean waved another card. "Christy and Brent."

A couple at the table across from us stood, the man cupping the woman's cheek, his tender smile almost making me weep. He kissed her long and hard, then performed a small bow amid applause and whistles.

I waggled my glass at Jake. "Quit hogging that Shiraz."

He nodded and poured me a generous portion before picking at his Chicken Kiev.

I sighed at yet another round of bells, glancing at the head table as Dara reached into the jar and handed another slip of paper to her new husband.

"Ah, this time our lucky couple is ..." Dean chuckled. "Ohhhhh! Jake Cavallaro and the lovely Amara Grant."

I froze, my glass halfway to my lips.

"Come on, buddy." Dean pointed at Jake. "I see you there."

Dara's eyes widened as she stared in our direction. In fact, every set of eyes in the entire room was on us.

Vivienne, the traitor sitting on Dara's right, was laughing behind cupped hands.

I slouched, sending a helpless look at Jake, whose knee bounced at a furious rate. "It's okay, we don't have to," I muttered.

"Kiss, kiss, kiss." Some guy across the room began the chant, thumping his fist in a steady beat. "Kiss, kiss, kiss."

I sank lower, peeking toward the head table, then back at Jake who was now massaging his temple.

Dean, the rat bastard, grinned as he waved the card in our direction. "It's just one little kiss."

Another deep voice rose from two tables over. "Kiss her. Kiss her. Kiss her." Feet stomped in time. "Be a man, Jake!"

The groom joined in, thumping his own fist and laughing, staring straight at me. "Kiss him. Kiss him. Kiss him."

"Dean, no!" Dara sprang from her chair, pinning his hand to his side. "Don't encourage this."

"Kiss!" More people took up the cry, the voices, thumping, and stomping carrying through the room like an endless wave. "Kiss her. Kiss her. Kiss her. Kiss her."

Jake closed his eyes for a moment before he stood, hauling me from my chair and slipping his arm around my waist. He leaned in, giving me a light kiss on the lips and drawing back.

A roar reverberated through the room.

"Boo! You call that a kiss? Do it properly!"

"Kiss, kiss, kiss!" Another wave of voices joined the fray.

Jake pressed his lips to my ear, pulling me closer. "They won't give it up until we give them the full show. Let's get it over with."

I stared into his eyes, tipping my chin and sucking in a breath just before his lips crushed mine. Nothing to do but accept that it was happening. It was only a kiss. A damn great kiss ... mm-mm ... his hair so silky soft under my fingertips ... his skin so warm ... his tongue so incredibly sweet ... that heavenly spicy aftershave ...

He pulled away, and I gasped for air, my knees trembling so hard they barely held me up. My cheeks burned as the room erupted with wolf whistles, cheers, shouts, and applause.

Jake lowered me onto my chair, me clinging to his arm and pressing my fingers to my lips, trying not to look at his wide-eyed sister with her hands clapped over her mouth.

Jake sat and leaned back in his chair, picking up his fork and stabbing a baby potato, shoving it in his mouth as the din died down. The buzz of conversation and silverware ringing against china resumed.

Luciana lifted her own fork and ate a dainty bite of her salmon, the corners of her mouth twitching.

I feared I'd unwittingly revealed how *not* over Jakob Cavallaro I really was. There was no way his little sister would ever let me forget it.

CHAPTER 3

Now that dinner was almost over, the couples we'd shared our meal with were either dancing or socializing.

Luciana sat back as the servers placed our plates in front of us and moved on to the next table. "Wow," she said. "That kiss sure was something."

The last of the wine chugged into Jake's glass. Even as the bottle thunked down, he tipped back the rich red liquid, already waving a hand at one of the servers.

His sister inspected the empty bottle. "You've had enough, Jakob."

"Mind your own business, Luciana."

She looked at me, then at her brother. "Is something going on here? I mean … why would they add your names to that jar as a couple? That's weird."

Jake lifted a shoulder. "Guess someone thought it would be hilarious." He tapped the golden caramel of his crème brûlée, breaking the crisp surface with a satisfying crack before taking a small, deliberate scoop. "It's good." After the second bite, he glanced at his sister and said, "It was only a kiss. Part of their wedding game. No biggie."

I kept my head down and dug into my decadent slice of chocolate cake.

"Huh." Luci pointed the tines her dessert fork at Jake. "A peck on the cheek is no biggie. Examining Amara's tonsils with your tongue is an entirely different affair."

Jake shovelled in his last bite of crème brûlée, then stood without even looking my way. "I should congratulate the happy couple." He tossed his napkin onto his empty plate and wove his way toward the head table.

Luci angled toward me. "Nothing to say about that bit of tongue wrestling?"

"I should … ummm … freshen up. Excuse me." I bolted, dodging through the guests. Glancing over my shoulder, I hurried into the coat check and ducked behind a rack of jackets.

The rustle of fabric and footsteps in the doorway had me holding my breath and crossing my fingers, hoping that Luci hadn't followed with the intent to grill me further.

"I saw you, you little sneak." Dara peeked around the corner, then threw her arms around me. "What are you doing?"

"Dar! Just needed a quiet moment." I hugged her. "You look gorgeous, amazing, and happy."

"Thanks for being here. It means everything that you travelled across the country to join us. I'm sorry we haven't had time to visit."

"It's your wedding day. You have better things to do than babysit me. Let's see that ring."

She presented her left hand with a flourish. "Isn't it incredible? Dean picked it himself. It's three carats!" Little prisms of colour danced across the extravagant princess-cut diamond as she turned her hand.

"It's stunning. You picked a good one." I tucked my own hand out of her sight, my thumb worrying the empty spot on my ring finger.

"I love him so much. To think I have you and Jake to thank for introducing us." She giggled. "Sometimes blind dates do pay off."

"Well, Dean thought you were adorable, and Jake had been on the lookout for the right girl for his friend."

"Was that so Dean could quit hanging around all the time? My guy always says you were lovely, never complaining about your third wheel."

I laughed and shook my head. At that time, I'd considered Dean as a playboy dating a string of women who seemed ditsy and self-centred and not even close to long-term girlfriend material. I formed the impression that maybe the guy liked it that way since it gave him plenty of excuses to avoid commitment. When Jake suggested a double date to bring Dean and Dara together, I'd dithered for weeks, but he'd been right in the end. Dean had simply been reeling from one too many bad love affairs, hiding his warm and gentle heart in hopes of avoiding further disaster. Once he'd shown himself, we'd become the closest of friends.

"Amara?"

"Sorry, just …" Drifting into the past? Not the place to be. Not tonight.

"Jake … the kissing thing … sorry about that," she said. "It wasn't my idea."

"It's fine. Not like we haven't kissed before."

"Well, clearly, but I'm apologizing anyway." She shook her head. "Dean and I had words about that stunt, and he's begging forgiveness from Jake right now."

"It's not your fault." I pictured the man's grin as he egged us on. "Your new husband thought it was hilarious. Typical Dean."

Dara rested her hand on my arm. "I'm sorry about you and Kyle."

"You heard. Well, we broke up months ago."

"Why didn't you call? I could have been there for you. Are you doing okay?"

"I'm fine. Really. Been out dating and everything. Mister Rebound's over and done."

"Ah. Ready to move on, then. Yay!" Dara clapped her hands. "I've missed you terribly. You never visit."

"I've missed you too," I said, holding back all the reasons why I'd withdrawn from our group. Who wanted to compete for space with the ex-boyfriend's new love, especially after the way I'd left? *But wait … crafty woman, sidetracking me from the real issue.* "Do I need to ask why Dean is busy apologizing?"

Dara wrinkled her nose. "This morning, my lovely husband insisted we seat you at Jake's table. Dean put the card in the kissing jar."

"Why would he do that?"

"You don't know? Even after last night's tryst? After the kiss Jake just laid on you?"

I crossed my arms. "Now that look Dean gave me makes perfect sense. Everybody knows?"

My friend waved her hand, bouncing lightly on her toes. "Yes, yes, well, obviously not *everyone* knows. Dean only told me after I dragged the reason for the last-minute changes out of him. I meant that you should connect those big ole dots. Jake's available ... You're available ... Dean insisted you sit beside Jake ..."

I matched Dara's light singsong tone. "Jake's wearing his wedding ring ..."

"How did I miss that?" Dara frowned. "The man needs a good talking to about that."

"Don't you dare. There are reasons why last night didn't happen, so don't get all excited or make this into something it isn't. I didn't sleep with Jake, no matter what *he* said."

"*He* didn't say anything of the sort, but it's not the worst idea ever. Maybe a session of hot, drunken mattress wrestling would soften that sharp edge. Jake's not seeing anyone, you're divorced, and he's as yummy as ever. No one would judge if you took advantage of the opportunity to tamp down that frustration. In fact, a little roll in the hay would do you both a world of good."

"Almost divorced."

"Bah." She waved a hand at me. "Says the woman who already admitted to getting Mister Rebound over with."

"Okay, then. It's not that simple."

"It kind of is, though. It's Jake. Buy him a drink, show him your legs, and invite him upstairs. Voilà. If that fails, which it won't, Dean will talk—"

"Ewww, no!" I grimaced. "Don't involve Dean. He'll stick his nose deeper into our business. I can't, Dara. Being Jake's second choice, his afterthought ... well, kill me now."

"Hoo, boy." She studied me. "You're still in love with Jake."

"Uh-uh. I'll always care about him, but I don't want to be his one-night stand. That's it."

My friend tilted her head. "Nice try, but it's love."

"Nope, but the man's kisses are hot. So what if it got overheated?"

"Ahh, so you admit you have the hots for him."

I narrowed my eyes. "Don't share any of this, especially not with Dean. Swear it, Dara."

"That'll cost ya." With a coy smile, she eyed me. "Swear you'll spend some time with Jake before you hightail it back to Vancouver. Have a proper conversation with the man. You can't duck him forever."

Want to bet on that? "Do I have to?" Did I have any other option? Judging by her stare, no, no, I had a zero chance of dodging my ex-boyfriend dilemma. I lifted my palms in surrender. "Okay."

Her smile widened, and she brushed two fingers along her lips. "Done. I won't say a word to Dean. Now, don't you dare renege on your vow. Talk to Jake about that kiss."

I hugged her. "Now quit worrying about me and Jake and everyone else and get back to your groom. Enjoy every second of this beautiful wedding. You deserve it."

"Thanks, it turned out better than I imagined." She rested her hands on my shoulders. "I look forward to hearing all about the convo between you and Jake when we're back from Aruba."

"Go cut that fabulous cake with your amazing husband. Love you, Dar."

She grabbed my hand, hauling me toward the door. "Quit hiding. This is my party. I demand that you have fun and live a little."

"Fine." I laughed as she towed me back into the reception hall. Why not? With a few more drinks, maybe I'd be able to forget and be one step closer to moving on.

❧

Within minutes of emerging from my tête-à-tête with his new wife, Dean sidled up to me. "Can we talk for a minute?"

"That took all of two seconds." I folded my arms over my chest and scowled. "What did Dara say?"

"Nothing," he said, raising his hands with palms flattened, "but Jake ripped me a new one, so I thought I'd better apologize. Sorry for seizing the golden opportunity to bring you two together."

I hauled him into the coat room I'd so recently vacated. "Yeah, you sound super sorry. Just be warned, you can't force broken pieces back together."

"You'll never convince me that you and Jake aren't meant to be. Everyone thought you'd be the couple who'd make it through. And I owe both you and Jake. You two did so much for me back in university, you know? You were sweet, letting me tag along when my life was at its worst. Then you introduced me to Dara. Look at us now."

"I'm thrilled for you, but until this weekend, Jake and I hadn't even spoken in four years. We had a university thing, and it's over. Let it go."

Dean scrubbed his hands over his face. "That's bullshit. You know it, I know it, and you can bet that Jake does too. No matter how much you both deny it, you have something worth fighting for. Just go for it. What do you have to lose?"

What, besides the carefully crafted life raft keeping me afloat? "Dean, I love you, and I know your intentions are good, but please leave it alone." I straightened his bow tie, then stretched and kissed his cheek. "Best wishes to you and Dara. Now, get back to your guests."

He engulfed me in a tight hug. "You are one of a kind, sweetheart. I've missed you. We all have. Promise you'll visit us in Halifax?"

I wiggled free and steered him toward the door. "I'll come and stay for a few days once you two settle into married life. Now, don't you have a cake to cut or something?"

"See you out there." He adjusted his tuxedo as he headed into the reception hall.

Wherever I turned tonight, the past smacked me head on, threatening to plunge me into an emotional meltdown. At one time I'd thought the same as Dean, that Jake and I would be the couple who slogged through every situation and emerged on the other side unscathed. But then, as it always does, life flattened us, setting us straight.

We hadn't deserved that much happiness when relationships crumbled around us, leaving us untouched and bobbing along in blissful oblivion. Yet, as we crept up on four years of dating, we'd seemed no closer to a solid commitment than we had six months in, still glossing over our issues and avoiding the toughest conversations.

Anyway, Jake wasn't interested in the least, and in two days, I'd return to the daily slog on my own side of the country. Further involvement was inadvisable, this I knew for certain.

I'd just accepted my cocktail from the bartender when an arm wrapped around my waist.

"Why aren't you out there dancing?" Vivienne asked.

"Why aren't you?"

"I plan to be soon." A sly smile touched her lips. "How was dinner?"

"Not you too."

"What? Ignore that smokin' hot kiss? That in-your-face chemistry with Jakey boy? Dreamer. Anyway, you two were the couple everyone wanted to be in university. Your breakup was a shocker."

"Whatever. It's nothing. Long over. Why don't you fill me in on your life since everyone already seems to know everything about mine? Anyone special?"

"My guy couldn't come this weekend." Vivienne wrinkled her nose. "Work obligations. He might be a keeper, though."

"Care to dance?" The deep voice and touch on my arm pulled my attention from my friend.

I smiled at the dark-haired cutie, who was certainly appealing with his blue eyes and dimples. Maybe he'd keep me from dwelling on Dara's words and my confusion about Jake.

"Go. Have fun. We'll talk later." Vivienne fluttered her fingers, leaving me no choice but to accompany the guy.

Not that it was so bad to socialize and enjoy, and the man turned out to be a great dancer. After several songs, he motioned to the bar. "Drink?"

I nodded. Time to honour my promise to Beth and have some fun. Not that I hadn't already gathered a ton of baggage to unpack after I dragged myself back to Vancouver, but I knew the messy situation with Jake wouldn't meet her uninhibited shenanigan requirements. However, a dalliance with my dance partner just might.

Christophe wasn't just a pretty boy. As we chatted about his escapades as a photojournalist, he became more and more interesting. The man was intelligent, well-travelled, and articulate. Just the kind of guy I'd been looking for now that the sharp edge of my impending divorce had faded.

"How do you know Dean and Dara?" I asked at one point.

"I'm a distant relative of Dean's. Some sort of obligation on their part to fill out the guest list, I guess. You?"

"Dara and I have been friends for years. We met at Dalhousie University."

To that he only nodded and smiled, turning the conversation to my life and work, focussing on the now rather than the past.

Finally, the expected and inevitable loaded question came.

"So, Amara, I have to ask—what's the deal with you and Jake? That kiss at dinner made me think you two are still a couple, but he's there"—he pointed at Jake who was chatting with the blonde woman again—"and you're here. So … are you two a thing?"

"No, nothing like that. We dated years ago, so someone thought the kissing would be funny." Heat rose in my cheeks, surely turning them to beacons of flaming tell-tale red. "You know, seat us at the same table, put our names in the jar. We're long over."

Christophe swirled his whiskey, studying me intently before he nodded. "That's it? You're single? Available?"

"Mmmhmm."

"Fair enough. Another?" He pointed at my glass, and at my nod, signalled the bartender. "Victoria and North Vancouver are only a short flight apart. Would you be interested in getting together sometime?"

"That would be nice."

"Do you mind if I excuse myself for a couple minutes? I'll be right back." He winked and headed toward the bathrooms.

Moments later, Jake looked my way and headed over.

"Amara." He flagged down the bartender and ordered a quartet of tequila shots. "Looks like you're having fun," he said, offering one tiny glass to me.

"It's a wedding. Isn't it for celebration and enjoyment?"

Jake's laugh—a sharp, short sound—combined with narrowed eyes. "I suppose."

"Besides, you've found someone to occupy your time." I eyed the other woman, who was talking to Dean and Dara.

"Who? Her?" He jutted his chin toward the trio. "That's Dean's boss. His married boss."

Oh. Oops. "Luci's done well for herself."

"How? By catching plenty of men to dance with?"

"Stop acting like the overprotective brother. I meant that you must be proud she graduated from medical school."

His face lit up. "I couldn't have raised Luci without Tía. She deserves the majority of the credit, not me."

"Tía's fantastic, but don't discount how much you did." I lifted my glass. "To the big brother who went to every parent-teacher conference and made sure Luci played soccer and always had lunch money."

We tapped glasses and tossed back the tequila.

I'd no sooner put down my glass when Jake pushed another into my hand.

"If we're crediting every contribution to Luciana's success," he said, "here's to the woman who took my little sister clothes shopping and out for girls' nights, taking on those touchy teenage girl conversations I never dared mention." He tapped his glass against mine. After we both downed our shots, he said, "She missed you after you left."

"I missed her too." The burn of tears stung my eyes. *Pull it together.* "I bet you're an amazing dad."

"Sarina is the light of my life," he said. "That sounds cheesy as hell, but my baby girl ..." A grin appeared. "Don't get me started."

"I'd love to see a picture."

"Would you really?" He eyed me but pulled out his phone. "This was taken last week."

The tiny girl's huge smile revealed a dimple, and she stared at the camera with wide amber eyes, the mop of dark, curly hair framing her cherubic cheeks. The next picture showed her sporting an impish grin, one finger dipped into the purple icing of a unicorn-shaped birthday cake topped with a single large candle.

"She looks like her daddy," I said, even as the pang hit. "What a cutie. Truly, Jake, she's adorable."

He smiled as he tucked his phone in his pocket. "How about you? Have you given any more thought to having a kid?"

The ache built in my chest as I lifted a shoulder.

"Hmm. The non-answer, answer." He squinted before he handed me another tequila and selected one of his own, downing it in a single swallow. "How times have changed. You used to want one. That was never a secret."

"How do you know I don't have a kid or two stashed at home?"

"Unlikely." He chuckled. "You'd have whipped out the pictures the moment we met at the bar last night, just to show off your perfect life."

Damn the man. "That was before." I welcomed the burn of alcohol as I sucked back my shot. "I've nothing to prove to you."

"All that impulsiveness is locked down tight, right? You've managed to convince yourself that it's under control, huh?"

"You want the low-down on my shitty life? My marriage crumbled, and I left him. There, satisfied?"

"Not in the least. It sucks that you're unhappy." He caught my hand, stroking my bare ring finger with his thumb. "What happened?"

"The usual boring stuff."

"Ah. He cheated?"

"Nah, nothing nearly so dramatic. Things didn't work out, and the baby never happened. Better we didn't have a kid in the middle to play tug o' war over, anyway."

"I'm sorry. You'd be a fantastic mother." Jake signalled the bartender and ordered another set of those sweet little glasses topped with lime curls and offered one to me. "There's a lot you're hiding." He peered over the rim before he tipped back his tequila, the empty shot glass hitting the bar with a thump before he cupped my face between his palms. "Tell me. What's the real story?"

The intensity of his scrutiny burned into me, and I wished I could draw back, but he pinned me with that intense amber stare, stilling me with his warm touch. I shut my eyes, hoping to shield my thoughts, my traitorous body responding as I leaned into him. Why did this man still affect me, making me lose track of why I'd left him in the first place?

I clutched his hand as I fought my internal battle, aching to pull away while pressing his fingers harder against my cheek. This was my Jake ... but not my Jake at all. So many memories and so many conflicting emotions lodged between us. "Why did you tell Dean about last night?"

He took a half-step back, dropping his hand to his side. "I don't know."

"There you are," Dean said as he approached with his arm around Dara. "We're leaving soon, but tonight wouldn't be complete without our final dances." He held out his hand to me as the first notes of a slow song reverberated through the room.

I smiled, following him onto the floor. "What a beautiful wedding."

"I'm glad you came, Mar. Our day wouldn't have been complete without both you and Jake being here, even if circumstances didn't allow you to stand at the altar with us. Thank you, from the bottom of my heart, for introducing me to the most amazing woman in the world."

A lump formed in my throat. I hugged my friend. "You two will be so happy. I know it."

Moments later, Dara, who'd been dancing with Jake, tapped my shoulder and slid an arm around Dean, drawing the four of us into a circle. Her eyes grew misty, and she smiled tearfully. "I miss the four of us together. I love you guys."

The MC's voice came over the speaker, announcing it was time for the bride and groom to depart, but that everyone was welcome to stay and enjoy a midnight buffet and more dancing.

"Have an amazing honeymoon." Jake hugged our friends, stepping back to let me say my own goodbyes.

Moments later, the couple were torn away and engulfed in the crowd, leaving Jake and I on the dance floor.

I wiped my eyes as the lights dimmed and the music level went up another notch.

Jake circled me and rested his hands on my hips, hesitating for only a moment before wrapping an arm around my waist from behind and cradling me against him. "We did good," he whispered. "You should see them together. It's amazing." His voice sounded a touch regretful, but I understood. The last emotional moments with our friends fed my acute longing to feel that same kind of love and joy.

I tipped my head back against his chest, comforted by his touch as we swayed. We used to dance like this, so long ago. I closed my eyes, savouring the delicious, familiar warmth seeping through the silky material of my dress and twined an arm around his neck to bring him closer. The woodsy masculine scent of his aftershave tickled my nostrils as he pressed his cheek to mine.

When the music changed and slowed, Jake caught my hand, twirling me out before drawing me tight against him, his lips grazing the tender spots on my neck, goosebumps rising on my flesh. His exhale was barely audible as he brushed my temple with his lips and rested his forehead against mine. "What you do to me, *Mare*. You're still deep and unpredictable."

My muddled mind flashed urgent signals, begging me to break free from this comfortably dangerous embrace. *Relax. It's just dancing …* No. With this man, it could never be *just* anything. The alcohol hadn't sufficiently dulled my senses to allow that fraught trek to the edge of sanity.

Yet all I could hear was Jake and his low, impossibly tender voice on that first night we'd slept together. *Mare*. The name he uttered only during our closest and most intimate moments. As he had last night. As he was now. Weakening my resolve. Testing my limits. Making me want him.

I wiggled free of the tender hands caressing my back and wobbled toward the safety of the bar. Contact with my beloved ex-boyfriend was a treacherous path leading to a rugged cliff that begged me to jump. Emotional injury was every bit as fatal as physical when it came to my vulnerable heart.

He caught my wrist, spinning me to face him. "Where are you …?" A pained look fleeted across his face. "No, you're right. It's ridiculous. I should go."

I clutched his hand. "What are we doing?"

His lips brushed my cheek. "Sleep well." He kissed me a final time, his fingertips grazing down my arm before he disappeared into the crush.

I stared after him, desperate to find a solution, a way to quell the ache. Slake my desire in a pathetic orgy involving chocolate and tiny bottles of vodka? Invite Christophe, the adventurous photojournalist, upstairs and attempt to satisfy my reawakened carnal cravings? A third option niggled at the edge of my consciousness. No. No bloody way. Time to shut that shit down. But … *Nothing and nobody will satisfy your needs like Jake. Just do it. Live a little. Enjoy some untethered, uninhibited shenanigans.*

I snatched my clutch from the top of the bar on my way toward the exit, pausing to scan for any sign of Jake. The sight of his broad back gave me hope. "Wait!" My heels tapped a rapid staccato beat against the shiny marble as I teetered forward, managing to slip inside the elevator just before the door closed. "Please, Jake," I whispered.

"Don't." He swayed and closed his eyes, rubbing his temples. "We both know where this ends."

"What was that at dinner?" Shuffling closer, I pressed my palm against his firm chest. "Only a kiss …?"

His entire body trembled as if he was scarcely a breath away from breaking down. One arm slid around my waist, and he pulled me against him.

There we stood, nose to nose, unblinking, our eyes and bodies locked. When our lips finally met, I was lost, incapable of anything except responding to him. Clinging to him. Right now, there was only me and this man, back to being that long-lost us.

The next minutes passed hazily. The ding of the elevator. The stumble down the hall. The endless kisses that left me gasping for air and searching for reason. Our silent trip was broken only by the click of the door to his suite, the whisper of my dress slithering into a silky pool, our heavy breath, and lips against sensitive flesh.

No words. No words. Just the tangling of tongues, and the smoothness of hot skin against hot skin. The familiarity of his touch, the brush of that sexy scruff against my navel, that perfect amount of rough and tender that had me yearning for more. The old feelings rose, engulfing me.

Desire … need … love … all intermingled. A perfect union, carrying me back to other times. Better times. Times when we were one and life was easy. Exactly as we were now, even if only for this moment.

CHAPTER 4

We lay entwined among the rumpled sheets, my head resting on Jake's chest as I traced the fine muscle definition with a fingertip. Life could be so beautiful and precious yet remain unpredictable and cruel. Here we were, but how long before he realized his mistake and walked out that door?

If only I could ask what he was thinking, but I didn't dare. A single sound might break the connection, and I wasn't ready for that. Not yet. I closed my eyes, sending a small thanks to the universe when he kissed the top of my head, stroking my hair as I welcomed sleep.

Sometime later, my eyelids flickered. I struggled to open them in the darkness. My body felt heavy with sleep, but something dragged me toward consciousness. Dread crept in. Something was out of place. *Harsh, ragged breathing.*

"Jake?" I rose to my knees, wrapping myself around him as he sat on the edge of the mattress, trembling. "Shh, Jake." I drew him into the bed and pulled his head against my chest, rubbing his back in gentle circles.

He sagged against me, the tension slowly releasing from him as his arm crept around me.

"Tell me." I brushed my lips against the salty sheen of his cheek, still stroking his back.

Jake shivered and drew in a shaky breath "Mar."

"I'm here," I whispered, drawing the covers around us, hoping my presence would banish his nightmares. What spun through his thoughts as we lay there in the dim room, I had no clue. I only knew that this phenomenon was new and uncharted, to be negotiated with care.

Eventually, his breathing quieted, and the silence around us deepened.

"Jake?" I sank lower and lower, a slow recline into the soft pillows, cradling the sleeping man against me.

Jake, always optimistic to the point of annoying, had earned his place as the level, solid, and strong half of our long-demised relationship, yet during the past hours, he'd barely contained his emotions. The man was scattered and unpredictable. A mess. What was I getting myself into?

For the first time in months, I woke up cocooned in warm sheets, curled against an even warmer body, which was pretty close to perfection. The best part? Even if I could never say it out loud, I was with the greatest love of my life. A love who was in no state to hear about my reawakened feelings.

The familiar adorable errant wisp of hair against his forehead beckoned me, begging to be smoothed into place, and I obliged, caressing him gently. Our gazes locked as he opened his eyes. Would our past mistakes get between us now that we were half-way sober?

After several blinks, he captured a curl of my hair in what seemed like agonizingly slow motion and wound it around his fingertip. *"Mare.* You're still here." He brushed the back of his hand over my face and shifted, drawing me closer, caressing my lips with a gentle kiss.

Even after so many years apart, our limbs intertwined naturally, our bodies instinctively remembering the countless times we'd made love. The comfort of my familiar lover, the soaking up of his sensual caresses, and the responding to his increasing demands brought me alive. I stroked his finely muscled back and dug in my fingertips, letting out a soft moan, encouraging his assault on my senses. How could I resist?

Full morning light brightened the room. After a luxurious stretch, I rolled over and reached out, patting the empty space. "Jake?" I propped myself on one elbow, searching for a sign.

He came around the corner, dressed in a casual button-down shirt, his damp hair sticking out at all angles. "Sorry. I didn't mean to wake you. I have to go."

"Is everything okay with Tía? With your daughter?"

Jake nodded. "Yeah, they're fine."

I sat and hugged my knees to my chest, eyeing the overnight bag on the floor by the door. "You weren't planning to say goodbye?"

He shoved his hands into his pockets and bowed his head. "Does that make me a coward?"

I nibbled my lip and tucked my chin to my chest, waiting for him to say something more. Something meaningful. The silence felt heavy and awkward. My eyes stung. I wiggled to the edge of the bed, hauling the sheet around my nakedness while scanning the floor for my clothing.

"Don't leave. Stay and enjoy the room."

I kept my head down, blinking hard as I hauled my dress over my head, shuffling toward the door where my designer shoes lay discarded. On the way, I paused to scoop my clutch from the floor, heart sinking as my expensive lacy lingerie, which had seemed oh-so-important yesterday, evaded me.

Jake advanced, one slow step at a time. "Don't cry, please?"

A burn crept into my cheeks. "Over you?" I dodged past, scarcely avoiding his outstretched hand, managing to hook my shoes with two fingers before fumbling with the lock. "Get over yourself."

"Don't make this—"

"Oh, don't worry. I get it, Jakob. I won't make it a thing." I slipped from his room, scurrying down the roughly carpeted hallway. At the sound of stirrings behind another door, I combed my fingers through my frightful tangle of hair, praying it wasn't one of the other wedding guests heading out for an early breakfast. Ugh. Please don't be Luciana, about to pop out and catch this embarrassing morning-after walk with her brother trailing down the hall behind me.

"Wait. *Mare*, please, let me explain."

"You're banned from ever using that name again." I poked the call button with my index finger. "Come on." I pushed it again, and then again. *Hurry up. Hurry up.*

"Where are you going?"

I prodded the button several times in quick succession.

"That never makes it come faster."

I dipped my head, staring at my bare toes, unable to stop their uncontrollable tapping against the rough grey carpet. "Who asked you?"

"Same old impatient Amara. Come back to the room."

The elevator gods heard my prayers and the door slid open. I stepped inside, lifting my chin and narrowing my eyes as I took one final look at the man who'd just ripped out my heart. The man who'd succeeded in making me love him again. "Sneaking away after playing me just so you could fit in that all-important wedding shag doesn't make you a coward, Jakob. It makes you a complete asshole." I slammed my hand against the button for my floor, grateful when I no longer had to look at him. *Shame on me for breaking my own rules.*

An hour later, my suitcase was packed, my online flight check in was done, and I'd ordered a sedan. Now all I had to do was make it to the airport, and I'd be on my way home. There'd be no faked smiles and endured gossip at the gift opening. No jokes and teasing about that hot wedding reception kiss. No pitying looks from all the disgustingly happy couples, either.

I hauled my bag to the front counter and set my room keys on top.

"Checking out?" The clerk smiled and took my keys, tapping something into the computer. "Was everything to your satisfaction, Ms. Grant?"

Definitely not. However, that wasn't this young man's fault. It was all mine.

"The room was lovely, thank you," I said as I scrawled my signature on the bill and pushed it across the counter.

"So, not quite over with Jake then."

I looked up at the man leaning against the counter.

"You ditched me last night, but I guess that's what I get for leaving an amazing woman like you unattended with an ex-boyfriend on the loose."

"Christophe." I straightened. "No, no. That's over. I promise."

"Hmm." He studied me, a smile flickering and growing. "You remembered my name."

Always. This man was certifiably adorable. As easy to remember as he was to look at. "I wasn't that drunk."

"Heading home?" He eyed my suitcase. "Time for a quick coffee?"

I shook my head. Jake might be over, but teeny twinges of guilt nipped at me. *What the heck was I doing, flirting with Christophe the morning after indulging in a one-night stand with Jake?* Now my ears burned.

"That's a shame." He stepped closer and pressed a business card into my hand. "If you're up for an adventure sometime, give me a call." He leaned in and kissed my cheek. "Safe travels, Amara. Hope I hear from you soon."

I clutched the card in my damp palm, watching until he disappeared around the corner. Call? Maybe. Maybe not. One thing was for sure; no Christophe until I banished my ex-boyfriend from my heart, or anything that might develop was doomed before it began. After tucking his card into my bag, I turned, managing three steps toward the sliding glass doors.

Jake loomed in my path. "You're leaving?"

"Not that it's your business, but yes, Jakob, I am." I sidestepped, scooting around him, hoping to avoid an awkward, stilted goodbye. Only a few more steps, and I'd be through the escape hatch, never to return.

"Can you wait? For a minute?"

Nope. No chance. The heels of my ankle boots tapped on the tile, my pace quickening as I spotted a black sedan pulling up to the curb.

"One damn minute." Jake caught my hand. "Please. That's all I want from you."

"Fine. One minute." I lifted my chin. "Use it wisely."

He tugged me toward the small seating area at the side of the lobby. "This morning wasn't my finest moment. I feel completely shitty for how that went down."

Here came the kiss off, but that had been inevitable all along. To believe otherwise would only be me deluding myself.

That damn wedding ring glinted as he swept his fingers through his hair. "Last night was incredible. Or it was, until the part where I-I …" He scrubbed open palms across his face.

Fucked up badly? Damn, damn. Now he was looking at me with those sad puppy eyes, twisting my emotions, this way, then that way. It would never end with this guy. "You lost your wife. You're sad and lonely. You needed someone in your bed. I get it. It was only one night." I cupped his face. "Call this weekend what it was. Closure. Goodbye, Jakob." Those words about tore my soul right from my body, but it was the right thing. I stretched and kissed him, caressing that sexy scruff, then turned to go.

"Mar." He caught my hand again. "You didn't let me explain."

I pressed two fingers to his lips, then bowed my head to hide my burning eyes. I brushed my index finger over his wedding band. "This tells me everything I need to know." Keeping my head down, I pulled away and headed through the exit, blinking hard.

"Ms. Grant?" The driver opened the car door as I nodded.

I slid into the leather seat, clutching my purse in my lap as the man stowed my bag in the trunk. Moments later, we merged into traffic, ending my second trippy out-of-body experience. I'd finally said my long-overdue goodbye to Jakob Miguel Cavallaro.

CHAPTER 5

When my phone rang and my mother's number appeared on the call display, I continued my task of dicing onion, swaying slightly and humming along to the playlist. As the rings faded to silence, I tossed the pile of veggies and garlic into the pot, enjoying the satisfying sizzle as I stirred.

Not hearing from my mom for a full seven days was unprecedented in recent history, but I figured going to the wedding had earned me a reprieve. However it had happened, I planned to enjoy it. Unfortunately, she was not going down without a fight—or at least an annoying amount of persistence. My phone bleated once, signalling a new message, and rang again.

I loved Mama. I did. It was the focus of this conversation I wasn't looking forward to. The questions I feared were coming.

I rinsed my hands and wandered toward the patio, stabbing at my phone with my index finger. "Hi, Mama."

"There you are. I haven't heard from you for weeks."

I perched on the edge of the wicker deck chair. "It's been less than two. I've been busy."

"I'd hoped you'd come our way while you were in Toronto."

"Next time." The drive to my parents' house was two hours from downtown Toronto on a good day, and this trip, I was unable to justify either the extra time off from work or the extra expense of a rental car. "How's Dad?"

"The usual." She sighed.

Ahh, my father was watching TSN, sinking ever deeper into the cavern he'd worn into the seat of his ratty beige recliner. One day he'd disappear entirely, never again to be seen. How she'd resisted smothering that cranky old man with a pillow boggled my mind. Maybe that day wasn't so far off.

"Who are the Leafs playing?"

"No idea. You know I don't watch sports." Her voice perked up. "How was the wedding? Did you see Jakob?"

"It was lovely. It was great to see the girls. Dara looked beautiful, and so happy."

"And your Jakob?"

I blinked and focussed on the spectacular view of the Lions Gate Bridge and the faint outline of Vancouver Island beyond. "The decor and flowers were amazing." I cringed, imagining what that comment would unleash.

"If only you'd let me arrange your ceremony." About now, her eyelashes would be fluttering, the usual dreamy expression reserved for discussions revolving around Jakob Cavallaro and weddings drifting across her face. "Piles of flowers, miles of lace and tulle." She sighed. "All at the Palais Royale. Jakob would have been so hand—"

"Don't start—"

"Why you married that other guy"—her tone frosted over, her lip surely curling—"when you could have had Jakob, I will never understand."

"Kyle, Mama. His name is … never mind …" I massaged my temples with my thumb and index finger. The ultimate irony. Enduring her judgmental comments about my choices while the woman withered away, married to a man who'd barely looked at her in years.

"That man never treated you right." She sighed. "How is … Kyle?"

"Fine." Truthfully, I had no clue. The relationship had deteriorated to the point where the only safe line of communication was through our lawyers, though I'd never share that tidbit with my meddling mother. "Let's talk later. I have a meeting."

"Promise? And send me some pictures of the wedding."

"I will. Bye, Mama."

The moment my phone was off, I stretched my arms above my head, taking long deep breaths before shaking it all out. With that over with, this precious sunny Saturday was all mine. I took another deep breath, sniffing the air and catching the aroma of lightly torched onion. *Crap.* I hurried back to the kitchen hoping to save the beginnings of my chili.

The late spring sunshine felt warm on my skin as I strode down the long hill toward Lonsdale Quay, sipping ice water and attempting to outrun both my unease and the clutter in my mind. My mom's phone call had yanked unwelcome thoughts of the wedding disaster with Jake to the forefront, along with the reality that I now faced the true end of my marriage to Kyle. Calling it quits heralded yet another failure to add to the growing list.

At one of the shops inside, I ordered a chai latte and a blueberry muffin. I sat at a table overlooking the boat slips, picking at my muffin as the SeaBus chugged across the harbour toward downtown Vancouver and seagulls hopped along the wharf in search of abandoned toddler snacks.

"Can I join you?"

"Luci. What are you doing here?"

"Thought I'd stop for a chai on my way to the Polygon Gallery and spotted you." She waggled her white ceramic mug before plopping into the seat across from me. "We missed you after the wedding. The girls had a fabulous night out, minus the bride, of course. Dean and Dara left for Aruba after the gift opening on Sunday. Where'd you disappear to, anyway?" She fiddled with her spoon. "Jake went missing too."

I set my lips in a flat line. "You found him, I hope."

"Eventually." Her bottom lip jutted out. "He flew home early because he was worried about Sarina. He missed her, or so he said."

"Why would you doubt that?" After a sip of tea, I said, "He seems like a devoted daddy, and she's a cutie."

"It's more than that. He seemed upset about something, and he's been even pissier than usual. Something major happened, but he won't tell me what. Funny. I swear I saw you both leave the reception around the same time."

"Did it escape you that he was in a foul temper for the entire weekend? He barely tolerated me."

"Really? You two looked darn cozy drinking at the bar. Everyone saw those moves on the dance floor, and then you both left within less than a minute of each other." She stared at me. "What happened? Did you fight?"

"Why do you think anything happened?"

"I know what I saw."

"And what's that?"

"The guilty look when I asked Jake if you might want to join us for breakfast. The avoidance in answering the simplest questions. The satin and lace lingerie, in your favourite colour, in his bag."

Heat crept into my face, travelling upward, flaming my cheeks and burning my ears. "Does he know you snooped in his stuff?"

"It wasn't snooping. It was sisterly concern." She cradled her cup in her palms. "I say this because we were close, weren't we?"

"We are still, aren't we?" I squeezed her wrist. "I love you, Luci."

"But not Jake? What did he do? I'd hoped that you two admitted—finally—that you're meant to be."

"Jake will always be here," I said, pressing a hand to my chest, "but we can't be together. Please understand, I'll care about him forever, but it's over."

"Don't you understand what he's been through?" Her keen gaze dug into me.

"No, and I don't pretend to, but I do know Jake. I lived with him for over three years."

"Then give him a chance. Please, Amara. Go home. Jake needs you."

"No. I've built a life here. I love my job, I bought my own place, and made friends. Should I drop everything and move to Halifax? For what? To barge, unasked, into Jake's life?"

Luciana's lip curled. "So, you sleep with him and dump him? Now, when he's at his lowest point, you use him like that?"

"That's what you think of me?" My head swam, and her words were an arrow to my heart, but mostly they fuelled my anger. "Grow up, Luciana. Your brother's a big boy who can take care of himself. Damned if I owe you any explanations."

Luci brushed her eyes with the back of her hand and bolted from her chair. "I hate you." She stalked toward the coffee kiosk, her mug hitting the counter with a thud, then she disappeared into the bustling crowd.

Hearing those words coming from Luci, someone I adored, stole my breath away. I tossed my muffin into the wrapper and shoved it into my bag. Maybe later I'd have an appetite.

❧

The next morning, the strident chime of my alarm woke me after another fitful sleep. The dim morning light barely seeped through the blinds. It was early, but I couldn't delay.

I stretched and tiptoed across the cool hardwood floor, stopping to scan the horizon. The brightening eastern sky promised a sunny day, the sheen of golden light covered with wispy clouds. The news from my western window was equally good, bright blue sky lingering over the Lions Gate bridge, extending far into the distance over the Strait of Georgia.

Some of my sadness at the way things had ended with Luci faded, my heart lightening further as I perched on my patio and savoured the mellow tones of my morning coffee. Despite the gulls' continuous mournful cries, I sensed hope.

At quarter to seven, I added high-energy snacks and a water bottle to my day pack and collected the last essential piece; my travel cup filled to the brim with fresh-brewed searing-hot coffee. Then I exited my cozy condo and rode the elevator to the main floor.

Beth waved from behind the wheel of the small silver SUV parked at the curb out front. "Morning." My friend's dazzling smile cheered me considerably as I buckled into the passenger seat. "I haven't seen you in weeks."

"Blame the wedding. It's good to see you, though." I adjusted the waistband of my formerly well-fitted joggers, tightening them an extra notch as they slid down my hips.

"You've lost weight." My friend frowned. "Again."

"Getting prepared for all the holiday eating."

She snickered, probably picturing the upcoming food fest created by the endless summer barbecues and long weekend parties. "Like you even need it. You'll disappear soon. Still not sleeping?"

"Not much." I cranked up the dial on the stereo as we turned onto the highway, adding my voice to the rock beat thumping through the speakers.

Beth joined in, swaying in her seat and singing along, while I enjoyed the escape from my thoughts.

An hour later, we pulled into the lot, the tires crunching over the gravel as Beth located a parking spot.

We climbed out, and I stretched my arms toward the sky, twisting to work out the kinks.

"How are things with Kyle?" Beth asked as she shouldered her pack.

"It's going. I'm sure I'll get the call to sign papers any day now." I forced one foot in front of the other as we trudged toward the trailhead. The air seemed to thicken, and the world pressed down on me, making it harder to draw air.

"I hate that he hurt you." A small frown appeared. "You're better off, honey. That man changed you, and not in a good way."

I lifted one shoulder and grimaced.

Beth wrinkled her nose. "Woman of few words, huh? How did the wedding go? Did you have fun reconnecting with old friends?"

"Well, basically Dara got her flawless fairytale wedding. Gorgeous, elegant, with the princess gown, perfect food, and amazing cake. I'm mostly glad I went, even though I didn't get to spend much time with either Dar or Viv."

"Mostly?" Her arched brow caused a flutter in my belly as an image of Jake flashed in my mind. "What happened?"

A hot flush took over my entire body, and I swore even my ears must be scarlet.

"Are you … blushing?" Beth's eyes widened and she grinned. "You're glowing. That can only mean one thing. Uninhibited shenanigans! Who was he?"

"Nobody." I cut in front of her on the trail. My pace quickened as I attacked the upward slope, putting several feet of space between us.

A low chuckle broke free from my friend. "I smell an unfolding tale." However, she said nothing further, the only sound the soft thud of our hiking boots on the trail's packed earth.

As the terrain levelled off, I sucked in the musky scent of old-growth forest covered by sparse shrubs. The occasional chirping birds and chattering squirrels soothed me after the sounds of the city. Under the canopy of the trees, the humidity and warmth of the sun filtering onto the pathway caused a trickle of perspiration down my back.

"Water break," Beth said as we reached a clearing near a small creek.

We found a flat rock and rested against it as we dropped our packs to the ground and uncapped our bottles.

After a long slug of water, I leaned back on my hands, tipping up my chin and closing my eyes, concentrating on the rustle of grass and soft burble of water. The outdoors with the expanses of sunny meadows and dramatic vistas ushered a ray of brightness into the dark mood that stalked me. "I needed this. Thanks for inviting me."

Beth patted my hand, smiling softly as she dug into her pack. "Want some?" She extended a bag filled with her famous homemade granola bites.

"My fav." I selected a tidbit and popped it into my mouth, savouring the crunch of sunflower seeds and almonds combined with the tart sweetness of dried cranberries.

We munched in silence, each lifting a hand in greeting as another small group of hikers trudged by on their way to the summit.

"You're awfully quiet about your romantic weekend in Whistler," I said finally. "How did it go?"

She hummed a few bars of something that sounded suspiciously like "Another One Bites the Dust."

"That good, huh. What happened?"

Beth shrugged. "Not much. He's just not that into me. I'm not that into him. So I broke it off and updated my dating profile. This nonsense is so exhausting."

"I'm sorry. What is it with these guys, anyway? They're all hot to date and seem to have their shit together, then suddenly, that shit is everywhere. Then they can't make a single phone call but send plenty of booty-call texts."

As we headed up the trail, Beth asked, "How are you really?"

I heaved a sigh. My respite had ended. "I slept with my ex. It got messy."

Her eyes widened, her lips parting slightly. "What the heck were you thinking? I thought you were done with that dumb ass."

My friend was probably picturing a passionate reunion with Kyle. Why wouldn't she? It wasn't a secret that the physical side of our relationship had never been a problem. It was everything else that made me pack my treasured wine collection and head for the door.

"Not that ex."

"Oh." Her brows drew together, and she halted, shooting her hand out to grasp my forearm. "Wait. You mean that sexy biology boy from Halifax?"

"Jake's a marine biologist." I shrugged her off, scanning the low shrubs around us, searching for one of the lumbering black bears that frequented the area in search of berries. Maybe a huge one would emerge from the scraggly underbrush. For sure that would sidetrack Beth's inquisition.

The crunch of her quickening footsteps and the skittering of loose pebbles pursued me. "Amara." Her hand landed on my shoulder. "You got down and dirty with hot biology boy?"

"Marine. Biologist." I refused to look at her, hoping to avoid her judgment.

"So that's a big yes. No wonder you're glowing. Must have been amazing to have you turning all shades of red." She giggled, then tilted her head. "Wait. Isn't he married? You did the deed with your married ex-boyfriend?"

"He's not married. Not anymore."

"Well, then that's okay, right? Good on you, girl."

"You think?" Good wasn't the word I had in mind. It had taken years and an ill-advised marriage to Kyle Weston to cure me of Jake Cavallaro, but now I was headed back to where I started; reeling from his rejection.

"Well, yeah. You've been moping over idiot banker boy for months. Now you're moving on. You got Mister Rebound over with. No harm in that."

My snicker escaped. My Mister Rebound had happened within a few short weeks of my split with Kyle. Jake was not that. He never could be. "Did you forget about Alex?"

"Oh, right. You did Mister Rebound already, so this is Mister Moving On." Beth giggled, then clapped a hand over her mouth. "Sorry."

"More like Mister Replay Bad History. Who do you think caused the Kyle mess to start with?" Ha. That would shut her up. Yes, that man could definitely fit the topic under discussion. Mister Dead End Relationship, Kyle, who I'd latched onto while I was floundering and miserable, hoping to find true love. Jake, on the other hand, married his new love and made a pretty baby, surrounded by the circle of our closest friends. A circle that had tightened to become their closest friends.

"He's single, so why the heck not?" Beth asked.

How about because of a dark-haired angel complete with amber eyes and adorable dimples, and the wedding ring welded to Jake's finger? Weren't those two insanely perfect reasons to run? "Because it ended with him trying to sneak out of his own hotel room after an all-nighter? And then everyone was sticking their noses in and commenting. Imagine this playing out in front of our two former best friends, at least three hundred wedding guests, and Jake's little sister."

"Ouch." Beth winced. "So, guess you're not planning on seeing him again."

"Not a chance. Anyway, he lives on the other side of the country," I said. "The topper to the whole episode was Luciana cornering me at The Quay yesterday. The little busybody lectured me on how I broke big brother's heart. Now she hates me."

"I'm sorry. Give her a few days to cool off and then reach out. Invite her to the club with us. We can have a ladies' night out next weekend. She's single?"

I nodded. "Yeah, but I can't be out meeting guys with Luci in tow. That would be super weird. Anyway, let's concentrate on getting to the summit before the trail gets busy and it gets scorching hot."

"Fine, but we're still going. Two singles at the club. Or three singles. Get in touch with Luci. No reason you two can't work it out. You used to be close, right?"

I allowed a noncommittal shrug and focussed on the steep climb ahead. Maybe Beth was right. Kyle was long over. Jake and I were done for the second time after a brief blazing inferno, leaving my soul scorched. The future, as bleak as it looked, was waiting for me, whether I wanted to live there or not.

Reaching out to Luci might be the right move. I'd invite her to join us for dinner and a night out. Make peace and move on. It was the only thing left to do.

CHAPTER 6

◍

B eth kept her promise and dragged me to the club on Saturday night, but not until after an afternoon of shopping at Park Royal to find a sexy little club-worthy dress.

And little this jewel-toned creation was, even if—as Beth pointed out—it played beautifully against my mocha skin. I tugged at the hem that continuously crept up, thrilled that I'd splurged on a new satin and lace ensemble to replace the ridiculously expensive set Jake had stripped from my body and was now, apparently, in his possession.

"Quit fidgeting. You look gorgeous." Beth slapped my hand away from my hem before she leaned across the bar and spoke to the bartender. She turned to me. "When did you become such a prude? Club dress. Strutting your stuff. Getting crazy. Remember? You were far more exciting before you married Mister Stuffed Shirt." She tapped a manicured nail on the bar. "Did Luci say she was coming?" she asked as she presented me with tonight's drink special saluting summer; an orange-coloured pink-tinged fruity concoction topped with a twist of grapefruit, a maraschino cherry, and a tacky paper umbrella.

"Nope. She ignored my texts, but at least she knows where we'll be tonight. Guess she's still sufficiently pissed and no longer wants to associate with this heartless bitch." I popped the cherry into my mouth before tossing the garish multicoloured decoration onto the bar and taking a liberal swig of the cocktail, wrinkling my nose and twitching as the tart-sweetness hit my tongue.

"Give it more time and try again," Beth said, scanning the room. "Don't let it ruin your night. He's in here somewhere."

He, in this case, being Mister Hot Guy, whose sole purpose was to rock my world and make me forget all about treacherous Kyle and sneaky Jake, though I still hadn't relayed the entire story. That tale would be for another time, once I'd let it settle and sorted it in my mind. Once I'd analyzed it to death, as Beth always accused me of doing.

I tagged along as she wove her way through the crowd, ending up at a high table beside the dance floor. When she leaned her elbows against it, staking her claim, I followed suit, watching the bustle of bodies. Closing my eyes, I relaxed, shutting everything out while I swayed to the beat.

"Don't get comfortable." Beth nudged me with her elbow. "One drink, and then it's dance time."

"Mind if I join you?" A tall man in a midnight-blue shirt and dark jeans set his drink onto our table, grinning at me before fixing his attention on Beth. "I'm Greg."

I studied him, trying to place the vaguely familiar man while sipping the drink clutched in my hands.

Beth batted her lashes and brushed her long blonde hair over one shoulder, gracing the man with a beguiling smile as she leaned in close, murmuring into his ear.

Small crinkles appeared at the corners of Greg's blue eyes as he returned her smile. He slid an arm around my friend's waist as he bent to say something back to her.

Turning my head away, I scanned the crowd. Leave it to Beth to pick up the hottest dude in the vicinity within seconds, but who could blame the powerless victim who'd succumbed to her lovely smile and voluptuous curves?

The occasional glance from Beth told me that the club's newest couple hadn't totally forgotten I lingered like an uninvited dinner guest. Still, I eyed the exit and then my watch, waiting for the right moment to sidle away and drift into the night.

The motion of Greg's rising hand caught my attention, as did the slight wave as he beckoned someone behind me.

Beth swayed toward me. "Scrumptious with a bonus," she said in my ear. "He brought a friend."

"Hey, Jake." Greg saluted the newcomer with his beer bottle.

"What are the odds? Jake." My friend smothered a giggle. "Must be something about that name."

Greg smirked at me and then averted his gaze as I narrowed my eyes.

Where had I seen Greg before? Then the heady scent of earthy aftershave wafted over me. It took superhuman effort to look up, my worst fear coming true. "Ohhh, no. Hell no!" I took two unsteady steps backward, colliding with someone behind me, the last of my drink sloshing over the rim of the glass and across the front of my dress, trickling down my bare thighs, straight into my shoes.

A low hiss came from whomever I'd stumbled into, accompanied by a sharp impact as they shoved me away. "Watch it, bitch."

The heel of my stiletto snagged—on someone's foot, I imagined, from the yelp—and I pitched forward, flailing as the surface of the table rose to meet me, but the arm slung around my waist caught me seconds before my face connected with the edge. My cheeks flamed as I wiggled free of Jake's embrace.

I slammed my empty glass onto the table and snatched up my clutch before hobbling and weaving through the crowd, focussed on the red sign above the door. Sucking in deep breaths and blinking hard, I barely managed to limp onto the street before the first scalding, salty drops splashed onto the screen of my phone.

"Amara."

"Leave me alone," I muttered, swallowing hard and swiping a hand across my burning cheeks. Each push of my thumb against my phone's home button resulted in a tiny screen jiggle. Damn. I pressed harder but with the same result. "Stupid fingerprint crap."

"Hey." Jake stepped in front of me and grasped my shoulders. "You're limping. Did you hurt yourself?"

"I was fine until you showed up." I wrapped my arms around myself, shivering at the peel of thunder followed by the first drops of icy rain landing on my bare skin. I shook off Jake's hands and manoeuvred past him.

"Relax." Jake shrugged out of his jacket and draped it around me. "Let me check your ankle. I'm a doctor, remember?"

"Ha. For sea creatures. Does the doctor angle work as a pickup line?"

"Like I need to pick you up. Anyway," he said with a wink, "I'm good at anatomy." He crouched, ignoring the damp concrete, and lifted my foot, removing my stiletto. He pressed my ankle with his fingertips. "Does this hurt?"

"A little." A masculine tang clung to every stitch of the enormous leather jacket engulfing me. I hugged it closer, soaking up his lingering body heat, shutting my eyes and inhaling, savouring his tender touch on my bare skin.

"Are you all right? Can you put weight on your foot?"

My eyes popped open, and I hunched my shoulders. "I'm fine. Where's a taxi when you need one?"

"I'll order a car." Jake stood and looped an arm around my waist, supporting me as I hobbled under the awning of a nearby store. He tapped the screen of his phone with one finger. "Hang tight. One's right around the corner."

"Why are you here?"

"Greg talked me into it." His soft laugh sounded a touch nervous. "He accused me of having no life."

"But why are you *here?* To see Luci?"

"Oh. My boss assigned me to a project," he said, his arm tightening around me as he motioned to the street. "That's our ride." Jake assisted me to the curb and into the car, sliding in after me. A droplet trickled down his cheek, and he slicked back his hair, dabbing at his damp face with the sleeve of his sweater.

The driver peered at us in the rear-view mirror. "Address?"

"West 15th, just off Lonsdale."

As our taxi pulled into traffic, I stared out the window, trying my hardest not to look at Jake, who looked adorably tousled in his blue sweater with wet patches. The light scruff on his jawline was absent, his hair trimmed. I longed for those silky soft tendrils that had curled against his neck. "You shaved."

"Hmmm?" His eyebrows rose as a smile touched the corners of those impossibly luscious lips. "Oh." He stroked his chin. "Someone always complained about my scratchy facial hair."

I clamped my teeth over my lower lip and looked away. Pitiful me, noticing the smallest change in the man. Next, I'd blurt out the words topmost in my mind. *I* hadn't said a discouraging word about his sexy scruff while he plundered my body. The exact opposite, in fact, as I'd welcomed the roughness against my tender skin during the night that I now sought to strike from my memory. Sometime, in the distant past, I might have complained … Heat crept up my neck. *It's not even about you, stupid. Why would he shave just for you?*

The moment the car stopped in front of my building, Jake assisted me from the backseat. Warmth seeped through my dress as he slid his hand under the jacket, pressing it against the small of my back, supporting me through the drizzle to the glass door.

"I'm good from here." As I dug for my keys, I brushed away the damp strands of hair clinging to my cheek.

He shook his head. "I'll make sure you get in okay with that mucked up ankle. As my reward, maybe you'll lend me a towel."

The small sigh left me as I unlocked the front door and crooked a finger in his direction. Not ideal, but how could I leave a soggy, chivalrous Jake in the rain?

Once we boarded the elevator, I leaned against the side, taking the weight off my ankle. "Poor Beth. I abandoned her with Greg."

"Ah. I wouldn't worry. Greg's a decent guy."

Of course, he wouldn't worry. He didn't understand Beth's fragile psyche when it came to love and relationships, or what a sucker she was for tall, blond charmers. I, however, knew better. "He seemed familiar."

"He was in my program at Dalhousie. You met him once or twice, but he took a job and transferred to a marine biology program here soon after you and I met." Jake followed me as I hobbled down the hallway, tilting his head as I fumbled with the keys. He scooped them from my icy hands and unlocked the door.

"Hmm." He scanned the space, drawing his brows together. "It's very ... posh."

"What? You don't like it?" *After all the hours I'd put in finding just the right furnishings and hanging the pictures I'd rescued from Kyle's West End condo?* I sank onto the bench by the door and tugged off my shoes, setting them carefully aside.

"It doesn't feel like you."

"Whatever that means. I'm still me. Always have been."

Jake kneeled in front of me, lifting my damaged ankle to his knee and performing another gentle probe with his fingertips. "It's swelling. You should elevate it," he said as I winced.

"I'm fine." I leveraged myself to my feet, sagging at the sharp pain. "Ouch."

Jake caught me. "Careful." He nestled me against his chest, and I looped an arm around his neck for the short trip to my couch. Pulling the ottoman closer, he propped my foot on a pillow, patting it gently. "Where's that towel?" He mussed his damp hair.

I pointed to the small linen closet outside my extra bathroom.

Jake peeled his sweater over his head on his way across the room, his denim-blue shirt pulling up and revealing fine washboard abs and a tapered waist above his low-slung jeans. He retrieved two small towels, using one to dab at his face before he rubbed it over his dripping hair. "You're shaking."

Despite Jake's jacket, a chill permeated my flesh. I struggled out of the wet leather and slung it over the back of my couch, wiggling and tugging at my rising hem.

"You're soaked." He brushed the towel down my legs. "And sticky. What was in that drink?" Jake tugged the bottom of my dress up. "Lift."

I raised my arms, shivering as he peeled the fabric over my head and tossed it in a soggy pile on the floor. Not exactly the sexy scenario I'd pictured when a certified hottie removed my clothing, but still, his intense stare raised goosebumps on my bare flesh.

Jake rubbed my arms and traced a finger over the lacy strap of my bra, then removed his shirt. He helped me into the smooth cotton and buttoned it slowly, leaning so close the warmth of his breath tickled my neck. "Looks good on you," he said as he straightened.

Nope. This couldn't happen. "Sorry for ruining your night. I'm sure you'd rather be at the club."

My shirtless ex-boyfriend scooped up my dress and hung it over one of the dining room chairs and his coat on another. "What, and miss out on your delightful company?" He proceeded to open and close my kitchen cupboards, fill the kettle and set it on top of the gas range, following up with unabashed digging in my drawers before he came up with a spoon. "I thought I'd make tea."

I thought he'd dry off and make himself scarce, but clearly, I'd been overly optimistic. *Nothing like making yourself at home, Jakob.* "What do you want?"

"Chai?" The corners of his mouth turned down as he inspected the glass containers of loose-leaf tea on the counter. "Or maybe black."

"Have you seen my phone?" I pushed myself partway to my feet. "I need to call Beth before she panics."

"Get off that ankle. I'll find it. Did you leave it by the door?" Jake disappeared around the corner, but soon reappeared, waving my phone. He handed it to me then headed into the kitchen to remove the whistling kettle from the burner.

Damned if he didn't move around with complete comfort as if he'd been here a million times. Little flickers of him cooking in our tiny apartment taunted me. This entire scenario was unraveling the memories I'd wound up tight and tucked into the back of my mind.

I tore my gaze away and read the string of texts from Beth. She stated she was fine—and still hanging out with Greg—but to please, please let her know I was okay. I tapped in a quick reply:

I'm fine and made it home. Jake's here, but he'll be leaving soon. Talk later.

I placed my phone face down on the side table. "Well, Jakob?"

"I'm surprised you still have this," he said as he filled my stoneware teapot. "Remember the day we visited Peggy's Cove?"

"How could I forget?" I said softly.

"You spent an incredible amount of time in that local shop admiring the amazing blue and grey patterns, so I drove back the next weekend to buy it for you."

"I still have most of the set, though one of the mugs got broken. Home is never home without my tea set."

"The extra trip was worthwhile." Jake glanced at me as he set two of the matching mugs on the counter. "Hope you're happy with chai."

I nodded, keeping my eyes averted as he delivered a cup to me.

"I added honey, just the way you like it," he said, sitting only inches away on the sofa.

This familiarity messed with my mind, making me want more from him than I could ever expect in reality.

"Look at me. Please?"

I set my tea on the coffee table and tried to tuck one leg beneath me, grimacing at the stab of pain.

"Stubborn woman." He repositioned me, lifting my sore ankle and placing it on his thigh, beginning a massage.

Mesmerized, I watched as he circled his thumbs, scrunching my nose as he dug into the flesh on the ball of my foot. *Pain. Exquisite, feel good, pain.* I focussed on my pink-polished toes.

"I'm sorry for what happened after the wedding." He rubbed the top of my foot before continuing the torture of my sole. "It was difficult to explain. You didn't seem to want to hear it, anyway."

My mouth grew dry. I closed my eyes, squeezing them tight before I opened them and inspected his left hand with its faint, pale outline on that certain finger. I cleared my throat. "Explain what?"

"Why I almost left without saying goodbye."

This should be good. "Bygones." I fluttered my fingers and tried to pull my foot from his firm, yet gentle, hold.

"What woman wants to deal with a guy who turns into a panicky mess in the middle of the night?"

"Jake." I looked straight into his eyes.

He caught my hand and nodded, staring at our entwined fingers. "When you wear something long enough, it becomes habit. You forget it's there. Sometimes it's to avoid the judgements, accusations, and assumptions that you haven't grieved long enough, or you've forgotten. Death is nothing like divorce where removing the ring is expected."

"It's okay."

"It's inexcusable. That weekend, I used it as a defence to back women off and give me space. Answering questions and dealing with the pity is exhausting."

"It worked."

"On the wrong woman. It gave you the wrong idea. If I had any doubts about how stupid it was, Dara cured me of them."

"She talked to you?"

"After you left, she caught me marinating myself at the hotel bar. Boy, did she rip into me, but everything she said was the absolute truth. Guess her sympathy wore out."

"She's a tattler."

"You talked to Dara?" He lifted a brow. "After you lectured me for telling Dean?"

"Don't shift the blame. You spilled your guts to Dean first, and now everyone knows."

"You're right. I shouldn't have said anything, but at breakfast before the wedding, Dean dragged it out of me. Then he played matchmaker, and by the time they pulled our names, I was half-cut. You tasted sweet and smelled delicious, reminding me of how we christened the dining room table in our apartment."

My breath caught, that long-ago moment playing in vivid colour. Cutlery clattering and papers fluttering as Jake swept the scarred pine top with one hand, the other lifting me, his bare back taught as I dug in with my fingertips. Our first twenty-four hours as roomies had been unforgettable. "You said our kiss was no biggie."

"Yeah … no. After that, I needed a cold shower. Don't tell me you didn't feel that kiss, 'cause for sure I enjoyed your delectable tongue in my mouth. And later, ripping those hot lacy panties off your fine ass with my teeth. Those slinky little scraps of lace are exactly the type to get me riled. You know that."

My entire body tingled, and I tugged at the cuffs of his shirt, trying not to inhale the remnants of aftershave too deeply or delve into why I'd worn that particular lacy thong and matching bra.

"Tell me you didn't enjoy our evening, and I'll walk out that door right now."

Fighting a smile, I said, "I hated every second."

Jake chuckled. "Stay, it is. With you, the sex is always amazing."

"Is that why you're here? For more fantastic sex?"

"Well, at least we've established that we agree about something." He winked.

"Stop." I narrowed my eyes. "Shameless flirt."

"Ahhh, fine." His grin faded. "That horrendous ending deserved more than a phone conversation. Luci mentioned the club invite, and I paid attention. Besides, calling meant you'd tell me to fuck off before we had a proper talk."

"So it was an ambush?" *Oh crap.* Those eyes. Stop, stop, stop looking at me like that, Jakob. I cleared my throat and pressed my lips together, looking away.

"It wasn't meant to be." He cupped my cheek, forcing me to look at him. "I screwed everything up, you're pissed, and you'll never forgive me for not realizing how it made you feel. Wearing my ring while we were together, so intimate ... I'm sorry. That was thoughtless and wrong in every imaginable way. The ring's off, forever."

"Where does that leave us?" Me, half-soothed, but still licking my reopened wounds? "Was it just a bit of weekend fun?"

"You're way off base." He tipped my chin with a fingertip. "I've missed you every single day, but now my life's impossibly complicated and fucked-up."

"Is that an apology? No need for more than that." *Please go before I do something I regret.*

"Have you ever wondered ... fuck, this is insanity, but what if ..." Jake leaned close, the essence of shampoo and fresh rain combining as he kissed my cheek. "This is wrong," he whispered, seconds before he captured my lips.

Rising to my knees, I curled my arm around his back and pressed my aching body against him. I tucked my face into the crook of his neck, soaking up the heady masculine scent of my

Jake, shifting to entwine my legs around his waist while kissing his tender flesh and ruffling my hands through his thick hair.

"My beautiful *Mare*." The mere whisper of his sweet endearment melted me, leaving me ready to be molded as he wished.

α

"Coffee?" Jake's minty breath brushed against my cheek. He kneeled beside my bed, waggling the cup cradled between his fingers, a delightful smile twitching his lips.

"It's Sunday. Why are you up?" The whiff of my rosemary shampoo and the sight of his damp, tousled hair launched me into high alert. "Where are you going?"

"I promised Greg we'd cruise up the coast and gather samples. That's the job I'm here to do. I'm working with Greg on a joint study." He waved a hand. "I won't bore you with details."

I sat and combed my fingers through my tangled locks, snagging the steaming coffee. "And then?"

"A late flight home."

"So soon?"

"I have ... responsibilities."

"Your daughter?"

He nodded. "Sari's a handful, so I can't be away too long. The single parent gig isn't the easiest."

"Well, it's back to reality for us." I stroked his cheek with my fingertips, then down to caress his rough, stubbly jawline. Our sweet interlude was ending. His child trumped everything. Besides, I had no right to demand anything. The man had only managed to remove his ring, which was hardly a commitment to me. *Yup*. I was an idiot for breaking my own rules.

He glanced at his watch, then dropped a kiss on my hair. "Greg's waiting. I'll call later."

The sight of his retreating back followed by the hollow click of a closing door caused a stab of indescribable pain. What if he didn't call? Or even more troubling; what if he did?

CHAPTER 7

J̲ake called late Sunday night as I rummaged through my closet, sipping a glass of white wine and preparing for my upcoming work week.

"I can't talk long. They'll be calling my flight."

"Did you get your samples?" I shoved aside several tops, spotting a pair of my navy work pants hanging toward the back of the walk-in closet.

"And then some. We had a busy day, and I'm beat." Muffled airport sounds followed by a tinny announcement carried down the line. "What did you do?"

"Not much." Nothing but drive myself crazy with self-doubt and avoid answering the numerous texts from Beth. "Just a little laundry, and I finished my online course."

"Oh, right. Updating your drug-pusher status."

"I'm not—" I rolled my eyes at his snicker. This man had teased me about my career aspirations in pharmacy from the first day we'd met in university. "Better than examining pond scum for a living."

Another low laugh issued from Jake, and I tightened my grip on the phone. How I missed that laugh, his voice, along with almost everything else about him.

"Is your ankle better?"

"It's perfect. Must have been that amazing massage."

"My pleasure."

I tipped back my glass, emptying the final drops. "What is this, Jake?"

"What do you mean?"

"This thing we're doing." I lowered myself to the edge of my bed. "Us. You live on the other side of the country."

"I have to go. Boarding call."

The small sigh escaped. I'd spent the entire day both dreading and anticipating this moment. Now I knew. *This* was a deep pit of nothingness. A dangerous quagmire dragging me underneath its murk. "Have a safe flight." I tapped disconnect and curled up on the bed, ignoring the insistent, periodic ringing of my phone by pressing my face into the pillow, inhaling the masculine scent lingering on my sheets. The only part of Jake that was truly mine.

Several minutes later, my phone dinged, alerting me to the text:

I hate that you're ignoring my calls. There's much more to say.

I stared at the tiny dots dancing across the screen, before the next message appeared:

I'm sorry. My flight is about to take off, so I have to turn off my phone. We still need to talk.

The dots danced again:

Sleep well. I'll call tomorrow night, okay? Please answer when I do.

I tapped my phone against my forehead. Okay, so maybe they really had called his flight. Maybe it wasn't a return to us avoiding the hard conversations. It still didn't mean anything.

I wandered into the kitchen, refilling my wine and settling on my couch.

"About time you called me back," Beth said when she answered my call. "I've been trying to get hold of you all day."

"Sorry, I had that course to do. How are you?"

"Ha." She snorted. "You mean you had a hot guy to do. What happened with Jake?"

I twisted a hank of hair around my finger. "What do you think happened?"

"Amara," she said softly, "please be careful with him."

"You thought he was great the other day."

"That's a gross over-exaggeration. I said, 'probably no harm in sleeping with him,' not that having a hot affair with an ex who lives on the opposite coast is a fantastic idea. Plus I've gained important new information. His wife died? That makes him a widower. A high-risk proposition."

"What else did Greg say?"

"Not much, aside from the wife's name—Alysa—and she died barely six months ago. Greg's a touch evasive about his friend's home life, but it seems the situation is complicated and messy. I interpret that as meaning the man has loads of baggage and avoids commitment."

"Who said I wanted commitment?"

"This is *the* Jake we're talking about." Beth let that zinger hang for a moment. "What happened to her?"

"Not sure. We haven't gotten into it, and it's not relevant since it's over. *The* Jake is on a plane to Halifax."

"That's it?"

"You're right. It's too complicated and messy." Even without the ring, everything about Jakob Cavallaro screamed emotionally unavailable and unable to commit. No matter that my love simmered in the background, my cravings reawakened. Tomorrow night, I'd have to end whatever this was, unless Jake ended it first.

❧

"You're cutting it close." Beth tapped her watch as I joined her in the queue for the theatre. "I thought you forgot our movie date."

"Sorry. Yoga ran long, and I had to shower and change." Balancing my bag of popcorn and water bottle, I wrangled my phone from my pocket and located my e-ticket. "I texted."

"One lousy line." She glared. "At bedtime." Her eyes narrowed. "I spent Monday worrying about you, and then you cancelled for Tuesday."

"Will you ever forgive me?" I did my best rendition of puppy dog eyes. "It's been crazy."

"Unless crazy is a euphemism for 'hot guy who's helping me get over my exes had me pinned to the mattress,' you're not forgiven."

I presented my phone to the sullen teenager at the wicket and followed my friend into the theatre.

"Is that what happened?" Beth asked as we located our seats. "Some random hot dude, making you forget all your troubles?"

I smothered a snort and shovelled a handful of popcorn into my mouth.

"Ah. Avoidance. As long as you didn't sleep with Jake, or contact Jake, or pine over Jake, you're forgiven." She looked at me. "Oh, crap. Pining. I knew it!"

"You sound surprised." What else would I do in this situation besides overthink, overanalyze, overreact, and then curl up in a ball and cry it all out for endless hours, periodically peeking at the massive bouquet from Jake? *Ha*. This woman called herself my best friend?

"Well, call me an optimist. Sue me for harbouring some hope that you'd broken out of your usual self-destructive pattern, realized the danger you're in, and ended it. You did, right?" The suspicion in her eyes told me she wasn't fooled. "Call him and end it!"

"I will. I've been busy."

"You're trying my patience. Get unbusy and do it. Tonight."

Well, touché. "Speaking of being pinned to the mattress, what's happening with you and Greg? That was some heavy-duty flirting, and you went home with him."

A delicate flush rose in her cheeks. "Not that you deserve an answer, but that man is not only smoking hot, but a total sweetheart. We're going for dinner on Saturday."

"Mister Blond n' Blue-eyes sucked you right in," I said under my breath as music blared and the previews began.

Beth nudged me with her elbow. "What was that?"

"Shhh. Oh, that looks good," I pointed at the screen.

"Yeah. Right." My friend adjusted her glasses and reclined her seat. "Don't think I'll forget," she whispered.

No, of course not, but there was still hope. Maybe my reprieve would last beyond the end of the movie.

As we dropped our garbage into the bins and exited onto the sidewalk, a gleam appeared in my friend's eyes. "What aren't you telling me?" Beth tugged me to a halt. "You did the deed with Jake again on the weekend, and now you're depressed."

"You did the deed with Greg. What's your point?"

"Greg's not my ex."

"Worse. You're getting all gushy over him. A one-night stand, fine, but you're winding yourself up for more. You're warning me to be careful with Jake when you should be taking care not to fall too hard for Mister Blond n' Blue-eyes. You barely know the man."

"You know his friend." A hopeful lilt coloured her voice.

"Do I?" That was debatable. The current grownup Jake was an enigma. Widower, now-a-daddy Jake existed on virtually another planet. At this moment, he was probably buried in childcare arrangements, diapers, and doctor's appointments.

"Why are you so against me being happy?"

I bit my lip, stalling all the things that wanted to fly from my mouth. "I love you, Beth, and you deserve a strong, loving man. A man who will put you first. Is Greg him? I have no idea." My lovely friend had been shattered by an endless stream of faithless lying cheaters. The aftermath was exhausting and painful to watch.

"At least I don't run whenever a guy pays too much attention."

Ouch. Is that what she thought? "I'm beat." I smothered a yawn.

Beth sighed, but fell into step as we trudged uphill toward home, a steady flow of vehicles swishing by us. Her downturned lips and shimmering eyes made me wonder if I'd been too harsh. This rare and precious woman deserved more than the spineless players that lurked in the dark corners of every club.

"I'm just Jake's diversion," I said when I could no longer ignore her sighs and sideways looks. "Maybe not even that. Even he admits that his life is messed up and us being together is wrong. You don't need to worry."

"Ummm ... I believe I do, actually."

"No. I'll tell him we shouldn't continue whatever this is." I focussed on the ground, kicking at a small stone and sending it skittering across the pitted cement as we headed toward the front door of my building.

"Amara ..."

"It's not running. It's being sensible."

"What is?" asked a deep and familiar voice.

"Traitor." I mouthed at Beth before turning toward the man leaning against my building with a small package tucked under one arm. "Why are you here?"

"Many reasons, actually, work being one of them," Jake said.

"I'm Beth." The traitor extended her hand. "We meet at last. Properly, at least."

Jake smiled, that adorable dimple in his right cheek appearing as he gripped her hand. "What has Amara been telling you?"

"Umm, not much."

That was at least partially true. Most of what she knew came from Greg or the bits she'd dragged from me during my self-defence mode. Besides, sharing too much would break my beautiful fantasy world. The one I clung to in those wee hours before dawn when sleep evaded me; the hours when I pretended a future with Jake was possible.

"Uh-huh." One of his brows rose the tiniest bit.

"I should go," Beth said. "Nice to meet you, Jake. I'll call you later, Mar." She hugged me, whispering in my ear, "Hell, he's even sexier in full daylight. No more shenanigans." As she walked away, she glanced over her shoulder.

Jake's smile faded. "Your friend's less than thrilled to see me."

"We watch out for each other."

"And I'm the dangerous, bad-boy ex." He leaned in, looping an arm around my waist.

"Hardly." I sidestepped, smothering a laugh at the suggestion that Jake—AKA Mister Responsibility—could even pretend to be the stereotypical bad boy. "Still, go home."

"I'm sorry." He scrubbed his hand through his hair. "That seems to be all I say lately, but I am ... sorry."

"Sure, until next time when you'll be sorry again. East Coast"—I pointed at his chest, then hooked my thumbs toward myself—"West Coast. How is that supposed to work?"

"Maybe we've both grown up. Maybe this is our chance." He glanced over his shoulder as one of my neighbours entered the building. "Can we go inside and talk privately?"

I shook my head. Alone with this charmer. Worst-ever idea. Somehow, we never ended up just talking. "There's a coffee shop around the corner."

"Lead the way."

CHAPTER 8

The warmth of Jake's hand against my back as he ushered me inside the door of the café made me shiver. "Chai latte, Mar?"

"Please." I draped my coat over one of the wicker chairs before settling into the chocolate-coloured faux leather seat.

Jake slung his jacket over the back of another chair and set the package on the table before heading toward the front counter. He extracted his bank card from his wallet, his chuckle carrying across the café as the barista batted big baby blues and smiled with a practiced coyness. Jake leaned in, shaking his head at whatever the woman said as she fiddled with the machine and, finally, she placed two mint-green ceramic cups on the counter, fluttering her lashes.

Moments later, Jake set my cup in front of me. "Why so serious?"

"Hmmm?" I forced the corners of my mouth up, ignoring the covert glances from the flirty barista. Checking for evidence of couple's chemistry and assessing Jake's potential availability, no doubt.

His brows drew together, but then smoothed, a tight smile appearing as he sat across from me. "I never can tell what you're thinking."

I lifted one shoulder, distracting myself with the artistry of the leaf etched in the foam.

"It's that flattering, huh?" Jake raked his fingers through his hair and stared at me, barely blinking, then pushed the box toward me. "Brought you something. Sorry, it's not wrapped with a pretty bow on top, but I had to put it in my carry-on bag, so …"

"What are you up to?" I removed the tab of scotch tape and unhooked the flap. "It's perfect," I said as I lifted the mug from the box. "I tried to replace the broken one, but I couldn't find any that matched."

"I used my superior sleuthing skills and tracked down the artisan. She remembered the design, so she made one for me."

"Thank you. That's sweet." I reached across the table and squeezed his hand, aching to hug him. But how could I? What kind of message would that send? Instead, I wrapped my fingers securely around my cup of chai.

"You wanted to know what this"—he waved between us— "is."

I scuffed the toe of my leather boot across the rough tile. "Maybe it doesn't matter. Go back to your life and forget about it."

"I can't." He pried my fingers loose from the mint-green cup and gripped my hand. "The question caught me unprepared." Jake brushed his fingertips over my palm, his light sensuous touch making me twitch. "I didn't know what to say, and then when I did, you ignored my calls. Did you get the bouquet?"

"Yes." I tugged free and clasped my hands in my lap. "Stargazers. Nice touch."

"Why the sarcasm? Remember when we'd lay on the beach for hours looking at the stars?"

"Yeah, and you're using that to get to me."

"Cynical." He shook his head slowly. "The florist had an amazing display of lilies, and I thought about you and how close you seemed on those nights, that maybe you'd remember how much fun we had, and the flowers might make you smile. Silly me."

"I'm sorry," I whispered, now feeling like the most churlish human in existence. I'd never forgotten the soothing shush of waves on the dark beach wrapping us in a secure cocoon, keeping my secrets safe even as I'd bared my deepest fears and feelings. "They made me smile, and cry, and miss you. I hated you a little, too, for playing that card."

Jake's smile was tinged with sadness. "It's not a play. I'm working my way through a bundle of confusing feelings, but you're not cooperating, at all."

"It's too complicated. That's why this thing is over."

"Is it?" He traced the jagged heart embedded in our table. "I wonder if ours is still there."

I gnawed my lip, picturing the perfectly formed heart Jake painstakingly carved so long ago in that Muskoka dock one hot night in mid-August. *J.C. + A.G. forever.*

"This is my first real relationship since ..." Jake closed his eyes, tapping a fingertip against the scarred wood. "Jumping into something, considering our history, is dangerous. I get that."

I considered my next words, debating, keeping one eye on Jake as I took a long lingering swallow of the perfect blend of chai and honey. "It isn't anything," I said, finally. "We can't let it."

"It might be something." That finger was in motion again as he bowed his head. "It seemed—seems—like everything."

It had to be said. Didn't it? Allowing him an easy out was the right thing. The kind thing. Wasn't it? Damn. Those eyes. Quit looking at me like that, Jakob. All that hope, that sweetness, that ...

"If we take it slow. Stay low key."

"Long distance?" My knee twitched, speeding into a nervous bounce as I slurped another mouthful of tea. "Like that ever works."

He brushed his thumb over my top lip. "Maybe if I was closer." That thumb travelled to his mouth, riveting me as it transferred that tiny lick of chai froth between those kissable lips.

I swallowed hard and gulped more tea before licking my own lips. "Are you moving to Vancouver?"

"I'll be here more often. I'm working with Greg for a while."

"And then?" *Deliver me from temptation.* An alluring idea was growing. What would it hurt to enjoy these moments with Jake, even if brief? I bowed my head, scooping the remaining foam into little piles on the surface of my tea, finally lifting my cup and peering over the rim.

His solemn stare met mine. "Forget it," he said. "Ridiculous idea."

My inner voice begged me not to get hurt. Not again. My weakness for this particular man could never change the actual facts. I swallowed hard. "Yeah, grief rebounds never work."

His grip tightened on his cup, but other than that, neither of us moved. "That's not how I see this, but ..." Jake looked down. "I won't pretend it isn't difficult and strange, but I want to start living again."

Imagining the pain this sweet man had endured, I covered his hand with mine. "Are you truly ready," I said as I traced my fingertips over the faint pale line on his bare ring finger, "to be with someone who's not her?"

Jake glanced up. "The hardest part is when people—especially women—look at me like you're looking at me right this second."

I straightened, swaying toward him.

"Conversations stop when I enter a room. Her name is never mentioned—at least not in front of me. You and Luci did it at the wedding. I could tell you were grilling her about me. Maybe about *her*."

"I'm sorry."

"It's always that sad pity combined with pathetic euphemisms." He lifted his head. "My wife died, suddenly and unexpectedly. I didn't lose her, she didn't pass. She died."

"What happened to her?"

"Can this be about us? Just for now? Everything in my life is about everyone else, but with you, I can be me. I want something real again, to see where it goes, just like I would with any relationship. I want that someone to be you."

My grip on his hand tightened. Maybe the thought of being with Jake wasn't so outrageous. At least he didn't seem to think so. Yet ... "Should it be me? You've had zero relationships since her. The very definition of rebound."

"Real. Not zero," he said. "None of them were you."

"Maybe I'm the worst choice. We have history." This felt too real, too intense. "You've barely taken off your ring."

"It's off because it's past due. My marriage was complicated and not always happy. It's time to let it all go."

"It's only been six months."

"I'm aware. The timing doesn't make my feelings for you less real or true."

"Are you sure?"

"Well, yeah. It's weird but taking off my ring lifted the weight and stress. All I've done these past few days was think about you, and me, and us, and our future."

"You thought about us? As a couple?"

He nodded. "Constantly."

Our fragile bond strengthened as we looked at each other, then faltered, his smile widened, but then faded.

My head bobbed, my body acknowledging what my mind scarcely comprehended. I drew in air, steadying my breathing against the staccato beat in my ears. Not too late to back out. But no. This was Jake. Even considering the challenges his young daughter and the distance added, this relationship might be worth the gamble.

"Want to get out of here?" I nibbled my bottom lip, hoping to send an alluring invitation. I'm sure I failed, but if what he said was true, he wanted far more than sex.

That familiar, adorable grin appeared as he rose to his feet and shoved his arms into the sleeves of his jacket. He hauled me to my feet and grabbed the box with my replacement mug, then urged me toward the door. On the street, he wrapped his fingers securely around mine as we hurried through the deepening darkness to my front door.

A giggle broke free as I fumbled with the key fob and pulled him into the lobby. Between kisses we stumbled into the elevator.

Jake propped himself against the side with one hand, the other curled behind my head as he leaned in and captured my lips again. "I've missed you, *Mare*." He pressed his lips to the tender flesh on my neck. "I've missed this."

As I tipped my head to the side and closed my eyes, the ache in my heart expanded. What if I'd never walked away? Then another little voice begged me to live in the here and now, where all things were possible.

In the now, Jake pinned me almost immobile, practically devouring me, not stopping until we reached my floor.

"Wait." I flattened a palm against his chest as I wobbled one step backward. "Wait …"

"Weren't we …?" He closed his eyes. "See? Stupid," he muttered.

"No, but let's slow down. We have all night." I unlocked the door and beckoned him inside, taking the box from him. "Make yourself comfortable."

"It's like our first date." He hung his jacket and slipped off his shoes.

"It's our first date for the second time." I moved through to the kitchen, unpacking my mug and setting it on the counter before selecting a bottle of wine and two glasses.

His warm breath brushed against my skin as he arrived behind me and leaned in, setting the wine bottle aside before his mouth was on mine again. He brushed the hair back from my face. "I love you."

"You do?" The little tingles running through me made me shiver, as I stroked his impossibly warm, smooth skin.

Jake caressed my hip, drawing me closer. "I never got over you. Not sure I ever will."

Maybe this was a fantastic dream, but no harm in letting this wonderful fantasy play out. I wound my arm around his neck as he pressed the entire length of his body against mine.

"Can we quit holding back and just do this already?" he asked.

I stared into his eyes. "Shut up and take me to bed."

He caught the bottom of my sweater and tugged it over my head, barely losing a beat before releasing my bra and attacking my neck with a fervour that made me weak in the knees.

The only thing I managed was to moan and yank at the buttons on his shirt, anxious for skin on skin. "Mmm, Jake." My entire body quaked.

Jake scooped me up and carried me to the bedroom, peeling off his shirt seconds after depositing me on the bed.

Damn. This man was beautiful. All lean toned muscle and smooth tanned skin, and not in the least bit shy as his jeans joined the rest of his clothes on the floor.

I squirmed and wiggled to free myself from my pants, Jake joining the tussle of pulling the dark-washed denim over my feet and discarding it in a heap.

His mouth engulfed my breast, hot hands skimming across my skin, then lifting my hips. Now there was nothing between us. Nothing to keep us apart.

Taking the second day off in a row made me feel a touch guilty, but how could I resist spending this precious day with Jake? Tomorrow he'd be on a plane to Halifax so many thousands of kilometres away, and we'd be relegated to days of text and phone calls.

Jake entwined our fingers as we walked down the hill, enjoying the warm and sunny afternoon. "Where are we going?"

"A cute little café that serves the most amazing comfort food. Like homemade mac and cheese, and ..." I wrinkled my nose, laughing as he smirked. "What?"

"You always did love to eat, but that's a great thing." His arm slid around me. "Remember that place down the street from our apartment?"

"Of course." As university students with heavy course loads, we often ate at the locally owned café. The food was amazing, and those forays doubled as a way to eat out and stay on budget. Our local haunt became our secondary study hall, where we'd quiz each other and pore over notes as we shovelled in their weekly special. Then we'd rush back to our snug apartment and make love, spending countless hours in each other's arms. "Having you here doesn't feel real," I said.

"Mmm, but I am." He rubbed my back. "What's the best dish on the menu?"

"That's a tough one. I love the—" My eyes widened as I spotted a familiar figure crossing the street in front of the Polygon Gallery.

"Amara," Kyle said as he halted several feet from us. His lips flattened, and he stared at our entwined hands, approaching slowly. "I'm Kyle Weston," he said, extending a hand to Jake.

"Jake Cavallaro," he said as the two men eyed each other.

I plastered on a smile. "What are you doing here?"

"I'm meeting the guys at the pub," Kyle said.

I nodded.

"Speaking of which, I'd better get moving. We're planning to watch the game." Kyle rubbed the back of his neck. "Can you call me tomorrow, if you're not too busy?" He dodged around us, practically loping up the steep slope.

"Kyle, huh?" Jake squeezed my hand.

I lifted a shoulder, nibbling at my lip as we entered the café and requested a table for two.

Once we were seated, Jake said, "That seemed a touch awkward for you."

"No ..."

His raised eyebrows had me shifting on the bench. "No?"

"Okay! It was weird for the two of you to meet like that. I was unprepared. It's been at least two months since I've seen him."

He set his menu aside and took my hand, stroking it with his thumb. "Was it a rough separation? He looked pissed about us holding hands."

"Like he'd give a crap about what I do in my personal life. He's just grouchy about the divorce papers."

Jake squinted.

"He texted me last week to hurry up and get to the lawyer to sign them, but I've been busy. They'll get done when they get done."

The man across from me rubbed his temples. "You aren't divorced yet?"

"It's not that big of a deal. He's been so indifferent, so emotionless, so ..." Stiff and unyielding.

"That look didn't say indifferent or emotionless. It said the man wanted to lay me out on that sidewalk. Just put the guy out of his misery and sign the damn divorce papers so he knows it's over. Or, if not for him, do it for yourself. For us."

"Bossy." I crossed my arms and sat back. "It'll get done."

Jake leaned back and mimicked me, crossing his own arms. "Why haven't you signed?"

Crap, crap. Now both Kyle and Jake were on my case. Jake practically had steam rising.

"It's not really your business," I said, narrowing my eyes.

"Refusing to divorce your husband when you and I are sleeping together isn't my business? Silly me, acting like we're in a relationship."

I shrank a little.

"You don't want to divorce him? Or are you running away, like always?"

"I'm not running."

"It's what you do. Avoid the real issues and then cut and run when it gets tough."

"I don't."

"Huh. Why did you sneak out of my room that first night at the wedding?"

"At least I didn't wait until after we had sex and then sneak out like you were some stray I'd picked up at the bar."

He narrowed his eyes. "Back to that, huh."

"If the truth fits."

Jake cupped his hands over his face, a long groan accompanying the tiny shake of his head. "This shit is getting us nowhere." He thumped a fist on the table, but his expression softened as our eyes locked. "I'm sorry for taking advantage of that situation. I'm sorry you thought it was less than it was. I'm sorry for being such a fucking mess. The woman I've loved for almost ten years showed up, all single, available, and desirable, acting so sweet and caring, and looking better than ever. I just ... wanted you in a way I hadn't wanted anyone in forever."

Damn, those eyes again. This man sounded so reasonable and lovable and vulnerable, digging deeper and deeper into my heart. "It was a strange situation, and we ended up in such an intimate position. But that damn ring ..."

"Okay, okay." He raised his hands. "I plead no contest."

A surrender of sorts. Maybe a signal that we'd ground this topic down to its roots and nothing further could be gained.

"Can we call this subject closed?" Jake asked. "You freaked, I acted like an embarrassed emotional mess, yada, yada, done. Okay? It still leaves us in the same place." He stared at me. "Do you regret leaving Kyle? Do you love him?"

I clamped my teeth onto my lower lip, blinking hard. "No." I curled into myself.

Jake sighed and then rose, only to slide into the booth beside me. He tucked an arm around me. "Divorce isn't easy, I get that, but if it's over, then finish it. If you aren't ready for that, then you aren't ready to start something new."

Unlike the day of the wedding, now I could lean into Jake and enjoy the security of his arms. I wanted more of that. I needed it. Longed for it.

"I spent a lot of time examining how ready I was," he said, "but I didn't consider that maybe you're not there yet. Maybe we should take a step back."

"Is that what you want?"

"Do you?" He kissed my temple as I rested against his shoulder. "Ah, my beautiful love, you are stubborn, and infuriating, and confrontational, and exhausting, but you're also strong, and independent, and incredibly sexy. A life with you will never be boring or routine. You're a challenge, a convoluted puzzle, which I love, even if it means working ten times as hard to keep this together."

"That's probably true, but it's worth it. I do want a divorce, but signing those papers means another failed relationship. It means admitting Mama was right about Kyle."

"What happened, anyway?"

I sighed, but I owed him at least a basic explanation. "In the beginning, we had fun, travelled, and spent all our time together. After the first year, it all changed. Kyle worked longer hours and hung out with the guys more often. Maybe he had an affair, but I never found any proof, so who knows? Anyway, I thought I could handle anything besides cheating, but it turned out I couldn't."

"Handle what, exactly?"

"The eerie silence and depressing daily dance where I was an afterthought, the sure thing, waiting for him to come home at whatever awful hour. I never figured out what I'd done to deserve his neglect, and he never explained why he stopped talking. Well, at least about anything real. So, I packed my wine collection and bought my condo."

"You made the right choice." He squeezed me tighter. "Endings are sad, but cut the cord."

"Maybe me not signing the papers isn't so different than you with your ring, me keeping everything and everyone at bay while I figured out how I ended up where I did."

"Maybe."

As I cuddled against Jake, the reality of the past five years faded. This felt right, our silence comforting and connected, so unlike the empty, oppressive silences with Kyle. My marriage often felt lonely, my husband growing more distant each day until he could no longer see me. Now I'd travelled full circle, perhaps ending up exactly where I needed to be. "Luci will never shut up about this. She's insistent we're meant to be."

"Yeah, about that. Maybe don't tell her."

"Meaning?"

"You said it yourself. My little sister will be all over us, wanting details and pushing her agenda. It's not a healthy way to have a relationship. Same with Tía. You two were close when we dated, and I'd hate to raise her expectations."

"Ah. So, we're a secret."

"Please don't." He tipped up my chin. "Those wheels are spinning, making my request into something it's not. Don't get stuck in your head. We've barely sorted ourselves and decided to give our relationship another go. Added pressure is the exact opposite of what we need."

"Dean and Dara?"

"More pressure and expectations. Can I just say, "wedding reception" and leave it there?"

"They did go slightly crazy." What else could I do but agree when the man laid it out like that? Ease into it. What was the harm in that? "For now, it's between you and me."

CHAPTER 9

I stepped out of the afternoon downpour into the shiny lobby, shaking my umbrella over the mats before crossing the floor and sliding it into the handy holder beside the front desk.

"Ms. Grant." The building's security guard's bushy brows waggled. "Haven't seen you in ages. Here to see Mr. Weston?"

"Yes, thanks, Billy. How are your girls?"

"Amazing. Tasha is …"

I smiled and nodded, struggling to follow the flow of words, but his voice faded into the background, Billy becoming a disjointed figure, his mouth moving soundlessly as he picked up the phone. I clutched my leather satchel, shivering as the dampness from the trip across the water pervaded my entire being.

"Ms. Grant?" Billy held out a security pass and motioned toward the bank of elevators. "Mr. Weston will see you."

"Oh. Thanks, Billy." I squeezed his wrist before taking the pass. "Say hi to Maggie for me and give your girls a hug."

"I will. Nice to see you again."

I nodded and squelched across the tile to the bank of elevators against the East wall. It was like entering that darn wedding all over again, except this time I couldn't even cling to that fantastically expensive and excitingly sexy dress. *Nope.* This afternoon I sported the drowned rat look, thanks to Vancouver's innate ability to produce limitless rainy days.

Sometimes it was a soft sprinkle. Some days it was a light and steady soaker.

Today it was simply torrential. A lot like my marriage, really. Relentless. Pain driving at me from above, the side, the front, and the back, drenching me from the ground up with ricochets, pooling, running in rivers, soaking me within minutes of leaving cover, a drenching downpour continuing throughout the slog from the beginning, right through to the bitter end.

As the elevator rose toward the fortieth floor, I squirmed and plucked at my raincoat, ruing the icy wetness seeping under my collar. It wouldn't be the first time Kyle had seen me looking like a scary troll doll, but today I'd aimed to look hot and unavailable. Not that he'd notice, anyway.

I sighed and straightened as the bell announced my arrival, and the door slid open.

"Amara!" Juliette bounced from her chair behind the reception desk and dashed across the floor. "Let me hang your coat. Poor thing. The weather's been beastly all week. Did you come across on the SeaBus?"

"I hate driving downtown. Parking is impossible." I shrugged out of the drippy jacket, and she draped it on the rack. "It's good to see you."

"You look amazing." Juliette hugged me. "He's been a real bear the past few months," she whispered. "What happened?"

"Why don't we go for coffee next week?" I grimaced and motioned toward the office. "Can I?"

"He's expecting you." Her faint but encouraging smile along with a little waving motion urged me forward.

Nothing for it now but to enter into Kyle's inner sanctum. I drifted closer to the door, tilting my head at the sound of his deep, low voice. For a sliver of time, I'd thought it the sexiest sound on the planet. But now? That was reserved for another. I tapped on the frame of the door and waved.

Kyle barely looked my way, holding up his index finger. "Yeah, email those figures. I'll take a look and let you know. Thanks." He set the receiver gently in the cradle and rose, running those strong fingers through his thick blond hair. He skirted behind me and pushed the door closed. "Sit."

I wrinkled my nose.

He sighed. "Please, Amara. Have a seat." Kyle headed toward the dark wood side table. "Coffee? Tea? I bought the chai you like. And local honey from that shop in Granville Island."

"Just water, thanks." I headed toward the cozy circle around the coffee table and sank onto the low chair, shrinking and wrapping my arms around myself as he approached, his six-foot frame looming over me.

He placed the glass of water on a coaster and sat in the matching chair to my right, squarely between me and my planned escape route.

I sipped the icy liquid and returned the glass to the table, looking around. *Yup.* Exactly the same as the last time I was here. Except now, my photo was no longer on display. I straightened, searching to see if someone else had claimed my spot of honour on his desk.

"What brings you here?" he asked.

Same old Kyle. Straight to the point with no side trips. I dragged my briefcase closer, pulled out the large envelope, and extended it toward him.

"Is this what I think it is?"

I nodded.

He took it but placed it on the table, leaning back and crossing his right ankle over the opposite knee.

"You're not opening it?"

"I've signed, you've signed, my lawyer will get paid to file everything," he said in a flat voice. "It's finished."

I pulled out the small case and extended it toward him. "You should have this back. I'm sorry for arguing over it." Especially as we both knew this stunning piece would sit neglected in my sock drawer for all eternity. Besides, ending this had been hard enough without creating more angst; something I seemed all too good at.

Kyle opened it, running a finger over the antique sapphire ring before he snapped the box close. "Thanks. My mom will be thrilled it's been returned."

"It is a family heirloom. You should have it."

"It's going to my brother. He and Candice are getting serious."

"Ahh." Of course, Kyle's mother would want someone to wear it down the aisle. Someone who would relieve the disappointment that I hadn't worn this magnificent piece of jewellery when I'd married her firstborn child. Oddly, the woman had nagged me to produce a grandchild. If only she knew the real story, but I'd never tell. "Maybe she'll hate me a little less."

"My mother never hated you. Your mother, on the other hand, detests me. She must be relieved I'm no longer her son-in-law."

What to say, what to say. Nothing could fix my family's dynamics. Kyle would see right through any subterfuge. I reached into my bag and pulled out a second velvet box. "Maybe you should have this back."

He reached out as I did, wrapping his hand around mine, squishing my fingers into the velvet. "That's yours. I'd never ask for it back."

I smiled sadly as he let go and tucked the tiny jeweller's box away.

Kyle rubbed his palms across his knees. "You're seeing the infamous university boyfriend, huh? Is it serious?"

"It might be."

"Your mother must be ecstatic you're with him again." He frowned. "Jake is why you finally signed?"

"No," I said. "You insisted I sign those papers."

He shifted, straightening his legs, only to bend them again. His lips set in a flat line.

"You seeing someone?" I asked. "Is that why you were in such a rush?"

"You really want to talk about this?" Kyle's eyes closed as he massaged his temples. "Now?"

"It was just a question." I fastened my briefcase. "Maybe I should go."

"Amara." Kyle rested a hand on my arm. "Please, just … no, I haven't been seeing anyone." He cleared his throat. "When did it start with him?"

"Does it matter?"

"Please. I need to know."

"In Toronto, at Dara's wedding."

"After we separated, then?"

"Long after." I tucked my chin to my chest, studying his shiny Prada loafers. My throat closed up, and I swallowed hard, blinking rapidly. *Don't cry, don't cry, don't cry …* "Jake isn't the reason our marriage failed."

"I'm not so sure about that. I've been asking for weeks why you haven't signed with no response. That guy shows up, and it's done within days. You look happier than you ever were with me."

"And you were so thrilled about our marriage."

"I could have been," he said softly. "I love you, but it was so damn hard for you to open up. To trust me. When it ended, you went on like it was nothing."

I lifted my head, no longer bothering to hide the tears gathering in the corners of my eyes. "It wasn't nothing, but you never wanted the same things."

"No, you rushed the process. You swung from impulsive to overthinking, full speed ahead to full shut down," he said. "For the record, I did want a baby, just not on your timeline."

"You should have told me that."

"I tried, but you were being classic Amara, seeing everything as black and white and ignoring all the shades in between."

We stared at each other for the longest time, all my conceptions—or misconceptions—about Kyle crowding my mind. The trouble was, I wasn't sure which were which. The argument over starting a family had been just one of our many hurdles, even though I'd tried to understand his viewpoint. Truly, I had.

What of all that I thought to be true? Had I really been set on one path, ignoring the other half of my equation? For all of my complaints, Kyle had never been abusive or cruel; just distant and unreachable.

"You're busy. I should go."

Kyle rose as I did, pulling me into a tight hug. "Take care of yourself, Marmalade. Be happy. You deserve it." He tipped up my chin and kissed me, lingering, increasing the pressure of his lips against mine.

I flattened my palms against his chest and pushed him back. "No. I'm with Jake."

"Then I guess that's that." He nodded slowly, his lips twisting. "I hope you fare better with your next relationship. Maybe take the time to listen to him as much as he listens to you."

"Yeah, thanks for the stellar advice. Maybe you should take it yourself. Or maybe just make her feel less like the invisible woman. Bye, Kyle." I trudged into the main office.

Juliette wasn't at her desk, so I scribbled a note on a pink sticky and tacked it to her computer screen before riding the elevator to the main floor and exiting into the pouring rain.

Was this what they called closure?

When I arrived home, I settled on my couch and dialled Beth.

"Hey, stranger," she said when she answered. "About time you got back to me."

"Sorry. I've been dealing with a crisis."

"Tell me."

"I signed the divorce papers and went to see Kyle. He wanted that ring back."

She inhaled sharply. "Your wedding ring? That's creepy."

"No, the heirloom platinum band with the sapphire and diamonds. His mother insisted on it. She always hated me." I said in a low voice as I paced in front of the floor-to-ceiling windows, stopping to stare at the gloomy grey sky. "I tried to give him my wedding ring. He didn't want it."

"Ahhh." The line crackled. "Why would you even offer? That sucker is worth a mint, and what would he do with it anyway? It's gross when a guy gives another woman their ex-wife's jewellery."

"Dunno." I twirled a lock of hair around my fingertip and swallowed a large mouthful of wine. "It's ridiculously expensive, but what will I do with it?"

"You earned that ring, sweets. Anyway, it's not like the guy's strapped for cash."

"I suppose. Maybe I'll pawn it to pay those legal fees."

"Kyle should be paying the lawyers. Jackass."

"That's me, Beth. He offered and stupid me, I refused. Damn. I wish I'd let him."

"Quit beating yourself up! It's done. Now move on."

I refilled my glass and swallowed a large gulp. "Juliette seems to think Kyle misses me."

"Well, too bad for him. You did the best for you. That idiot doesn't deserve more than that."

"Thanks. Are we on for our movie this week? I really need to get out. Jake won't be back for a few days."

"Jake is away a lot."

"He'll be back next Sunday," I said. "So, movie?"

"Yeah, I'll see you Tuesday." Beth sighed. "I hope you know what you're doing. Long distance relationships are a killer."

"How are things with the amazing Gregory?"

"Well, amazing, of course." She laughed. "We've been seeing each other almost every night."

"I'm happy for you. Maybe it's time for a double date. Then you'll see Jake isn't as bad as you think."

"I never said he's bad, but he's bad for you. Widower. Lives on the opposite coast. Remember?"

Single dad. Though Beth had yet to suss out that fact. "What does Greg say?"

"About Jake? Let's see. Jake's a great guy. It's sad about his wife. Greg needs to respect Jake's privacy. So basically, he tells me nothing that doesn't involve work. What does Jake say about Greg?"

"That Greg's a great guy, but not much beyond that. They're following the same playbook."

"Ha, right? See why I'm concerned? Something dark lurks beneath the surface."

"Nah. I've known Jake forever." I glanced at my watch. "Speaking of, it's time to call."

"And so it begins." Beth laughed. "See you Tuesday."

After a quick trip to the kitchen to pour more wine, I set my laptop up on the coffee table for our nightly video chat, settling cross-legged on the couch.

"Perfect timing," Jake said as he appeared onscreen. "How was your day?"

"Well, I did it," I said. "The papers are signed, sealed, and delivered."

"That's great news." He grinned and lifted the goblet in his hand. "This calls for a toast."

I laughed and lifted my own glass. "How did you know?"

"Amara Grant lounging at home without her libations? Does such a travesty ever occur?" He chuckled. "To us and new beginnings."

I tapped my glass against the screen. "To us."

"I miss you. Only a few days, and I'll be there."

Always being apart was the hardest part of this for me, but still, I was all in. If I kept moving forward, things would work out. Or at least I could hope they would.

The next Saturday, I headed across the water again to have lunch with Juliette.

She waved as she wove between the tables, sporting a big smile as she arrived at the booth and set her bags on the bench.

I stood and hugged her tight. "I'm so glad you called."

"Awww, honey. I've missed you. The office parties aren't the same without my partner in crime." She air kissed me and hung her coat on the hook beside our table. "I wanted to make good on my promise."

The server came by bringing water and menus, and we both ordered coffee.

"How have you been?" Juliette ripped open a raw sugar packet. "It was a shock when Kyle said you were divorcing."

"Was it really?" I tapped a finger against my pursed lips.

A small grimace appeared. "He seemed super happy with you, so yeah, it was."

"Funny. He spent loads of time at the office. Most nights it would be eight or nine before he got home."

"That's early, considering he was a junior partner." She picked up her menu. "What happened last week? After you visited, Kyle cancelled every single meeting for that afternoon and holed up in his office."

"Has Kyle been talking about me?"

"Only a few passing comments, and just to me. Nobody else, as far as I know."

I pointed a finger at her, waving it. "Is there something going on between you and him?"

"Uh-uh," she said with a humourless laugh. "He's my boss. An office romance would ruin our great working relationship. I've been his assistant for seven years. You get to know a man."

"I've known him almost four."

"But do you truly know him?" Juliette shook her head. "Before you, he often slogged at the office until midnight. Work was his life for a long time. Kyle's a driven man, but for you, he made sacrifices."

"Right." I snorted. "Mister Romantic. I should have clued in when he wanted the quickie no-frills wedding."

The other woman tipped her head down and stared into her cup, fiddling with her spoon as she finally looked up. "Maybe I shouldn't share this, but he's wrestling with something. He's in the office late every night. Over the past two weeks, I've counted five times where he was sacked out on his couch when I arrived. He's been showering in the partners' lounge and then diving in for another eighteen-hour day."

"Yeah, I'm sure he's heartbroken over little old me." I wrinkled my nose, even though some of these words were ringing true.

"Always the little self-deprecating comments. Stop doing that and recognize the man is devastated. He loved you, but he had a hard time showing it. Or maybe he couldn't show it in the way you expected. My theory is that the quickie wedding was self-defence before your ex-boyfriend showed up and took you back."

My mouth dropped open. This was the last thing I expected to come out of this woman's mouth.

"Why so shocked? Weren't there good parts to your relationship?"

What had drawn me to Kyle Weston? And how did Juliette know how he felt about me? Even I hadn't comprehended that during our separation and divorce, and barely during the second half of our marriage. From his actions, I'd assumed his feelings for me had died, followed shortly by our entire relationship.

A thought niggled at me, though. There had been times in the early months of our relationship when he'd beat me home, and we'd go out—dinner, a movie, or an evening walk along the seawall. Those had been the best of our days together. One weekend we'd visited the Okanagan Valley to tour wineries, and he surprised me with a romantic dinner on a patio overlooking the lake. Maybe my infatuation had faded. Maybe the love wasn't real to begin with, even if I'd wanted Kyle to be the one. Maybe he just checked those perfect little boxes. Gorgeous? *Check.* Educated? *Check.* Successful? *Double check.* Wealthy? *Triple check.* Would make me happy for the rest of my life? *Massive question mark.*

"It shouldn't be that difficult to answer that. He could have given you the world. What could you possibly need that he didn't offer?"

His undivided attention? A scrap of affection? A happy family? Nope. I couldn't say any of that to Kyle's administrative assistant. He'd hate me forever if I divulged my grievances to his staff, even if this woman was once my friend. *An office friend.* Not a spill-all-my-painful-secrets friend like Beth or Dara. "I don't know," I said softly.

"If you ask me, you gave up too soon."

Had I? Even if I had misread Kyle and the depth of his feelings for me, the one thing I couldn't mistake was how I'd felt when I was with the man. That compared to Jake ... well there simply was no comparison. Jake was my person. "I hate that Kyle's hurting, and I never meant to hurt him, but our marriage wasn't working on so many levels."

That was the truth. *My truth, even if it wasn't his.* As much as ending my marriage sucked, it was exactly right. My heart wasn't in it, or at least not on the level it needed to be to overcome the issues we'd been facing. Now, with those experiences—both joyous and devastating—behind me, I was ready to give Jake everything.

CHAPTER 10

T he tune just wouldn't get out of my head and the bounce in my step became more pronounced as I strode down the stark hallway. I stopped humming as one of the RN's rushed by with a chart in her hands.

A sly grin accompanied her perky, "Looking good, Amara. Who is he?"

I turned to respond, but she'd already disappeared through the double doors. Continuing my trip, I exited into the sunny afternoon, glancing at my phone as I hurried toward home, Jake's short text making me smile:

On my way home. Can't wait for our date tonight.

Home. For three glorious days, Jake had been staying at my apartment, and we'd sunk into an easy routine; one that grew more comfortable with each visit. The beat of my heels against the pavement increased. The return to the sweetness of being loved by Jake had planted a permanent grin on my face.

I'd barely gotten in the door when my phone rang, heralding Jake's return from work.

"Come on up," I said before tapping nine to release the front door.

It was almost six. Just enough time for a quick shower before we were due to meet Beth and Greg at the pub. On the way to the bathroom, I stripped, dropping my clothes in a pile before entering the glass shower stall.

"Hey," Jake said as he arrived in the bathroom. "Room for one more in there?" His shirt joined the pile of clothing on the tile floor.

I chuckled as his pants landed on top of his shirt. "Like you would take no for an answer?"

"And miss this?" He rested a hand on my hip, using the other to push aside my hair to nibble at the nape of my neck.

"We'll be late for dinner," I whispered as a delicious shiver raced down my spine. "They'll be waiting."

"I'm willing to risk it." The heat of his body against mine was welcome, as was the hand gliding over my bare belly.

I turned my head enough to kiss him. *Yup*. We'd definitely be late.

⌀

We strolled into the restaurant forty-five minutes later. My warm and contented feeling grew as Jake's hand glided across my hip, coming to rest on my lower back as we approached the table.

Beth stood and hugged me. "You're practically glowing," she whispered in my ear. "What were you two up to? Or do I need to ask?"

Like the glow, my smile could barely be contained. Not with Jake's lingering touch on my back as he pulled out my chair, accompanied by the kiss to my temple. I turned to Greg, who looked completely comfortable and relaxed with one arm slung over the back of Beth's chair, and not at all bothered at our lateness. "How are you?"

"Good, good." An easy grin surfaced as Greg looked at me, then at Jake, and then back to me. "Ahhh. I see how it is. You two …" He motioned back and forth between us before chuckling. "Thought we'd be eating alone."

"It was just a slight delay." Jake picked up his menu.

"Is that what we're calling the quickie now?" Greg sipped his wine.

I buried my nose in my own menu, letting the conversation roll over me as I scanned through the options, my belly rumbling. "I'm starving."

Once we'd ordered, Jake said, "We should do that kayak trip before the weather turns."

"Sounds amazing. What do you think, Beth?" Greg asked.

"Urgh, no." Beth wrinkled her nose. "I love the great outdoors but being stuck miles from civilization in a tiny unmanned campsite with wild animals stalking the perimeter is not my idea of paradise."

I hid a smile. It wasn't the bears so much as the several kilometres of fathomless frigid water between her and the campsite, all of which would be negotiated in a tippy kayak. "Have you ever seen *The Proposal?* That movie with Ryan Reynolds where he says—"

"Oh! Let's go to that new movie after dinner." Beth narrowed her eyes in my direction. "Greg and I were just discussing it."

My friend knew exactly where I was going with my comment. She and I had gotten serious mileage out of the quip about the boat. I smothered a giggle, but maybe keeping Beth's intractable phobia to myself was the best plan. It might prove the tipping point for Greg, who spent most days navigating open water.

"Sorry, no can do on the movie." Jake glanced at his watch. "I have a flight to catch."

"Tonight?" Beth frowned. "Where are you off to?"

"Halifax."

"You spend an awful lot of time back east. If I didn't know better, I'd think you had another girl waiting."

"He does, and she's adorable." Greg winked at her.

Beth opened her mouth then snapped it closed again, tilting her head.

"How is sweet Sarina?" Greg asked.

"Good. Tía sent me this today." Jake turned his phone and showed us a picture of his cherubic baby girl.

"How old is she?" Beth squinted at the screen then frowned at me.

"Fourteen months." Jake tucked his phone into his pocket.

"She's … cute." Beth rose from the table. "I need the ladies' room. Amara?"

"I'm fine—"

"Now." Beth grabbed my hand as she widened her eyes and hauled me from my seat, dragging me toward the bathrooms. "He has a kid?" she asked in a low voice as she shoved me through the door and then leaned back against it. "You didn't think that was important to mention?"

I shrugged. "Lots of guys have kids at thirty-three."

"He's a widower with a kid in diapers!"

"What's the issue?"

"What's the—" She straightened, planting her hands on her hips. "Oh, no, no, no. You have to stop seeing him. Immediately."

I scoffed. "I thought you were okay with it now, after what he said. He took off his ring."

She wagged a finger at me. "You failed to mention the *extra* excess baggage. Bad enough that his wife died, but he has a kid too? Never, ever get involved with a single dad of any child under five, or next thing you know, you're changing diapers and picking preschools." Beth clutched her hair, shaking her head. "Red alert! Abandon ship before it founders."

"Relax. I haven't even met Sarina."

"Wait." Beth cocked her head. "You've been messing with him for"—she squinted, tapping her fingers against her palm—"six … seven weeks, and he hasn't mentioned when you'll meet his daughter?"

I shrugged. "The travel is too much for a little girl."

"Then go to Halifax and meet her."

"He hasn't invited me."

"You don't see the big flashing danger sign? Open your eyes." She grasped my shoulders. "The ink isn't even dry on your divorce, and you've launched yourself into a relationship with a widowed father of a child barely a year old." She pursed her lips. "Has he told you what happened to his wife?"

"We'll get there."

"It must be bad." Her eyes widened. "What if he's one of those guys where everyone says, 'he was such a nice quiet neighbour' and all the while his wife's buried in the backyard. Or, he dumped her in a tank of piranhas at the aquarium to destroy the evidence. Jake, the black widower."

"You know that's not true." I swatted her arm. "I've known him since university. Even at his angriest—and believe me, we had some ragers—he never laid a hand on me. Jake's not that kind of guy."

"Maybe not, but enormous revelations lurk behind his secretive behaviour. You're charging full speed ahead without considering how bad it could be. Coupled with the fact he's avoiding the intros with his daughter ..."

"He's amazing." I crossed my arms. "Good looking. Successful. Educated. Sweet. The guy actually wants to be with me, yet you say run?"

Beth nodded. "Yeah, Amara, that's exactly what I'm saying. Something isn't right."

"I like him."

"It's far worse than like." She stared at me. "You're a goner, taking the hard and fast plummet onto the rocks of *l-o-v-e*. Just like the last go-around with this guy, you'll need intensive care when he packs up and leaves town."

With this attitude, who knew what my friend would say if we factored the "don't tell Luciana" ultimatum into the equation, or the fact that his daughter held a priority position in his life? Right now, I might turn her opinion around, but that chance would evaporate the moment Beth learned that Jake had vowed me to silence about our relationship outside of our circle of four.

"What?" She eyed me. "There's something else, right?"

"Nope." Lifting my chin, I straightened. "I'm not breaking up with him. Don't hang around us if it bothers you so much."

"You're too stubborn." Her shoulders slumped. "From that look on your face, you're determined to continue this, so that's all I'll say. Just promise you'll be careful. Please?"

I nodded and hugged her quickly. "We'd better get back out there before they send a search party."

ɑ

My keys clanked onto the tray inside the front door, and I hung my coat, smiling when Jake wrapped his arms around me from behind, pressing his face against my hair.

"This sucks." His embrace tightened. "It gets harder every time I leave."

I nodded slowly. The nights without him in my bed and the days without him in my life seemed intolerably long and lonely.

"Is everything okay with Beth?" he asked.

"Sure." Any hope I had of Jake not mentioning my friend's disapproving silence vanished.

"Hmmm." He turned me, tipping up my chin with his fingertip. "Your friend doesn't like me. What did she say about Sarina? She clearly didn't know about my daughter."

My wrinkled nose made him sigh.

"That good, huh." He caught my hands in his and squeezed. "If Sarina's an issue, we should get it out there."

"She's not."

His brows lifted and he tilted his head, staring at me.

"It's not that Beth doesn't like you, and she loves kids. She's a teacher."

"She's clearly not a fan of the dead wife/toddler combination."

"Beth's worried I'm jumping in too soon, considering our history and my fresh divorce."

"Yeah, well, Beth should save her breath. I only care what you think. Is it too much to date a guy with a toddler?"

"It bothers me that I haven't met the toddler. Why don't you bring her on your next visit? We'll set up a crib in my guest bedroom. Or I could come to Halifax for a few days."

"I'm not sure that's a good idea."

"Which part?" I pulled free and headed into the kitchen, stopping to fill the kettle.

Jake rested his hands on the edge of the island, shoulders hunching.

"Ah, I get it." I blinked hard as I shuffled around the kitchen, keeping my head down as I selected a canister. "I'm making chai."

"Mar." Jake rounded the counter and caught me around the waist, pulling me close. "Please understand. Travelling back and forth would be too stressful for a toddler."

"Don't you wish you could see your daughter more often? Isn't it difficult to be away?"

"Hell, yes, but this is my job. You want the low-down on *my* shitty life? After Alysa died, I uprooted my daughter and moved into a tiny house a quarter of the size of my other one. I can't afford to fly Sari back and forth or pay the added expenses for childcare in Vancouver. Working on the other side of the country while balancing the needs of a baby bites. I miss my daughter every single damn day, but this contract was too good to pass up. Next pay day I might even put a dent in that towering pile of bills."

"I'm sorry. I had no idea." I placed my palm against his chest. "I get it. I do, but …"

"But what?" He held me in place, keeping my hand against his chest. "I want this to work, but can we take it slow?"

If only slow could work, but our relationship was cranked to all-ahead-full. Jake spent more and more time here whenever he was in town, and when he was back home, we talked. Daily. Sometimes more than daily. Yet still, he held back important details.

"What happened with Alysa?" I asked softly.

Jake closed his eyes and shook his head. "Can we talk about it later? It's not a three-second conversation."

"Maybe not, but whenever I bring it up, you change the subject."

"Do I?"

"Don't pretend, Jakob. I shared with you about Kyle, now it's your turn."

"I'll be back in a few days. We'll talk about it then, okay?" He kissed my nose. "Sorry, I should head to the airport. Are we okay?"

I stared into those beautiful eyes and wondered how I could ever refuse this man anything. There was no denying it. My heart was in danger, our forced separations intensifying everything when we were together.

"Please, *Mare*. Tell me what you're thinking."

I held up a finger before I spun and hurried to the table in my foyer, tugging open the drawer. "Hold on … I think … yup." I held up the chain, the silver jingling as I extended it toward Jake.

He inspected the fob, a slow grin appearing. "My own set of keys? Thank you." His genuine smile and big smacking kiss quelled my misgivings, if only a little.

Don't make me regret my vow to be all in, Jakob. Please, please don't break my heart.

❧

After Jake left for the airport, I tidied my apartment and tossed a load of towels into the washing machine. Anything to keep my mind off Beth's fatalistic words and Jake's evasion of the looming issue about his wife.

I wanted it to be okay, but was it? His reluctance about me meeting his daughter and his refusal to share our budding relationship with anyone but Greg and Beth was an ominous sign. I'd made an enormous leap, launching into a relationship with the man of my dreams—or at least the one he'd become four years after the fact—all the while crossing my fingers and hoping my heart would survive.

Jake's book sat on the side table, and I carried it into the den. I tucked it onto my overloaded shelves, all the while eyeing my laptop. Maybe he'd consider it an invasion of privacy, but wasn't everything on the internet free game? Our relationship status gave me the right to know. Didn't it?

The screen came to life as I started my laptop, sinking into the office chair and swivelling back and forth. One tap opened the browser. *Should I? Shouldn't I. Should? Shouldn't. Do. Don't.*

I stared at the screen, then sprang from my chair, paced three steps, and sat again. *Blink. Blink. Blink.* The steady pulse of the cursor taunted me. I drummed the tips of my fingers lightly against my forehead and closed my eyes, then peeked at the screen again.

"Argh." I bolted, stomping into the kitchen and digging in the fridge, coming up with a chilled bottle of Riesling, taking my time pulling a clean glass from the rack and pouring an inch. I tilted my head, doubling the portion. Better. *On second thought* ... I tucked the entire bottle under my arm.

I sidled back to the tiny den, taking a liberal swig of wine and setting the bottle within easy reach before resting my fingertips on the keys.

Once this was done, I wouldn't be able to take it back. If I were patient, maybe Jake would open up and share.

Ha. Right. His reluctance showed no signs of abating. What if Beth was right? I huffed out a breath and closed my eyes, shaking it out before allowing my fingers to fly over the keyboard. My index finger hovered over the enter key for barely a moment before it dropped with firm resolve. A few more taps and ... there she was. *Alysa Marietta Cavallaro, Halifax, Nova*

Scotia. A petite blonde woman, posed in front of a stone fountain in some park or other, smiling brightly.

I scrolled down the page, reading the details of my lover's deceased wife, holding my breath until the end. Nothing. There wasn't a single clue to the cause of her sudden, traumatic death.

The family requests donations to the specified charities in lieu of flowers … I skimmed over the words. *Please respect the privacy of the family during this time …*

The other search results contained only snippets of information, giving no further clues. Well, that was it then. Unless Beth could wheedle some extra information out of Greg, I was out of luck. Nothing to do but bide my time and hope one day soon my man would be willing to discuss it. With a big sigh, I closed the search window, shutting down both my laptop and the idea that Greg would ever let anything slip. If he hadn't already, he probably never would. Anyway, I refused to put Beth in a position that might ruin her new romance.

I scooped up my glass and the bottle and shuffled through to the living room and slumped onto the couch. In a few hours, Jake's plane would be touching down four thousand kilometres away, and he'd be anxious to get home to his daughter. Did he miss his wife? That perky smiling woman in the photo?

Stop it, Amara. Just stop. No good could come from stalking his former life. No good at all. Yet the question remained. What had happened to his wife? Why was he being evasive, avoiding the topic with practiced finesse?

He'd be back in a matter of days, and I vowed to learn the truth, no matter how devastating or painful.

CHAPTER 11

S uddenly, I was awake, aware of the restless man beside me, his leg twitching as he struggled against the tangled sheets.

"No, no," he mumbled.

"Jake. Wake up." I shook him. "It's a dream. It's okay." The false words hurt, as truthfully, I had no idea if he was okay, but for now, my only aim was breaking him free from his nightmare and calming that harsh breathing. "Hey. Open your eyes," I said in a level voice, venturing what I hoped was a reassuring smile as he complied, staring at me for several seconds.

"Shit. Shit." Jake sat, running his trembling fingers through damp hair, kicking to free himself from the covers. After a moment, he pushed to his feet. "Sorry I woke you," he said, stumbling toward the door.

I took several deep breaths and followed the rattles and clinks to the kitchen, making it just in time for a view of his broad back as he retreated onto the patio.

The French doors wobbled in the early morning breeze, the blinds rattling and tapping against the frame. I left them ajar as I approached the hunched figure in the wicker chair, pausing for a second before crouching and taking the empty tumbler from his hand. "That's three nights in a row." That I knew of, anyway, because that was the exact number of nights he'd been sleeping in my bed this time around. "Talk to me. Please."

He clenched his eyes shut, shaking his head. "It's just a stupid dream. I'm fine."

"Are you?" The smell of orange liquor wafted over me, and I sniffed the glass, wrinkling my nose. "Yeah, just fantastic, right? Whiskey at three in the morning? That's anything but fine."

"How about your three glass a day wine habit?"

"We aren't talking about me or the wine I drink to unwind. This is about constant nightmares, not sleeping, and the dark bags you have packed there." I pointed to his red-rimmed eyes. "Why don't you trust me enough to share what's bothering you?"

"It's nothing."

Sure, sure. However, my instincts and knowledge of this man told me not to push and drive him deeper into his silent brooding.

"Just being here with you makes everything better." Catching my hands, he pulled me to my feet. His bear hug crushed me against his chest, and then he scooped me up, already in motion, heading toward my bedroom. "Back to bed. We have an early morning."

Rearing its ugly head was a classic case of avoidance tactics, so I'd bide my time. Tomorrow we'd be on the water, which was his happy place. Once he'd relaxed, maybe he'd be willing to share whatever torment disturbed his sleep night after night.

❧

Jake set his small pack on the chair, then wrapped his arms around me from behind as I put the finishing touches on the food stash for our paddle trip up the coast.

"Who was that on the phone?" I smothered a yawn. "Geez, five feels early this morning."

"Greg. He's battling the flu, so a day in a kayak would be too much." He turned me, cupping my face. "You don't have to come if you're not up for it."

"No, no. I'm fine. Besides, it's safer with a paddling buddy." I ran my thumbs in a gentle arc across his cheekbones. The deepening of the dark circles underneath those red-rimmed eyes was surely the after effect of the two hours of restless half-sleep following his startled awakening. I wasn't even sure I'd slept at all. "Are you sure you're up to this? You look exhausted."

"I'm okay." His faint smile did little to reassure me. "A day on the water is just what I need. Are you ready?"

"Almost." After a quick kiss, I hurried into the bedroom and yanked open my top drawer to sift through my socks. All through my shift yesterday, I'd been looking forward to having a full day with Jake. Now I wouldn't even have to share his attention.

"Can I borrow your laptop? I need to do a final check on the weather before we get on the water, and this thing," he said as leaned in the doorway, waggling his phone, "is dead again. I need a new one."

"No problem. You know the passcode." After stuffing the change of clothes and extra socks into the dry bag on the bed, I stopped to straighten the duvet and plump up the pillows. Glancing over my shoulder, I picked up the sweatshirt Jake had slung over the chair and pressed my face into the soft cotton, inhaling deeply. I'd spent an interminably long week missing the man while he lived his life on the opposite coast, and this little reminder that he was here soothed me.

The slight whisper of feet against the floor made me look up. I folded his sweatshirt and set it on the chair, wrinkling my nose at the man standing in the doorway. "Oh, is the weather turning?"

"It's passable, but we should go as it might rain later. The bonus is that the waterways should be quieter today. If I'm to get those samples today, I have to leave. You sure you want to brave it?"

"I won't melt from a little rain. Give me two minutes, and I'll be ready." No way would I pass up a full day alone with Jake. Anyway, I'd committed to digging for the truth. To move forward, we needed to delve into the past.

Three hours into the trip, and I was in deep concentration, intent on keeping up with Jake, whose strokes were clean and strong as he skimmed across the water. The man could put on the power, and the sight of his taught muscles straining under his paddle gear certainly made for pleasant viewing.

He glanced my way. "Time for a break," he said, turning toward the rocky beach.

The rays of late morning sun filtered through greyish clouds, and I shielded my eyes with one hand, squinting toward the shoreline.

"Almost there." Jake smiled, lightening both his expression and my mood. "Don't give up now."

"Wasn't planning on it." I set my lips in a flat line as I fought the grin. "Race you." My kayak shot across the waves as I dug my paddle in deep, pouring my last dregs of energy into the drive toward shore.

Jake's hearty laugh echoed across the water behind me. "Good thing you got a head start. I'm coming for you." The bow of his red kayak caught my eye just before he skimmed past. "Still can't beat me." He smirked as he pulled his craft onto the beach.

"Yeah, yeah." I jabbed him with my elbow as I stowed my kayak beside his. "Such a tease."

"But you still love me." He winked as he slung an arm around my waist.

I shoved him lightly before retrieving my pack and the thermos of coffee.

Several feet above the beach we found a large flat rock to perch on. I offered him one of the loaded turkey ciabatta buns and opened the container of veggie sticks.

"Thanks." He took a bite of his sandwich and scanned the horizon. "Look."

I leaned in and peered down his arm toward the seals cavorting in the water. "They're so cute."

"If we keep watch, maybe we'll see otters."

I munched on a carrot, motioning at the seagull as it hopped up the beach toward us, its beak open and its beady eyes trained on my loaded ciabatta. Scooping it up, I cradled it close. "None for you. Go catch a salmon or something."

"That'll convince him." Jake chuckled. "Good thing it's not fish and chips."

I shuddered and hunched my shoulders, my skin crawling. Those long wings flapping around my head, beating against my face as that greedy gull swooped in to snatch my portion of crispy battered Halibut straight from my fingers, was something I'd never forget.

"You'd think you were being murdered."

Rubbing at my cheek, I glared at Jake. "That sucker was huge, and he dive bombed me from behind, walloping me on the head, and all you did was laugh."

"Well, it was funny." He chuckled as he wrapped an arm around my shoulders. "It was quite a sight, you shrieking and ducking, fries flying across the boardwalk, and the gull taking off like a bat out of hell with a beak full of your lunch."

"Greedy vulture, calling a swarm of his friends in for the cleanup crew." Now I was laughing too, though in the moment, I'd been terrified. I still had a healthy respect for the speed and cunning of these creatures and probably always would. I leaned into him. "Afterwards, you shared your lobster roll and bought me ice cream. Caramel swirl on a waffle cone."

"I'm good at sharing." He winked. "Don't worry, I'll protect you. Eat up."

"Good to know." I bit into my sandwich, still keeping a keen eye on the bird, noting its tilted head and rapt attention. "It's plotting. Waiting for that window of opportunity."

"Relax." Jake rose and moved toward the creature, waving his arms. "Move along little fella. No free lunch today." Once it had scuttled down the rocky beach, he returned and sat beside me. "We should head out so we can get there and back before dark."

I finished my last bite and scooped up the silicone bags from our early lunch, stuffing them into my pack, the loose pebbles skittering under my feet as we headed back to the kayaks.

Jake scrubbed a hand through his hair before returning the red cap to his head. "Thanks for coming with me, *Mare*. I'm glad we have an entire day all to ourselves."

Soon we were back on the water, paddling against the current. I shivered at the slice of chill wind and eyed the gathering bank of clouds on the horizon. They scuttled across the sky, obscuring the sun in a dark blanket.

"Damn," Jake tipped his chin up. "That doesn't look good. It's coming in quick."

I dug in my paddle, increasing my stroke rate as we bobbed through the growing surf, adjusting my path with a slight turn to avoid broadside hits from the waves.

Jake powered toward me. "This is bad. Head to shore."

My nod showed him I'd heard, me being unwilling to spare a single breath or drop a single stroke. As hard as I paddled, the line of trees along the shore remained a distant goal. I fought the treadmill, never advancing but endlessly running in place.

"Okay, Mar?" The note of worry was apparent in his voice even as a gust of wind whipped his words away.

Lightning streaked across the sky followed by a loud cracking sound, and the clouds opened up. Tiny spears of rain cut into my tender skin, a ferocious wind burning my cheeks. I tucked my chin to my chest, struggling against the power of the surf sloshing across my bow.

I blinked hard, striving to clear my vision as the torrential rain pounded me, ricocheting from every direction and streaming from the brim of my neon-pink sports cap. My fingers cramped, and I longed for the neoprene gloves tucked into my storage cubby, but I couldn't afford to pull them out. If I stopped paddling for even a second, I'd lose triple the ground I'd just gained.

A large swell hit, and I clung to my paddle, sucking in a large breath seconds before the surf rushed up at me, plunging me into a glacial bath and leaving me suspended upside down. I thumped against my boat, yanking at the cord of my spray skirt. *Damn, damn.* The skirt remained stubbornly in place, though I kept tugging, my lungs burning.

Relax. Stay calm. You've got this. Letting out a fraction of my air, I took a moment to centre myself, then jerked the cord, grateful when the spray skirt released. I wiggled free and struck for the surface, immediately reaching for my kayak.

"Amara!" Jake grabbed the bow of my boat while, hand over hand, I worked my way to the stern. "Are you okay?"

I nodded, managing an awkward thumbs up with the hand still clutching my paddle.

"I was about to come in after you. You were under a long time. Ready?"

As a team, we righted my kayak, Jake steadying both boats as I hauled myself into my seat and pumped out the water sloshing inside the hull.

"That sucked," I said, reclaiming my paddle from Jake. "Almost lost it under there." And now the shore seemed farther away than ever.

"You look done in, and this current is brutal." Jake pulled out his towline, handing me one end. "Hook on to me, then I'll link to your bow."

"You don't have to haul me in."

"No arguing." His lips set in a flat line. "Hook up. Now."

I attached the carabiner to the tow loop on his PFD and then let go, waiting while he turned and fastened the other carabiner.

He nodded and aimed for shore, paddling with strong, sure strokes.

I regained my own stroke, relieved when we finally gained some ground, courtesy of Jake and his tow line.

It seemed like forever, but finally we neared the shoreline. Jake arrived first, sloshing into the water and then overhanding the rope, drawing me in as I spent the last of my energy for those last few feet of gain. When he was within reach, he steadied my kayak, allowing me to slip over the side before we waded toward the rocky beach, hauling our boats with us.

Jake beached his kayak high above the crashing waves, then hurried toward me, helping me negotiate the last few feet over the slippery rocks. Once my kayak was stowed, he cuddled me against him. "That was close."

"Don't worry, I'm fine."

"I'm sorry, Mar. You almost died."

"No, no, my skirt got stuck, that's all. You taught me well, I knew what to do." I clung to him, waiting until his breathing calmed and the pounding of his heart faded to a steady beat. Whatever he'd been thinking during those few minutes I'd been submerged, he'd hidden until this moment. This panic was something I'd never seen from Jake, who'd always been so under control, no matter the circumstances. Another after-effect of his wife's death? I had to find out. Soon.

α

Jake removed his share of the emergency camping gear from his storage cubby as I emptied mine, each of us hauling a load to a flat spot just under the tree line. My man, the consummate planner, always insisted we carry the proper gear, right from the first time we'd kayaked together, and this trip was no different. *"Never paddle unprepared. The ocean is unforgiving,"* he *always said.*

By the time I set down the bundles in my arms, Jake was unrolling our shelter. "Let's set up so you can change," he said. "Unfortunately, no campfires for us. They're not allowed here, even if we could get one started."

"I know the drill." I linked the poles as Jake spread the tent, and within minutes, we'd pitched our snug accommodations. Taking care to keep the sleeping pads and bags safe from the rain, I transferred them into the tent while Jake selected some food and stowed the rest in a dry bag.

He hoisted our cache into a tree several feet from our camp. "The food's safe from the critters," he said. "Now, out of those wet clothes."

"I bet you'd like that." I wrinkled my nose.

"Yup. Get naked. Leave your gear out front." He patted my butt, but turned to sort the last of the gear, throwing a light tarp over the pile as I slipped off my shoes.

I peeled off my leggings and top and crawled inside the tent.

By the time the nearly naked Jake arrived, I'd donned my extra set of clothes and crawled into one of the sleeping bags, drawing it up to my chin.

"Here." He handed me the thermos and a bag of high-energy snacks. "Might as well dig in. Even if this blows over, it'll be too late to paddle back, so we're here overnight. I hung our gear in the little alcove, so hopefully it will be reasonably dry in the morning."

He pulled on sweats and a t-shirt and crawled into his own sleeping bag while I poured coffee and opened a bag of granola bites. "Thanks," he said, tossing a couple into his mouth.

Though the tent shook and quivered as it was buffeted by gusts of wind, and rain pelted the top and sides, we were snug and dry, safe on solid land until this storm let up. No small thing, as these violent outbursts of weather could take either mere minutes or numerous hours to end. One never knew.

"I'm thrilled to have something hot." I cradled my coffee between numb fingers as Jake moved closer, holding out his arm, encouraging me to rest against his chest.

"Sorry I risked those conditions."

"You checked the forecast, and that's all you can do. Anyway, no harm done. There are far worse things than cuddling in a tent." I set aside my empty cup, sinking further into his arms. "Why were you so panicked when we got to shore?"

His shoulders barely lifted, but his jaw clenched, and his knuckles whitened around his mug.

"You never lose it like that, and you know I'm trained for kayak recovery. You're the one who taught me what to do when I capsize, so what's the issue?"

"My total lack of judgment scared me." He cleared his throat. "Today we cut it close, mistaking the severity of that storm, and it's unacceptable. We should have used Greg's power boat." He sighed, resting his cheek against my hair.

"What is it?"

"What is what?" he asked in a gravelly tone.

"That thing that's leaving those dark circles under your eyes and has you second guessing. This isn't you, Jake. You're not this uptight, overly serious guy."

"Being a father changes everything. I can't take stupid risks with a baby at home."

"We both know there's more to it than that. What about the nightmares?"

"Stop." He scrubbed a hand over his face then shifted me, reclining and tucking an arm under his head.

I lay facing him, reaching out to cup his cheek in my palm. "Can't you trust me with whatever is bothering you? How can we move forward if you won't talk to me?"

Jake stared at me, expressionless. Then that tiny crease appeared. "It's a lot."

"But nothing I can't handle. Let me prove it."

The tiny shake of his head accompanied his hitching breath.

"Please." I stroked his rough, stubbly jaw with my thumb. "Let me understand what keeps you awake at night. Tell me what causes those nightmares."

"It's always the same." He closed his eyes, inhaling roughly. "All disjointed and dark. A baby wailing, and I'm running through a dark house, but I can't find her. So many locked doors and stairs and halls that go nowhere in a convoluted maze that leads on forever. Then the crying stops, and I see her, so pale and still. I can smell it, taste it, so weirdly pungent and sickly sweet, gagging me."

I pressed my hand to my mouth, my eyes burning, nausea stirring in my belly.

"Reality seeps into everything, even my dreams, creating a nightmare." He bit his lip, his breathing heavy and halting. "The moment I got home, I knew something was wrong. I found her on our bed."

"Her?" I whispered. "Alysa?"

"She did it while I was at work. Emptied two bottles of her medication. Sari was in the playpen, making these weird little noises as if she'd run out of breath to cry. Judging by the mess in her diaper and the soaked sheet, it had been hours."

Tears trickled down my cheeks, and I wrapped my arms around him, pressing my face into his chest. "Jake. That's unimaginable. I'm so sorry."

"I thought she was getting better, that the counselling sessions and medications were working." He pressed his face to my hair. "I was worried about all the bills and went back to work."

All I could do was hug him tighter. The words forming in my mind seemed horribly inadequate.

"Alysa ran out of hope, but I didn't see it." Jake's shoulders hunched. "My daughter is motherless and suffered a horrible trauma. I can never make that up to her. I should have figured it out, but I didn't."

We lay there for a few minutes, me rubbing his back until his tense muscles relaxed a little. "It's not your fault."

"Isn't it? I should have checked on her. For sure, I should have known she couldn't be trusted to be alone with Sari, that I couldn't count on Stella to follow through with her promise to check on them."

As the wind whipped around our little tent, I wished there was something I could say or do to ease his pain, but everything seemed trite and paltry. Jake had surely gone down every avenue in his own mind, torturing himself with all the what ifs, leaving me little to comfort him with.

"So now you know. Maybe this is unfair. Me, being selfish, and now you're tangled up in my crappy life. It's hardly what you signed on for."

"This doesn't change how I feel about you or us," I whispered. "It makes us stronger, because now I understand."

The hard truths about Jake's loss were finally seeing the light of day, leaving me relieved yet fearful. The death of his wife was as bad as Beth had imagined, though for different reasons. Things like that caused trauma, leaving unseen scars on the psyche. Right now, the man needed patience and love, the only things that would make it possible for us to move forward. I renewed my resolve to be there for him, to not panic and run.

❧

As I unzipped the tent and peered into the darkness, the cool night air surrounded me. "Jake? Where are you?" I hugged myself, rubbing my arms through my sweatshirt. The only sound was the steady chirping of crickets. "Did a bear eat you?"

Jake's low laugh had me straining to spot him. "Luckily, no. Come out here."

I grabbed the small wind-up flashlight and flicked the switch, getting only a faint beam of light.

"You're ruining my night vision."

"How can I join you if I can't find you?" I muttered, turning off the light, though I kept it clutched in my hand as I stepped out and zipped the tent. "Talk to me."

"Over here. To your right, on the beach. Just be careful."

I picked my way through the stones and branches littering the landscape, shapes emerging as my eyes adjusted to the low light. Soon, I found him propped against a weather-worn log, wrapped in a blanket. "What are you doing out here? It's freezing."

"I'll warm you up." He pulled me onto his knees, folding me inside the secure confines of his embrace. "Better?"

"Perfect." I curled up in his lap, my head resting on his chest. "Another nightmare?"

"Nope. The wind died down and nature called. When I got out here, I saw that." He pointed up. "The Milky Way and Aurora Borealis."

"Incredible." Leaning back against his shoulder, I watched the continuous waves of colourful light dance across the vast black canvas above us. "Now that's a show. Almost as good as the one during our camping trip to Kejimkujik. We hiked so much I thought my feet would fall off, but it was amazing, seeing all the seals and birds on that beach."

"That was St. Catherines River Beach. I'd like to camp at Kejimkujik again when Sari's older." He cuddled me closer, resting his cheek against my hair. "That was our favourite weekend trip with Mom. She'd take us to the tidal pools at Seaside, and we'd explore all the different trails, making a game of spotting the petroglyphs, and we'd kayak the lakes and rivers. It's sad that Sari will never experience adventures with her abuela."

I rubbed his arm. "I wish I could have met your mom. She'd be proud of you and Luci."

"I hope so, though I fear I've made far too many mistakes." He sighed. "Mom's been gone almost seventeen years, and I still miss her. Marisol's amazing, but my mother had this innate wisdom. There were many times I wished I could ask her what to do."

"I'm sorry," I whispered, my fingertips continuing their travels up and down his arm. It might have been years, but there could be no time limit on grief or loss, and Jake had experienced more than his fair share.

"Mom would have loved you, *Mare*." He kissed my temple.

It was hard to imagine who Jake would be now if his life played out differently. I stared up at the vibrant lights snaking across the infinite space above us, sinking into the comfortable silence and the warmth of our blanket cocoon. At this moment, anything seemed possible, but I knew from experience that every choice, no matter how tiny, would impact me in ways that could never be foreseen.

I held out the bag of trail mix to Jake as he tucked the final bag of gear into his kayak's hold. "Want some?"

Jake straightened and stretched. "Thanks." He tossed a handful into his mouth, then finished the last swallow of our morning coffee. "Got to love those travel stoves. Morning caffeine is essential."

"Thanks for breaking down the camp and packing." I squinted toward the water. "Time to pull out the sunglasses," I said, tucking my ponytail through the back of my cap.

"Mmmhmm." The man stepped toward me, pulling me against him with one arm wrapped around my waist. "How is it you look so amazing this morning?" He nibbled my neck, and then pressed his face against my hair. "You smell incredible."

My giggle couldn't be contained, growing into full laughter as he plied me with more kisses, tickling me before his lips finally landed on mine. I ran my fingers through his hair, enjoying both the salty taste on his tongue and the way the heat from his body warmed me even more than the early morning sun.

"I smell like you," I whispered before going in for another kiss. Today I was surfing that postcoital wave, an aura of hope floating around my heart that had overtaken the edge of sadness for what this man had suffered.

"Or like us," he murmured as he rested his cheek against mine. "Whatever it is, I like it."

"Me too."

"Thanks for last night. For listening. For not freaking out."

"It means everything that you trusted me." Cuddling against his chest felt so right, like we were closer than we'd ever been. Maybe he felt it too.

He stroked my hair and held me, our breaths melding as we lingered in that perfect and oddly peaceful moment. Finally, he sighed and kissed my temple. "Time to get those samples and head home. I tried messaging Greg, but there's no reception," he said. "If we aren't back this afternoon, they'll worry. Anyway, I have to call home and check in."

"Let's go, then."

"Wait." He pulled out his phone, holding it at arm's length and pressing his face against mine. "Smile, beautiful." After a quick inspection of the photo, he turned and captured my lips again for a long kiss, then patted my ass. "Better get moving."

We hauled our kayaks into the water and settled into a steady paddle stroke. The idea of another day on the water with Jake was pretty much perfect. Today was my chance to let last night's revelations sink in, far away from the distractions of our usual routines. But maybe that was what we needed; our opportunity to seek our new normal, whatever that might be.

CHAPTER 12

T he moment I opened the door, Beth stepped inside and
wrapped her arms around me. "You're okay. I worried
when you weren't back from kayaking on Monday night."

"I told you I was fine." I shared a conspiratorial look with
Jake over my friend's shoulder and mouthed, "Told you so."

"I took good care of her." Jake pushed both of us toward
the living room, allowing the hovering Greg space to enter my
apartment. He and his friend exchanged fist bumps. "Feeling
better?"

"Much, now that I've had a couple of days to recover."
Greg patted Jake's shoulder as they hugged. "Sounds like you
enjoyed a little adventure, but I told Beth to relax, that you'd
never let anything happen to her friend."

Beth rolled her eyes. "Apparently, Jake's a proverbial Boy
Scout when he's on the water."

"That's the everyday Jake, but who says I need a big strong
man to take care of me? You all act like I've never paddled in
my life." I folded my arms over my chest and glowered at the
three who were now crowded around my kitchen island,
munching on my carefully assembled appetizers. "Those
emergency camping supplies were mine, by the way."

"Ha, yet he still rescued you from an icy bath." Beth
dashed the back of her hand over her eyes. "You could have
died."

"Actually, she rescued herself with a seamless kayak recovery." Jake slid his arm around my waist and pulled me closer. "You two should join us next time."

Beth's eyes widened. "Noooo."

"Turns out Bethie isn't fond of open water. Or boats." Greg dipped a chip into the guacamole, scooping a healthy dose. "This is the best guac I've ever tasted." He loaded another chip with the mixture of creamy avocado and cherry tomatoes that I'd whipped up after I'd gotten home from work.

"Oh. Thalassophobia," Jake said.

"Thala-what-what?" Beth giggled.

"Thalassophobia. Fear of open water." Greg started on the veggies and dip.

"Figures you two would know that." I wrinkled my nose, which Jake promptly kissed. "Guess they did teach you something during those ten years of university."

"Sass." Jake swatted my butt. "Too bad, Beth, you're missing some great times on the water."

"I'm good with the solid land kind of fun," she said.

Jake laughed. "Well, salut." He lifted his glass. "To amazing friends, and Amara's incredible cooking skills. Glad you two could join us tonight."

I raised my brows at Beth, but she just smiled.

"Did you get those results from the water testing?" Greg asked after everyone had devoured most of the appetizers.

"In the office." Jake set aside his glass. "Want to review them?"

"Oh, here we go," Beth said. "You promised no shop talk."

"I need the figures for our Thursday team meeting. It won't take more than five minutes."

"Better not," Beth said, accepting Greg's kiss before he and Jake headed toward the den. The moment the door closed, she giggled. "I thought they'd never leave. What happened with you and Jake. You two seem settled and domesticated."

"And I see your star-filled eyes and that lovey-dove glazed look." A snicker escaped. "Maybe I should worry, but you haven't been this happy in forever."

"I'm beyond happy." She fluttered her lashes. "Greg's great, and he didn't even blink when I told him I hated boats.

Even guys who make their living from the ocean love a bit of dry land now and then."

"True enough, though given what Jake does, it's nice to understand his love of the water." I topped up her glass. "While we were stranded, he shared about his wife."

"Ohh, tell me." She grabbed my hand. "What was it? Car accident?" Then she frowned. "Oh, worse?"

"Much. She overdosed," I said. "Jake found her."

"That poor man." She pressed a hand to her mouth. "No wonder he wasn't talking. Was it intentional?"

"Yeah. She was battling severe depression."

Beth swirled her wine and took a long swallow. "He probably has PTSD. Didn't you say he has nightmares?"

"Don't get all social worky, okay? No analyzing my boyfriend."

"I can't help it. I've dealt with kids who've lost parents and siblings. The fallout isn't pretty, especially in the case of suicide. How's he handling it?"

"Not alone, that I can guarantee. When I said all in, I meant it."

"So, now you'll meet his daughter?"

"One hurdle at a time." In my view, Jake finally opening up about his wife was a major step forward; time to break my own mold and exercise extreme patience.

"Well, you seem more like you when you're with Jake."

"Do I?"

"Yeah, you do. The man's a conundrum. On one hand, he brings out the best in you, but it's concerning that you two are playing this waiting game over his kid." She eyed me. "It's bugging you to no end, isn't it?"

"I'm exercising patience."

"Sure you are. Meanwhile, frustration simmers under the surface, building pressure."

"It's fine."

Beth lifted a hand. "Ha, right. Jake needs to get his act together. Are you sure he's ready to be dating? How serious can you get while you're four thousand kilometres apart?"

Well, that was the big question, wasn't it? How could I be all in unless Jake joined me?

Shortly after ten, Beth and Greg said goodnight and headed home.

I filled the sink with hot soapy water and started washing the few dishes that hadn't landed in the dishwasher. "You have an early morning, so go to bed."

"You have to work at seven, no?" He selected a fresh towel from the drawer and set to work drying the moment I set a dish on the rack. "So, what's up?"

I lifted my shoulder. "You want to discuss this now?"

"Spit it out. If this is going to work, we need to have open communication."

I swirled the dishcloth around the pot, pausing to scrub a spot of tomato sauce. "It's time to tell people about us. I feel like a crap friend because I'm evading Dara's text, your little sister flat out hates me, blaming me for your disappearance after the wedding, and I'm ready to meet Sarina."

"Ah." He wiped the blade of my carving knife and shoved it into the butcher block before he slung the dishtowel onto the counter. "Guess I asked for that."

"Yeah, you did." I scrubbed harder, nibbling my lip. "Nothing to say?"

"Hey." Jake pulled the cloth away and forced me to turn, drawing me close and cradling me against his chest, oblivious to the dishwater dripping from my soapy fingers. "Can you let this be for a little longer? I'll talk to Luci, though, and find a way to smooth out your relationship with her."

"How, if you won't tell her about us?"

"Maybe I'll just say I'm dating someone." Jake chuckled. "That usually gets your name into the conversation."

"Luci talks about me? What does she say?"

"That she misses you. She doesn't really hate you, you know, but it hurt when you left, and seeing you brought up those feelings again." He rubbed my back.

"I've tried to fix things. Why do you think I invited her to the club that night? She never answers my texts or messages."

"Well, she's a medical resident, so it might be that she's busy."

"For weeks? No, she told me outright. She detests me for what happened at the wedding."

"Don't worry. By the end of the week, she'll be dying to call. Trust me, she just needs to see me happy. To see that I don't blame you."

"Why not open up about us?"

"Soon, I promise. I love you, *Mare*, but my life in Halifax isn't simple. Our time together is a break from all of my responsibilities. Please?"

What could I do in the face of these hopeful words but agree? His state was fragile still, but he'd started to open up, and if that was any indication, I needed to stay the course. No doubt having time away from his complicated world was needed, allowing him time to reflect and heal.

The next evening, we'd barely finished dinner when Jake's phone buzzed. "Time for my nightly video chat. I'll take it in the den." He stopped to kiss my cheek as he headed toward the small room situated to the right of the kitchen.

I watched his retreat from my spot in the overstuffed chair by the window, tucking the bookmark into my novel.

"There's Daddy," the woman said. "Can you say hi to Daddy?"

"Hi, Sari. Are you …?"

As his voice level dropped, I tilted my head, shifting to better overhear the conversation. Not that I was proud of eavesdropping, but I was curious. The most I'd learned about Jake's daughter was that she was an adorable toddler, but only from the occasional comment and the ever-changing pictures he used as screensavers.

The little girl squealed, but Jake's reply was muffled.

I rose and tiptoed into the kitchen.

"… I miss you, Starfish," Jake said, his voice clearer now. "How has she been?"

"Exhausting. She misses you, Jakob. When are you coming home?"

"Tomorrow afternoon."

"That's almost a week you've been away. It's not good that you're gone so much."

"This is where my work is right now." Jake's tone changed, became steelier. "I don't enjoy travelling every week, but I have no choice."

"You sold that beautiful house, so you could work less. Where are you? That doesn't look like a hotel."

"This isn't the best time for this conversation. I appreciate all you're doing for Sarina. Bye, bye, Starfish. Daddy loves you."

I crept back to my spot and picked up my novel, the words on the page blurring as his low tones told me he was wrapping up his call.

Some rustling and the distinctive snap of his laptop closing carried to my spot. Seconds later he appeared, rubbing the back of his neck. He stopped in the kitchen for water and the bottle of acetaminophen.

"Headache?" I lifted my head only briefly before tucking my chin to my chest.

"Mmmhmm." He tossed back the tablets and narrowed his eyes. "How much of that did you hear?"

"Starfish. That's cute. With you, it's always nicknames related to the sea." I failed to quell a horrible thought; *what cute sea-inspired name did he have for his wife?*

Jake shook his head and reached for his phone. "Sari earned her nickname during her time in the NICU." As he flicked his index finger across the screen, he said, "My daughter arrived seven weeks early by emergency C-section." He perched on the arm of my chair. "See? Our first photo."

I accepted his phone, examining the picture of the baby cupped against his bare chest, tubes and wires sprouting from every angle. "Aww, she's so teeny and sweet."

"Sari was barely three pounds," he said softly. "The pediatrician said holding her against my bare skin would be beneficial, so for several hours a day I sat with her, staring at the name tag stuck to her incubator. It had starfish along the edges."

I pressed a hand to my chest as he showed me a picture of Sarina inside her incubator wearing a tiny hat covered in pastel sea creatures, and then another of him feeding her from a bottle, again bare chested, but this time with a receiving blanket tucked around his daughter.

"The nurses told me to talk to Sari, that she'd recognize my voice and it would help with her development. It seemed strange to have a conversation with a sleeping baby," he said with a chuckle, "so I told her the adventures of a starfish who lived on a coral reef, thinking the storytelling was good practice."

The burn started, and I swiped a finger across the corner of my eye.

"The doctors and nurses listened in on the tales of Sarina the Starfish, and everyone started calling Sari 'Baby Starfish.'" The softness of his expression as he scrolled through the pictures melted me inside. "Anyway, I practically lived in the NICU for five weeks before the pediatrician said Baby Starfish was ready to go home."

"That's a tough start." Closing my eyes, I imagined the bustle of the NICU staff, the bewildered parents, and the steady beeping of multiple machines. Sadly, I'd witnessed incredible devastation as well as overwhelming joy during my visits to the NICU to counsel parents on various prescribed medications. "I'm glad she's okay."

He blew out a breath. "Watching a crowd of doctors and nurses hovering over your child, prodding and sticking needles and tubes into your helpless baby"—he shivered, his lips twisting—"it hurts just thinking about it."

I kneeled on my chair, sliding my arms around him. "It's over. She's healthy and happy." It struck me that he hadn't mentioned his wife. "Did Alysa ever come to the NICU?"

That familiar crease knotted Jake's forehead. "Never. After three days, the doctor discharged Alysa, and Stella took her home. It wasn't so bad, though. I had Tía, Dean, and Dara, so when I took Sari home, at least I had a chance to shower, eat, and catch some sleep. Between the three of them, they filled my fridge and freezer and provided small breaks. I didn't cook or buy groceries for weeks."

"Wasn't Alysa there? You said home."

"Stella and Ben's home. Alysa struggled with postpartum depression and with the realities of having a premature baby." Jake took my hand. "I haven't been completely upfront, but I didn't know how you'd react."

I eyed him. "To what?"

He lunged to his feet and traced his earlier path, scrubbing a hand through his hair as he paced.

"You're scaring me." Heaviness settled on my chest.

"Once Sari stabilized, they did a ton of testing."

I nodded. Further tests seemed brutal after all the necessary interventions, but I could recite the standard list. Vision, hearing, cognitive … "Jake?"

Jake halted and turned toward me. "Turns out I spent hours telling Sari stories that she couldn't even hear."

"She's deaf?"

"Acute hearing loss is what the doctor called it, though they don't know how or why. Now she wears hearing aids in the hopes she'll pick up at least a few ambient sounds. The audiologist is constantly assessing her, and we've been to see numerous specialists and therapists." The sad smile was accompanied by the slightest shrug. "It's a lot, right?"

I shook my head, peering at him. "Idiot." At that moment, I didn't know who in this mess made me the angriest; Jake for keeping secrets, the selfish woman who'd checked out without any concern for her family, or me for letting this man suck me in with a line of half-truths and omissions. "How could you not share that earlier?"

He stood there, arms dangling at his sides, shoulders stooped. "You're angry."

"Stellar observation." I folded my arms across my chest as I rose and planted my feet. "You didn't trust me with crucial information."

"It's not the leading statement I make when I talk about Sari. She's a little girl, like any other."

"No, she's absolutely not like any other, and I'm not just anyone, am I?"

He straightened, his eyes narrowing. "You know the answer to that, but it seems her deafness is a dealbreaker."

"Are you ashamed of her?"

"Don't be crazy. Sari's amazing. I can't imagine life without her."

"Oh, so you just believe I'm shallow and uncaring. That I'm incapable of loving your daughter because she can't hear."

He bowed his head, shaking it slowly. "Not everyone can accept Sari as she is. Her own mother rejected her. Her grandmother wants to fix her, like Sari's somehow broken."

That burn behind my eyes grew again. I covered the few steps between us, lifting one hand.

Jake flinched, hunching his shoulders and turning his head away.

"Hey." I moved slowly, gently, cupping his cheek in a caress and forcing him to face me. "What was that?"

He drew shaky breath, his almost inaudible sniff accompanied by two fingers pressed to the bridge of his nose. "Nothing. It's nothing."

We stood there for several seconds, neither of us moving. His reaction concerned me, but now was not the time to dig into causation.

I filed my question away for a better time, instead asking, "Fix her how?"

"Surgery. An implant, even though it's not the best thing for Sarina. Stella refuses to learn sign language and is so damn impatient. Sari gets frustrated and overwrought and acts out, then Stella calls her bratty. It takes me hours to calm her down after she's been to Nana's house."

"Why let Stella take your daughter if she can't accept her as she is?"

"You say that like I have a choice. If I refused access, Stella would come at me, fully armed, guns blazing."

My head bobbed as I absorbed the facts. Jake had an entire life I was barred from and, therefore, may never fully understand. A case of tactical segregation; the splitting of his life in two. Taking his video calls in another room. Avoiding telling his family we were dating. Refusing to let me to meet his daughter. The list was endless.

All of those reactions were completely opposite to the first time we'd dated. The man had dragged me to a family dinner at the earliest opportunity, eager to introduce me to his tía and little sister. "Is that why you don't want anyone to know about me? It'll upset her family, right?"

He shoved his hands into his pockets. "Does that bother you?"

I lifted one shoulder, not trusting myself to speak, lest every frustration tumble from my unguarded lips.

"Yeah, stupid question. How could it not bother you?" he muttered as he began to pace again, mussing his hair with his fingertips.

"Jake—"

"See? This situation is all sorts of fucked up. Now you'll definitely dump me." He glanced my way before he continued stalking back and forth between my couch and coffee table. "The crazy complicated wreck of a boyfriend, getting a lecture from … ahhh!" He stopped in the middle of the room, covering his face with his hands.

With two strides, I reached him. "Breathe. Just breathe." I slid my hands up his chest, manoeuvring so his arms dropped to his sides, and I could cup his face between my palms. "This is weird, yes, but I'm all in, remember? Look at me."

He opened his eyes slowly, staring without blinking. "How do I deal with her family? If you heard Stella, you know she'll freak when she finds out. It's only been eight months."

"They have to know you'll move on. If her family cares anything about you and your daughter, they'll not only support it, but encourage it."

"Eventually, maybe, but it's too soon. How long before a parent stops grieving their daughter?"

I blinked hard, wrapping my arms around myself. "Are we rushing this? Do you even want to move forward?"

"I do, but the worst part is, Stella's right. Being away this often isn't great for Sari."

Ah, right. Alysa's family would have expectations. They were still buried in grief. Sarina would always be their grandchild. They'd want constant contact with her. They demanded a say in Jake's life and in how their grandchild was raised. *Jake was bowing to their demands.*

"Oh, Mar." He wrapped me in an embrace. "I have no excuse for being such a disaster."

The soft kisses he was now giving me, the way his lips lingered on mine, weakened my resolve.

"What about us?"

"Please let me sort things with her family. It won't be forever, but just for now."

"It's important that I meet your daughter, but I'll try to be patient." Clearly, Jake hadn't reached a place where he trusted me enough to let me all the way in. Whether or not Sarina liked me was the make-or-break piece of our puzzle, but for better or worse, this was how it was; I had little choice but to follow his lead.

Late the next afternoon, I kissed Jake goodbye amidst promises he'd be back in a few days. Shortly after he left, I settled in my office and searched for an American Sign Language course. Now that I knew about his daughter, it made perfect sense to learn a few basic signs. Maybe that would convince him I could be trusted with his precious Baby Starfish, and that I was ready to welcome her into my life.

I'd been immersed in practice for almost an hour when the text popped up:

Are you still alive out there? I still haven't heard what happened with Jake!

How should I respond to Dara when Jake insisted on keeping our involvement on a need-to-know basis?

How about that fabulous honeymoon? Tell me all about Aruba.

My phone rang almost immediately.

"The trip was amazing," Dara said the moment I answered. "Dean told me you promised to visit once we were back. How soon can you be here? We have a guest room."

I laughed, struggling to control the quaver in my voice. "Well, let me look into that." Halifax. That wasn't remotely feasible given the Jake situation. He'd view that as me pushing to meet Sari before he was ready to let me in. "It's good to hear your voice."

"Back at ya." Her light laugh carried down the line. "Maybe Viv will join us for a spa weekend."

"I'm down for that." *Darn. Why did I so easily fall into line?*

"Perfect. Send me some possible dates." Her long breath carried down the line. "Did you hear that Jake has a contract in Vancouver? You should hit him up. I'll text you his number."

I shifted on the couch, tapping a finger against pursed lips. "It can't hurt to talk to the man. He doesn't bite."

Ha. If she only knew. "I'm good," I said.

"You'd be proud of him. Jake's an amazing dad, and on top of that he completed a grant proposal for an environmental study on water pollution. He's involved in a project to protect Kejimkujik."

What ...? What was happening? Grant approval? Water pollution? Kejimkujik? "What about his contract in Vancouver?"

"That's almost finished. This grant allows him to work full-time in Halifax and be home for Sari at night, and he'll be doing important work. One of our own, fighting the good fight."

I blinked hard and gnawed at my bottom lip.

"Isn't that fantastic?" Dara light lilt brought me to the edge of tears.

I reached for the glass of ice water beside me and gulped down a mouthful, swallowing hard. "Yeah. Amazing." Forcing a dramatic yawn, I said, "It must be bedtime for you."

"Too much Jake talk, huh?" She chuckled as a text arrived on my phone. "I sent you his number. Call him. He'll be stoked to hear from you."

"Night, Dar. Love you."

"Sleep well, Mar. Send me those dates."

The woman was a terrier, never letting go. It would be even more difficult to dodge her inquiries in person.

Even harder would be managing my own reactions and keeping myself in check during Jake's next video call. Surely he'd bring up this amazing grant soon, wouldn't he?

CHAPTER 13

I managed to hold back my questions, waiting patiently, hoping Jake might mention the spectacular achievement of winning a grant, but nope, not a peep. Not during the video chat when he told me he'd stay at his sister's tiny basement suite this week, not tonight over dinner, nor did it come up during our pillow talk, though there was still time.

Jake pressed his lips to my temple before I sat and propped myself against the pillows.

"Guess what I learned last week?" I asked.

"Hmmm?" He tilted his head my way, blinking sleepy eyes.

"Hi. How are you?" I said, signing along with the words.

"Not bad. Where did you learn that?"

"Online. I'm doing a little every day, half an hour at a time."

"Keep at it." Jake slid from my bed.

"Come back. There's more."

"Luci's expecting me." He tugged his t-shirt over his head.

"Since when does your baby sister set your curfew?"

The little smirk revealed his dimple. "She's a tyrant," he said with a chuckle, but his smile faded. "I promised I'd spend time with her. The last two trips I've stayed with you, barely seeing her at all. Anyway, I work early tomorrow."

"Fine. Go." With a waggle of my fingers, I sank into the sheets, pressing my face against Jake's pillow and inhaling the tangy remnants of man scent clinging to the soft cotton.

"Love you, *Mare*." He nuzzled my neck before giving me a long, satisfying kiss. "See you tomorrow night," he whispered against my lips. "Sleep well."

"Mmm." I wrapped my hand around the back of his neck. "Don't go."

"Wish I didn't have to, but tomorrow night, okay?" He loosened my grip and retreated. Seconds later the apartment door clicked shut behind him.

It felt like he was drawing away, slowly separating himself from our entanglement. I feared that one day soon he'd just stop calling. Was this just a bit of fun? A convenient cure to his loneliness? I wasn't sure my heart could take it.

❧

Late the next morning, when I entered The Quay and spotted Luciana with her companion, my stomach lurched. There was no mistaking the mass of dark curls or those eyes. I'd have known the little girl anywhere, even if she was the last person I expected to see here. *Did I still have time to run? Could I duck behind the greenery and text Luci that something had come up?*

Luciana smiled and beckoned from the small table beside the bank of tall windows, then she turned toward the baby girl in the highchair.

The young woman's call early on this sunny Tuesday morning had been a welcome diversion on my day off. *"I've been busy at the hospital, but I hope we can meet for coffee. I'm sorry I overreacted before, and I hate that we aren't talking. Please, please call me back!"*

Well, why not fill in my empty day and take the opportunity to mend my relationship with Luci? Tonight's date with Jake would be a late dinner, though he'd probably leave my bed before midnight, just like last night. Now his speedy exit made perfect sense.

I approached slowly, carrying my cup of chai. Jake wouldn't freak about this, would he? *Right.* He'd be as calm as a ballistic missile, coming in hot before detonating, leaving massive carnage with no survivors.

Sarina stared at me, not blinking as she grasped a chunk of muffin between chubby fingers and crammed it into her mouth.

"You look great." Luci rose to hug me. "This is Sarina."

"Of course, it is," I said and settled into my seat. I angled toward to the girl, making sure I looked straight at her. "Hi, sweet girl." I signed along with my words, hoping I was getting it right. "Enjoying your muffin?"

"How did you know?"

"Her resemblance to Jake." No need to expand on the statement or admit I'd seen her latest photo last night as I shared pillow talk with her big brother.

"Well, yeah, who else's child would I be babysitting, but how did you know to sign?" She tilted her head. "Who told you about her hearing?"

"Jake."

Luci's brows rose.

"At the wedding."

Sari crammed another chunk of muffin into her mouth, leaving a streak of blueberry across her cheek.

"Huh." A crease appeared in Luci's forehead as she dabbed at her niece's cheek with a napkin. "He rarely shares so quickly. Guess he trusts you."

I lifted one shoulder and sipped my tea. *Yeah, trust oozes from his pores.*

"Do you want kids?"

"Someday." The someday that Kyle had avoided. The someday I ached for.

"You'd be a great mom." She eyed me. "Jake's working, so he entrusted me with Baby Starfish last night, and I'll have her again tonight. Must have another hot date with his mystery woman."

"Good for him."

"You think?" Luci wrinkled her nose. "I begged him to bring my darling niece this trip. Last time I saw her was the month before Dara's wedding. It's too long until the holidays, if I'm even able to beg time off to visit Halifax."

I bit back my questions and my tears. Jake had omitted the crucial facts, all sweet parting kisses and promises as he dressed, leaving a slight dent in the pillow and a cooling spot in the sheets. Maybe that was the cruelest deception of all.

"Sorry." She patted my hand. "It's weird, right? Stupid of me to bring up the other woman, but … he's playing it cool. He refuses to introduce her, which is weird. I should know something about her by now."

With a forced smile and a tip of my chin, I bobbed my head. Luci's words stung, and again, I considered where Jake and I were headed. Even worse, today's invitation seemed less like an opportunity to reconnect and more like a chance for this young woman to get in some digs about how Jake was over me and dating with abandon.

"Are you seeing anyone?" Luci asked.

"Nobody special."

She nodded slowly, studying me.

"Stop it, Luci. Quit overanalyzing my life. Use those psychology classes on someone else."

Sarina whined, a chunk of blueberry muffin whizzing past me as she shrieked and kicked her feet.

"Let's take this little miss somewhere she can run. Do you mind?" Luci swiped at the little girl's face with a damp cloth from the small bag slung over the chair beside her. "Babysitting probably isn't what you had in mind when you agreed to meet me for coffee."

"Jake might be upset about me spending time with his daughter."

"Nah." She waved a hand before releasing the toddler from the confines of her seat. "Why would he care? He's overprotective, but you're not a stranger or anything."

No, this was much worse than being a stranger, between Jake's omissions and Luci's dismissive attitude. I busied myself with tidying the table and returning our cups and then we exited into the sunshine, strolling toward the nearby playground. "You're good with her."

"She's a complete doll." Luci ran a hand over the girl's dark curls before setting her niece free at the edge of the park. "Amara? I'm glad you came. I've missed you."

Now I was thoroughly confused, but I'd hang in there and see where this was headed.

a

We'd been chasing the little girl around the playground for half an hour when Luci's phone rang. "It's the hospital. Can you keep an eye on Sari?"

I nodded, moving closer and steadying Sarina as she negotiated the steps to the slide, then holding her hand as she slid down.

Several steps away, Luci paced back and forth, talking in a low voice.

"Go again?" I pointed at the slide, laughing at Sarina's emphatic nod and following as she toddled toward the stairs.

Luci rejoined us, frowning. "I have to check on a patient, but Jake won't be back until after five. Taking Sari to the hospital isn't the greatest idea, and she'll need a nap soon. Would it be too much to ask you to watch her?"

I blew out a long breath, raising my brows at Luci. *If only she knew.*

"Sorry." Luci combed her fingers through her hair, a despondent look appearing. "It's too weird for you to be around her given how things ended with Jake, right? Never mind, I'll take her with me."

"No." I lifted the little girl and rested her on my hip. "We'll do fine, won't we, Sari?"

The girl twirled a lock of her hair around her finger, one thumb finding its way into her mouth.

"She's exhausted." Luci draped the diaper bag over my shoulder. "I'll be back before Jake finishes for the day, so you don't have to deal with him."

"I'll take good care of her."

"Was there ever any doubt?" Luciana planted a kiss on the girl's head. "Be good for Amara," she said before she headed in the direction of the hospital.

Holding Jake's child in my arms felt strange, but I loved the crisp outdoor scent that clung to her hair, and the way she wrapped her arms around my neck and rested her head against my shoulder. I snuggled Sarina close and strolled toward my condo, wondering if this blissful feeling would reappear when—*if*—I eventually held my own child.

Her eyelids drooped, one fist rubbing at her eyes. A snack followed by a nap was needed by this little starfish.

I stared blankly at my book, struggling to shut down the thoughts whirling around my brain. Would Luci tell her brother about this afternoon? As the lock turned in my front door, I straightened.

"Are you home, Mar?" Jake's voice brought me out of my chair.

Shooting a look toward my bedroom, I hurried toward the front door. "You're early."

"Aren't you happy to see me?" he asked, catching me around the waist and hauling me against him. "Greg had a meeting downtown, but he had it covered, so …" His lips were enticing, soft and warm as he kissed me, dancing us toward the bedroom. His keys landed on the island with a clatter.

"Stop." The firm push against his chest did little to dissuade him, but the only thing worse than him finding his daughter in my apartment would be him finding her curled up in the middle of my bed enjoying her afternoon siesta as he stripped me naked, intent on luring me into that very bed. "Really, we can't."

He pressed his face into the crook of my neck, groaning, still guiding me toward my bedroom, one slow backward step at time.

"Jake."

He stopped just short of my room and stared into my eyes. "What's wrong?"

Sarina's tiny feet pattered against the hardwood as she toddled toward her daddy, lifting her arms.

He narrowed his eyes, but a bright smile appeared as he scooped up his baby girl, tossing her in the air and peppering her with kisses. "Starfish! Did you have fun today? What happened to Tía Luci?"

The little girl patted his cheek, followed by an open-handed thumb tap to her forehead with her right hand. She squirmed and pointed toward the living room.

Jake set her on her feet, and she raced away, plopping onto her bum beside the board book we'd looked at before her nap. "Why is my daughter here?"

"Good question. Why is she here, Jakob?"

"Where's my sister?" He crossed his arms.

"Luci got called in to work and asked me to watch Sarina."

"You should have said no."

"And tell her that you demand that I stay away from your kid?"

"No, but this isn't—" He eyed my phone as it rang.

"That's probably Luci," I said, glancing at the number—the one linked to the building's intercom system. "What should I do?"

"Damn. Let her in? You can't ignore her."

I answered and released the door, still observing Jake.

The man stared at his blissfully unaware daughter, tense and poised, appearing ready to snatch her up and bolt from the apartment at any moment.

"It's not that big of a deal. Just tell her I called you to pick up Sari."

"Why would you do that? In her world, we aren't even speaking, let alone having chummy phone convos while you babysit my daughter."

"Then tell her we're seeing each other. It's time."

As my front door opened, he pressed a finger to his lips and covered the few feet to my bedroom, slipping inside and closing the door only seconds before his sister appeared.

"How did it go? Oh, Sari's awake."

"It was fine ... good. She just woke up from her nap."

Luci tilted her head, her attention caught by something behind me as I leaned against the island.

"How was your patient? Okay, I hope?"

"The patient ... oh, fine, great, yeah." Her head bobbed. She glanced at her niece, then fixated on the island again, smirking. "Sari looks perfectly content."

"It went well. She ate a snack and had a long nap." Though I tried my hardest not to look down, I couldn't resist. *Damn, damn, damn.* The keychain with its distinctive Hawaiian koa wood turtle shone like a beacon.

"Good. Are you and—" She clamped her teeth onto her lower lip, squinting at me as she shook her head. "You lied straight to my face. Nobody special? I thought I was imagining things, but his leather jacket is on the rack by your front door and that"—she pointed to the keys the counter—"is his hand-carved turtle from Maui."

I blinked, hard. This is not how I imagined revealing our relationship to his family.

"You two almost had me, but Jake protested too much about not being ready, and you sat there with that pained look while I fed you details about his fictional love life. Ha!" She pointed her finger at me, her eyes lighting up as she grinned. "And you magically know sign language?"

I clapped a hand over my mouth as the woman performed a victory dance, hips swinging, arms waving, and hair flying, her laughter filling my kitchen.

Sari turned, watching her aunt, wide-eyed.

"Such a lousy actor. My big brother is here, right now, lurking behind that door, hanging on every word we say." Luci tipped her head toward my bedroom. "Jakob! You're busted!"

Sarina pushed to her feet, waving her book as Jake stepped from my bedroom.

"You think you're so sneaky, big brother, but you can't hide that look you get whenever I mention Amara." Luci covered the few feet into the living room and scooped up her niece, peppering the little girl with hugs and kisses. "Good job, *Starfish*, you reeled her in. And now"—she set the giggling toddler onto her feet—"my work is done, so I'll leave you two to whatever you were doing. Just keep it PG, 'cause I'm leaving the toddler. Tata." The woman fluttered her fingers and skipped toward my front door.

"Wait." Jake bolted after her. "Don't tell Marisol. Not yet."

"Why ever not?" Her voice level dropped, as did Jake's, making it impossible to catch anything but the occasional tidbit of conversation.

Sari wandered into the kitchen, clinging to the edge of the counter with one hand as she tapped her lips and pointed to my banana tree.

"Eat?" I mimicked her sign.

She nodded and signed again.

"Banana?" I pointed my index finger and repeated her motions. After setting her on the island, I peeled the bright yellow fruit and broke off a chunk. "Here you go, Baby Starfish." I tipped my head, straining to hear what was being discussed in my hallway, but their voices were low and muffled.

"What? No way, no how am I assisting with your ludicrous crap. Deal with it, Jakob."

The door slammed.

Jake shuffled into the kitchen and held out his arms for his daughter. "Come on, Starfish. Let's get you home for dinner. Sorry, Mar, we need to cancel."

"You don't need to leave."

"Yeah, I do. Sari needs dinner and a bath, and I just lost my sitter."

"We could ..." The firm set of his lips warned me not to bother offering. "Fine. Go." I waved a hand toward the door and wrapped my arms across my chest.

"Luci will settle down," he said. "I'll call you tonight."

"Why bother? So you can drop by for dinner and a quickie? You're hiding us from everyone. That little performance made it obvious what this is ... and what it isn't. I wanted to be all in, but I'm doing all the giving. This secret half-life is exhausting."

"Please don't run from this."

"I'm not the one who's running."

He shook his head. "Don't overreact."

"Where am I in all of this?"

"Right here. We're together."

"If we were a real couple, me spending a few hours with your daughter wouldn't freak you out. You would have told me she was with you this trip."

"It's not that." He peered at me over the head of his daughter who had settled against his chest, arms wrapped around his neck.

"You know, when I was married, things seemed really good for a while. Kyle isn't a horrible person, but still, his needs always mattered more than mine."

"You're comparing our relationship to your shitty marriage? That's great, Amara. Just"—his lip curled as his jaw tightened—"great."

"No, but skulking around the corners of your life isn't fulfilling." I bowed my head. "Sarina is the single most important person in your life. I don't even rate a distant third."

"You know the situation. What do you expect?"

"A man who's there for me. Someone who doesn't need me to tell him how much it hurts to be shut out of the most important parts of his life. Someone who wants the same things I want. I turn thirty next month and someday soon, I want my own baby. Can you see that in our future?"

"I don't know if I go through that again. I love Sari, but ..."

I closed my eyes, tears burning and seeping from under my lids. The one thing I wanted most was still out of reach. "Shame on me for doing exactly what I swore I would never do again."

"What are you saying?"

"That I rescheduled my entire life for you. I changed my shifts at work as you weren't here for weekends, so I could spend more time with you, even though that ended up a bust. I clung to the ridiculous notion that after everything, you'd want me to meet your daughter." And bent and twisted and shaped myself into that minuscule space the man allowed for me in his life. "When were you planning to tell me about the grant?"

He sighed.

"Just say it. The grant you never told me about was approved, so all work is now scheduled on the east coast."

He nodded.

"No more trips to Vancouver."

He shook his head.

"Fantastic."

Jake closed his eyes, turning his head away.

"I mean," I said, concentrating on softening and levelling my tone, "congratulations. You've worked hard for the opportunity. You'll change lives for the better."

"And my own life?"

"Seems you're all set. No point in hanging on while you promise me more and more when it's never going to happen. I see that now." I lifted my chin. "Leave your keys on the counter. I'll pack your things and give them to Greg or Luci."

Jake bowed his head, rubbing Sarina's back.

Nothing to say. No fight left in him. All I longed to hear was that he understood, that I was wrong, that we did have a future. That he would try harder. But the humiliating moment dragged on, the uncomfortable silence smothering my last bit of hope. Cutting away this little slice of me, sending this man away, would be painful but, ultimately, it was necessary for both our sakes.

"Bye, Sarina." I waved and kissed her rosy cheek. "Be good for your daddy." Now, walk away. *Walk away. Walk away.* Finally, my stubborn feet obeyed my command, step after step, until finally, I shut my door and crawled under the covers, burying my head and my tears in my pillow.

CHAPTER 14

Two hours later, once my apartment had descended into that empty quietness that came of being truly alone, that silence that offered no hope of my someone arriving to fill the space, I trudged into the kitchen.

I opened my snack cupboard and shifted packages, coming up with a half-empty box of stale croutons and a bag that offered ten pathetic nacho chips—the woeful remains, thanks to Jake's constant raids on my munchie stash.

Tears flooded my eyes. *Wine.* I still had the expensive Sauvignon I'd selected expecting to share tonight's dinner with Jake. A huge chunk of the afternoon I'd invested preparing food I now had no appetite to eat.

I frowned as the lock in my front door turned, followed by voices.

Seconds later, Beth and Luci appeared, both with armloads of grocery bags.

"Wha—" My words were muffled by Luci's tight embrace and tiny snuffles.

"I'm sorry. It wasn't supposed to end like that." Luci pulled back, still holding my shoulders. "For a brilliant man, Jake's incredibly stupid. And clueless. I love my brother, but … aaaargghh!" Her fingers curled as she lifted her hands in a pantomime, shaking them exactly like she actually had them wrapped around the offender's throat.

Beth was next, her warm hug and silent back rub making my eyes well up, even though I had no clue how, since I'd emptied gallons of tears into my pillow.

"You told me. Why didn't I listen?"

"Because you had hope." She kissed my cheek. "I'm sorry, sweets, it really did seem promising."

Luci was already emptying bags, littering my island with packages. "Okay, so we have the essentials. Tissue," she said, holding up two brightly patterned boxes, "and of course, assorted chips and gummies." She tossed several more packages onto the island. "I ordered two loaded pizzas."

"Chocolate?" I asked.

Beth produced three packages of my favourite Belgian dark chocolate from her bag, waving them before setting them with the other snacks.

"I have wine." I turned toward the cabinet against the far wall.

Luci motioned to the assembled ingredients on the counter. "Nope. We have drinks covered. Welcome to Margaritaville," she said, hefting a bottle in either hand. "All we need is glasses."

α

Soon we were gathered in the living room, sipping cocktails and munching pizza and snacks.

"How did you know?"

Luci sighed. "My big brother called from Greg's and gave me hell for the Sari babysitting fiasco. He's inordinately pissed and refuses to stay at my place. Anyway, Beth sneaked a look at his phone to get my number, and we organized our rescue mission."

I reached for a tissue.

"It was stupid for me to interfere."

"No." I shook my head. "It would have ended sooner or later, so sooner is better. Thank you for dragging me into the light." Prolong my agony by pining over the man while he enjoyed his summer surrounded by friends and family, well, that would have just about killed me.

"Would it end, though?" Luci tilted her head. "He loves you, but he's still struggling to sort out his life. He told you how Alysa died?"

"Eventually." I sucked back the dregs of my Margarita.

"Damn it, Luci, he's in the wrong." Beth refilled our glasses from the frosty pitcher on the coffee table. "No matter how awful, and devastating, and heartbreaking her death was for him, he doesn't have the right to start something he can't finish." She turned to me. "You did the right thing, sweets, you deserve so much more than a dead-end long-distance farce. Ugh, selfish jerkity jerk, jerking you around."

Luci picked at her nail, head bowed. "It doesn't change how he feels about you. Be patient. He'll get there."

"No, he won't." The air rasped down my raw throat. "He doesn't want another baby."

"Baby! You're pregnant?" Luci straightened, reaching for my drink. "Put that down! Did you tell him? Did he walk—"

"No!" I yanked away from her, sloshing margarita across the hardwood. "Seriously. Do ya think I'd be sucking back tequila if I was knocked up?" My hand trembled as I pressed it to my belly, the ache growing. "A baby is in my plans, but it sure the hell isn't in his, so … we're done."

"That's a deal-breaker," Beth said as she hurried into the kitchen and grabbed some paper towels. "Never give up your chance for a family." She returned, kneeling to dab at the sticky puddle on my floor.

"That doesn't sound like Jake," Luci said.

"Then maybe you don't truly know your brother. Anyway, if he doesn't trust me with Sarina, why would he even consider a child with me? It's done. There's nothing left to say." I poured another liberal serving from the pitcher, gulping it down my parched throat. Nothing would persuade me to discuss this any further with Jake's sister, especially after a few drinks. Who knew what I might say?

❧

Fingers brushed across my hair, tucking a strand behind my ear. "Hey, sleepy, wake up."

I forced my eyes open and stared at the man sitting on the side of my bed. "Who let you in?" My alcohol-addled brain was already sorting out the answer and adding up the facts. Jake. Keys. He'd taken his keys.

"Someone had a big evening." Jake shook his head, the corners of his mouth twitching as I smacked my lips, rolling my tongue around in hopes of banishing that disgusting murky taste. "You three did some serious damage to a massive bottle of tequila."

Yup, and now I longed to do some serious damage to a massive glass of ice water.

"You never returned my calls."

The damp pillowcase stuck to my cheek. *Ick.* I wiped the back of my hand over my mouth, loathe to make the slightest move, sympathetic to my queasy belly. How would that be for a colourful good morning to my newest double-exed boyfriend?

"Now I know why. My little sister is passed out on your couch, and I assume Beth met the same fate in your guest room." He sighed as he retreated. "Maybe you really are that done with me." The door snicked shut as he exited my bedroom.

Excellent. Back to sleep for me. Anyway, this was probably a bad dream. A horrendous nightmare. I pressed my face deeper into the delicious, masculine smelling softness of well-worn leather, hugging it tighter and tighter ... leather? Dreaming. Yes, dreams. Nightmares. Hallucinations, maybe?

"Mar."

Mmmm. Warm hands on my arm, shifting me. An arm sliding around me, propping me up against a firm chest. The cold rim of a glass pressed to my lips. Ohhh, heaven. Icy water tumbled down my tortured throat as I took greedy gulps.

Jake pulled the glass away. "Slow down, or you'll hurl. Wearing last night's celebration or cleaning you up isn't my idea of a good time." He chuckled. "Wouldn't mind showering with you, though."

Ha. Ha. Funny guy. Enjoying my abject, hung-over misery, much? I squinted at him through aching eyeballs. Wouldn't be the first time Jakob Cavallaro held back my hair while I kneeled at the porcelain altar, but that scenario was far less acceptable at this particular moment. Did I want him here, seeing me as a mucky, maudlin mess? Him smirking while I wished for a hasty death to eliminate the awful pounding in my head? Nope. *Go away. Far, far, away. It's all your fault, asshole.*

"The place is a disaster. Did you stage a raid on the convenience store down the street?"

I tugged at the sleeves of the blue cotton garment engulfing my body as a vision of last night flickered into my consciousness. The second, then third pitcher of margaritas, then ... tequila shots? The crazy dance to that late-night pop mix pouring through the high-end speakers, the flood of tears followed by a lurching path to my bedroom, stripping off my clothes, and ... I bowed my head, my cheeks flaming as I picked a speck of lint from the front of the oversized sweatshirt. Jake's black Dalhousie sweatshirt that I'd nicked from his drawer when I'd left those many years ago.

"You," he said, his voice flat but firm, "really packed my things."

Ahhh. Yup. I'd done that, avoiding Luci's accusing stare as I raced around my apartment, stuffing her brother's socks and boxer-briefs into his bag before slinging it to the floor by the front entrance.

Followed by ... ohhhh, crapola. *No-no-no.* A vision rose; the contents of my purse scattering as I fumbled for the business card and stupidly performed the dreaded drunk text. I hadn't even thought of Christophe since the wedding all those months ago. What exactly had I said to him? In front of Luciana, no less. Had she ratted me out to her brother?

Jake propped himself on one hand, peering at me in the dim light filtering through the blinds. "No further discussion on the matter? It's just over, huh?"

Guess not. No yelling from Jake. No berating, livid, betrayed words, either. I wiggled toward the edge of the bed, pushing the crumpled pile of leather to the floor. Geez. Caught cuddling his jacket, wearing his stolen clothing. Forever branded as the psycho, obsessed, twice-exed girlfriend who couldn't quite let go, even as I shooed him out the door.

Jake caught me around the waist before my feet touched the floor. "Amara."

"Just go." *Leave me to my miserable, single, baby-less, bereft life.*

"Please." The mattress sunk as he kneeled, wrapping his arms around me from behind.

I froze, my body rigid. I could feel everything. The firmness of his chest against my back. The thud of his heart. The warmth of his arms. His sweet minty breath as he pressed his face to my hair.

"I love you," he whispered. "That might not be enough, but please give me another chance. I fucked it all up, again, and I'm sorry."

My breath hitched in my chest. Hold strong. Stay firm. Don't let him toy with your emotions. Cause that's what men did. What Jake excelled at. Avoiding commitment. Forming our relationship based on his own terms. Just like our last go 'round.

"You were right, but also wrong. I'm not running, but maybe I've been avoiding decisions. I've thought about Sari, a lot, but that next step is huge and changes absolutely everything. I'm sorry for not telling you she was here, but I expected to be part of that meeting when the time was right. It should have been my decision, not my sister's. And ..." His voice quavered. "Those months before Sarina was born were some of the worst in my life, the spot where everything fell apart. I don't want that for us. It could all be different with you and me, but what if it isn't?"

What was he even saying? My heart pounded.

"Don't say anything, please. Just take some time and decide if you can still deal with the mess that is me. Because I am. Nothing is simple and making this work won't be easy. Maybe you won't be up for what's waiting, or the challenges we face, but I hope you are."

I was stuck. Unable to move. What was happening here?

He drew away, the move followed by jingling. "This is for you." He set an envelope on the bed and placed his keys on top. "Look at it when you're ready." He brushed back my hair, his warm fingers lingering against my face as he leaned in and kissed my lips, then my cheek. "Bye, my beautiful *Mare*. Take care of yourself."

Moments later, my front door closed behind him.

CHAPTER 15

Just because I'd poured innumerable ounces of booze into my system, and now suffered the worst hangover in recorded history, it didn't give me a free pass on work. My boss showed great understanding during those confusing months after my separation from Kyle and submitting her to another round of abject depression courtesy of Jakob Cavallaro would be unfair.

When I entered the kitchen an hour after her brother's departure, fully dressed and ready—well, sort of ready—to tackle the day ahead, Luci eyed me while I fumbled around grinding espresso beans and frothing milk for my morning latte.

"What did he say?" she asked.

So. *Not* passed out on the couch. More like faking, completely aware that her brother had returned to the scene of his crime. Maybe she'd lurked in the hallway with a glass pressed against my bedroom door. *Uh-uh.* No way would I explain or relive those final sad moments. Anyway, I'd cried myself out in the shower, eventually pulling myself together so I'd arrive at work before eight in a semi-respectable state. "None of your damn business."

"Who's Christophe? Have you been sleeping with him too?"

"Also not your business."

"It is when you're cheating on my brother."

"I've never cheated on your brother. Ever." I jangled the extra keys that had so recently been Jake's, yanked open the drawer of the ornate side table, and dropped them inside. "Anyway, cheating implies a relationship. One without secrets and lies and sneaking around. One where my boyfriend treats me as more than his bed warmer." For good measure, I slammed the drawer.

"Then leave my brother alone. I take it all back. I don't want you as my sister. Not anymore." The little meddler grabbed her purse and scurried toward the foyer, muttering under her breath. Moments later, the door slammed behind her.

"Of course, idolization of the asshole. He can do no wrong." Nothing had changed with Luciana Cavallaro, except now she despised me twice as much.

I packed my lunch, sniffling as I sucked back my latte, and then followed it up with a double shot of espresso, using the strong brew to wash down two acetaminophen tablets, fuming at the injustice. Fighting the searing pain that made it almost impossible to breath.

Finally, I wrapped my arms around myself and slid to the floor, curling my knees to my chest, letting it pour out in heavy sobs, gasping for air.

"Sweetie." Beth's warm embrace was welcome as she hugged me and rubbed my back. She peered at me through bleary eyes, her hair in disarray. "Oh, girl, you look rough. Call in sick."

"And sit here all day stewing about him?" I wiped my eyes with my sleeve.

The only thing that might keep me sane was focussing in on work and zoning out on the unopened letter in my bag while ignoring my confusion over Jake's actions. Ignoring the ache caused by the attack from his little sister as she informed me I was no longer welcome in her family.

And Jake. *I love you, and I hope this will work, but here are your keys, and see ya later?* Crap. Utter nonsense and complete bullshit. Hot and cold. Here or there. In or out. Over and done.

"Amara?" Beth handed me a box of tissue. "Are you going to be okay?"

Better get used to that question, yet again. Tomorrow, I might just beg for that day off and take another one of Heather's yoga classes, calming diffuser blend and all. Who knew? It might actually work this time. It might drag me through the worst of another heartbreak.

Maybe it would get me over Jake. Not that I had a choice.

By the end of my shift, I was ready to drop, but I only had myself to blame. To make matters worse, I received an email from my boss, asking me to see her before I started work the next morning. Stepping things up would be a good idea or, based on my recent troubles, my job might be in danger.

I trudged down the street, making a brief stop at my favourite family owned Indian restaurant to pick up dinner, mildly excited at the thought of a quiet evening at home. After I cleaned up the destruction from last night, of course.

To my surprise, a soothing silence and lemony freshness surrounded me as I set my keys on the tray inside my door. The evidence of last night's wallowing had disappeared without a trace. Every dish, crumpled napkin, snack bag, and sticky Margarita puddle.

Beth, no doubt. That wonderful woman. Thanks to her, I could relax, enjoy my evening meal, and nurse my vague, lingering headache.

After stopping for a glass of ice water, I carried the takeout into the living room. Better forgo the wine habit tonight. In my current state, I'd down the entire bottle and pass out on the sofa.

The city lights twinkled from across the water as I stabbed one of the vegetarian samosas and bit into it, chewing slowly. Usually, I loved my impromptu meals from the little Indian Fusion restaurant, but tonight the savoury bites appealed as much as the three-day-old ciabatta buns lingering on my counter.

I forced down a few more mouthfuls before setting aside my fork and wiping my fingers on my napkin. That stupid envelope would haunt me until I satisfied my curiosity. The man knew that when he left it. He got me. Understood my silly little quirks. Opening it was irresistible, even with hurt and anger clouding my viewpoint, something Jake surely counted on.

I stomped toward the table and plucked the letter from my bag. "You win, Jakob. You always win." It stared me down, the looping script smirking at me as I smoothed the envelope between my fingers and set it on the coffee table. Maybe I'd open the bottle of wine after all. I definitely needed a liberal dose of liquid pain reducer.

Three minutes later, I settled on the couch again, sipping the rich red liquid, tapping a fingertip against the crystal, inspecting each and every letter. Finally, I slid a fingernail under the seal of the dreaded envelope, slitting it open one tiny bit at a time. Inside was a single sheet of paper. I unfolded it slowly, staring at it for a moment, pressing my fingertips to my lips.

An itinerary. The dates and times of the flights blurred together. The handwritten note read:

> *"I'll be at the airport waiting for you when you arrive. That is, if you decide to accept my invitation and spend a week with me and Sari. I hope you will. Love, Jake."*

I squeezed my eyes shut, clenching the paper in my fist. Now he wanted me to be there? How could he just book this without asking me first? I crumpled the note, shuffling into the kitchen and slinging open the lower cupboard. The note landed in the white trash bag, the lid of the can thunking as it closed.

Then I refilled my glass. Time for a movie. Something light and funny. Or at least something hopeful.

α

My eyes popped open in the darkest hours before dawn. I'd curled into a ball on my couch, and now I trembled and sobbed, fat, scorching, salty drops flooding down my face and smothering my every attempt to catch a breath.

Jake. The charmer. Wiggling back into my heart only to rip it straight and unceremoniously from my chest. He had no right. None whatsoever. Toying with me and my fragile psyche was beyond cruel.

It took an ultimatum and a solid ass dumping before he admitted wrongdoing and acknowledged my feelings. Where had I seen that jackass move before? *Right.* My ex-husband.

Exed-ex-boyfriend and shithead-ex-husband. Two exes, each intent on messing with my hard-gained perfect system in their own mind-fuck ways. Yet, only one had true power over my decimated heart. Considering all the possible outcomes and how he could strip me, take it all, leaving nothing but an echo of who I'd fought so hard to become, left me weak and weary.

The moment I'd seen Jakob Cavallaro and that dimple so many years ago, I'd been lost. Hopelessly and deeply in love. Nothing had changed. Maybe it never would. A picture of the perfect life swirled into formation and danced along, slightly beyond my grasp. A return to our past and the forty-two months that sealed my fate.

Mornings of floating into his kitchen, blissful, wearing nothing but a t-shirt that smelled like him, cuddling against his firm chest as he handed me fragrant coffee to be sipped on the tiny deck. Days of sailing up the coast on the tiny borrowed boat, the stops in the small bays, salt on the breeze as we explored the beaches. Long leisurely paddles in the kayaks from the boat rental where Jake worked, our budget-friendly escape from the daily demands of part-time jobs and full-time studies, just for a little while. Walks along the waterfront boardwalk at sunset, hand in hand.

More than that, the remembrance of being held, valued, loved for exactly what and who I was—that was the missing factor in my entire life.

The impossible dream taunted me. Him holding me as our child snuggled close to my chest. That miracle he'd witnessed without me, the birth of his child shared with another.

I clenched my jaw, tears still seeping from under my lids, soaking my cheeks until I felt I might drown. I hugged his jacket around my shoulders, sucking in the warm earthiness of him while struggling to breathe, to grip reality. My heart filled, not with joy, but with cavernous, starless pain.

How could I fit into the life he'd built with his beautiful daughter? Such a huge mistake to have met her. Too soon. Far too soon. The fatal mistake; allowing total captivation by the wave of tiny fingers, bright smiles, amber eyes, and that mop of curls. No mistake. Sarina was Jake's child, not mine, and he simply didn't want me interfering in that part of his life.

Too late for retreat. I was spinning. Tumbling deep down that rabbit hole, maybe never to be seen again.

I swept away my tears along with my nonsensical half-awake brooding and rolled from the couch, landing hard on my knees. Wrapping myself tighter in the leather, I stumbled toward the kitchen, retrieving the crumpled paper from the bin. I pressed it flat against the counter, sweeping my palm across it, then tracing his familiar script with a fingertip. *I'll be waiting for you.*

Perhaps he would be, but why subject myself to further heartbreak? Maybe this time it made actual sense to avoid the entanglement, rather than me reacting to a situation. I balled the paper up, cramming it into the pocket of Jake's jacket. The buttery leather slid easily from my shoulders, and I hugged it to my chest, savouring the smell of him for a final time.

With a sigh, I rolled up his coat and shoved it into the storage basket in the recesses of my walk-in closet. *Goodbye, Jakob. You'll be missed.*

◌

The next morning, as requested, I stopped by Trina's office before the start of my shift and tapped on the door.

"Amara." My boss beckoned to the seat in front of her desk. "How are things?"

My forced smile surely didn't fool her, but it was worth a try. "Great." I perched on the edge of the chair. "What's up?"

Trina steepled her fingers under her chin, swivelling her chair from side to side. "Well, something major has come up."

My mouth dried as I straightened. *This couldn't be good.*

"I've been offered an administrative position with the Health Region. It's a huge promotion, one that I've been working toward for years."

"Wow. That's amazing. Congratulations." My smile was genuine. This woman had been an incredible advocate and mentor over the years. "You're leaving? When?"

"I start at the end of August."

"You'll be missed."

"My new office isn't far, so I'll be around." She slid a paper across her desk. "The search for my replacement starts tomorrow. You're the ideal candidate."

My eyes widened.

"Don't look so shocked. This is the inevitable next step in your career. One you deserve. I've taken the liberty of writing a recommendation letter that you can include with your application."

"Thank you." *Huh*. Not what I expected. "I'll consider applying."

She laughed. "Don't be crazy, Mar. Apply. The job is your perfect next career step, plus it's more money—a lot more money—which never hurts, either."

A salve of sorts on my open wound, but my boss was right. A perfect opportunity had presented itself; one I'd be crazy to pass up. Maybe this challenged would add a new sense of purpose in my life and lift me out of my funk over Jake.

❧

That evening, I updated my resume, filled out the online application, and attached Trina's written recommendation, a sense of satisfaction washing over me as I hit Apply.

The last thing needed to turn things around was to have *that* conversation. As his phone rang, half of me hoped he'd answer, while the other half wished I could avoid this ending.

"Hi," Jake said, his voice soft and low. "How are you?"

"Surviving."

"That's it? Just surviving?"

"How do you expect me to feel?"

"I can't even begin to guess."

"Really, I don't know what we were thinking in starting up again. Long distance never works and brief visits every seven to ten days aren't nearly enough to sustain a serious relationship."

"Then we agree. It's serious. Maybe it's time things changed."

I let the silence hang, biding my time. *Let him fill the space.*

"Have you ever thought about moving home?"

"And do what?"

"We have hospitals and pharmacies in Halifax."

"We have an ocean in Vancouver." The moment the words left my lips, I knew that could never happen, considering Jake's life situation as a widower with a young child. My promise to myself solidified; this time my needs had to rate on an equal footing.

"It's beautiful one, but if I tried to leave Halifax, it would not go over well with Ben and Stella. My support system is here. Marisol. Dean. Dara."

"Not to mention that fabulous hard-won grant. I get it."

"Will you consider moving?"

My needs. Stay firm. "You haven't been totally honest. You've kept me apart from your life. You freaked about me seeing Sari. We're still an inconvenient secret to almost everyone. I want more. I want a family. That's non-negotiable."

"So, that's it?"

"I'm sorry. I love you, but …"

"You're not even willing to try?"

Tears built and my throat ached. "I have tried!"

"Don't do this, Mar. Not again."

"It's futile to chase what can never be."

"This could work if we were in the same city."

"My boss is leaving. I've applied for her job, which is a huge promotion and more money." Silence fell and dragged on for several seconds.

"Well, that's what's important, right? Your career?"

"Like yours isn't? You're all set on this grant. You get to save Kejimkujik."

Another long silence. "I never told you it was Kejimkujik," he said, finally.

"Yeah, exactly my point. Tell me again, whose career is more important? Whose needs come first?"

"For me, it's about supporting my daughter and digging myself out of a trench. I'm not sure it's the same thing."

"Do you love your career?"

"Yeah, of course," he said softly.

"Well, so do I. Just because I don't have a child doesn't mean my dreams are any less important, Jakob. My struggles might be unimportant to you, but I've still poured my heart and soul into making something out of my life."

"I'm not saying—"

"Yeah, you are. I'm the woman, so I should bend, sacrificing what I need in favour of what you need, including forgetting my wish to have a child. Even worse, you won't let me all the way in, keeping secrets, leaving me hovering on the fringes."

"That's not—"

"But it is. I could love her, you know, but you never gave me the chance. Even learning ASL and being there for you wasn't enough. What's changed? That you moved the goalpost, so I should fall into line? Forget it. We're done."

"Mar, please don't—"

"Take care of yourself. Be happy."

The brief sound of fuzzy dead air was followed by a click. Not that there was anything left to say. I curled up on my bed and watched the images on my digital photo frame. Me with Jake at Lonsdale Quay. The two of us on the rocky beach the morning after being stranded while kayaking. The picture he'd taken of us on a hike in Deep Cove. Mixed in were several from the recent wedding in Toronto.

A few from our time together in Halifax, along with one of our many visits to Peggy's Cove, had worked their way in too. Those reminded me of another lifetime; a time when we were young and carefree. During the past weeks, we'd proven you could never go back. Trying to relive the past and rekindle the flame was impossible, at best feeding the illusion that you had actual control over anything.

I rose from the bed and unplugged the frame, tucking it in my bedside table. My time with Jake was something to treasure, but now it was officially over.

CHAPTER 16

The next few weeks were excruciating, not only waiting for the answer on the promotion, but fighting the urge to contact Jake. But I'd righted my life and moved on, at least as far as work was concerned, as I'd accepted the job offer. My emotions, however, were still in shambles.

Beth lifted her glass and tapped it against mine. "Congratulations on the promotion. You deserve it."

"Thanks."

"Why don't you look more excited? Still thinking about Jake?"

I shrugged as my phone lit up. "He's forgotten all about me," I said, glancing at the text:

Hi, stranger. How are things?

"Not likely." Beth waved toward my phone. "Is that him?"

"Why would it be?" Keeping my head down, I tapped in my reply, hitting enter with a flourish. "It's Christophe. Tenacious, that man."

"They usually are in the beginning. Doesn't it concern you that he knows Jake's best friend?"

"That's only a minor a complication."

Another text appeared:

I'm in Vancouver on Friday. Can I buy you a drink?

I shifted on my bar stool and sipped my wine.

"A little soon to be flirting, isn't it?"

"It's been six weeks. High time to move on." Burning tears gathered behind my eyes.

"I hate to see you like this." My friend looped an arm around my shoulders. "It's not too late."

"For what? To move to Halifax, all the while crossing my fingers and hoping that whatever it was with Jake pans out? That he magically changes his mind about having another child? Meanwhile, I trash my career by ditching a huge promotion and start over in another province, ending up no happier, without a chance at my own family."

"I'll support you whatever you decide, as long as you're happy. I'd miss you, sure, but being with the man you love isn't a ridiculous idea."

"Except it is ridiculous. Why should I sacrifice my needs for a man who has no intention of giving an inch? No, thanks." I straightened and reached for my phone again. "Anyway, who says he's the least bit interested in hearing from me?"

"Did you forget who I'm dating?"

Ha. That would be impossible. As evidenced by her blatant attempts to push me toward Jake, the woman was too far gone, her ear taken by a man when she should be on my side. "What does Greg's opinion have to do with anything?"

"It's not about Greg's opinion. It's about you being on the verge of leaping into another one of those dead-end relationships you complain about when the man you love is madly in love with you."

"Isn't refusing to settle a good thing?"

Beth levelled an unamused look at me. "Jake hasn't rushed into a new relationship."

"Goody for him," I said as I texted Christophe:

Sounds lovely.

Christophe's reply arrived seconds later:

I'll come to North Vancouver. Say around 7? I'll make reservations.

"Nothing wrong with a friendly drink or two with an eligible single guy."

Perfect. Looking forward to it.

"Have it your way, then." Beth signalled for refills. "Get it out of your system."

"Maybe Christophe is the one."

Beth wrinkled her nose, but only shrugged.

"You said it yourself. Don't compromise on what I want. Being with Jake means giving up the promotion, my apartment, and never having my own baby. Sometimes love can't bridge a deep divide."

"So, you admit you love him."

My glare silenced her, at least for now. I'd never denied loving the man, but my decision was final. Time to let go of what might have been.

Just before seven that Friday night, I followed the server onto the patio.

A grinning Christophe stood as we approached, looking sharp in dress pants and a button-down shirt. "Wow." He took my hands, pressing warms lips to my cheek. "You're even more gorgeous than I remember."

"Thanks. Back at you," I said as he pulled out my chair, waiting for me to sit before returning to his seat.

After the server had left with our drink order, the man ran slim fingers through dark hair. "How have things been? You've gone quiet since our text chat. That was what? Seven weeks ago?"

I dipped my chin, hoping to hide the flush of red tinging my cheeks. "Sorry about that. Drunk texting isn't usually my style."

"Ah," he said, waving a hand, "it's fine. I was happy you hadn't lost my number."

"It wasn't the greatest night. Life kind of blew up." I bit my lip. *Shut up, shut up.*

The man leaned back and draped his ankle across his knee. "I did get that impression. Is it resolved now?"

"Completely."

"Then you've ended whatever relationship put you into that tailspin?"

"Uh-huh."

Christophe stroked his chin. "How long were you together?"

"A couple of months."

"So, nothing too serious then?" The emerging smile coincided with the arrival of our drink order.

"Nope, nothing serious," I said, even if saying it felt like a lie. Just a tiny white one, though. Jake and I were done. This time, there was no going back. The only way now was forward.

The next Tuesday, I headed straight to the theatre after work to meet Beth for movie night.

When she spotted me, she waved from her place at the refreshment counter before turning back to the cashier and swiping her card over the reader.

I headed toward her, stopping short as Greg appeared at her side with a handful of napkins and three straws.

The man picked up the bag of popcorn while Beth tucked a package of chocolate candies into her purse and retrieved the drinks, fiddling with her straw as they joined me.

"We have snacks." My friend handed me a cup of iced tea. "It's so good to see you." Her awkward hug was accompanied by a whispered, "Sorry."

"Hi, Amara." Greg waved. "Thanks for letting me be the third tonight. Beth knew I wanted to see this one."

"Oh, no worries." I forced a smile, sipping my drink as we moved into the queue to enter the theatres.

Beth chattered to Greg as the teenage boy at the wicket scanned the e-tickets on our phones, and we proceeded inside and took our seats.

I shook my head as Greg tipped the popcorn bag toward me, locking the sigh in my throat. I'd looked forward to the usual girl talk with my friend, but how could I dish about my date with Christophe with one of Jake's closest friends hovering? Instead, I checked my phone, feeling almost invisible as the two discussed their plans for the upcoming weekend.

Finally, Beth nudged my side. "Phone away."

"Sorry. Work."

"How's the new job?" Greg asked as he tossed popcorn into his mouth.

"Good. Busy. I spent the day with Trina, getting up to speed. How was your day?"

We launched into mindless small talk, sharing the minutiae of daily life.

Usually, I enjoyed visiting with Greg, but this seemed stiff and awkward, as if Jake sat between us. When the previews started, I almost cheered, finally relieved of the duty to make nice with the uninvited guest to our girls' night. I sank lower in my seat, angling away so I didn't have to watch the two cuddle and whisper, their heads bent close together. The entire movie felt like its own brand of torture, a reminder of everything I didn't have.

As the final credits rolled almost two hours later, Greg said, "We're heading for a late-night snack. You should join us."

Forcing a yawn, I smothered it and shook my head. "Thanks, but I'm totally beat. I'll take a rain check."

"Are you sure?" Beth asked, linking her arm through her boyfriend's.

"Yeah, you two go on. Have fun." I hugged my friend and waved at Greg, starting my solo trudge up the long hill, keeping my eyes averted as a happy couple's laughter rang across the busy street.

If only Christophe lived closer. Finding a great guy who lived in the same city seemed impossible. Though even if he had lived in Vancouver, the man travelled extensively. Right now, he was in Rio de Janiero on assignment.

On my way into my building, I stopped at the bank of mailboxes and opened number twenty-four, sorting through the pile and disposing of the junk mail. That left me with a thick legal-size envelope sporting the distinctive logo of Kyle's investment firm, and a thin letter-size envelope showing my lawyer's return address. Clever, hiding a bloated legal statement in this non-threatening smallish envelope.

I tapped them against my palm, reluctant to open either. These days, my mail never contained good news, usually containing unexpected and unwelcome extra bills. Not the greatest way to top off my busy day and disappointing movie night.

I hung my keys on the hook inside my front door, shuffling into the silent space. Tonight, it felt even emptier. Over the summer, I'd become accustomed to arriving home to find Jake lounging on my couch or cooking in my kitchen. Everything still reminded me of his presence, no matter how hard I tried to forget.

With a heavy sigh, I dropped the mail onto the island and dug into the fridge, pulling out a container of leftover Indian Fusion and popping it into the microwave. While the small appliance hummed, I selected a Pinot Noir I'd been saving and poured, filling the glass almost to the rim. I leaned against the counter, sipping the rich wine and staring through my open blinds at the winking lights across the water.

Despite spending not only Friday night but also Saturday with Christophe, and the fact he'd already invited me to Victoria for the upcoming weekend, I felt lonely. My work colleagues were mostly just that—colleagues. On occasion we'd go for Friday night drinks, but most had husbands or wives or kids to hurry home to on a weeknight.

Beth had become more and more immersed in Greg, and without Jake, our interactions were becoming fewer and further between. That she'd allowed him to encroach on our sacred movie night without even asking made me reluctant to go to the next one.

The microwave beeped, and I grabbed a hot mitt to wrangle out the steaming butter chicken. I heated some rice and mixed the two dishes together in a pasta bowl, hunching over the island as I ate.

I inspected the two envelopes, weighing the pros and cons. Bad news first or worse news first? Taking a large bite, I chewed slowly, slitting the flap of the thin envelope with my fingernail and slowly unfolding the contents, preparing myself for acute sticker shock.

I swallowed hard and blinked, double checking the balance at the bottom, sure I had missed something. The total consisted of three neat zeros, suggesting someone had made a grievous accounting error.

Now I'd need to call the law office. A mishap like this had the power to circle around and take a chunk from my ass if it wasn't rectified immediately.

I washed down another forkful of butter chicken with a mouthful of wine, then slit the flap of the second envelope. To my surprise, the contents of this one also had neat zeros in the balance column, but zeros that combined with a sweet pile of numerals.

Of course, I knew Kyle had deposited retirement savings under my name, taking his rightful tax deductions, but this balance was far higher than I'd anticipated.

I flipped through the stack of papers, picking off the yellow sticky note affixed to the last sheet:

Amara,

These are the statements for the Registered Retirement Savings I deposited for you during our marriage. I took the liberty of adding some funds for this year and opening another account in your name for the future. I deposited a sum in the cash account in case you want to pay off your condo. I've asked my colleague Matt to take over managing your investments, so call him if you have any questions. His card is enclosed.

P.S. Thanks for returning the ring. My mother's grateful and sends hugs.

P.P.S I paid the legal fees for the divorce.

Kyle

So, *not* an accounting error, but a goodwill measure from my ex-husband. I pulled out a stool and sat, pouring through the numbers in more detail, my eyes widening at the amounts. My credit card was already performing a happy dance, my mortgage melting away.

I picked up my phone and dialled, my foot tapping a beat against the hardwood floor.

"I bet you opened your mail," Kyle said.

"Good guess. Wow, I don't know what to say, except thank you."

"Thank you is sufficient," he said, a smile in his deep voice. "We battled over some stupid things during the divorce, but I didn't want this to end on a bad note."

"Well, success, then. This was totally unexpected. Maybe I should say no and send it all back."

"Now that's crazy talk. You could have skinned me by taking half of everything and forcing me to pay alimony for infinity, but you didn't. That's what I love about you."

"What, that I'm kinda thick?" I laughed softly.

"No, you're brilliant, with the biggest, kindest heart, and it feels shitty that I took advantage of that. So, there we go. It's karma. Your integrity paid a few dividends."

"Well, thank you, karma, and thank you, Kyle. The investments certainly make life easier."

"You're welcome. Oh, and Matt's the best, but do what you feel, including changing firms if using mine is uncomfortable."

"I'll talk to Matt and see, but I'll probably leave it for now. Stellar returns, Kyle. I'm impressed."

"Investment rock star, at your service," he said, but then he lowered his voice. "I made you feel invisible?"

"Not at first, but over time, yes. You'd come home and barely look at me, stay late at the office, or go to the gym. I'd plan something for the weekends, but you'd hole up in your office instead. I wondered if you were having an affair."

"No, I promise, that wasn't why."

"What was it, then?"

"I wish I knew," he said softly. "You're beautiful and sexy and sweet. Far too good for me, but you married me anyway. I'm sorry for everything I never gave you."

"I'm sorry too. I should go."

"Bye, Marmalade. Be happy."

I hung up, surprised by his use of that name again. He'd stopped calling me Marmalade eighteen months into our marriage, with things deteriorating quickly afterward. Maybe he did still care for me, just a little. Or maybe this was a payoff for an affair he would deny until the end of time, or maybe it truly was an attempt at good karma for his future.

I still didn't have any real answers, but maybe why didn't matter, it only mattered that he'd taken steps to make my life easier. For that, I'd be forever grateful.

I spent a few minutes working through the statements and coming up with a solid financial plan, then I tucked Matt's card into my wallet. Tomorrow I'd call and set things in motion for my brighter financial future.

a

My stomach did a flip as the tiny seaplane touched down in Victoria. The flight, arranged by Christophe, had given me moments of incredible exhilaration combined with a touch of abject terror.

Christophe waved as I disembarked, striding toward me and sweeping me into an exuberant embrace. "How are you?" He planted a kiss on my lips. "You look amazing as always. Let me get your bag."

"That was crazy, but fun. I've never been on such a tiny plane."

"Glad you enjoyed it." He wrapped an arm around my waist as I admired the view of the parliament buildings, which were only steps away. "We can come here tomorrow if you're interested, but tonight we have reservations for dinner."

"I'm starving. I went right from work to the air terminal." The journey hadn't been long, being only a quick ride on the SeaBus to downtown Vancouver, which was the location of the Harbour Air terminal, but it still hadn't left me time to eat.

"Excellent, because this place has fantastic seafood and a gorgeous view of the water." He put my bag into the trunk of his black Acura.

"How did your assignment in Brazil turn out?"

"I took some amazing pictures. Later, I'll show you." He guided me toward the waterfront. "It's a short walk. I hope you don't mind."

"Of course not. It's pretty down here." As we approached a quaint eatery on the wharf, my smile widened. "Reservations, huh? How did you know I love fish and chips?"

"Ah, Halifax girl, of course you do. Question is, which fish is your favourite?"

I tapped my pursed lips as I considered the menu. "Halibut, please."

"My kind of woman." He winked and ordered, adding two cups of chowder.

When our order came up, we claimed a nearby bench and looked over the water as we munched on the crispy battered fish, thick-cut fries, and tangy slaw.

"This is delicious. I thought we'd end up inside some fancy restaurant, but this is much better." I tipped up my chin, enjoying the salty breeze and the sunshine kissing my cheeks.

"You do seem like someone who enjoys adventures, though I suspect you haven't had enough of them. How do feel about ziplines?"

"They're fun," I said, immediately thinking about the trip Jake and I had taken to Whistler in early July, and the amazing feeling of freedom as we'd soared over the treetops at high speeds.

"Perfect. I have just the place, and to make it extra special, we'll add a little twist."

"Sounds daunting."

"You'll love it. Trust me. A Saturday night you'll never forget."

Now I was wondering what I'd gotten myself into by agreeing to spend the weekend with the man. However, I was ready to have a bit of fun, and why not? The man had been nothing but generous and kind.

❦

Shortly after six a.m. on Sunday morning, I padded downstairs dressed in the t-shirt Christophe had left draped over the chair in his bedroom. The main floor seemed deserted, but the patio doors hung open, letting in fresh morning air. A mug sat on the counter beside a silver carafe. I poured a steaming coffee, leaning against the counter and taking a ginger sip.

Christophe's home was a modern space with sparse, masculine furnishings and cupboards containing a few functional dishes, but not much else. His ultimate bachelor pad was complete with a bike hung from a wall rack and a big screen TV attached to an adjustable mount. Of course, he spent much of his time living out of a backpack-style travel bag, holing up in whatever accommodations were available, from a five-star hotel in Paris to a simple tent on the Serengeti. This lock-it and leave-it condo suited him perfectly, containing the bare necessities and nothing more. The man didn't even own a plant.

I wandered to the row of framed photos hung on one wall, particularly drawn to the forlorn girl of around five crouched on a pile of rubble in the middle of a devastated village. Wide, sad eyes stared at me, tears creating shiny rivulets on her filthy, mud-caked cheeks. Her story, as told by Christophe, was heartbreaking. That pile was the remainder of her home after an attack by rebels, her parents and two brothers missing and presumed dead.

On Saturday morning, he'd shown me his collection of albums and several magazine spreads featuring his work. His tales at the wedding were no lie; he travelled everywhere and seen things I'd never imagined. Nobody could deny his compassion and courage, his work unsuited to the faint hearted.

After topping up my cup, I headed onto the sunny patio.

"Good morning, beautiful," Christophe said without pausing his movements. Tai Chi, he'd told me the day before when I'd found him practicing the dance-like moves before the sun had even risen. He'd offered to teach me, but I hadn't managed to drag myself out of bed at five a.m. to take him up on it.

I settled into one of the loungers, enjoying the sight of the man's tanned, well-toned chest. "How do you have so much energy after last night?"

"To which part are you referring?"

"All of it." Ah, the rush of adrenaline as we flew over the forest's canopy in near darkness, followed by his enthusiastic and energetic lovemaking had me all turned around. "It was a good night."

"Good! That's all I get?" He stretched before strutting over and planting both hands on the arm of my lounger. "I must try harder." Setting my cup aside, he hauled me out of the chair and tossed me over one shoulder as if I weighed the same as a feather. His deep laugh rumbling, he pinned me there and strode inside.

I kicked and squirmed, pummelling his back with my fists as he carried me up the stairs, dissolving into giggles as he tossed me onto the bed.

"Ah, Marley, you have some fight in you," he said in a deep, growly voice. "I love it."

This big bear of a man dove into everything with exuberance, existing in perfect simplicity. That appealed in an inexplicable way, yet left me off-balance and questioning everything.

❂

That afternoon, we explored the downtown before he took me to the air terminal for my return flight to Vancouver.

"Now what do you have to say?" He narrowed his eyes, but his lips twitched, his eyes twinkling.

"Amazing." I kissed him, smiling inside as he hugged me tight. "I had a great time. Thank you."

"My pleasure. I'm on a plane tomorrow morning, but I'll be back for the weekend. Maybe we could find a new adventure near Vancouver."

"I'd like that."

After another long kiss, he handed me my overnight bag. "See you next weekend." He retreated and sat on a nearby bench, waving as I stepped onto the seaplane.

I sank into the seat and closed my eyes, exhaustion overtaking me after our whirlwind weekend of sightseeing and adventure. When I looked out the window again, the city had disappeared into the distance, and I wondered if I'd drifted to sleep during takeoff.

Christophe was fun, but I questioned the stamina level it would take to keep up with him.

CHAPTER 17

T he dreaded call came at the end of October, just as the first sets of twinkling, festive lights began to appear.

"Have you booked your flights yet?" my mother asked after we'd exchanged our usual greetings.

"I'm not travelling east this year, remember?"

She sighed. "I wish you'd reconsider. Martin and Michelle are bringing the kids."

Oh, joy. If there was anything my mother could have said to ensure I'd avoid the holidays in Toronto, that was it. My rambunctious eight-year-old nephews were hazards to life and limb.

"When did you see them last?" she asked.

"The time of the great turkey disaster," I said as evenly as I could manage, picturing the flaming inferno that had ended our last family Thanksgiving feast two years ago.

"Oh … right. At least it was only a small fire."

"Ah, Mama. You're so forgiving. The little monsters torched your dining room."

"It was Thanksgiving, Amara. They're family, so what could I do?"

Send my brother the repair bill? "I'm sure you'll all have fun. Just don't light any candles. Anyway, it's my turn to cover the holidays at work. I'll visit in the spring."

"Promise? I miss you."

"I miss you too, Mama."

"Oh. One more thing." Her voice level rose. "Dara sent us a video of the wedding and reception."

I scrubbed my palms over my black leggings. "That was sweet of her."

"So was that kiss between you and Jakob. Why didn't you tell me you spent time with him at the wedding? Are you still in touch?"

Dara had a video of that? "No, it was just a stupid wedding game, and the groom thought it would be cute. Jake and I don't talk."

"That's too bad," she said. "Anyway, I'll be sure to send your gifts before the end of November." Her tone dropped an octave as another voice sounded in the background. "That's your father, bellowing about something. Bye, darling."

It still broke my heart that my father seemed to look through her, much like Kyle had looked through me, but I doubted it would ever change. Nothing to do but hope she was happy enough while ensuring not to repeat my own mistakes.

Two hours later, Christophe arrived by seaplane.

"Marley, my gorgeous goddess." His passionate kiss prompted a long, low whistle from the pilot who was readying for his next flight. "He's jealous." Christophe winked and slung his bag over his shoulder. "Oh, you know what we should do this weekend?"

The man launched into his list of suggestions as we strolled toward the SeaBus terminal. "I heard that—"

A shriek split the air, a small boy who looked barely two bursting into one of those screams that developed into a full-blown tantrum, complete with stomping feet and a full body sprawl across the sidewalk. "Hungry, Mommy!"

"Shh, buddy." The woman jiggled a stroller as the occupant's tiny whimpers escalated into a full-on wail. She ducked her head, her face reddening at the blatant stares coming from all directions. "We'll be home soon. Please, get up, or we'll miss the SeaBus."

"Oh, man." Christophe rolled his eyes. "Keep it under control, lady."

I smacked his arm. "Have some compassion."

The young mother struggled to lift the screeching toddler to his feet while peering over the canopy at the baby, continually shooting anxious glances toward the boat that was less than five minutes from docking.

"Maybe she should keep them home."

I heaved a sigh and pulled free of his grasp, heading toward the unfolding chaos. "Hi, I'm Amara," I said as I approached. "I work at the hospital in North Van."

"Sorry, sorry, it's just that …"

"Don't apologize. Managing two little people is challenging. Can I help?"

She stared at me wide eyed, her head bobbing slightly. "It's been the worst day. We missed lunch and nap time."

"Can I?" I motioned to the stroller, waiting for her nod before I lifted the screaming baby, draping her blanket over my shoulder before cradling the tiny girl against my chest. "Shush, darling. It's okay." I rocked, adding a tiny bounce as I rubbed her back.

The woman, keeping her eye on me, retrieved a granola bar from her overflowing bag and crouched beside the boy, offering him a chunk as the baby's cries turned to hiccupping sobs. "We'll miss the boat, buddy. Can you get up?"

The boy frowned and folded his arms across his chest, but then reached for the offered snack.

"Up. Let's go." His mother wrangled him to his feet, brushing dust from his pants. "Ugh, meltdowns. They're the worst."

"They sure are."

"How many kids do you have?"

"None," I said, shrugging, "but I love them. One day soon, I hope." I motioned to the terminal. "We're headed your way."

The woman's shoulders sagged as she took charge of the stroller and her red-faced boy, tugging his hand to set him in motion. "You're an angel," she said as we walked toward the terminal as the loaded water taxi pulled away from the wharf. "Sorry, you missed your ride."

"We'll catch the next one." I smiled, still cuddling the sweet little baby.

"I'm Laney. I almost lost my mind back there." She glanced toward Christophe who'd fallen into step beside me.

"How old?" I peeked at the baby in my arms.

"Six weeks." A smile brightened her features. "Tyler the terror"—she motioned to her son—"turns two next week."

"You poor thing," Christophe muttered.

I glared at him before turning to Laney. "Ignore him. What does he know, anyway?"

"Enough." He nudged me with his elbow.

"I won't keep you, but thanks …?" Laney raised her brows.

"Amara." I transferred her child into her arms. "You have a lovely family." With a wave at Tyler, I caught Christophe's hand, and we continued our journey.

"You're too much," he said, squeezing my fingers, "but in a good way. I never would have considered stopping." The man grimaced. "The rugrat left a little something," he said, flicking my shoulder.

"Oh?" I scrunched my nose at the smear of milky drool, laughing softly as I fished a tissue from my bag. "Wipe it for me?"

"Eww, no. That's just … yuck. No offence, but you smell a little gross."

A snicker escaped. "Unsanitary conditions in third world countries and photographing guerrillas are routine, but baby drool is offensive?"

"It's about my perfect record." He lifted his chin, a rather proud grin appearing. "I've never wiped drool, sopped up baby puke, or changed a nasty diaper. Life. Is. Good."

"Sounds like you need some practice for the future."

"Hell no! Have you seen the state of the world? No way will I bring a child into a society that can barely handle the humans already in existence. There are too many orphans and neglected kiddies already."

My heart sank a little. "What if it happened, though?"

Christophe shrugged. "It never will. It's been taken care of with a quick snippety-snip. Medical marvel, that."

A heaviness settled over me. "What about adoption? Taking care of one of those orphaned or neglected kiddies?"

"Who me?" The man shook his head. "I'm a nomad, Marley, and I like it that way. Babies suck the life out of you, demanding all your energy. You and I, we could travel the world, living new adventures every single day. Doesn't that sound better than diapers, preschools and white picket fences?"

I forced a smile. "You forgot to add the sleepless nights."

"I did not, because those I enjoy, as long as they don't involve whining, puking two year olds."

We paused as the next vessel docked, then we boarded, selecting two seats by the window.

"What's going on in there?" The man tapped my forehead. "Do I want to know?"

I bit my lip, considering the combined upheaval and excitement of the past six weeks. "We never discuss the future."

"We are now." He took my hands in his. "I'm serious, Marley. Anytime you like, join me on a trip. Check out the world. Broaden those horizons."

"Maybe." Travelling with Christophe would take me to unimaginable heights, launching me into the ultimate adventure, but was it the one I wanted? Committing to this man meant veering away from my intended path, leaving my dreams further behind or reimagining my entire life. Would that even work? It was simply too soon to know.

Even at two a.m. the city lights sparkled, the occasional hollow wail of an emergency vehicle breaking the silence.

I swirled my glass before taking another mouthful of rich red wine. The tart, fruity tones didn't quite hide the tang of sour milk clinging to the sweater I'd slung over the back of the patio chair earlier. Christophe dragged me away before the soiled garment had reached my laundry. Even now, it didn't bother me. Babies were babies, and the patch of drool would disappear in the wash.

Christophe's adamant position about kids hadn't truly surprised me. The clues were all there, if I'd bothered to examine them. Maybe I hadn't wanted to, instead busily shaving off layers of stress and despair, enjoying the excitement of a new relationship.

Now, in the earliest hours, sleep evaded me, leaving me no place to hide from the problematic revelations of the day. I liked Christophe, and I enjoyed our time together. No, he didn't want a traditional life or family, but I understood his logic. I couldn't even argue against it.

The slight rustle, followed by a pair of warm arms slipping around me, made me look up. The man pressed his cheek to mine. "I wondered where you'd gone." He lifted the bottle sitting on the low table, peering at the label. "Serious wine for serious thoughts?"

I sank into his embrace, tears gathering in the corners of my eyes.

"Ah." He kissed my hair and perched on the wicker chair beside me. "I'd hoped for a longer reprieve," he muttered.

I twirled my glass around and around, studying the red liquid as it clung to the sides.

"The moment you held that newborn, the inevitable *tick-tock* of that damn clock started." He stilled my restless hands. "You want a baby?"

"Yeah, sorry." I wiped my eyes, then summoned the courage to look at him. "Why did you assume I didn't?"

Christophe slumped further back in the chair, picking at a nail. "It's not that I assumed. I didn't want to disappoint you by admitting I'd already taken permanent measures." He took my hand. "Seeing all those camps, all that death and destruction, all those orphaned and starving kids solidified the fact that this world is not a kind place. Even in the richest countries, there's too much suffering."

"I understand. Maybe I didn't want to look too hard, either. It's the breaking point, and selfish me, I wanted to have fun, but one day soon I want a child."

Christophe soft rumbling laugh made me smile. "Oh, Marley, you have a big beautiful heart. You always did. That's why I harboured an insane, crazy crush on you from afar, but you only had eyes for one guy. These weeks have been my dream come true. I'll never regret our time together."

I squinted. "You're from Halifax?"

He nodded. "They used to call me Topher."

"Wait." My eyes widened. Topher, the young guy who trailed after Dean and … *ohhhh, crap. Jake.* "Asshole. You could have mentioned *that* earlier."

"Not if I wanted to be taken seriously." He sighed. "Talk about impossible crushes, especially considering the competition. Anyway, I asked if you were involved, and you said no."

The look in his eyes, that dreamy expression ... I wasn't sure whether to be royally pissed or immensely flattered. *Oh, hell.* "I thought you were sweet, though you barely said a word." I sucked back the last of my wine and poured another glass. "You're a great guy, Christophe."

"Just not for you, right?"

"Sorry," I whispered, leaning in to him as he put his arm around me.

"Why aren't you with him?"

My sideways look was met with a deep sigh.

"It's a fair question, considering the big-ass ring and the love letter in his leather jacket."

"Oh, a liar and a snoop."

"You asked me to get you a sweatshirt yesterday, and I saw them. Surprised you could lift that piece of ice. The jacket I recognized right away. He's still in love with you, and I'm thinking you love him too."

"That ring didn't come from Jake."

"Oh, right. Your ex-husband."

I shrugged.

"I'd like to be your friend when this is over, but I'm gonna say it anyway. Jake's a great guy. He was always nice to me, even when others weren't."

"What—"

"Marley, just listen. No guy wants to be a placeholder."

"You're not."

"Yeah, I am. I deluded myself into thinking you could be mine, continuously forcing myself into that tiny space left by another man." Christophe angled toward me, my skin tingling as he cupped my face. "Just tell me, why did you two break it off?"

I stared at him for several seconds, then said, "Turns out he doesn't want another kid. That's my curse. To remain childless."

"Is it?" He cocked his head. "Depends on how you look at it. Jake has a kiddie, so you wouldn't be childless. Giving birth doesn't make you a mother, Marley. Being there, every day, makes you a mother."

I stared into his eyes, my heart pounding. "What?"

"You love him. You always have, so why are you here and not there?" Christophe captured my lips in the gentlest of kisses. "Get past the biological part of the equation, and you have everything." He stood and headed for the door. "I'll pack my things."

"Christophe?"

He halted, one hand resting on the door frame.

"I'll miss you."

His chin dipped down. "Goodbye, Marley. It's been fun."

Dara led me upstairs to the second floor of the home they'd purchased before their wedding, a big bright two storey in a quiet neighbourhood not far from downtown Halifax. She stopped at the second door on the left and motioned to the small but impeccable room, the dark wood of the queen bed contrasted by feminine, yet not fussy, linens. "The bathroom is through there." She pointed.

"Thanks, Dar," I said as I set my bag on the chair.

She hugged me. "I'm so happy you're here. Come down when you're ready."

"Okay." After she left, I peered out the window at the postage-stamp of a backyard already blanketed in snow. Ugh. November on the East Coast.

Two hours after the abrupt end of my whirlwind affair with Christophe, after buckets of inexplicable tears, I'd longed for my closest friends and I'd turned to the logical choice; Dara.

Beth, being wrapped up all things Greg, left me feeling abandoned as I rattled around my beloved condo. Anyway, what could she say except, "I told you so?" We'd worn our conversations about Jake and Christophe down to the core, heading twenty miles underground if we dug any deeper.

Two days later, my tickets were booked, and two weeks later, here I was, still fighting the dense fog clouding my thoughts. Of course, being here played double duty, though I wasn't sure I'd have the courage to approach Jake. He hadn't made even a single attempt to contact me, so his message was clear. In his view, we were over.

CHAPTER 18

Dara squeezed my hand as we entered Seaport Market. "I'm glad you're here. When was the last time you were in Halifax?"

"Over five years." A myriad of familiar scents assailed my nostrils; baking bread, French fries, and coffee, along with the pungency of raw shrimp, scallops, and fish from the seafood vendor. "It doesn't feel like much has changed."

My friend held up a hand. "Hold that thought." She beelined to the right, ducking into the hallway with the large Washroom sign above it.

"Again?" I muttered, but shrugged it off, treading my own path with crossed fingers, delighted to find the stand in its usual place, but not so delighted with the usual line up. "Two, please. Chocolate, with caramel," I said once I'd reached the front of the queue, watching as the young woman beside the cashier popped spindles into the mini-oven. The tantalizing scent of fresh cake made my mouth water as I paid and stepped to the side.

"What a surprise, finding you buying Chimney cake. Chocolate?"

I curled my damp palms into the cuffs of my over-sized sweatshirt. "With caramel." After a deep breath, I dared look up. "What are you doing here?"

"Shopping for dinner." Jake waggled a package wrapped in brown butcher paper. "Dara finally talked you into visiting."

"She's pretty convincing." Shuffling my feet, I tipped my chin down, holding my hand stiff at my side. It took everything in me not to stare, and even more effort not to brush away the errant wisp of hair curling across his forehead. "What are you making?"

"Surf and turf," he said. "I'm on my way to pick up shrimp and scallops."

"Yum. Haven't had that since …" *The last time you barbecued on my patio*. I bit my lip and peeked at him. My entire body ached as our eyes met and locked.

"How long are you here? Maybe we could—"

"There you are! Ready to head home?" The petite blonde rested one hand on Jake's then linked her arm with his. Her bright smile made me nauseous. "Hi. I'm Lianne."

A dropping feeling and sudden weakness in my knees made me sway. "Amara," I said, pasting on a smile. Fortunately, my order landed on the counter. "I should go. Dar will be wondering where I went." I scooped up the Chimney cakes and hurried back the way I came, weaving through the crowd of shoppers, relieved when I spotted my friend sitting on a wooden bench.

"Thought I lost you." Dara smirked as she accepted one of the cardboard trays. "Should have known you'd indulge your chocolate cravings." Her eyes narrowed. "You're pale."

"I'm good." I sat and crammed one end of the cake into my mouth, savouring the whipped cream filling.

"Hmm." She bit into her own cake, eyeing me as she chewed. Finally, she said. "Maybe your mood has something to do with Jake."

I lifted one shoulder and took another massive bite.

Dar snorted. "I saw you talking to him at the bakery, so drop the pretence. Seeing him bothered you."

"Uh-uh."

"Liar. Double liar, in fact. You and Jake, canoodling in Vancouver, but nary a word to me."

"The rat told you?"

"Are you referring to my husband?" Her arched brow accompanied a twitch of her lips. "My beautiful, kind, loving man pried the truth out of our wonderful, yet thoroughly depressed, friend. Jake slaved over his grant proposal for months, and we expected tears of joy when his funding was approved, but instead, he got moody. Talk about waving a red flag."

"Ah." What could I possibly say to that?

"Then I heard about you messing around with Christophe." Dara wagged a finger. "That guy? Really?"

"What? He's nice!"

"No, not nice! I bet he was all over you. He's not a good guy, and if I'd known he was moving in, I'd have warned you."

"I disagree, but you're Team Jake, so naturally you'd say that."

She folded her arms over her belly. "Damn right. Jake went ballistic when he found out."

"Hypocrite." I crumpled my napkin and dropped it into the empty wrapper. "Jake's soaking up all that's Lianne."

"Ahh. You're jealous!" Dara looked oddly pleased, but she only patted my knee. "Let's round up the stuff for dinner. Dean will be tracking me down soon."

"What, your beautiful, kind, loving man can't be without you for two hours?" I tossed our trash into one of the silver bins. "Come on. Let's do this."

⍺

After a sumptuous dinner of grilled steak and twice-baked potatoes, we set out on a tour of Dean and Dara's neighbourhood.

"Beautiful houses." I stopped and looked up at a two-storey red-brick home. "I'd die to own a house like that, but Vancouver prices are brutal."

"Halifax is affordable," Dean said. "In fact, there's a gorgeous two-storey for sale a block over that would make an excellent family home." He waggled his brows at me.

"Subtle. Real subtle." I muttered as ringing bike bells had me side-stepping into the park, frosty red, orange, and yellow leaves crunching under my runners.

Two girls raced by on purple bikes, clutching the handlebars with gloved fingers, laughing and chattering in those high-pitched teenager tones.

I paused, inhaling the crisp fall air, memories assailing me. With eyes closed, I savoured the frosty, almost-winter, earthy tang hanging on the wind. With it came a vision of that day I'd wandered the streets of a neighbourhood not far from here, secure in the knowledge I'd found the one, his arm looped around me as we made up stories about the families inside the houses.

A smile lifted my lips, but the image faded when I opened my eyes.

Dean and Dara were both staring at me.

"What?"

"It's time you moved home." Dara caught my hand. "We miss you."

"Awww." Grinning, I threw my arms around her. "Back at you, honey bunny, but you know it's impossible. I have my condo. I took that promotion."

"Some things are more important." Dara clung to me, sniffling. "There are no guarantees, so job be damned. Do what makes you happy."

I freed myself from her clutches. "Why do you think I'm unhappy? I have a life."

Dara swiped a hand across her eyes. "Having our friends close is important. Now more than ever."

Now this was getting weird. "What's wrong?"

"Nothing, I promise, but I have a huge favour to ask. Please listen before you say no." My friend fixed her red-rimmed, misty eyes on me. "We've invited Jake for brunch tomorrow."

I folded my arms over my chest. "We're not getting back together. So stop."

"No, it's not about that. It's something else, and we need to discuss it with both you and Jake. Please?"

My breath caught. "Dara? Are you both okay?"

"We're amazing." Her soft words and tearful smile loosened the lump in my throat, but only a touch. "It's nothing to be concerned about, but it's important. Can you deal with Jake for a couple of hours?"

"Does it mean that much to you?"

Even as Dara nodded, I knew I could never refuse her anything.

"Okay. Best behaviour. I promise."

Early the next morning, I escaped for a run along the boardwalk, intent on burning the nervous energy rampaging through me. When I returned just after nine, I tiptoed up the stairs, hurrying past Dean and Dara's room, blocking out the giggles and low voices by turning up my music.

As a couple, these two just worked, immersed in bliss while navigating their dual existence. I was happy for them, truly, but feared I'd never have the chance to be half of the deliriously joyful couple in perfect step. The man I'd hoped was that second half simply wasn't, but I ached for him anyway.

Once I'd showered and tugged on dark-washed jeans and a cable-knit sweater, I skipped down the stairs. "Smells wonderful. What can I help with?" I asked as I fixed my hair in a messy bun.

"Good morning, Ms. Bundle-of-Energy, out at the crack of dawn." Dean stirred the pan of homemade hash browns on top of the silver gas range. "Want to set the table?"

"You're disgustingly perky." Dara rubbed bleary eyes and sipped from her steaming cup. "Wish I felt like that."

"It was only ten kilometres." I stopped to massage her shoulders for a moment before accepting a tray of cutlery and glasses from Dean and carrying them to the breakfast nook. "You look done in."

"It's early." She smothered a yawn. "Not everyone can be lively at the crack of dawn."

I scrunched my nose and smirked at Dean, who seemed unfazed by his wife's uncharacteristic grouchiness. "Says the woman who dragged me to bootcamp at five in the morning. Married life making you lazy?"

"Something like that." Dara's face whitened and she bolted toward the stairs, leaving the tall stool wobbling in her wake. She charged up to the second level, her feet thumping against the laminate in the hallway, followed by a slamming door.

"Is she hungover? I don't remember her drinking much wine at dinner." While I filled an ornate pitcher with ice cubes and filtered water from the fridge, I tried to remember if she'd had anything at all. "The woman's acting mighty odd."

"Don't worry about Dar." Dean adjusted the heat under the pan, then looked my way, his eyes reflecting too much concern for my liking. "You ready for this?"

"For what, exactly?" I strived for an easy tone while struggling to keep the water from slopping over the side of the jug. "Seeing Jake?"

"Well, that, yeah." He bent to peek into the oven, then straightened. "I'm hoping you'll go easy on the guy, considering what happened with Alysa. Did Jake mention he lost the house?"

I claimed the stool beside the one Dara had vacated. "He said he sold it. The bank foreclosed?"

Dean leaned against the counter. "No, but the bank forced him to sell at a loss," he said softly.

"I'm surprised a planner like Jake didn't have life insurance."

"They had plenty, but suicide tends to complicate everything." The man sighed. "Losing the second income, taking months off work to be with Sari in the NICU, and the extra expenses bled Jake dry. I offered to help, but he refused. That's Jake, always with a huge smile on his face, while underneath he's drowning." Dean levelled a look at me, barely blinking.

"That hasn't changed," I said in a low voice. "He's lucky to have you and Dara."

A knock sounded on the front door, followed by a blast of cool air.

"Speaking of …" Dean jutted his chin toward the foyer.

"Morning!" Jake strode into the kitchen and set a terracotta pot containing a delicate purple orchid on the counter. "Where's our lovely hostess? I brought something to add to her collection."

Dean sneaked a look at me. "She'll be down soon. Coffee?" He reached for a mug and started pouring. "Silly question. When have you ever said no to a caffeine infusion?"

"Never?" Jake laughed and turned to me. "How are you?" He leaned in and kissed my cheek, leaving a waft of sexy man scent in his wake. "Did you get out for a run? It's beautiful by the water."

"I hit my mandatory ten. You?"

He shook his head. "No time today. I drove Sari to stay with Tía for a few hours."

Dara bounded down the stairs, and headed to Jake, throwing her arms around him and planting a smacking kiss on his cheek. "So happy you came," she said with a wink at me.

"It's ready, so everyone sit." Dean motioned toward the table as he loaded plates with toasted English muffins, topping them with crispy pancetta, poached eggs, and Hollandaise, adding a side of crispy hash browns.

"Let me help." As I served the plates, Dean put the finishing touches on the fruit plate, and Jake poured fresh-squeezed orange juice.

"Looks amazing," Jake said once we were all settled around the table. He raised his glass. "Cheers."

Everyone clinked glasses before tucking into brunch.

After a few bites, Dara's fork clunked onto the side of her plate. "This is so great." She sniffled and dabbed the corners of her eyes. "It feels like old times."

"No tears." Dean slid an arm around his wife's shoulders and kissed her.

"I-I can't help it."

"You're so emotional." I giggled. "What's up with you? You're all hormon—" My eyes widened as I clapped a hand over my mouth, feeling like an idiot. All the signs were there, but I'd been too busy stewing in my own drama and misery. "No! Are you?"

Dara nodded. "Sixteen weeks this coming Monday."

"Congratulations!" Springing from my chair, I hugged her and then Dean, but avoided looking at Jake.

"Sixteen? How am I the last to know?" Jake grinned. "That's amazing."

"You two are the first friends to share the good news." Dean held his wife's hand. "We wanted to keep it to ourselves for a while, but it's time."

"Is everything good?" Jake asked. "You're not expecting twins, are you? The baby's healthy?"

"The baby—singular—has a strong heartbeat, and I feel great, aside from a bit of fatigue and morning sickness." Dara exhaled a long breath. "We love both of you so much. I know this might be weird, but …"

I slid to the edge of my seat, holding my breath.

"You two aren't together. We get that. Even though Amara's been far away, and it hasn't been the easiest time for Jake, we still need ... want"—Dara glanced at Dean—"to ask a huge favour."

"I'll never forget what you did for me during university, or how Amara jumped in with Luci during those tumultuous teenage years." Dean cleared his throat. "Jake, watching you with your daughter now ... you're an incredible dad."

Dara looked at me, then at Jake. "Will you be our baby's legal guardians?"

"Who?" I pressed a hand to my chest, my face flushing. "Wait, you mean Jake, right?"

"Well, both of you." Dean set down his fork. "We want two strong role models for our child."

Silence dropped over us as I sneaked a look at Jake. "Is that the best idea? I mean ..." My gaze travelled to Jake, then to the hopeful faces of our friends.

My ex-boyfriend squinted at me—surely taking in my stunned expression—then sat back in his chair, arms folded across his chest. "Anything for you two. Even if Amara isn't on board, I'm a yes."

Anger flickered, but I bit back the scathing words about to erupt. "It wasn't a no, Jakob," I said in the levelest tone I could muster, "but it's not a commitment I take lightly. Nor should you."

"Is that what you think?" He rubbed the back of his neck.

"I'm sorry." A large tear tracked down Dara's cheek. "It's just in case, you know? Please don't fight."

Nausea tickled my belly. Making my friend cry was not on today's agenda. "No, I'm sorry."

"Don't be sorry, Dar," Jake said. "This is unexpected, so maybe we need a moment to absorb your news." He rose and pulled out my chair. "Amara?"

My knees wobbled, but I managed to follow.

The second we were outside, he closed the door, keeping his back to the glass. "Way to go, making her cry. Couldn't you have bottled your negativity for once?"

"Oh, shut it. 'Will you raise my kid if I die' differs from 'can you water my fern while I'm on vacation.' Anyway, what happened to you not wanting another kid?"

"It's hardly the same thing. If it's too much, then say no. I'd manage on my own."

"It's not too much, but I live in Vancouver. What if something did happen? How would that even work?"

"Wow, that nugget again?" He hunkered over the railing, and muttered, "This is their backup plan. Have faith that if it ever became a reality, we'd act like a couple of grownups and figure it out."

I stared at his back, then moved beside him, resting my forearms on the cold aluminum. "You're right. Probably never happen."

"We can hope not, but Dean's my best friend and I love Dara, so I have to do this."

"Yeah, they're amazing. You're right. They would be there for me if I asked anything." I peered at Jake. "It's a yes?"

"Definitely, a yes." He caught my fingers. "It's good to see you. How are you, really?"

"I started my new job."

"I heard you're dating again."

"I was, but that's over."

"Music to my ears," he muttered.

I stared over the tiny yard. "How are things with Lianne?"

Jake shrugged. "We've only gone out twice." He rubbed his thumb over the back of my hand. "It's nothing, really. When I heard about you and that guy, I figured … you know?"

Yeah, that I understood. Rawness and pain tumbled through me just thinking about Jake with another woman. "You made *our* special dinner for *her*."

He shook his head. "I'd never."

"Then who'd you make surf and turf for?" I yanked my hand away.

"Not for Lianne."

"Right. You're busted, dude."

"Am I?" His brows rose as he brushed his fingers against my cheek made me shiver. "Those two," he said with a nod toward the house, "made damn sure to mention you'd planned a visit, and they coerced me into coming for brunch so they could drop the baby bomb. Coincidence?"

I stared at him, floating in a disjointed limbo caused by those gorgeous, soulful eyes.

"Our meeting at the market was my sad attempt at making you jealous."

No-no-no. The steady drip-drop of my heart melting into a puddle sent me reeling, reaching out to steady myself and bracing my palm against his solid chest. As I opened my mouth, he placed a finger over my lips.

"I'm not done."

"Jake ..."

"Ah!" He added a second finger. "Please join me for dinner. Tonight. At my place."

I widened my eyes, my head shaking automatically.

"Before you drag out a ton of crazy excuses, Sari will chaperone. Anyway, our good friends are asking for full involvement with their child. That means birthday parties, anniversaries, and other family gatherings. Why not overcome our differences now?" He moved his warm fingers to cover mine; the ones glued to his pec.

Damn the man. How could I fight straightforward logic? Anyway, not much could happen with his baby daughter there. "Just me?"

He nodded. "I doubt those two voyeurs"—his gaze flicked toward the house—"will object."

Barely moving my head, I peeked at them. Every few seconds, either Dean or Dara stared through the window, then averted their attention to whatever they pretended to be doing. "Not very convincing, are they?"

His low laugh sent a shiver through me. "Not in the least, but they mean well. It's hard to get angry with them. They've been total rocks during the worst of times."

"Let's do this, then." I pulled free and shuffled toward the door with Jake close behind.

The moment we entered the house, Dara perked up, back to her smiling, even-tempered self. "All good?"

I hurried to her straight away, drawing her into an embrace. "I can't wait to meet this little person," I said, cupping a hand over the slight rounding of her belly.

"You'll do it?"

"Of course." I blinked hard. "I'm honoured."

Dean was next in line, wrapping his arms around me. "Thank you. It means everything that you agreed."

"Anything for you two," Jake said.

"Appreciate it, man." Dean hauled his friend in, his eyes taking on a suspicious sheen.

Dara pulled me toward the two men, creating a tight circle. "Group hug!"

Being squished in between my friends, especially the feeling of Jake's arm curling around my back, had me grinning. *This. This feeling was everything.* I missed us, in a breath-stealing, sharply acute way.

CHAPTER 19

As I waited on the front porch of Jake's tidy, though tiny, bungalow, I strained to hear any sound from within, stepping back and taking a cleansing breath as the lock turned.

"Come in." Jake, looking adorable in dress pants and a burgundy button-down shirt, motioned and moved to the side. "You found the place okay?"

I slipped into the foyer, cradling the wine I'd purchased along the way in the crook of my elbow. "Dara's Acura has GPS. Anyway, Halifax hasn't changed that much."

"Amazing. She barely lets Dean drive her car."

"It's a small thing after she asked me to take their kid."

"Us, you mean." Jake retrieved the bottle, allowing me to shrug out of my coat. "Don't forget about me."

Unlikely, when my heart raced at the very sight of that dimple.

His gaze swept over me as I hung my coat on one of the hooks by the door. "You look nice."

Nice? That's all the man could muster? His best friend had wolf-whistled and winked when I appeared wearing this sexy number. I'd even paid extra attention to my hair and makeup, adding the diamond earrings Jake had given me on our second Christmas. The man's bland reaction felt anti-climactic after the hours of angst.

"Make yourself comfortable." He led me into the living room, the oak hardwood floor creaking. Holding up the bottle of chilled Gewürztraminer, he said, "Thank you. It's from one of my favourite wineries."

"Your place is charming." The lines of the modernized living space were simple, but the patina of the floorboards gave it a classic feel. The furniture was sleek, yet looked comfortable. The bookshelf tucked along the far wall displayed a shelf of children's books plus a collection I recognized; the treasured first edition novels Jake's mother had left him. A white and navy-blue teepee sat in one corner, full of bright pillows, completing the eclectic look. Electronic sounds echoed down the hall. "Is Sari in her room?"

"Yeah." He glanced at his watch. "I encourage a few minutes of quiet play when I start dinner." The man beckoned and headed through an archway at the far end of the living room.

I arrived in the small, yet functional, kitchen as he popped the cork on the wine. I peered through the large window at the brightly lit patio, its furniture draped in blue covers. The only exception was the stainless steel barbecue, waves of heat emanating from the hood into the chill air. Beyond that was an ocean of darkness.

"The yard's huge. In the spring, I plan to put up a swing for Sari and build her a playhouse." He handed me a glass of wine.

"She'd love that, I bet." With a self-conscious smile, I shuffled into the living room, the row of photos on the mantel over the stone fireplace catching my eye. I chose a silver frame—a photo of Jake with Sari—turning my back on Alysa, captured in a sideways profile holding a sign proclaiming *Six Weeks!* "This is a beautiful photo of you and Sarina."

He moved behind me, standing a touch too close for my liking. "Sari barely sat still long enough for the poor photographer."

"She's not even two. It's not in her nature to be still." I returned the photo to its place, averting my burning eyes from Jake and Alysa—him in a sharp suit, his arm looped around her trim waist as they posed in front of a restaurant. An ache built as I noted the feminine touches in the room, perhaps unnoticeable to some, but bright beacons to me. The colourful throw pillows, the perfectly hung art, and the ornate candleholders on the mantel didn't speak much of Jake. Those were definitely chosen by the woman whose pictures dominated the space.

I jumped at the loud thump, turning as footsteps pattered down the hall toward us.

Sari stared at me wide-eyed, soon scuttling to her dad and pressing her cherubic cheek against his leg.

In one smooth motion, Jake lifted her. "Playing shy?" He tipped Sari's chin up with one finger and said, "It's Amara. Remember?" He signed smoothly as he spoke to his little girl. "Say hello."

Sari fluttered her fingers, then hid her face, peeking as I approached.

"Hi, Sari. What a pretty dress." I filled in the words with signs where I could. "Did you pick it?"

She nodded and rewarded me with a tiny smile before pointing at the easel set up in the corner of the living room, following with a hand motion.

"You want to colour?" Jake set her on her feet.

Sari tugged at me, pulling me toward the easel.

"I guess we're colouring," I said, allowing the little girl to lead me. I kneeled beside her, taking the marker she held out. "Why, thank you. I love blue."

Jake was observing, I could feel it, but he soon headed into the kitchen. He peeked around the corner and motioned to the platter in his hand. "I'll just put these on." Seconds later, the sliding door off the kitchen squealed and clicked, followed by a clank that sounded like the lid of the barbecue.

The little girl tapped my arm, grinning as she created a swath of purple across the paper, then chose a fuchsia marker, adding to the colour.

"It looks like a rainbow." I nodded and smiled while making a mental note to look up the sign for rainbow.

Soon the slider squealed and clicked again, and Jake appeared, raising his brows as he caught my eye. "Okay?" he mouthed.

I smiled and nodded, fluttering my fingers in a "we're fine" gesture, and he retreated into the kitchen.

Sari dropped her marker into the easel's tray and toddled to the nearby bookshelf. She stared at the selection then chose a glossy green board book, waving it at me before crawling into the teepee and beckoning.

"Oh, dinosaurs," I said as I sat cross-legged on one of the large pillows. "You like these guys, huh?"

She looked at me with bright eyes, motioning with her hands, then making a sweeping motion over the book with her fingers.

"Okay, second one, was read, right? What's this?" I copied her first motion.

Sari pointed at the dinosaur on the front cover and motioned again.

"Dinosaur?" I clapped my hands. "Clever girl. You're teaching me to sign. How do you know so much?"

"We take classes," Jake said from the small dining area adjacent to the living room. He winked at me as he arranged the cutlery. "You're a fast learner."

"Not fast enough. She wants me to read. What do I do?"

"Let her look at the pictures, then when she looks at you, point at the picture and sign it. If you don't know the ASL, you can spell out the words, or ask her what it is. That's Sari's favourite book, so she remembers most of it. Oh, and use lots of facial expressions."

Sari patted my knee, then jabbed at the book. She lifted both hands, tapping the tips of her fingers together.

"Oh … more?" As I copied the movement, a small laugh escaped. "Sorry. Pay attention, right?"

Sari made the "more" motion again and pointed to the first page.

"Happy dinosaur." We worked through page by page, me signing some, but I often asked Sari, amazed at how many signs I recognized from my online course.

Jake disappeared again, the now familiar squeak and click telling me he'd gone to check our dinner. "I have to fix that door," he said when he returned. He crouched in front of us, waving to catch his daughter's attention. "Hungry, Sari?" He tapped his lips.

Sarina nodded and patted his cheek.

"Do you want to eat?" he asked, repeating the signs.

His daughter nodded again, but this time she tapped her lips.

"It's important to encourage her to sign everything. Can't let up for a second." He ruffled the girl's hair. "Can you help her wash and put her in the highchair? The bathroom is down the hall."

"Let's wash those hands." I carried her to the bathroom and stood her on the low stool in front of the sink.

She rubbed her hands together and stretched on tiptoe toward the taps.

"Yes, wash," I said, mimicking her motion before turning on the water, watching as she picked up the small bar of soap, creating a lather. "Good job." Once she was done, I followed her into the dining room and buckled her into her seat, mimicking her again as she tapped her lips.

"Daddy," I said, flattening my right hand and tapping my forehead with my thumb, "is bringing dinner."

"Still learning online, huh?" Jake set a plate with tiny bits of steak, potato, and carrots in front of his daughter and headed toward the kitchen.

"I got in the habit. It only takes fifteen minutes a day."

Jake returned, balancing plates on one arm with the skill of a professional server, a bottle of wine grasped in his other hand. "I wish her grandmother would adopt that attitude."

I sat back as Jake placed the loaded plate in front of me. "What's this?" With narrowed eyes, I poked at the steak before turning the skewer of shrimp and scallops.

"Dinner?" One brow rose as he poured a portion of burgundy liquid into my glass. "It's not up to your discerning standards?"

All I could see through my tear-filled eyes was *her*, the other woman, sitting in this very chair, eating our special meal, surrounded by the deceased *her*. It took full effort to avoid the accusing stare of the woman clad in cream satin, holding a multi-hued bouquet of pink peonies.

"I was kidding." Jake turned my chair, crouching as he pressed his palm against my face. "Talk to me."

I swept away the salty drops. "Sorry, it's lovely."

"But?"

"Nothing. It's nothing."

"It's something." He stroked my damp cheek with his thumb. "Please, tell me."

"It's stupid," I mumbled, "but you made this for her last night. Here."

"Her? You mean Lianne, right?"

I nodded, sniffling.

"A woman has to be extra special for me to cook them dinner in my home, and only a complete rock star gets to meet my daughter. That's you, *Mare*."

"Only me?"

"This is everything I bought at the market yesterday. I'm a stupid fool, desperate to make up for acting like a complete idiot over you seeing Sari in Vancouver. It's a belated thank you for taking such good care of my daughter that day."

Now I felt like a stupid fool for making a big deal over a steak and a few shrimp. "Sorry. I didn't mean to be dramatic or seem ungrateful for all the hard work you put into this. It's not my place to comment on who visits your home."

Our gazes locked, Jake's fingers trailing along my jaw in a slow and tender arc. "I don't bring women here, ever."

Bang.

Instantly, Jake was on his feet, rescuing the hard plastic cup from Sari's grasp and placing it out of reach. "None of that," he said. "We don't bang cups on the table. How about eating your dinner?" Pushing the plate closer to his daughter, he scooped a bit of roasted potato into her mouth.

The next bite Sari helped herself, cramming a tiny piece of steak in with her fingers.

Jake picked up his cutlery, slicing into his steak, observing me as I worked the seafood and veggies free of the skewer. "I'm glad you came," he said. "I wasn't sure you would."

"Me either." I wrinkled my nose, then ducked my head, doing my best to avoid the photo of the happy couple on their wedding day. The woman who was now buried, but clearly not forgotten. Having this small insight into his world made my concerns valid. He'd removed his wedding ring, but he was far from ready to move on.

Once we'd finished our meal, Jake freed the girl from her chair and opened the toy box. "Okay, Starfish, be good while Daddy does dishes."

Sari crowed, clapping her hands before pulling out a yellow plastic truck. She pushed it toward the easel, stopping to load the markers into the back.

"Can I help?" I asked as Jake stacked our plates with the cutlery on top.

"I'm good." He hurried into the kitchen, leaving me stranded in this domestic hinterland.

I perched on the edge of the sofa, still avoiding the smiling dead-wife images and feminine touches imported from their home. The sharp, cutting edge of reality. Did I belong in Jake's life?

For Dara and Dean, I did. Anything for Dara, the friend who'd step in front of a bus for me. I counted myself fortunate to have such people in my life. Anyway, this was a formality. A peace offering from Jake to make our future interactions easier. One I needed to accept. I closed my eyes, repeating the mantra, over and over.

"Five-minute warning."

"What?" I stared wide-eyed at Jake.

He chuckled and kneeled in front of Sari, repeating his words, accompanied by signs. "Bedtime," he said. "Time to clean up."

"That's my cue to head home."

"I'll only be a few minutes." He handed his daughter another toy and pointed to the wooden box. "Maybe … Sari," he said, "can Mar help with pyjamas tonight?"

The little girl nodded, then toddled toward me, holding out her hands. And just like that, I was caught, contentment working up from my belly as she wound her arms around my neck.

"First door on the right. The starfish pj's in the top drawer are her favourites, naturally." Jake's light tone had me grinning as I carried Sari down the hall.

I admired the coral reef with the colourful sea creatures playing against soothing blue walls. Laying Sari on the change table, I inspected the neat stacks, one of diapers, one of pull-ups, keeping a hand on her belly. "Diaper? Pull-up?"

"Diaper for nighttime," Jake said as he opened the dresser's top drawer, "otherwise I end up changing sheets in the middle of the night."

"This is a great room. Ocean themed, what a shocker."

"That was Dara, the decorating miracle worker. This place is a bit of a fixer upper, but I set her loose, and she turned it into a home."

"Dara decorated the house?" I wrangled the squirming Sari into her pajamas.

"Yeah, aside from Sari's furniture, not much else made the cut," he said in a low voice. "It seemed best to leave all that behind."

Tucking Sari against my hip, I turned to Jake, "I'm sorry you lost your home."

Jake shrugged. "It was just a house. Probably would have sold it anyway." He held out his arms. "Let's brush those teeth." He carried his daughter into the bathroom across the hall. His low voice and Sari's giggles carried to me as I contemplated the new information.

Somehow, I refused to believe Dara had approved the multitude of pictures in the living room. Not based on how she'd reacted to him wearing his ring. Not that it mattered. He wasn't ready to move on.

I moved to the low bookcase in the corner, running my finger over the spines of the books, examining a few of the titles. One of the slim volumes caught my eye. "I can't believe you have *The Very Hungry Caterpillar*," I said as Jake returned with Sari. "It was one of my favourites."

"She loves it almost as much as she loves her dinosaurs." He hugged his daughter, then handed her to me. "Time to say goodnight."

"Sleep tight, little starfish." I embraced her and kissed her rosy cheek, practically melting inside.

One thing for sure, Jake was an amazing father. This glimpse into his life proved why Dean and Dara had chosen him for a major role in their child's life. I hoped I could do even half as well in fulfilling my role as honorary auntie.

Jake eased the door closed on a sleepy Sari, and we tiptoed to the living room.

"She's adorable. I love her." I followed him into the spotless kitchen.

"Thanks." Jake pulled a bakery box from the fridge. "Maybe I'm biased, but she's amazing."

I moved closer, peering inside as he selected dessert plates from the open shelf above the counter.

"Tiramisu? Is it from the amazing bakery on Water Street?" I searched the box for the curly old-style lettering etched into the simple black label. "Oh, I'm in heaven. I've missed that place."

Jake reached for two glasses and a large bottle of chocolate ale. "I couldn't find our usual brand, but this one's better."

"Wouldn't be hard." I laughed. Once a month, we'd scrounged coins from the change jar on our dresser to buy one portion of the decadent dessert and a single dark ale. No matter the weather, we'd sit on the same waterfront bench, sharing our treat straight from the box with cheap plastic forks.

"We were broke university students." He handed me a slice and portioned the ale into two glasses. "Let's sit in the living room."

Once there, I found my perch on the sofa and took a small sip of ale and a tiny bite, keeping my gaze focussed downward. The only sounds were the occasional rattles of silver forks against stoneware.

Jake set aside his empty plate. "Why so tense?"

"I'm not."

"You're never this quiet. Isn't it as good as you remember?"

"It was delicious."

He took my plate from my trembling fingers. "You're edgy, ready to bolt. Why? I'm not expecting anything to happen."

"Nothing could." I glanced at the photo on the end table. "Not here."

"Not here, why?" He tucked a finger under my chin. "What's got you spooked?"

Now I had nowhere to hide, and surely he read the conflicting emotions consuming me. "You took off the ring, but your house is a time-warp mirage of a happy little family. It's full of mixed signals, like you want something but have no idea what that is. Nothing's changed, Jake. You're nowhere ready, and I'm exactly what I never wanted to be. Your rebound girl."

"You're wrong." He caught me hand, but I yanked away.

"Don't. Just … no."

He rose and paced, back and forth, back and forth, occasionally glancing at me before finally halting with one hand resting on the mantel. "Sari never bonded with her mother," he said in a low voice. "There has to be some connection for her. I can't pretend Alysa never existed."

"Of course not, but this room is overwhelming, full of her, leaving no space for anyone else." My cheeks burned. "I should go." I crossed to the front door and slid on my ankle boots and coat. "Dinner was lovely. Thank you."

"Amara, wait."

"Goodbye, Jake." Snatching up my purse, I bolted through the door, refusing to look back.

❁

I crept into the foggy November morning, still bleary-eyed from a night of tossing and turning. I trotted down the stairs and began a slow jog toward the local park a block down. Once I was safely out of sight of the house, I performed my stretching routine.

After leaving Jake's house, I'd driven around town, stalling until I was sure Dean and Dara would be tucked into bed. Sorting out my feelings would take time, and discussing what I'd found last night, no matter how astute Dara was with advice, was not something I relished. Besides, I already knew what she'd say.

Tucking my earbuds in and cranking my playlist, I sank into an easy stride, feet pounding on the pavement. *What would Jake be doing? Did he sleep last night?* Scenarios raced through my brain, and I picked up the pace, pushing myself harder, faster, sweeping a trickle of perspiration from my brow.

What about Sarina? Did my presence confuse her? As I sped down the path, another inevitable thought invaded. *She's not even two, dummy. In two days, she'll forget you.* I veered sharply right, heading toward the waterfront, a flock of startled seabirds fluttering and squawking as they took flight.

Now, if only these brewing thoughts would disappear into the sky. Easier said than done when with each stride my brain circled round and round, my thoughts churning, as turbulent as the waves in the harbour. Inconvenient, this thing called love. Completely unsettling, all thanks to a series of serious misjudgements.

I levelled up to a full sprint, forcing my concentration to good form, measuring each breath as the chill air rasped down my throat, racing into the eerie glow created by a feeble sun fighting through fog.

Finally, I slowed, sucking for air as I halted and hunched with my hands braced against my thighs. Time to head back to the house and face my hosts. I'd live up to my commitment, deal with the entwining of my world with Jake's, but I could avoid him most of the time. Couldn't I?

I straightened and stretched my arms toward the greyish skies, cherishing the numb tingle of my skin in the misty breeze, then turned back.

In some ways, I missed this tiny city perched on the edge of the mighty Atlantic. At one time, I'd planned to live here forever. Yet I also loved the West Coast with its numerous parks, mild weather, and breathtaking vistas.

Maybe it was just the man fuelling my yearning for my former home province. *Yeah. No denying that sad truth.*

The last part of my run, I slowed, delaying, yet resigned to reaching my destination. At the sight of the illuminated white wire reindeer on the lawn, my will faltered, and I stopped, staring long and hard at the massive white door tucked under the brick archway. My friends were living their dreams while I navigated my nightmares.

After several long breaths, I trudged up the steps and into the house, slipping off my shoes and setting them on the rack. I tugged my earbuds free and tucked them into my pocket. "Dara? Dean?"

Huh. Maybe the lovebirds were still upstairs. I tiptoed down the hall into the kitchen, heading straight for the glasses. "Ah!" I clutched my chest as a figure rose from the living room sofa. "Holy crap. I just lost a life."

Jake bowed his head. "Sorry, didn't mean to scare you."

"Why are you here? Where are Dean and Dar?"

"They took Sari for breakfast."

"Oh." I poured a large glass of water, leaning against the counter as I gulped down half of the glass. "You're not hungry?"

"Not particularly." He moved toward me, blinking his red-rimmed eyes. "We need to talk."

CHAPTER 20

The remaining water danced against the side of the glass clenched between my fingers.

"I thought about what you said." Jake gripped the edge of the island. "How uncomfortable you seemed. It shouldn't be that way."

"I overstepped. It's none of my business."

"You deserve an explanation." Now he stood in front of me, inches away, me twitching as he pried my drink free and set it on the counter behind me. "My daughter will never know her mother. It took weeks for the medication to kick in and months for Alysa to come home. Our marriage was long over by then, but given her mental health, my options were limited; end our marriage or hold it together for Sari's sake."

"I'm sorry." Without thinking, I reached out and stroked the roughness of his stubbly jawline.

"The bond between them was tenuous at best, and then Alysa was gone." He closed his eyes, pressing his cheek against my palm. "Sometimes, it's overwhelming. A weight dragging me under."

Shards of pain sliced through me. I searched for some simple words to comfort him, but everything seemed forced. Hollow. "Tell me."

"Everyone says it's not my fault, but maybe they say it to keep me from imploding."

"Depression is a tricky illness. You know it"—I placed my other hand over his chest—"in here."

He slid his arms around me, resting his head on my shoulder. "I want to give you everything, but I'm scared," he whispered. "I'm stupid, lying to you. I wanted something to happen, even if I have no right to expect anything. Being with you makes everything better. It's not over between us."

"It's okay." Holding him in my arms after these long weeks, I knew to my core that he was right. We weren't over. Fighting my feelings was a futile exercise. A lost cause. I slid my hand down to his, tugging him toward the stairs, feeling only a slight twinge of guilt.

Without protest, Jake followed me to the guest room. I pushed the door shut with my foot, still unsure if this was the right thing, but I hated to see his pain. I could even understand it a little. How many nights had I felt hopeless and alone? Yet my big tragedy was divorce, which was nothing when compared to death.

"Mar," he said, his voice low and almost breathless.

I peeled my top over my head and tugged my hair free of its ponytail. Not breaking our eye contact for a second, I slid my hands under his sweater, caressing his smooth skin.

He exhaled heavily, tipping back his head as his eyes sank shut.

Moving closer, I lifted his sweater, bringing it over his head and tossing it aside. I shivered as he caught me around the waist, pressing his face against my neck.

"Mmmm, sweet and salty. I miss your taste. Your smell." His kiss sent me spinning as I clung to his broad shoulders.

Even if this turned out to be my biggest mistake, it was worth it. Right now, all that mattered was him and me. Us.

In a calm sea, I paddled toward fish in varying shades of yellow and blue, the occasional flutter of my swim fins jetting me over rocks and coral. The tropical sun beat on my back, the water caressing my skin as I hovered, inspecting the starfish splayed across a rock only inches away. A clump of seaweed drifted against my shoulder and wrapped around me, tightening into a vice as I brushed at it, but it refused to loosen. I swatted and pried as the clump tightened, creating ripples as it shook me.

"Wake up." A disjointed voice echoed, surrounding me.

The tropics dissolved and I opened my eyes, greeted by antique-white walls in a dim bedroom.

"You were mumbling." He cuddled closer, his bare chest pressed against my back as he curled his arm over my waist.

I angled my head. "What time is it?"

"Almost one."

"In the afternoon?" I giggled, but then reality crept in. "Oh, crap. We fell asleep." Rolling, I stared at an adorably mussed Jake, his hair sticking out at all angles.

Something thumped, the sound reverberating throughout the house, followed by the whir of Dara's stand mixer.

"She's making cookies," Jake whispered. "I'm starving."

"Cookies? We had sex in their guest room, and you're worried about what she's baking?" I clapped a hand over Jake's mouth as he laughed aloud. "Shh. What do we do?"

"Shower and dress?"

"If we go down there, they'll know."

Jake widened his eyes. "Oh, the horror!" He swept his fingers over the sensitive spot on my belly.

I shrieked and curled into a ball, breaking into full-blown laughter as he launched into tickle mode. "Stop." Gasping for air, I lunged at him, but Jake caught my wrists in one hand, continuing his assault with the other. "Oh, stop. They'll hear us."

"Like they missed that high-pitched squeal?" After planting a kiss on my lips, he rolled from the bed, gracing me with a view of his firm ass. "Care to join me?" He glanced over his shoulder when he reached the doorway, wiggling his brows.

"Incorrigible." I threw back the covers. "Warm it up."

Straightening the tangled mess of sheets brought order to the room, but it did nothing for my tangled nerves.

Jake combed his fingers through his damp hair. "Ready?"

"You go." I plumped the pillows and tucked them under the duvet.

"Uh-uh." He hauled me into the hall, steering me forward. "We're in this together." Just before we reached the top of the stairs, he twirled me into his arms, rocking us in a slow dance. "That was amazing, *Mare,*" he whispered against my hair.

"Buttering me up?" I wrinkled my nose, but still, the man put a smile on my face. One that endured the short trip to the main floor.

"Ah, there you are." Dara kept her head down as she placed spoonfuls of cookie dough onto the tray, but nobody could miss the twitch of her lips. When she finally looked up, her eyes sparkled. "Did you leave some hot water in the tank? Longest shower, ever." She snickered as she set the mixing bowl in the sink.

"Where's Sari?" Jake asked.

"In the den, napping." Dara slid the tray into the oven and set the timer.

Jake rubbed my back on his way to the rack of finished cookies. He snagged one and took a large bite. "Delicious."

Dean rounded the corner as Jake helped himself to a second cookie. "Hey, we need to move a few things out of the extra bedroom. Someone"—he winked at his wife—"is anxious about decorating the nursery."

"Yeah. Let's do it." Jake shoved in the last of the second cookie and followed Dean upstairs.

"I'm craving a cup of tea." Dara set the kettle on the gas range, then circled the island and sat, patting the seat beside her. "They'll be a few minutes."

"What are you planning for the nursery?"

"Oh, I don't know." She swivelled the stool toward me. "I asked Dean to keep Jake busy for a few minutes."

"Ah. Divide and conquer?"

"It isn't like that." Dara drummed her fingers on the counter. "Things seem better with Jake. The man can't stop grinning, where this morning he looked like he'd been mowed down by a train."

"Trust me, I noticed. Right now, he needs my friendship, and I'm giving him that."

"Nothing wrong with a casual romp, but seriously? This is Jake, so I doubt friendly applies." Her brows rose. "If that's what you call it, you're misreading his intentions."

"I assure you, I'm not misreading anything. The man's not exactly subtle about his needs."

"Now you're looking all panicky and backing away."

"Not at all. I gave him exactly what he needed. He was sad, lonely, and overwhelmed. Now he's not. Tell me, how is that a bad thing?"

"So that's it? I mean …" She massaged her temples. "What about the wedding? Or … or"—she jabbed a finger at me—"or those visits to Vancouver?"

"Yeah, those really built our relationship, him with that damn ring and segregated life. Even last night was just about getting laid. He's a mess, so just let it be what it is. That's the sum total of us these days, lots of amazing no-strings-attached sex and hours of cuddling, but it ends the moment one of us gets on a plane. It's impossible for it to be more."

"Do you even hear yourself? The man is crazy in love with you. Sex seems to be what you're willing to give him, but you're holding back the part he wants. Come home. We need you. Jake needs you."

"Really, Dar? I love you, but understand, I went through a shitty divorce because I didn't insist on having my needs met from day one. Jake's unable to compromise, so why would I move across the country?"

"He's letting you in. All the way in. What else could you want from him?"

"No, he's making nice. Some of that's for your benefit, I might add." The kettle whistled, and I sprang to my feet, circling around the island to turn off the burner. "Let me make that tea."

"You didn't answer the question."

I held a jar in each hand, waggling them back and forth. "Chai? Or herbal?"

"Herbal." The oven timer beeped. "Can you take out the cookies?"

"Of—"

"And-promise-to-spend-more-time-with-Jake?"

"… course." Glaring at the woman who'd managed to rush her question in between my words, I yanked open the oven and slid out the tray of golden-brown cookies. "Sneaky."

Now she was gloating, her cheeky grin making me roll my eyes as I fiddled about, adding tea leaves to the shiny filter and popping it into the teapot.

"Where's the honey?" I inspected the neat rows of baking supplies in the pantry cupboard. "Geez, are these cans sorted alphabetically?"

"Did you expect less from me?"

"Certifiable, you are. Honey?"

"On the counter in the little black and yellow pot. Glad you're so agreeable about Jake."

"Spoons?"

My friend pointed at a drawer beside the oven and then cupped her palms against her belly. "For my unborn child, Auntie Amara?" She circled over the slight roundness, keeping her wide eyes turned my way. "Auntie Mar and Uncle Jake. Such a nice ring to that."

With a sigh, I dribbled a teaspoon of honey into each cup and set Dara's blue mug in front of her. "Yes, I will spend more time with Jake. Satisfied?"

"Thank you." Her voice dropped to a whisper as footsteps and laughter heralded the return of the men. "He's not as big of a mess as you seem to think. His feelings for you, that's what sent him spinning." She peered at me over the rim of her mug as the guys arrived, mouthing, "Be nice."

I squinted at her. *What exactly did she think I'd been doing for the past three days?*

"All done with the furniture, thanks to Jake." Dean planted himself on the stool, eyeing me with an inscrutable expression.

"I'm taking Sari to the play gym after her nap." Jake looked directly at me. "Anyone interested in coming?"

Dara widened her eyes, and she stared at me without blinking, giving her head the slightest bob.

"Sure," I said. "Sounds like fun."

Dara stretched and yawned. "I need a nap. Growing a tiny human is exhausting." She rose, cradling her tea as she shuffled toward the stairs. "Enjoy."

"Oh, I'd better prep those walls for the first coat of paint," Dean said. "You two have fun." He leaped to his feet and hurried after his wife. "Let me carry that upstairs for you."

"Well, I guess we're on our own," Jake said. "Better get Sari up, or she'll be awake half the night."

"Let me know when you want to leave." I sat to drink my tea, pondering this swift turn of events. When I'd woken up this morning, the plan was to hang out with Dara and tame my silly thoughts about Jake, but our friends worked their unsubtle agenda, pushing to reunite us.

Dara was getting her payback for my avoidance of her question, but our conversation did the opposite of what she'd intended. It reminded me there were still serious challenges in our relationship.

❧

An hour later, after dropping Jake's SUV at his place, we tucked Sari into her stroller and boarded the ferry for our journey across the harbour.

"You'd think there'd be something closer," I said as we joined the queue to disembark on the Dartmouth side.

"Well, there is, but Sari loves riding the big boat. It's an adventure for her. Anyway, this place is huge, and sometimes we run into Sari's friend from daycare." He adjusted the cover of the stroller, peeking in at his daughter. "As her mom is deaf, Julia's learning sign language. It's nice that Sari has someone close to her age who also signs, and Julia's mom, Steph, is amazing."

I nodded. "I never considered the challenges in arranging playdates. How will it work when Sari's old enough for school? Like, where will she go?"

"I don't know. We'll make that decision later."

"Jake Cavallaro, fully domesticated. Never thought I'd see the day." I caught his hand. "'Tis a good thing."

"Uh-huh. Get used to it." He entwined our fingers, still keeping perfect control of the carriage. "I'm glad you decided to keep us company."

"It sounded like fun." I pointed at a bright green hut near the water. "What's that place?"

"The touch tank, a land-based tidal pool. Sari loves it, but it doesn't open until summer."

"Already training her to follow in Daddy's footsteps as a marine biologist?"

"You expected less?" He peeked at his daughter, who pointed at the shack and kicked her feet. "The indoor playground is just down the block."

At the play centre, Jake unbuckled the little girl and set her loose. He kissed me then followed his daughter.

I pushed the stroller to the side, smiling at the young woman who sat on the bench rocking a baby against her chest.

"Your little girl is beautiful," the woman said.

"She's ... thank you." Explaining our complicated situation to a stranger seemed silly. "He's sweet." I peered at the baby snuggled in her arms. "How old?"

"Three weeks. Matty's big sister is over there." She pointed at a girl, about four years old, bounding across the mats. "Your husband looks like he's having fun. Enjoy it. Too many dads can't be bothered."

"Yeah, he's pretty great with his daughter." I wandered toward Sari and Jake, watching him chase the little girl, sending her into a fit of giggles as he caught and threw her over his shoulder. After seeing him with his sister in her teenage years, and observing the many kayak lessons he'd given to the local kids during university, I wasn't surprised he was so natural with his child, or that he'd become an amazing father.

Jake beckoned to me. "Get in here, Mar."

Sari pointed at me then made some awkward shapes with her fingers.

"That's right, Starfish." Jake crouched in front of his daughter, making similar, smoother signs as he said, "M.A.R." He hugged his daughter, smiling at me. "She's learning your name."

I kneeled beside him, clapping my hands and smiling as I said, "Great job, Sari."

Those warm arms wrapping around my neck combined with the brief resting of her head on my shoulder had me fighting for control. All too soon, she wiggled free and jumped up and down, her fingers in motion. She toddled to the tunnels, turning and beckoning.

"Coming, Sari." I brushed at my misty eyes, hoping Jake hadn't noticed my near breakdown.

ɑ

It was near dinnertime when we returned to Jake's house, so I texted Dara to let her know they should eat without me. Her return message made me roll my eyes:

> *I figured you'd be late, if you made it at all, so no worries. Having fun??*

"Everything okay?" Jake asked as he fed Sari noodles.

"Oh, yeah, all fine. Typical Dara, gloating because I'm with you."

"Ah." He released his daughter from her highchair, cradling her as she whined and squirmed. "Someone's exhausted. Could you order a pizza or something while I put her to bed? My laptop is in the kitchen, and my wallet is in my jacket if you need my credit card. That place on Young is still my favourite."

"Right. Salvatore's." I started toward the kitchen, then stopped. After a moment, I performed a slow spin in the middle of the living room, searching high and low. A sob caught in my throat, and I circled again to be sure. Aside from two silver frames on the mantel, the others had disappeared, leaving only photos of Jake and Sari.

I cupped my hands over my mouth. *In ... one ... two ... three ...* My head spun as I struggled to control my breathing. *Out ... one ... two ... three ...* He'd done this without saying a word. Without making it into a power struggle. *Don't make a deal of this. Just go with it.*

In the kitchen, I opened Jake's computer and placed the order. I selected a bottle of Zinfandel from the rack, decanted it, and set out plates and napkins, finally relaxing in the peaceful living room while the muffled sounds of Sari's bedtime routine carried down the hall. Right now, he'd be brushing her teeth and playing silly games to get her into some cute pj's.

The man was making this difficult, wrangling me into submission with his adorable toddler along with his damn listening skills and sensitivity to my feelings, doing all those little things that twanged the heart strings.

The doorbell rang, and I leaped to my feet, hoping the sound wouldn't keep Sari from settling for the night. Then I caught myself. *Silly. She can't hear that.* Especially now, when her hearing aids would be docked in the charger, stowed safely on top of the white dresser in the corner of her room. Sarina never wore them to bed.

"Thank you." I tapped my credit card on the machine offered by the delivery guy, barely getting the pizza to the coffee table before Jake entered the living room.

"Oh, smells great. What did you get us?"

"Pizza alla Siciliana and Pizza Miguel. Large for both, so you'll have leftovers."

"Excellent." He poured two glasses of wine, handing one to me as he swirled the glass and took a long sniff followed by a small sip. "Dry, slightly fruity. Bet it's awesome with pizza."

"When did you become such an aficionado?"

"Have to keep up with my little wino." He winked. "Dean and I took a course at the specialty boutique downtown."

"I am impressed." *Damn. Damn! What was he doing to me?* I raised my glass. "Cheers."

Jake appraised me over the rim of his glass. "Did you drink an entire bottle already?"

"Can I not be in a good mood?"

"Sure." But still, he kept looking at me as we ate, but finally relaxed as we sped through the first decanter, soon starting on a second and then a third.

As we talked and laughed, memories of how it used to be assailed me. Our differences melted away, and all I could see was Jake. The old Jake, not the stressed-out single dad, even though reality would soon return with a resounding thump.

"I'm stuffed." I flopped back on the couch, patting my belly.

"Still the same amazing food." Jake combined the leftovers into one box and carried it off, soon returning with a fourth bottle of wine. He topped up my glass.

"Don't think I'm getting back to Dar's tonight, if you're as drunk as I am." I wobbled to my feet and stumbled down the hall with the glass in my hand, ducking through the second door on the left. "Oops. Missed the bathroom."

"There's one right there." Jake lifted the goblet from my fingers and steered me through another doorway into the small but tidy bathroom. "Take your time."

"So, so drunk." I bent over the sink and splashed water over my face, soaking my sweater in the process. Without a second thought, I hauled it over my head and draped it over the glass shower stall. Clad only in my lacy bra and jeans, I stepped into his bedroom. "Uh, got my top wet."

Jake looked up from his seat on the bed and groaned. "Fuck," he muttered, scrubbing his jaw. "You wearing stuff like that makes it hard to behave."

Swaying my hips, I stepped forward, tugging my ponytail free and shaking my head, sending my curls tumbling over my shoulders.

He tracked my path through half-closed eyes, his breath growing heavier as I stopped in front of him and ran my fingers through his silky hair. Reaching out, he spanned my waist with splayed hands and rubbed his stubbly cheek against my belly. *"Mare,"* he whispered, planting one, then another tender kiss on my bare flesh. "Gorgeous woman."

My gentle push against his chest sent him backward onto the bed, leaving me room to work on removing his pants, now eager to have this man naked between the crisp cool sheets with my legs wrapped around him. I quivered as he discarded my scarlet bra.

Jake hauled me onto the bed and flipped me, rising up just enough to peel off my jeans and toss them aside. "You're so, so"—his voice grew deeper, lower—"fucking beautiful." His eyes darkened as he ran a warm hand down my body, starting between my breasts, caressing my belly, working lower and lower, hovering over me.

I slid a hand up his chest, staring up at this man who stirred me to the point it was almost unbearable. "Jake?" I rose up to meet him, nipping his bottom lip and pulling him down with me, one hand curled around the back of his neck. Ahh. This man was a feast to my senses, all sweet salty kisses, earthy masculine heat, and smooth hot skin. I pressed my face against his hair, sucking for air. "I love you."

That fleeting second of stillness before he brushed his hand along my arm, entwining our fingers and squeezing ever-so-gently, was the only sign he'd heard.

ɑ

The vague remembrance of Jake kissing me and leaving the bed while I floated somewhere in between the states of consciousness brought on a soft, contented smile. In the span of time between then and now, the light had brightened, but still, I snuggled deeper into my cocoon, loathe to leave the warm bedding that smelled deliciously of him.

The occasional clatter of dishes alerted me that it must be time for breakfast—or maybe even past. I crawled from bed and headed for his dresser, snagging a pair of his sweatpants and a t-shirt.

Still rubbing sleep from my eyes, I padded into the main room, taking in the scene; Sari at the coffee table scribbling on a colouring book page with a fat blue crayon, and Jake in the kitchen, stirring the hash browns sizzling in the frying pan.

"You look rough."

"Gee, thanks, but I'll admit I'm slightly parched."

He tapped the wooden spoon on edge of the pan before setting it on the ceramic rest. "Come here, you."

I shuffled into his welcoming arms, content to cuddle against his chest, my eyes closing as I soaked up his soothing warmth.

Jake kissed my temple and tipped my chin with a fingertip. "Okay?"

"You let me sleep."

"There's nowhere we need to be." He rubbed my back. "It's been a gruelling weekend." His embrace tightened as he pressed his face into my hair. "You never said it before last night."

"Hmmm?"

"On some level I knew, but it's not the same as hearing it. Or being able to say it out loud." He tucked a finger under my chin. "Tell me again."

I stared at him. "What are you talking about?"

"What you said last night. Was that just in the moment? Those four bottles of wine speaking?"

Oh. Ohhhhh. Had I really never said those words out loud? I'd thought them plenty of times when we were together and even more often when we weren't. They'd run through my head non-stop while I'd agonized over seeing him during this trip, weaving themselves into my dreams.

"Mmmm." He sighed. "Gotcha."

"No, Jake …" The patter of feet was followed by little hands slapping at my thigh. I looked down as the little girl wrapped herself around her daddy's leg, then stretched on tiptoes, reaching for him.

"Ready for breakfast?" Jake released me and scooped her up. "Could you put her in her chair?"

"Come on, Sari." While I settled her at the table, Jake filled our plates and poured coffee.

"Marisol called," he said once we were seated. "She wants to see you, if you'd be okay for a visit this afternoon."

"You told her about us?"

"Well, the short version. The one where I've seen you a few times, leaving out the juicy bits."

"Ah. I see." I contemplated him for a moment. "I'd like to see her, but Dara and I have plans this afternoon, and I have an early flight in the morning."

"She'll be disappointed, but I'm sure she'll understand."

"About earlier …"

He shook his head. "Leave it, Mar. Please."

Round and round we go. Every time we took a step forward, something forced us back. That brief moment of optimism had flickered but was soon shattered by reality.

CHAPTER 21

I sank lower in the leather seat, staring at the city lights glittering through the curtain of rain pattering against the windshield. The wipers swept back and forth across the glass, a pattern building in my foggy brain. *Squeak. Thunk. Squeak. Thunk. Squeak.*

Jake's drumming on the steering wheel didn't help. Nor did the punctuation of heavy sighs coming from his direction.

My temples ached, my head bobbing in time. Last night's wine overindulgence and lack of sleep, added to this steady influx of mindless noise, created a soporific effect that even the three cups worth of caffeine coursing through my veins could barely overcome.

"Mar?" The drumming stopped for a blissful moment, Jake jabbing my shoulder with his finger. "Are you listening?"

"Hmmm?" I rolled my head to the left. "What?"

"I asked if you're spending Christmas in Toronto with your parents."

"No."

"Big plans, though, right?"

I hugged myself, picturing the upcoming holidays. I'd had plans, until Christophe broke up with me. "No."

"Are you cold?" He fiddled with the heating controls.

"No." I tugged the cuffs of Jake's sweatshirt over my fingertips.

"You're quite the conversationalist this morning. Are you still drunk?"

"No."

Jake rolled his eyes, but the corner of his mouth twitched as he placed one hand over mine. "How is it an amazing woman like you isn't booked up over the holidays?"

"I was," I said, bowing my head, "but now I'm not."

"Ah." His lip curled. "Guess that was a stupid question. Why, out of every guy in the world, did it have to be a douchebag like him?"

"It really bothers you."

"Fuck, yeah. Out of the thousands of guys in Vancouver, you had to pick Dean's cousin? And now you say, 'But Jake, we were broken up.'" He shuddered. "It makes me want to puke."

"Well, join the club. I'm sure you haven't been celibate, either. What about Lianne? You've had her company."

Jake grimaced. "I haven't *had* Lianne, but thanks for that sickening confirmation of what you've been doing in my absence."

My mouth dried, taking on that woolly after-the-party feeling. "Surely there's been someone."

His knuckles whitened as he focussed on the road. "Yeah, because supervising a research team, preparing data, and raising a deaf toddler leaves me loads of time to fuck around."

I fought the urge to apologize. We'd broken up, hadn't we? I'd never promised anything to this man, because he never promised anything to me. "I didn't set out to hurt you. You know that, right?"

"Maybe not, but it still bites." He flipped on the signal and turned into Dean and Dara's picturesque neighbourhood, not even glancing my way.

"We can still talk. You have my number. Anytime you need to talk, call me."

"Talk. Fuck, yeah, that's what we need. More stupid, meaningless chatter. That's not nearly enough for me, but good to know you're all about the talk."

Maybe it wasn't enough, but it was all we had, considering in a few hours I'd be winging my way to the opposite coast. I pried his right hand from the wheel, entwining our fingers and squeezing, but he shook me off.

Jake pulled into the driveway, the SUV gliding to a halt. He bowed his head, running his hands up and down the steering wheel. "I'm sorry for losing it. This can't be how we end this." He looked at me, his brows lowering, drawing tighter, his entire expression relaying an echo of my own pain. "I'm trying to make this right."

"I appreciate that, but I'm not convinced you're ready for a serious relationship. I can't uproot my life or put my needs on hold while you figure it out." Leaning across the console, I kissed him and brushed my fingers over his lips, lingering for a moment. "I love you, Jake. I always will, but this isn't our time. I'm sorry." I exited into the drizzle and opened the back door, waving to catch Sari's attention, signing as I said, "Bye, sweet girl. You be good for Daddy. I'll miss you."

Sari waved, giving me a toothy grin.

"I love you, both of you." I closed the door and, keeping my head down, hurried toward the house.

"No." Jake caught me by the elbow and stepped into my path. "You don't get to say that and walk away." His embrace surrounded me, and he hunched, burying his face in the crook of my neck. "Did you mean it?"

My breath hitched as I clung to him. "So much it hurts," I whispered.

"Come for the holidays. Stay with me and Sari."

Oh, if only it were that easy. "I'm not sure that's a good idea. It's painful to leave now. The holidays would only dig us deeper."

"So what? This is home, *Mare*."

"It's not fair to any of us. Not to you or to me, and it's especially unfair to Sari. I can't be popping in and out of her life."

"No, but if you spend more time with us, maybe you'll fall in love with this life again. Maybe you'll never want to leave. What would make you stay?"

"Oh, Jakob." I extracted myself, my eyes overflowing, tears mixing with droplets of steadily falling rain. "I've already told you. You just weren't listening." Spinning, I dashed up the steps.

"You still don't know, do you?"

I paused, chancing a look over my shoulder. "Know what?"

"Why you left? Why you run whenever things get serious? Ever consider that maybe you're the one who's not listening? Don't forget, I know you better than anyone. But yeah, run away, because that's what you do. Just figure out your shit before you spin another poor guy through the Amara wringer." A second later, the car door slammed and tires crunched over the loose gravel and pavement as he backed out of the driveway.

Once inside the house, I leaned with my back against the door, smothering the sobs.

The sound of footsteps coming down the staircase had me drying my eyes, and I swung around, turning my back to the hall as I removed my shoes.

"Out all night, huh? Someone had some fun." Dara's voice was cheery, my friend oblivious to the tornado of emotions raging through me. She peeked through the glass insert at the side of the door. "Jake left? You should have invited him in."

"Please leave it alone." I said in a low voice, avoiding her curious looks as I headed down the hall.

"What's going on?" She trailed after me. "Did you two fight? You can't leave it like that, sweets."

I slumped onto the couch. "We had an amazing time. Sari is adorable. And tomorrow, I'm on a plane back to reality."

Her heavy sigh was accompanied by running water, followed by the swoosh of the gas burner. "Seems things already got real."

"This is a borrowed life. A fantasy. The real one is waiting for me on the other side of the country."

"You want to talk about it?"

"Not sure there's any point, but maybe later." As she sat beside me, I said, "How are you feeling?"

"Today hasn't been bad. The nausea is all but gone, though I pee constantly." She leaned back, the outline her growing bump noticeable under her loose blouse.

"Can I?" I motioned, and at her nod, I touched her belly. "Talk about unreal. Soon you'll be a mommy."

"I'm so excited, but also slightly terrified. Then I tell myself I have Dean and my friends to help me through this." She covered my hand. "Remember how we vowed to raise our babies together? Take them to the park and share those wonderful big family dinners we never had as kids?"

"How could I forget?" I drew in a long breath, my shaky laugh making Dara frown. "I'll visit all the time so I can be a good auntie."

"Oh, sweetie." My friend looped an arm around my waist. "It'll happen for you too. Just give him a chance. The man is crazy about you."

Yeah, the man was crazy … to think I'd bend on having my own child.

"Hey," she said, patting my knee, "my friend sent me a posting for a senior pharmacist at Dartmouth General. With your education and experience, you'd be a perfect fit." Fluttering lashes accompanied her wide grin. "Then you can be here for the birth and for … everything."

"I'll visit when you're due and help with the baby."

She sighed. "Boy, you are one tough sell. Let's go for lunch and choose some stuff for the nursery. That'll cheer you up."

"Absolutely. Boy or girl?"

She shrugged, but her lovely smile lifted my mood. "Do you have holiday plans? It would be amazing if you joined us. My parents are coming, and they'd love to see you. They missed talking to you at the wedding."

"Really? I mean, I'll have to see if I can arrange it. No promises." Being in the middle of Dara's happy family for the holidays would soothe some of my wounds, but I wasn't sure I could bear being near Jake. "Let me change, and we can head out."

"You could wear that cuddly sweatshirt." She hugged her arms to her chest. "Don't tell Dean, but Jake smells yummy, all the time."

I scrunched my nose, trying to block those subtle warm and masculine scents rising from soft cotton encasing my body. Feeling so close to him emotionally, but still so disconnected, was a leaden weight, dragging me into the abyss.

All the more reason to change. Maybe then I could forget that I already missed the man.

Even with the emotional upheaval over the past few days, Dara's joy as she showed Dean our afternoon's purchases made everything worthwhile. It highlighted just how much I'd missed while I'd been gone.

"Look what Auntie Amara bought!" She draped the baby wrap over one shoulder, stroking the soft cotton. "It's perfect. Baby wearing is so good for their development."

"That's amazing, Bunny. And I agree. I heard all about it when Sarina was born, remember?" Dean winked at me. "Jake got some ribbing from the guys over his cute baby wrap."

"Ha!" Dara laughed. "They were jealous, because he got loads of attention from the ladies, who, by the way, thought that wrap was adorable and more than a little sexy."

"Oh, did they now?" Dean curled an arm around his wife. "You were eyeing my best friend?"

"Not me, silly." She batted her lashes. "I only have eyes for one man."

"Sure, sure." Dean snickered. "All right, Bunny, put your feet up and I'll get your loot out of the way so we can eat dinner." He gathered up several bags and headed toward the stairs.

"I'll help." I scooped up the large bag of crib linens, hurrying after the man.

"Thanks," Dean said as I caught up to him. "Let's put this in the extra room for now." He flicked on the lights and started a neat stack of parcels on the bed. As I added my load, he said. "It means a lot to Dara that you actually came. She's missed you terribly."

"I've missed her. I didn't realize how much until this trip. I'll visit as often as I can." I pushed aside the blinds, peering out the window onto the brightly lit street. "Dean? Can I tell you something? Like something confidential?"

"Of course." He sat on the edge of the bed and looked up at me.

"What I say has to remain between us. Promise?" I levelled my gaze at him.

"Sounds serious."

I leaned back against the dresser, nodding. "I'm concerned about Jake."

Dean straightened, his full attention on me.

"What you said, about him being all smiles while drowning, it's right on the mark. He's in the middle of an existential crisis, sending out mixed signals."

"Yeah, I'm aware." Dean sighed. "Jake never came out and said it, but I suspected you two had reconnected. He hates being away from Sari, but those trips to Vancouver ... I swear they saved him."

I covered my face with both hands, shaking my head. "Please, please don't say that. I can't be his emotional crutch. Maybe our relationship is comfortable for him, like I'm an old pair of shoes, but it isn't healthy."

"No, no, you have it all wrong." He pinched his nose, scrunching his face. "What he's feeling is anything but comfort. Jake's on that ride, the one with the out-of-control plummet, one that you long for but at the same time, you dread its ending. He's been running blind and scared, second guessing every single decision he makes, because his daughter's life depends on it."

"I fear what we've been doing hasn't helped that situation."

"Well, it sure as hell didn't hurt. You know, I'd love to lock you two in a room and leave you there until you work out your shit, but we both know what you two would be doing. Not talking, that for damn sure."

"Ugh. Dean. Stop."

"You know, that's always been the thing. You two have this off-the-charts chemistry, but you just can't figure out how to get on the same page. There are these flashes of it, but it never quite gels."

"Yet you two are determined to keep pushing us together."

"Well, I'm all about the science. Facts. Before the wedding, Jake was sinking fast, barely getting through the days. Part of it was the process. The grief, the guilt, the turmoil of dealing with suicide, none of it's easy. I admit, sometimes I was terrified he'd collapse under the weight, but he's a fighter." He scrubbed at his hair. "That little push at the wedding tested your connection and *bam!*" He smacked a fist into his palm. "You two lit up like a pair of Roman candles, and I knew we needed you back."

"Did you now." This astute man might be talking some sort of sense, even if I didn't want to hear it. He'd been there through it all, and I hadn't, so maybe I should consider his words.

"You're his magical antidote." Dean nodded. "Keep loving him, keep supporting him, and he'll get there."

Just where did he mean?

The man chuckled. "Don't look so concerned. We're looking out for him until you come home."

α

Far from setting me at ease, the conversation with Dean only raised more questions, though I trusted my words had heightened his vigilance. The man seemed calm and collected, but I detected a note of concern underneath his smooth words.

Shortly before ten, noting Dara's smothered yawns and surreptitious eye rubbing, I stood and stretched. "I should finish packing. Early flight tomorrow."

Dara's eyes grew misty as she hugged me. "It went too fast. Promise you'll come for the holidays?"

"I'll do my best. Thank you for inviting me. I had fun." I kissed her cheek, then found myself engulfed in Dean's bear hug.

"Love you, sweetheart." He squeezed me tighter and whispered, "I've got him, Mar, but I expect you to haul your ass home soon. My beautiful Bunny needs her best friend, too."

I kissed his cheek, grateful yet again that this couple had welcomed me back into their lives. With a small wave, I retreated to the guest room, holding back my sniffles as I tucked my makeup bag into my suitcase.

At ten thirty, I checked in for my flight and scanned my text messages, but there was nothing from Jake. Not that I expected anything after his outburst today.

The more I thought about it, the more torn I became. Being here for Dara to share her excitement was enticing, but every interaction with Jake became more painful. What if I accepted and he backed away, opting out of the holiday gathering? How could I take away his support system? Halifax was his home, not mine, and he'd need his friends. Grief and holidays often combined into a depressing combination.

I pushed away the pillow that still smelled like him and closed my eyes, practicing my relaxing breaths until I drifted to the edge of sleep. Every now and then, little sounds invaded. The murmur of voices in the hall, the click of a bedroom door, the rush of warm air through the heating vents. Thoughts invaded too, but those I pushed away, restarting my meditative countdown and breathing.

The mattress quivered, and something brushed across my hair. "Mar," a deep voice whispered. "It's me."

I'm dreaming, hearing his voice everywhere. In … and out … ten … nine … eight …

Heavy clothing rustled and dropped to the carpet, and the bed jiggled, followed by warm arms encircling me. *"Mare,"* he whispered. "I'm sorry for going off on you."

"Jake?" I wiggled onto my back, staring at the dark figure beside me. "How did you get in here? What is it with you sneaking into bedrooms?"

His warm breath carried a waft of alcohol. "I have keys, just in case."

Of course, he did. "Are you drunk? Where's Sari?"

"With Marisol." He tucked his cheek against my neck. "I hate how that went down, me yelling, you running. I swear, we've always invented our own issues, engaging in stupid fights, and endless, meaningless arguments about nothing. Well, not nothing. I'm pissed that you slept with him."

"We'd broken up." I pressed my face against his shoulder.

"Yeah, I get that. I love you, and I forgive you."

"Forgive me?"

"Yeah, for being with *him.*"

I bolted upright. "Don't you dare waltz in here pretending to be some saint and acting like I need forgiveness. You have two choices. One"—I pointed my index finger—"get over yourself and accept I dated someone after you decided your needs were more important than mine, or two"—I added another finger—"walk out that door right now and never see me again. Ever."

"I didn't mean—"

"Oh, didn't you? Does it hurt your fragile male ego that someone might want to be with me? That he might find me more worthy than you do?"

"Fuck. Topher doesn't find you more worthy, he just wanted to piss me off. Don't you remember him, always hovering around, creeping on you and Dara? He couldn't wait to move in on you, even though he knew we'd been involved. Disgusting."

"Not only am I disgusting, but I'm a pawn to make you jealous?"

"No!" He cupped his hand over his face. "Stupid, stupid, stupid, to think I could explain, and that you'd understand why I'm struggling with it."

"You're misjudging Christophe and assuming he had an ulterior motive. Maybe he actually liked me. Maybe he's sweet and fun. Maybe you should pack up that oversized ego and get out!"

"You drunk-texted him before we broke up, so maybe you do need forgiveness, 'cause that's real faithful."

I cupped my hands over my face, cursing Luci. "She told you," I whispered. "When?"

Someone tapped on the bedroom door. "Is everything okay in there?" Dean asked.

I wiped my eyes and padded to the door, opening it a crack, but I kept my head down. "I'm fine." My voice trembled. "We're working things out."

"Yeah, that thing I said about the room? I didn't mean in my house, at two a.m., but careful what you wish for, right?"

My cheeks flamed. "Sorry, he'll go."

"Jake doesn't have to leave, but maybe stop shouting. Makes it more interesting when we have to speculate about what's happening in here." The man waved a hand before heading down the hall.

I closed the door, concentrating on keeping my voice low and level. "Fantastic. They heard everything." Dropping onto the bed cross-legged, I picked at the duvet, glad that tomorrow I could escape our friends' disappointment.

"Sorry, I shouldn't have said any of it." Jake perched on the edge of the mattress. "Maybe you're right and I'm wrong, and I'm just a victim of frustration and jealousy, but it's better that you know that I know, and... I love you, so maybe we can get past our stupid mistakes. Forgive each other and work through it."

Tugging his hand, I drew him onto the bed. "You're choosing option one?"

"Well, option two sucks. There's no way to make that work." His faint smile lightened my heart.

I crawled under the covers, hugging his hand over my heart. "Ah, Jakob, life would be dull without you. I get it now. I didn't set out to hurt you, but I did, and I'm sorry. I'm even sorrier for the drunk text. I was angry and hurt and disappointed that you didn't find me worthy of meeting Sari."

"Yeah, I didn't really rise to that occasion, did I? I'm sorry." He stretched out and wiggled closer, until he was spooned against my back. "I'm not rich," he whispered, "and our life would never be glamorous, but we could be happy. Please come home. I need you. *We* need you."

We. Jake, the single dad, responsible not only for his own happiness, but for that of his precious baby girl, here offering his version of what I craved. "I don't know if enough has changed."

"Will you consider it? Let me prove that I deserve you?"

"It's not that simple."

"Love can be simple if you let it." Jake shifted, drawing me closer. "I can't stop loving you. I just can't."

"Shh. Sleep. No talking. Just cuddling."

His arms felt secure and comforting, as did the kiss pressed to my temple.

Why wasn't what he offered enough? Being with Jake meant playing a role in his daughter's life, even if I wasn't clear on what that role might be. We could be a family, just not the one I'd always imagined.

CHAPTER 22

The early afternoon sun peeked through the greyness. I lifted my chin, sucking up the fresh breeze. A few feet later, I stopped to inspect the shiny inscription plaque on the tribute bench, one of many situated along the old Vancouver Seawall. *"Come sit with me awhile."*

"Thank you for the invitation," I said under my breath. "I accept." I'd sat here many times, staring over the foamy waves breaking the surface of the ocean, contemplating the possibilities for my future.

I tightened my scarf and zipped my coat to my chin, balancing my cup of coffee from the café in Dundarave. The past days started their usual running loop. Would yet another replay of his last words give me the answer to my dilemma?

Give me a sign. Anyone? Anyone at all?

Two days and counting since my return from Halifax, and still, I was begging for the elusive clarity that would decide my entire life. Not quite ready to talk it out, I'd managed to dodge the calls from both Beth and Dara. I suspected their advice would only add to my confusion.

Beth's message had been a gentle *"Call me when you're ready to talk."*

Dara's message had been filled with excitement. *"Have you booked flights? Please, please come. I need you here."* Of course, I wasn't naive enough to believe she hadn't coerced the low down on the rest of my conversation with Jake out of her husband.

Jake had maintained radio silence after leaving me early that morning with a kiss and a long text:

Walking away was my worst moment in a long time, but I get it. Trust me, I do. Maybe you're right. Maybe I have a ways to go before I can be what you need and give you what you want. Maybe there are things you need to sort out too. So I won't push, even though I'm certain you belong with us.

Thank you, my beautiful Mare. For being you. For being wonderful and amazing with Sari. For being exactly what I needed these past days. For tolerating my half-cut ramblings and allowing us what we needed most. Time. That means everything. You deserve everything.

I hear you. I love you. I'll be patient until you've sorted things out and you're ready to talk.

I blinked hard. Who said I'd ever sort anything out, especially myself?

With a sigh, I rose and ran my hand over the bronze plaque, sending silent thanks to whomever had inspired the bench. Sometimes the sentiments lifted my mood, even for the briefest span of time. Sometimes they just created the space and inspiration to dig deep, be introspective, and reconsider everything one thought to be true.

I wandered along, stopping now and again to admire the herons, stare at the endless waves, and then to contemplate another inscription, moving further to the right at the sound of feet slapping against pavement.

"Amara." The light touch and familiar voice made me look up. "Glad I caught up with you. I saw your car in the lot at Ambleside."

I eyed the man as he matched my stride and plucked out his earbuds, tucking them in his pocket. *Hmmmm, making yourself comfortable at my side, are you?*

"You look amazing. Ready for the holidays?" he asked.

"Mmmm, fine. You?"

My ex-husband was flourishing from the looks of his broad smile and tanned face. Perhaps he'd visited some tropical paradise. *With a new love, perhaps?*

Kyle ran fingers through his artfully messy hair. "So-so. Took a quick trip to Belize, did some Scuba diving, gathered my thoughts." His lips twitched, then settled into a flat, serious line. "Re-evaluated my life choices."

Must be something in the water. Or maybe it was rote for the approaching end to another year, an event that always seemed to encourage people to revisit their expectations and dreams. "Hope you have it all straightened out."

"Yes. But no. Soon, perhaps." He peered at me. "Still doing the long-distance thing with that ex-boyfriend?"

I lifted one shoulder. *Was I?*

"Ah. Trouble in paradise?"

Was he … grinning? Jerkity, jerk, jerk, jerk. Some things never changed. I wished I had some witty retort at the ready, one that would wipe away his annoying smirk, but the man stared at me, showing no sign of buggering off into the gloomy winter afternoon. "What?"

"You have …" Kyle gripped my arm.

I hunched as he ran his strong fingers through my hair, moving so close that the puff of his warm minty breath touched my cheek.

"Relax." He waved his hand into the breeze. "It's just fluff."

Weird. The man's actions were decidedly un-Kyle-like, including the way he held my shoulders with firm tenderness, rubbing his palms over them. Caressing me. Leaning closer and closer.

"Maybe some of my decisions were too hasty." His eyes widened a touch, his pupils dilating.

"You lost me." *Truly, what had this man been drinking?* Appearances might be deceiving, but his cheerfulness screamed *half cut!* Hmmm, actually he might be on to something. That sweet bottle of Riesling sitting on my island beckoned me from afar, but Kyle rambled on.

"… the divorce." He cleared his throat. "On that, we moved too fast. On the other thing … the family … we moved too slow."

A numbness crept over me, starting in my cheeks, moving down my body, making me shiver. Starting a family? Now was his ideal moment? Worse, he dug it in, the gritty particles stinging my open wound, the wave of everything I longed for threatening to sweep me away. Take a beat. *In … one … two … three …* "Who is she?"

"Huh?" Kyle tilted his head. "Oh. No, no, no." His grip tightened. "It's not about another woman. It's about you. What I gave up when you walked out that door. You're amazing, even if you don't realize it."

My breath caught. Frozen, I could only stare into those wide unblinking eyes. Me. He'd been thinking about me? "Kyle—"

"Now I'm sidelined, watching the woman I love falling for some pretty boy ex who lives on the other side of the country. No surprise, really, that he reclaimed you. Losing you to a guy like me must have burned his ass. Some things never change, and here you are without him. Again."

"Jake. His name is Jake."

"Where is he? Not here. That's obvious from the sad look on your face."

"But—"

"Uh-uh." He pressed a fingertip to my lips. "Just consider the possibility. Whatever you need, it's yours. Just come home. Let's try again."

I swallowed hard, my throat dry and scratchy, my eyes burning.

"I'm certain you belong with us." Jake's words, repeated over and over in my ravaged brain, sinking in deep.

"Such a fool, I let you go. Screwed it all up because of fear." He exhaled, long and slow. "There. I said it. The thought of forever, the wife, the family … it's terrifying. Completely and utterly terrifying."

"You were scared? You're never scared of anything."

"Yeah, well, it's easier to pretend, you know?" He shoved his hands into his pockets. "But who isn't frightened of something, sometime? It's a huge responsibility taking on a wife, and then adding on a baby … well shit, the relationships around me at the office were cratering left, right, and centre after babies came into the picture. That's terrifying. I didn't want it to be us, but you left anyway."

Terrifying. Yup. That made complete sense.

"Sorry. I'm messing this up but seeing him with you bothered me." His tone softened, and he brushed my cheek with a tenderness he hadn't shown in forever. "It'll be different, I promise. No more long hours at the office. No more hiding. I'll give you everything you ever dreamed. We can start that family. Counselling is our first stop, though."

Everything? Counselling? Kyle's lips were moving, the sound muffled, sending the earth spinning, the wind screaming, my head shaking, negating the words spilling from his lips.

"Stop! You can't promise those things. We can't go back."

"Wrong. We can do anything we want. Have everything we want." He shuffled closer, slipping an arm around me. "I still love you. I never stopped."

I blinked hard, sure I was dreaming. I dug my nails into my palms and scrunched my eyes closed. *Nope. Not working.* He was still here. And serious. Dead serious. "I can't. It wouldn't be fair to either of us." I flattened my palms against his chest, pressing and forcing him to create a space between us. *Gentle. Gentle.* This man had finally shown his truest, deepest feelings, even if the revelation came far too late. That level of vulnerability took immense courage. "Thank you, Kyle."

"Thanks, but fuck off, huh?" He tipped back his head, scrubbing at his hair. "I'm an idiot. You never loved me. It's all about him."

"Not true." *Ah, the pain.* Unexpected, but still a genuine, honest agony. We'd shared some wonderful times, this man and I, but our inability to navigate the difficult, hurtful times defined us. "I did love you, but it's over. Our ending has nothing to do with anyone but you and me and our mistakes. You'll find someone better. You're an amazing guy."

"Sure I am. That's why you ran."

"No, that's a me issue." As I swayed toward him, my mind cleared. "It's my fault as much as yours that we didn't make it. My own fears stepped in and broke us."

"Yeah, right. The typical break up line. The truth is, I'm too late. You've always loved him more, and"—he held up his hand—"I accepted that and took a gamble on us. One that never paid dividends, 'cause here we are."

"Yes, with you restoring my faith in love."

"That's what you got out of this?" He shook his head. "You, Amara, are one of a kind. It's really no, isn't it?"

I smiled sadly, nodding. "We can't be together. It's too late."

"Ah, if only we'd had this conversation months ago, maybe then we could have worked it out. You deserve the best. Don't let anyone tell you otherwise. Never settle."

"Back at you." I stretched to kiss him lightly, then stepped back. "You take care of yourself." With a final wave, I turned toward Ambleside, intent on reaching my car. As odd as that encounter had been, it felt like closure on my marriage. And maybe, just maybe, the universe had prodded me with a sign. *Terrifying*.

❧

Once I reached home, I hung my jacket and headed for the den. The job competition closed bright and early on Tuesday morning, and with tomorrow being a full day at work, this was my last chance to get the application completed.

After attaching my resume and cover letter and tapping Apply, I checked my email, snickering as I read the job postings that Dara had sent while I was out.

Well, why not? I set to work, methodically completing each one before opening my video chat and calling Dara.

"Do you really want me in Halifax that bad?" I asked the moment my friend appeared on screen.

"You got my emails."

"Yeah, all five of them. Are you alone?"

"Dean's in the garage, and I'm in our bedroom. Why?"

"I love him, but that man blabs. This is hush-hush. Got it? Jake can't know."

"Oooh, secrets. Just a second." She disappeared and a door clicked, then she dropped onto her bed, cross-legged. "What are we not telling Jake?"

"Or Dean," I said in my sternest voice, wagging a finger.

"Just tell me already."

"I applied for the job at Dartmouth General, plus the other five."

"Yessssss!" Dara bounced up from her seat, flitting in and out of the frame as she danced, pumping her arms and swinging her hips.

"Dara? Dar! Get back here."

"Sorry, sorry." She leaned close to the screen. "I'm just a little bit excited."

"Me too. Hey, how's baby?"

"Growing. Look." She stood and adjusted the screen, angling herself to give me a profile view. "Strong heartbeat, and I feel amazing."

The sight of her caressing her rounded belly brought on a flurry of emotions. I cupped my hand over my mouth, blinking hard. "You look beautiful," I said. "My mission is to be there in May to greet your little darling and be the best auntie ever."

"I'm holding you to that. I'll send you a picture after our ultrasound on Tuesday."

"I can't wait." I twirled a lock of hair around my finger. "Have you talked to Jake?"

"Ha. I can barely get rid of the man." She wrinkled her nose. "It's adorable, really. He's always checking in, asking how I'm feeling, bringing me treats from that bakery on Water. Yesterday, when I told him I was too tired to cook dinner, he brought pizza. Seriously, the guy's more attentive than my own husband."

"Dean's going to wonder about you two."

"Nah." Dara waved a hand. "Jake's madly in love with another woman, and Dean knows it. I suspect part of this attention is about wiggling details out of me about a certain somebody's holiday plans. One word about inviting you, and boy, relentless."

"Speaking of which—would you be upset if I didn't stay with you?"

"You better not be talking about no hotel, sweetie."

"That's not what I had in mind."

"My, my, full speed ahead." My friend tilted her head. "I still expect you here on Christmas Day, early. Not that it should be an issue, since I've already invited Jake and Marisol."

"Deal. Who says his offer is still open? Maybe I'll show up on your doorstep."

"There's only one way to find out. Sounds like you have another call to make. Bye, sweetie, talk soon."

"Bye, Dar."

What would he say? Our last interaction left things in limbo, and I had much atonement ahead. My dear friend's words gave me some comfort, though. If Jake still loved me after everything, I was a lucky woman.

☾

Ten days later, I lingered in my cozy den, the jacket of my sharpest power suit slung over the back of my chair. The second interview I'd just finished with the head pharmacist at Dartmouth General played in a loop, me revisiting and second guessing everything.

Had I seemed too cheerful? Too eager to abandon my seniority and high position and take a voluntary demotion to a mere worker bee in the hive?

I knew what both Beth and Dara would say. Quit overthinking this and embrace new opportunities. But I'd had no opportunity to tap the brakes, the days blurring as I did the work of searching my soul, followed by a lot of second guessing my decisions.

A text arrived from Dara:

Have you told him yet? I'm about to burst. It's December, so I hope you've booked your flights.

Done, and done. At least the flights, anyway. The Jake part, not so much. Telling him would make things so final.

I'll email you the information.

I signed into my airline account and pulled up my itinerary, adding her email address, then adding the CC to Jake. One small step accomplished.

Another text arrived just as I hit send:

Please, please, talk to him. It's getting seriously awkward. Anyway, are you just planning to appear on his doorstep?

That would be interesting, though I might get a door slammed in my face. Not that I'd blame him.

Settling in my chair again, I checked my messages from the office and then opened the schedule, making adjustments where needed and sending it out to my department.

A notification bar slid in from the right as my laptop connected to an incoming call. An unfamiliar number with a Nova Scotia prefix. I smoothed my hair and put a smile in my voice. "Amara Grant."

"Well, hello there, Amara Grant," Jake said in a low, level tone. "You sound perky this afternoon. I hope it has to do with your email."

"Jake. Sorry, I thought you were someone else. What is that noise?"

"The sonar. I'm on our research vessel, so I'm using my sat phone."

"Sorry if I bothered you at work."

"No bother," he said. "It's great you're coming out, but you're planning to stay with Dara, right?"

"Is that what you want?"

"You sent this to both of us, but you haven't called, so I—"

Another voice cut in, an indistinct, garbled mash up in the background.

"Hold on." Jakes voice faded and became muffled. "No ... this call is important, so can you give me a minute? Close the door? Thanks, Josh." He sighed. "My research assistant, asking a ton of questions. I love being the boss, but sometimes I hate being the boss."

"Tell me about it. Anyway, this can wait. Call me later."

"No. Tell me what you're thinking, otherwise I'll be fixated on this all afternoon."

"What if I wanted to stay with you? I'm not sure where we are, you know?"

"If you stay, we could figure that out."

"So it's okay?"

"Hell, yeah, it is." His voice grew lighter, almost bouncing over the airwaves. "Call you tonight?"

"I'll be here. Talk later."

"Bye, *Mare.*"

I reclined in my chair, tipping my head and tangling my fingers into my hair, the tension draining out of me as I stared at the ceiling. I'd been driving myself insane, worrying, all for nothing.

Another notification slid in at the top of my screen:

Still can't concentrate. So much I need to know.

I closed my eyes, picturing his inquiring look; his eyes dark and serious as he paced and mussed his hair.

With a click, I opened my message app on my laptop and replied:

Know that I love you.

Sitting back, I watched the dancing ellipses:

I love you more.

Then a second text arrived:

Damn, I must be walking around with the stupidest grin on my face. Josh just asked, "Is she coming for the holidays?"

I pressed my hands to my chest, as if that could keep everything I felt contained. Then my fingers were flying over the keyboard:

I had a second interview for a job in Dartmouth. That's who I thought was calling.

Staring at the screen, I held my breath, waiting as the ellipses danced, stopped, and then began again before disappearing. *No message?* Of course not. Me applying for jobs there made this too real.

Slapping my phone onto my desk, I stalked into the kitchen, clunking my mug onto the counter, immediately lifting it and inspecting the bottom for cracking. *Phew. No damage.* I planted my feet shoulder width apart, thrusting my shoulders back with my arms bent and raised. *Breathe in.* He's at work. *Breathe out.* He's busy. *In.* You're the panicky party. *Out.* Give the man a minute.

My eyes popped open as ringing echoed down the hallway, and I lurched forward, slip-sliding down the hall to my office. Almost stumbling over my chair, I snatched up my phone just as the ringing stopped. The Missed Call notification displayed Jake's number.

I poked at my screen, clutching the phone to my ear as it rang once, then twice, then …

"You're moving home?" he asked in a breathless voice. "Why didn't you tell me?"

"I was sorting out my life."

"You've figured things out?"

This is not how I wanted to have this conversation, yet … "Enough to know I can't overthink this. I love you, and I love Sari. That's all I need." A deep silence fell. "It's too much, right? Not what you want?"

"I do want that. It's just …" He cleared his throat. "You're too far away. I can't wait to see you."

"I miss you all so much."

"We've missed you," he said. "Just a second." Muffled voices followed. "Damn, sorry. Josh has a problem with the sonar readings."

"You'd better go."

"Tonight, okay? Love you, *Mare*."

"Yes, tonight." I hung up, about ready to dissolve into a gooey mess of happy tears.

⨎

Beth greeted me at her front door, arms wide open. "I'm glad you called," she said as she hugged me. "It's been forever."

"Greg here?"

"No, he beat a rapid retreat due to the threat of extended girl talk."

"Eww, girl talk! The poor guy must have been horrified." I followed her into the living room, grateful when she poured two glasses of Pinot Grigio and handed one to me. "Thanks. You read my mind."

Beth snickered. "Yeah, I'm a magician."

"Close enough." I gulped down half of my wine and sighed. "What has Greg been saying?"

"Not much. He's remarkably tight lipped, not wanting to get stuck in the middle." She shrugged. "I have no insight into the Jake situation, though Greg did say you visited Halifax. How am I the last to know?"

"Sorry about being a crap friend. That's me, avoiding all the mushy stuff between you and your man."

"It's okay, I get it. When you told me about Jake tripping over himself to be with you at the wedding, I had a jealous moment, considering how sucky my love life was at the time." Beth topped up my glass. "I'm sorry I've been preoccupied. I believe I'm in love."

"I'm happy for you. Have to say, I like the guy."

Beth giggled. "He's pretty great, except when he leaves toothpaste in the sink."

"We all have our thing. I leave little balled-up sock piles under the coffee table. Used to drive Kyle nuts." I sipped my wine. "Speaking of, I ran into Kyle on the path near Dundarave," I said. "He wants to get back together. Have a baby."

"Wha—what?" Beth's eyes widened. "You're not considering it."

"No, but I had an epiphany. What if I'm too quick to give up when things get tough? That made me reconsider Jake's offer. We've broken the communication barrier, and we're owning our feelings." I grinned. "I'm moving to Halifax. I accepted an incredible job offer at the hospital in Dartmouth, and I start at the beginning of February."

"Oh." Her eyes misted, but she hopped up and hugged me. "That's huge. Are you sure? I like Jake, but you'll be trying to blend a family and take on a toddler."

"I adore Sari."

My friend tilted her head. "Yeah, she's cute, but there are considerations, like the extra time and expense involved in raising a deaf child. And who will be taking care of Sarina when Daddy's out on that research boat chasing dolphins and analyzing pond scum? Are you ready for that?"

"Lots of spouses travel, leaving the other to take care of the kid, so how is this different? Sure, it'll be a challenge, but Jake and Sari are worth every moment."

"Ahh, you're finally listening to your heart instead of your head. I approve."

"This from the woman who cautioned me about the dangers of the single daddy widowers?"

"I was wrong. Jake's good for you. Embrace all those big, beautiful feelings, and let yourself be in love." She beamed. "Guess you won't be joining us for Christmas dinner."

"Nope, this third wheel is out. I'll be on a plane on the twenty-first." Wiggling my hips, I performed a happy chair-dance. "I'll be back after New Year's to finish packing up my condo and, hopefully, sign a lease with a renter. We'll go for dinner."

"Bring Jake with you. Greg would love to see him, and we can celebrate."

I wrinkled my nose. "Cross you fingers that I don't revert to old habits and screw up my last chance."

"Uh-uh." Beth wagged a finger. "Positive thoughts only."

My entire body bundled into knots, my heart racing at the thought of reuniting with Jake. In only a few days, I'd be stepping into a brighter future.

CHAPTER 23

Jake groaned, scrubbing a hand over his face as a steady *tap-tap-tap* echoed down the hall. He patted the side table, then held up his phone, squinting. "It's only four. Usually, she allows me until five."

"Is Sari making that noise?" I rubbed my eyes.

"When she needs something, she taps on the crib rail."

"Weird. Most kids scream or cry."

"Well, she does that on occasion, but she's clever. She figured out that tantrums only work on Nana Stella. At home, she finds better ways to get attention."

"Interesting." I ruffled his hair. "You have to work today, so go back to sleep. I'll check on her." I slipped from the bed, pulling one of Jake's oversized sweatshirts over my head and stuffing my feet into my slippers.

"Mmm. Could get used to this." He puffed up his pillow and closed his eyes as the *tap tap tap* started up again. "Call if you need me."

When I tiptoed into her room, the little girl pressed her face to the gap between the spindles, her eyes wide and bright.

Sari pulled herself up and fluttered her hand, then tapped her mouth with three fingers. She reached for me, arms open and raised.

"Ah," I said, recognizing the sign the darling duo of Jake and Sari had taught me last night at dinner. Curling my fingers into a *c*, I tipped them toward my face. "Drink?" I repeated her mouth tap. "Water, right?"

Sari bounced and nodded, curling an arm around my neck as I lifted her from her crib. As we headed toward the kitchen, she pointed toward Jake's room, following with an open-handed thumb tap to her forehead.

"Daddy's sleeping." With her balanced on my hip, I swayed, slow dancing into the kitchen, to the cupboard for her cup, and then toward the fridge.

Sari patted her chest and grabbed the cup.

"Oh, you want to do it?" I steadied her hand, helping her press the filter switch on the fridge. "You have that all figured out."

This little girl continually surprised me, but as I added the months in my head, I realized she wasn't a baby anymore. She was fast approaching her second birthday, an age where children wanted to do things for themselves. I kissed her mop of curls as she slurped her drink. "You are too sweet. I wish ... I wish ..." *That I'd known you sooner.* Jake and I had reconnected over eight months ago, yet I barely knew his daughter.

She rested her head on my shoulder, the cup tilting and sending a dribble of water down the front of my sweatshirt.

"All done? Let's get you back to bed." I tiptoed down the hall, stopping to change her diaper before lifting her over the side of her crib.

Sari frowned and shook her head, pushing at the rails with her feet, her back arching. She pointed to the door, then tapped her forehead.

"Daddy's sleeping." My second attempt at putting her into bed had her squirming and shaking her head, followed by her signing for her daddy. "Does Daddy allow that?" *Rules, rules. What were the rules?* I had no clue.

She clung to me and signed again, pointing at the door.

"All right." I grabbed her blanket and stuffed bunny from her bed. "Daddy it is."

Jake had his arm curled over his head when we entered the bedroom, not moving as I set the girl down.

Sari scuttled beside Jake and lay down, hugging her bunny as she closed her eyes and crammed her thumb into her mouth. She didn't even twitch when I covered her with the blanket.

Her daddy cracked one eye open, running a hand over her dark curls and kissing her forehead before he snuggled down in the covers, his steady breathing relaying he was unconcerned and drifting into sleep.

My job done, I slipped under the covers, watching the slow rise and fall of Sari's chest, and the way her thumb slid from her mouth as she shifted and sighed.

This scenario was something I'd never experienced, and I'd given up hope that I ever would. Maybe I could do this and be the step mommy, setting aside the desire to cuddle my own newborn baby. Sari was easy to love. Her daddy was not so easy to handle at times, but I certainly loved him. Maybe this was my family, right here, perfectly made, just for me.

𝒶

A light smack to my face woke me, and I reached up, coming into contact with tiny baby-soft fingers resting against my cheek.

The bathroom fan whirred, a steamy mist escaping as Jake appeared in the doorway, a towel slung around his hips. "Ah, you're awake. Are you sure you'll be okay? Tía will watch Sari if you'd rather not." Already, he was tugging a t-shirt over his head, followed by a heavy sweater. "I feel bad for leaving you on your first day and saddling you with the toddler."

"I'm excited to spend time with Sari."

"She'll nap around eleven, but don't let her sleep past one, or we'll pay for it tonight." He chuckled. "Then you can catch your own nap."

"I might unpack, and make use of those drawers and the closet space you cleared for me." I propped myself on one elbow, smothering a giggle at the sight of the little girl in the middle of the bed, her limbs flung out at all angles. "She even sleeps like a starfish."

"She does have a habit of taking over the bed."

"So, it's okay I gave in, then? She insisted on seeing Daddy."

Jake strapped on his watch and reached for his phone. "Yeah, sometimes she refuses to sleep in her room." Chin tipped down, he eyed me. "If you want the truth, it happens two or three times a week. Even more if I've been away for a few days. Sometimes I don't have the energy for a toddler battle, and she sleeps better with me, anyway."

"Your trips upset the balance here?"

"The first days at home were a bit hellish, can't deny it. Even worse was leaving again." He sat on the edge of the bed and pulled on his socks.

I moved behind him, resting my chin on his shoulder as I wrapped my arms around his chest. "What you're saying is not only did you have a grouchy baby here, but you had one waiting in Vancouver too? Sorry if I made things harder for you."

He turned his head, pressing his cheek against mine. "You couldn't have known. Anyway, I enjoyed our alone time, *Mare*. With you, I feel more like me."

"Back at you," I whispered. "I love you."

"I love you." His lips lingered against mine. "Damn. I have to go. Your house key is on the hook by the door. Call if you need anything, and you have Marisol's number, right?"

"Yes, yes. Go, but be careful."

"Back before you know it." He winked and headed for the door, but hesitated, looking back at me, at his child who he'd now entrusted to my care.

"It's okay. I'll keep her safe."

"Yeah, yeah, of course, but ... doesn't any of this scare you?"

"No? I mean ... what are you ...?"

"Never mind. It's nothing." He dashed across the room, kissing me one last time before he retreated down the hall, the door thunking as he exited the house.

The next morning, Jake let me sleep in as my reward for a job well done.

My sassy *"See? The house is still standing, and your child is still alive"* when he'd returned in the late afternoon had been met with a chuckle, but I wondered what was going through his mind. *Scared.* Should I be frightened? Of what? If only I had the courage to ask him what he'd meant.

This morning after a late breakfast, a certain little someone had taken over our day, which led to this moment, with me sputtering and clawing disintegrated snowball from my freezing lips. "I give." I raised both arms.

"No way." Jake dashed across the yard, catching me around the waist and ducking behind me. "Save me."

Sarina wobbled along behind him, coming to a halt only inches away, bending awkwardly as she gathered loose snow with mittened hands. She screwed up her face and tossed the tiny scoop toward us, bursting into giggles as the breeze blew it back, sprinkling her upturned cheeks with icy crystals.

"Does that tickle? Here, let me help." I wiggled free of Jake's grasp, helping the little girl collect more snow and form it into a soft snowball. "Let's get him." Moving beside her, I steered her forward, making sure she could see me as I spoke and motioned. "Throw it. Get Daddy."

As the snowball tumbled onto his boot, Jake performed a dramatic collapse, hauling me down with him. "Ah, no fair." He groaned as Sari launched herself across his belly. "I'm wounded." His deep laughter rang out as he hugged his little girl.

"Snow angels." I flopped onto my back, spreading like a star, swishing my arms and legs back and forth.

Sari propped herself on Jake's chest, watching me for several seconds before she pushed herself up, then plopped into the snow beside me, copying my moves.

Jake hauled himself to his feet. "Beautiful job, Sari."

She reached out to him, and he grabbed her hands and pulled her straight up, taking a moment to brush away the snow clinging to her toque.

"Time for lunch?" He tapped his fingers to his lips which elicited an emphatic nod from his daughter. Tucking the girl on his hip, he reached for my hand. "I'm glad you're here. After lunch, we'll pack up and go to Tía's."

"We're staying overnight?"

"Yeah, it'll be easier since she's watching Sari tomorrow. Anyway, Tía's excited to see you."

"I can't wait to see her. So, what's on the agenda for tomorrow?"

"Not telling," he said. "Be patient, and all shall be revealed."

Patience. Not my strong suit, but in this case, I was willing to play along.

❦

I left Jake asleep in the double bed, hauling on leggings and Jake's sweatshirt before padding from the guest room into Marisol's kitchen, absorbing the silence. Aside from the addition of a high-end espresso machine, nothing in this homey kitchen had changed. The grey stoneware cups were still in the same place, awaiting the early risers. A matching baking dish sat on the counter, promising the succulent treat of fresh *bollos* spread with the homemade strawberry jam sitting beside them. The oven ticked as it preheated.

I fiddled with the machine, creating a frothy, invigorating latte. Curling my fingers around its warmth, I stared through the frosty window, shivering at the fresh blanket of whiteness covering the yards, streets, and leafless shrubs. The harsh Maritime climate took some getting used to, and this chilly morning made me question my determination to move back.

The dry heat of the corner wood-burning stove drew me into the living room, and I snuggled under one of the wool throw blankets with my novel. Mornings like these were perfect. I hadn't even realized how much I'd missed Marisol's welcoming home until now.

Twenty minutes later, the front door clunked, followed by stomping feet and Marisol's soft tones. Jake's tía appeared in the archway and set Sarina onto her feet. "Sari and I built a snowman in all that fresh white stuff out there."

Extending my arms, I said, "Morning, Sarina. Did you have fun with Tía?" I hugged her tight, enjoying how she snuggled against me for those few moments before wiggling free and heading for her toy box.

"Is my nephew still lazing in bed?"

"Should I wake him?"

Marisol shook her head. "He'll be up soon." She hurried into the kitchen and popped the tray into the oven.

"Can I help?"

"You know how to work that thing?" She pointed at the espresso machine. "Jakob bought it, but I haven't figured it out."

"One latte, coming up."

"Oh, it's so good to have you back." She planted a kiss on my cheek and then pulled a bowl from the cupboard. "It's wonderful you came home for the holidays, sweet girl. I haven't seen you in years. It's too bad Luci couldn't get time off. She's sad to be missing this holiday with us."

What could I do besides nod and smile? If Luci hadn't aired her grievances over my relationship with Jake, it was best left alone, especially given that Jake and I were still in testing mode.

"How is your family? They must miss you."

"They're good." Miss me? Maybe, but only because fewer women slaved in the kitchen. My brother and father would plant themselves in the twin loungers, yelling at uniformed refs and watching skate-wearing men chase a disk of vulcanized rubber around the ice, only rousing themselves when the laden platters hit the table.

"We've missed you terribly. I've noticed the changes in Jake since you've been back in his life. He's unmistakably happier these days."

Sari toddled into the kitchen, holding her arms up to me. I tucked her against my hip, retrieving the bowl of yogurt and banana Marisol had prepared and settling at the table with the girl in my lap.

"Anyway, why shouldn't he find love again? My nephew deserves a strong woman. An equal partner." Marisol jutted her chin toward us. "Someone who loves his daughter. Someone his daughter loves."

"Tía … Did you know about us?"

The woman eyed me. "Dara's mother showed me a snippet of the reception when she visited last month. Remarkable clarity those little phone videos have."

"Don't they just? My mother said the same thing."

"So sweet of Dara to send copies."

"Yes, because I needed my friends and family to have blackmail material on me."

"Oh, my dear. No shame in a passionate lover's kiss. One day you and Jakob can show it to your own children." She clasped her hands to her chest. "Having another baby in the house would be divine, but no rush. Wedding first."

"I'm not sure I'm ready to get married again, or that it's something I need. Anyway, marriage is just signing a piece of paper, accompanied by an expensive party."

Marisol placed her hands on her hips. "Oh, none of that. I raised Jakob right, to take those sacred vows seriously. He will marry again. I'd have it no other way."

Jake shuffled into the kitchen, raking his fingers through damp, tousled hair, stopping to kiss both me and his daughter. "Morning." He pointed at my empty mug. "Can I make you another latte?"

"Thanks, but I should shower and dress."

Marisol's lips twitched into a self-satisfied smile as I transferred Sari into her arms. "You'll never want for anything, sweet girl," she whispered, "not for the important things, anyway. You belong here, with him. The rest will settle into place."

"Can you be ready in thirty, Mar?" Jake asked, seeming oblivious to his tía's machinations. "It's a bit of a drive."

"Absolutely!" I hurried down the hall, excited to learn where he was taking me. Jake's surprises were always fun. His spontaneity was one of the things I liked best about him.

❧

By lunchtime the sky had cleared, the gloomy clouds giving way to weak, mid-winter rays of sun. As I pushed through the door, exiting the charming and slightly rustic dining room of the Sou'Wester, I wrapped my scarf around my neck and tucked the ends into my jacket. My booted feet sent bits of sand and gravel skittering across the pavement as I walked toward Jake, catching a flash of something black disappearing in the depths of his pocket.

He adjusted the bottom of his winter coat as I approached. "Ready?"

"I knew it was risky to leave you alone in the gift shop." I brushed my fingers along his leg, digging for whatever had disappeared into those dark-washed jeans. "Let's see the contraband."

"Ah!" Jake batted away my fingers. "I promised I wouldn't buy any useless crap, and I didn't." Catching my gloved hand, he tugged me across the parking lot toward the narrow boardwalk on the far side. "Let's walk to the point before the sun goes down."

"You're really not going to show me?"

"Later." He chuckled. "Nosey little thing."

Hand in hand, we wound our way through weathered boulders and patches of snow-covered earth toward the white-washed structure perched at the edge of the Atlantic.

"This was a good idea." I peered up at him. "The lobster is every bit as delicious as I remember, and the view is twice as beautiful."

"Yup, and I got my lobster roll all to myself."

"Ha ha, funny guy." I snickered, but scanned the sky, happy none of the scavenging white birds were anywhere in sight.

We stopped near the iconic Peggy's Cove lighthouse, and I stepped forward and lifted my arms, tipping my chin toward the pale blue sky. The chill breeze swept around me, making me feel as if I were about to fly off the edge of the world.

"That's close enough. It's slippery," Jake said, wrapping his arms around me from behind, "and I don't want to lose you to a rogue wave. I only got you back."

"You'll keep me safe." I crossed my hands over his, mesmerized by the flumes spraying high into the air as the ocean beat and churned against the wave-worn rocks only a few feet below. "The power of the ocean always amazes me." As beautiful and captivating as the prismatic colours created by the arcs of water were, I knew better than to venture onto the black rocks.

The weathered plaque posted beside us on the side of the lighthouse issued a stern but much-needed warning: *Injury and death have rewarded careless sight-seers here. The ocean and rocks are treacherous. Savour the sea from a distance.*

"You're as obsessed with the ocean as I am. That's one of my favourite things about you." Jake pressed his clean-shaven cheek to mine. "Some of our best memories happened right in this very spot."

A melty, cozy feeling enveloped me, and we swayed together, a gentle connected motion. *If only every day could feel this blissful, my heart full and content.*

"Soon, we'll stay at that bed and breakfast again. Remember that weekend?"

I bobbed my head. The weekend when we'd stood on these rocks, savouring the breezy summer evening, my heart racing as this man finally said those three magical words I'd been dying to hear. At the time, I'd thought hearing those words could never be sweeter, but I'd been proven wrong.

"That day I realized I'd love you forever." He tightened his grip. "Today feels so right. So perfect."

My mouth grew dry, my head tipping back against his chest as he kissed my temple and shifted, tucking something into my gloved hand.

Angling my head, I looked up at him. "What's this?" I asked as he cupped my fingers in his palm and lifted. "Jake?" Now I stared at more sparkling prisms, these ones coming from the ring nestled in the soft velvet of a black box.

"I love you, *Mare*," he whispered. "Marry me."

CHAPTER 24

My breath caught in my chest, the ocean swirling around me as I stared at the ring, my knees trembling, about to give out and leave me in a quivering heap on the icy rocks. *Holy crap.* The morning's conversation with Tía flitted through my mind. *Did she know he was about to propose? Where in the hell had he found the funds for the magnificent, sparkly rock sitting in my palm?*

I blinked, sucking hard as chill air rasped down my throat, leaving me frozen and unable to utter a single word. *In ... one ... two ...*

Slowly, the disembodied feeling lifted, replaced by the warmth of his arms, the gentle brush of his breath against my cheek, and the thundering beat of his heart. "It's ... wow." I scrunched my eyes closed and reopened them, greeted by blurry glints and flashes.

"Too soon?" he said softly.

"No ..." *Who was I kidding?* "Yes ... maybe?"

"It's okay, *Mare.* I'll never give up on you, because you're the one. You've always been the one, and you forever will be."

Such certainty and tenderness, without a hint of doubt. "No." I turned, resting my palm against his chest. "I mean, yes. Yes."

The smile, hesitant at first, brightened, the adorable dimple in his right cheek showing itself. "Yes? As in ... *the* yes?"

"Yes."

Jake gazed at me steadily, catching the tip of my left glove, tugging until it slid free. "Just a second." Closing his eyes, he exhaled a long breath. "Sorry. Don't want this"—he waggled the box—"to end up in there." He jutted his chin toward the frothing waves. Then he winked, his wicked grin shattering the tension. "Was that a forever yes?"

"It's the forever and ever and ever yes. Hope you can handle it."

"Yeah, I'll manage." He slipped the ring onto my finger, nodding. "What do you think?"

I wiggled my fingers. "It feels weird, but amazing. It's just what I would have picked myself."

The frown was fleeting, morphing immediately into a smile as he leaned in and captured my lips, laying a kiss on me that I wouldn't soon forget. We lingered, kissing and cuddling as the light faded.

"Time to check in," he said, finally.

"Check in?"

"At our B&B. Time to celebrate, without a toddler chaperone." He slung an arm around me and steered me toward the boardwalk.

Now this I could get used to.

❧

The next afternoon, Jake pulled into Dean and Dara's driveway, nosing his SUV in close behind Marisol's silver RAV4. He smiled and lifted our entwined hands, adjusting the sparkly rock on my ring finger.

Sharing a conspiratorial look with the man who, twenty-three hours ago, had become my fiancé, I asked, "Does Dean know about the ring?"

"Sure, but I swore him to secrecy. I love Dara, but that woman blabs."

I burst out laughing. "That's what I said about Dean."

Jake chuckled. "I feel bad, making them keep secrets from each other. Maybe we should stop doing that, since it's probably not good for their marriage." He hit the hatch release. "Head in, I need something from the back. Just hold her off until I'm there to see how long it takes her to spot it."

"Not long, I assure you." I stepped onto the driveway, which was rapidly disappearing under a blanket of white.

Dean bounded through the front door as I reached the bottom of the steps. "I've shovelled twice, but it looks like I need to go in for round three." He held out a hand, steadying me as I negotiated the slippery concrete stairs.

"Thanks. Jake will be right in."

He kissed my cheek and slipped by, heading toward my fiancé. "Hey, man. Glad you got back safe."

I stamped the snow from my boots, brushed down my coat, then stepped inside, immediately assailed by those wonderful smells of the holidays; fresh baking, cinnamon, and the tangy sweetness of Marisol's homemade apple cider.

A little head peek around the corner, and an adorable toddler charged toward me, pursued by Dara.

"Darling, let Amara get in the door." Dara scooped Sari up and peppered her rosy cheeks with kisses. "I'm so glad you made it back. They're calling for several centimetres this afternoon." She grimaced. "My parents are flying in from Toronto tomorrow morning."

"It's really coming down, so I hope their flight is on time." I took Sari, hugging and kissing the squirming toddler. "Were you good for Auntie Dara?"

The girl nodded, and the moment I set her on her feet, she ran straight for the family room, the clatter of blocks following seconds later.

"Talk about a bundle of energy. Where's the off switch?" Dara reached for me. "You're positively glowing," she whispered. "Is it from being in love, or from being loved up? Either way, you look fantastic."

"So do you." I followed her to the kitchen, keeping the diamond hidden in my palm.

Marisol bustled toward me. "Thank goodness, I worried about you two. Did you have fun?"

"The bed and breakfast was fantastic. Better than I remembered." I wrapped the petite dark-haired woman in a warm embrace. "Thank you for watching Sari overnight."

"I love that little monkey to death." Tía patted my cheek. "Oh, the pies!" She hurried into the kitchen as Dean appeared.

Jake entered moments later, with a bag that looked suspiciously like the ones from the Sou'Wester gift shop tucked at his side. He grinned as his daughter launched herself at him, motioning furiously. "I missed you too, Starfish."

"Jakob." I wagged a finger. "I thought you said—"

"That I didn't buy any crap." He pulled out a sturdy wooden ship and gave it to Sari. "I couldn't resist. It looks like my research vessel, and it's locally made."

"Oh!" Dara's gasp made me turn. "The baby kicked. Feel this." She grabbed my hand and guided it to the left. "Wait for it … there!"

A little lump travelled under my hand, and I followed it until it disappeared. "That's neat, but freaky." Cupping both palms over her belly, I leaned close and said, "I can't wait to meet you, baby."

"What's that?" Dara stared at me.

"What?" I straightened as she turned my left hand.

"Ohhhh." Her eyes widened as she examined the ring. "It's gorgeous. You're engaged?" She fanned her face, blinking furiously before bursting into tears. "You're getting married."

"Awww, Bunny, don't cry." Dean cuddled his wife against his chest. "Damn hormones," he mouthed over her head, then winked at me. "About damn time."

Marisol beamed at me, but soon turned her sparkling eyes toward her nephew. "That's wonderful. Jakob, have you phoned your sister? Amara, your parents must be thrilled. When is the wedding? Oh! We should have the ceremony at Saint Mary's."

My heart raced as I stood in the middle of the room, practically wilting under the weight of the attention. Already it started, less than a day after I'd said yes, and my muscles tensed, ready to vault me into rapid flight.

"Tía, relax." Jake motioned downward with flattened palms. "Everybody calm down. Dates, venues … that can wait. Let us catch our breath."

I hurtled across the room, flinging open the door and rushing into the snow in my socks. Hunched over the railing, I sucked for air, swallowing hard. *In … one … two …*

The door behind me thunked, and Jake draped a blanket over my shoulders, then crouched and worked my feet into

Dara's fleece-lined leather slippers. "Better?" He wrapped an arm around me, drawing me close.

"Just tired. It was stuffy in there. And hot. Wasn't it hot?"

"More overwhelming, but close enough." His gentle kiss to my temple almost brought me to tears. "Is this rushing?"

"No," I said, examining the delicate beadwork on the toes of the slippers, "but being engaged feels strange. Marrying again is pure craziness. My relationships have all ended in disaster."

"It'll be different this time. Life may not be glamorous, with few jet-setting holidays, but we'll be happy." He ran his thumb over my ring. "I wish I could give you more."

"Are you kidding? It's gorgeous. Perfect." I wrapped my fingers around his. Just looking at this lovely ring filled me with a happy glow. "You know me, Jake. This," I wiggled my fingers, "proves just how well. Someone was paying attention."

"Well, all those bridal magazines with the dog-eared pages, and those markings in the jewellery catalogues worked."

"That was years ago." I laughed, but still, it was impressive that he remembered. "Dara and I sure obsessed over the big white wedding with the perfect dress, didn't we?"

"Oh, yeah." He chuckled. "Current issues of those magazines popped up again when Dean and Dara got engaged. I'm prepared for my fate. Bring it on."

"I guess, since we can't disappoint Tía or my mother. You saw the way she lit up last night during the video chat."

"What can I say? Your mother loves me."

"She likes you more than she likes me. Anyway, she's probably planning the guest list. What do you want to bet she's already checked availability at the top five venues in Toronto?"

"Wait. Isn't the big white wedding the ultimate dream?"

I shook my head. "Stupid, right? Dara's wedding was amazing, but it was over the top."

"Glad it wasn't just me thinking that. Dean complained about their wedding turning into a runaway train. He and Dara fought constantly and spent way too much money to make their families happy." His lips set in a grim line. "They almost didn't make it to the altar."

"I'm glad they did. They're happy, aren't they?"

"Deliriously. And we'll join them." He held up his fist. "United front. We do it our way."

Curling my fingers tight, I bumped them against his. "When we tell my mother there's no Palais Royal, sweetheart necklines, or oodles of tulle, expect tears and tantrums."

"Yeah, I can picture her rolling on the floor kicking and screaming, but this isn't about her. It's about us building our life together."

"I love you." Stretching on tiptoes, I entwined my fingers in his hair, kissing him long and hard. "I want more of this, but my socks are now icicles."

"Can't have that." Jake scooped me up and lugged me across the patio, fumbling one handed with the door before stepping inside the cozy house. He set me on my feet and rubbed my arms.

Across the room, the low conversation between our friends faded, and Dean looked up from dicing potatoes, pausing with the knife poised above the cutting board. He smirked and opened his mouth, but Dara shook her head at her husband. The man tucked his chin down, the blade picking up its steady *tap-tap-tap* against the cutting board.

Dara slid from her stool and headed my way with a pair of socks. "You must be frozen."

"My toes are." I folded the throw and hung it over the back of the sofa, accepting the soft wool socks and peeling off my soggy ones.

"Marisol's hiding upstairs, worried she created issues," she said in a low voice. "Everything okay?"

"Yeah," Jake said. "I'll check on her." He strode to the stairs and loped up them two at a time.

"It's good, right?" Dara's brows lifted.

"We're terrific. Don't worry." I squeezed her hand and headed to open the large box beside the sofa with Jake's distinctive scrawl across the top, and add our gifts to the growing pile. The small rectangular package for Sari with its colourful sea creatures and silver curling ribbon made me smile, thought I tucked it deep beneath three other elaborately wrapped parcels.

Dara sidled up beside me. "No question who that's for, but why are you hiding it?"

"He'll ask me what it is if he sees it."

She kneeled beside me, pretending to adjust the tree lights. "What is it? I won't tell him."

"I know." I fiddled with the ornaments. "It's expensive, and I don't want him to be upset with me."

She sat back, staring up at the twinkling lights. "You'll be Sari's stepmother, so maybe he won't mind."

"I hope he doesn't." I glanced at Dean, who still seemed immersed in dinner prep. "It's a tablet with a gift card, so we can buy games for Sari."

"That's thoughtful. You'll be the best step mommy ever." Dara straightened my ring. "That's two carats of fabulous, that is."

I turned my hand, admiring the prism of colour. "I almost fainted. He's worried it's not enough, when I'm thinking he spent way too much. It's gorgeous and perfect, like it came straight out of that display case. Remember the day we tried on rings? This one is so similar to the one I loved, it's eerie."

My friend scrunched her nose, nibbling at her lip as she sneaked a look at me.

"What? You don't remember?"

"I remember," she said softly. "You know, that's the exact ring you tried that day, right?"

"Impossible!" I giggled. "That was years ago. Anyway, that ring was phenomenally expensive, way more than a university student could …" My eyes widened. My friend wasn't smiling. In fact, she didn't look the least bit amused. "No. He didn't. Did he?"

"Jake saw the brochure and bought the ring on layaway."

I closed my eyes, remembering how I'd looped a big red heart around the picture, tucking the incriminating evidence inside a bridal magazine and cramming the works into the back of my desk drawer.

"The tips from the extra shifts he worked at the restaurant and the fees from those weekend kayak tours paid for that lovely diamond on your finger."

I cupped my hands over my face, so many questions crowding in. "Jake kept it all this time?"

"He hoped you'd be back, like all the other times you two blew up at each other, but you dropped off the map. Then he heard you'd married some rich dude in Vancouver. That wasn't pretty."

"It sure wasn't," I muttered, though I knew Dara was referring to the fallout Jake endured because of me. Now I'd come full circle, drawn back into the fold, finally realizing that while I'd been gone, everything had changed. "And Alysa?"

"Alysa was cute and fun, and I liked her most of the time, but I often questioned why she stayed. She knew his heart was never hers, but they got in too deep, and then Sari happened. Jake refused to abandon them, to his own detriment, even though he never stopped loving you."

"I'm trying to deserve him," I said in a low voice. "Dar? I'm sorry I wasn't here for you. Were things rough during the wedding planning?"

"Nah, it wasn't so bad."

I raised my brows.

My friend shook her head and looked away.

"Please? Talk to me."

"I'm not sure you want to hear it," she muttered, before she glanced over her shoulder at Dean, who was still busy in the kitchen.

"Okay, Bunny?" he asked.

"Just wondering where Jake and Marisol were."

"Upstairs. Need something?"

"No, it's all good." She turned to me and lowered her voice. "Okay, here's the real deal. It sucked. You should have been my maid of honour, you should have been by my side picking flowers, tasting cake, and trying on wedding gowns. Viv was amazing, and I love her, but she's not you. I'm still hurt and angry, but I'm doing my best to forgive you, because I love you, you big jerk." She grabbed a throw pillow and, holding it in both hands, bopped me on the head, sucked in a long breath, then bopped me again. "That's for Luci. The poor girl cried for a solid week. You left a swath of destruction a thousand miles wide."

I sat there, stunned and barely able to draw air. "I'm sorry," I whispered, finally. "You're right, I'm a big, stupid jerk, and I'm sorry."

"Why?" She sniffled. "How could you just walk away from everything? From us? We were more like family than your actual family!"

I wrapped my arms tight to my body, wagging my head. "I got scared. Then I got in my head and panicked. That last fight with Jake gave me justification to cut and run, and I regret it. I'm sorry for hurting you and everyone else."

"You always did overthink everything." Dara reached out and rubbed my back. "I'm glad you came to our wedding."

"I was surprised you invited me. Was that a test?"

Dara shrugged. "Maybe, yeah, I guess so. I figured if you actually came, I'd try to forgive you, and if you didn't, I'd put it to rest and accept the loss. So you did, and you were as sweet as I remembered, so I pushed for you to visit, and you came. It was like we'd never been apart, and I knew right then what I wanted. You're like my sister. I love you, and even though you did something stupid and hurtful, underneath I know you love me too. Through this whole thing with you and Jake, I've been terrified, trying desperately to make you see it without pushing too hard."

Tilting my head her way, I asked, "See what?"

"That he'd forgive you for everything and do anything to make you happy. Whatever happens next, you absolutely can't freak and run. These next months will challenge your relationship, and you have to stick with him, as if you've already said those vows. Weddings are wonderful, but they're also a pile of stress. Promise me, whatever issues come up, you'll stay and work it out."

"I promise." Kneeling, I threw my arms around her. "I love you, Dar."

"I love you too, jerk." She sniffled. "Finally, I have my bestie back, and even better, you'll be here for the birth of our baby."

"You couldn't drag me away." I released her and lay back, staring at the silver ornament slowly spinning above one of the lights. "Your bestie is thrilled to be home."

Dara tucked the throw pillow behind her head and worked into a half-reclining position beside me, rubbing her belly in tiny circles. "Close your eyes."

"Why?"

"Just do it. You owe me, so no questions."

"Fair point." Closing my eyes, I took a long cleansing breath and relaxed.

"Picture one of your favourite memories of Halifax. Preferably something recent."

I cracked one eye open, only to be met by Dara's huff and wagging finger.

"Did I say to open your eyes? No?"

My lips twitched. "This is hard. There are so many great memories from this trip alone."

"Excellent. You shouldn't have any trouble, then."

"Mmmm." I sank into the pillow, images flowing through my mind. Jake and Sari meeting me at the airport. Our snowball fight in the back yard. Sari, her captivating smile and sweet bedtime hugs. I concentrated harder, imagining the little girl's proud attempt at signing my name, and Jake's deep, joyful laugh at his daughter's antics at the park, and then his intimate whispers, meant only for me. *I love you, Mare.*

"Ah, you've got one. I see it in your smile," Dara murmured, squeezing my hand. "Whatever happens, the love and joy you feel right now is why you'll always stay and try harder. You'll never leave us again. This is home."

❨

Four hours later, the house was a hive of activity.

"Can I help?" I hovered near the island.

"No. We've got this." Jake topped up my glass of wine and handed a fruity spritzer to Dara. "You have your assignments."

"Stay out of the way?" I laughed.

"Well, that, but you have the crucial task of keeping order while we clean the kitchen." Dean grinned. "Dara's task is to put her feet up and stay hydrated."

Dara inspected the pies sitting on the cooling racks. "Tía's amazing. These smell divine."

"Oh, watch out, or those will disappear before we get any," Dean said in a light tone.

"Don't judge." Dara squinted at her husband. "This"—she pointed to her bump—"is your doing. It leads to constant cravings and hunger."

"Easy, easy." Dean rounded the island and sank to his knees in front of his wife, laying his head against her. "Tell Mommy not to be mad at Daddy, 'cause he loves you both, so much." He slid her shirt up and planted a resounding kiss on her bare belly.

I sneaked a look at the couple, then at Jake, but he seemed intent on finding something in the fridge. "Geez, Dar, when will we eat all of this?"

She tugged her husband to his feet. "Go help Jake. Maybe stow the pies in the extra fridge if you're worried about me snarfing them down before tomorrow."

"I'm kidding, Bunny, but I'm serious about you getting off your feet. Amara?"

I snapped a salute, then guided my friend toward the living room. "Put your feet up, and then we can decide which presents we'll open tonight."

"Oh." She rubbed her hands together. "My favourite custom. Sari should open the one from you."

"Maybe not. It's been such a great day. Look at him."

We both looked toward the kitchen where Jake and Dean were playing Tetris to get the leftovers into the fridge.

Jake caught my eye and winked before handing Dean the next container.

"Yeah, exactly. What better time than after several glasses of wine, a delicious dinner, and a night full of mind-blowing engagement sex. Mm-mm, the wattage on that smile says someone is sa-tis-fied."

"Dara!" I bobbed my head toward Marisol, who was only a few feet away helping Sari colour a picture.

"Oh, please. She'll tell you to hurry it up and make that sibling for Sari."

Damn, damn. I pasted on a smile, wondering how I'd make it through the next few months. At some point, the truth would sneak out. I wasn't sure if that would make it better or worse.

I patted Dara's belly. "We'll let her enjoy this bundle of joy first."

My friend glowed, her rosy cheeks and radiant smile making me want to laugh and cry all at the same time. "Not for long, though. My little bundle needs a playmate," she said.

Marisol looked over, her excitement plain to see. Already, she'd be dreaming it was me with the big belly and Jake as the doting husband who couldn't keep his hands off it. The constant prodding and encouragement to have kids would test my limits, of that I had no doubt.

"Yay." Dara clapped her hands as Dean dropped onto the couch beside her, drink in hand. "Time for our Christmas Eve gift. Amara? Why don't you start?"

❦

During the drive home later that night, Jake seemed pensive, drumming idly on the wheel, sending occasional glances my way.

"Sorry for the end run on Sari's gift. I shouldn't have given it without your agreement. I overstepped."

Jake lifted my hand, transferring it to his knee. "Except she freakin' loves it, and those games are amazing. So thank you, but"—he looked my way—"next time, let's discuss expensive gifts first."

The tires crunched across the fresh snow as Jake pulled up in front of his house. He peered over the seat at Sari, her mouth moving slightly as she slept. "Hope she doesn't wake up."

"I'll get the bag and the door, you get her. If we're quick, she'll sleep through it."

He nodded and slid out of the car, moving to unbuckle Sari.

I gathered her bag and pulled out my key as I hurried toward the house. This had started to feel so domestic, our little family coming together seamlessly as we exercised our teamwork.

Jake followed me through the door, toddler draped over his shoulder as he kicked off his boots and headed down the hall.

Immediately, I turned the lock and shed my boots, snagging her stuffed bunny from the bag, tiptoeing down the hall and into her room.

"I wonder what she's dreaming about," I whispered, placing her bunny beside her. "Snowball fights? Tía's apple pie? Cuddling with Daddy while he reads stories?"

"I'd bet it's about the hugs and love from her family." Jake moved behind me, wrapping his arms around my waist. "I have something else I want for Christmas."

"Your gifts are under the tree."

"There's one you could still give, but it's a big one." His embrace tightened. "I want you to adopt Sari. Be her mom."

"Really?" My heart felt even fuller, if that could even be possible.

Jake pulled me from the room, turning me toward him. "Before you answer, take some time to think about it."

"Why would I need to think about it? I'll be her stepmom, fully involved in her life. Adoption isn't much different."

Jake shook his head. "It's entirely different, and with the in-law's family dynamics, it might be a total shit show. You'll be front line in the war zone."

"Surely it won't be that bad."

"Don't count on it. The ring alone will set off fireworks. They'll be taking Sari tomorrow afternoon, and I want to introduce you. Are you ready for that?"

I nodded. Really, how bad could it be? They'd have to accept his decision to move on, and they couldn't prevent me from adopting Sari if it was what Jake wanted. Though I hadn't considered adoption as an option, instinctively I knew this would be good for all of us, giving both Jake and Sari some much-needed security.

CHAPTER 25

His words were prophetic as my ring set off fireworks, but not with the parties he imagined.

Just after seven, Jake set his laptop on the coffee table and answered Luci's video call, holding Sari on his lap while I hovered out of camera range.

"Hi, Sari!" Luci signed smoothly as she spoke, pausing while her niece signed back. "Precious girl, you're so big. Wow, and your signs are so good. Tía Luci has been taking lessons, just like you."

"The improvement's noticeable, right?" Jake grinned as Sari wiggled from his lap and beelined for the tablet sitting on the end table.

"It's incredible. You absolutely have to bring her to Vancouver. I miss you guys."

"I wish you were here." Jake blew a kiss to his sister. "Did you talk to Tía?"

"She's my next call. You're going to Dean's today? I heard the amazing news about Dara."

Sari headed my way, waving her new gadget.

I crouched and helped her open one of the games we'd downloaded the night before.

"What's that noise?" Luci asked as Sari tapped at the screen, eliciting sounds from her game. "Did you guys open a gift last night?"

Jake nodded. "Sari got a tablet with some educational games."

"Fancy. Who's that from? Auntie Dara, perhaps?"

"No, Amara bought it for her."

"Why would she buy that for Sari? Is she in Halifax?"

"She's moving back in January."

"Why? She's already messed up your life. You should send the thing back."

I kept my head down, focussing on the bright colours on Sari's screen.

"Luci—"

"Stay away from her, Jake. She's poison. I can't watch you go through that again."

"I appreciate your concern, but you're wrong." Jake looked at me, then back at the screen, his lips set in a firm line. "She's here, and she wants to talk to you." He beckoned to me.

I gnawed my lip, shaking my head at Jake.

"Like … she's there, in your house, listening to our conversation? Are you for real?"

"It's totally real. We're getting married."

"Wait. You and her? Have you lost your mind?" Her tone dropped. "No. I won't. Not after what she did."

Jake bowed his head, fingers steepled against his forehead.

"She hung up on you?"

"Yup. Don't worry. She'll calm down."

"She hates me," I whispered. "I thought she was okay, you know? During the wedding, and after the Sari thing in Vancouver, she acted like she wanted us together, but then it all fell apart."

"She's confused, but she loves you." He pulled me in for a hug. "She gets like this when her feelings are hurt. Give it time, and she'll be okay."

"Will she? It seems that Luci's hidden her anger at me for what happened when I left."

"It was tough on her. You were the big sister she never had, and she was rather pissed at me too. Eventually, she got on with it and forgave me. She's hurt, but beneath all of that, she loves you and she'll forgive you. Don't give up."

"How do I make it up to her?"

"Just be there. Be open when she's ready to talk." Jake kissed my temple. "You have a big heart, *Mare*, and she'll see that with you, I'm happy. Don't worry, I'll call her tomorrow, and we'll sort it out. Trust me, she'll be at our wedding."

Around and around I went, my past choices circling back to bite me when I least expected. As I clung to this man I loved, I sent out a new wish to the universe. *Please, please make it all okay.* Now that I was here, I never wanted to leave.

❡

At least when we arrived at our friend's house an hour later, I received a warm welcome, though Dara's shimmery eyes spoke of disappointment.

"What's wrong?" I asked as we exchanged hugs.

"My parents' flight was cancelled. They're hanging at Pearson, hoping to catch the next one."

"It's okay, Bunny," Dean said, cuddling his wife. "If they don't make it today, they'll be here tomorrow. It's supposed to clear up by then."

With Dean's encouragement, Dara headed to the table and we all gathered for our family breakfast.

Jake nudged me. "Should we tell them? You know, the thing from last night?"

I nodded. "They should know."

Dara perked up. "Big news? Oh!" She slapped a hand over her mouth. "Are you pregnant? You are, right?"

"No. You really have baby on the brain, Dar." Jake cocked his head, looking at Dara then at me, then around the table. "I asked Amara to adopt Sari. We'll start the proceedings in January."

"That's big," Dean said. "It's a fantastic idea. You'll be an amazing Mommy to Baby Starfish."

Marisol patted my hand. "Sari needs both of you. It's wonderful seeing you with her, sweet girl."

"Well, I approve, but you two need to board the baby train." Dara bit into a slice of toast slathered with strawberry jam, examining both Jake and I with bright eyes, her head bobbing.

I bowed my head, intent on cutting into my frittata, but picturing the acute disappointment all around when Jake and I failed to provide the expected baby. One day soon, that conversation would be needed, though I dreaded the day.

At eleven-thirty, the doorbell rang, and Jake rose, taking the tablet from his daughter and setting it aside. "Come on, Sari. Nana and Papa are here."

This moment was expected, but still, I clenched my hands in my lap, nervous it had arrived so soon.

Jake tucked Sari on his hip and held out his hand. "Ready?"

I rubbed my thighs then reached for him, taking comfort in his warm grip as we walked down the hall.

Jake's reassuring smile eased my nerves a little as he opened the door, letting in a blast of winter. "Come in out of the snow."

"There she is." The tall grey-haired man stepped inside, waving a massive hand at his granddaughter, followed closely by a woman with silver hair who could only be Alysa's mother. The woman had the same crystal eyes and petite frame.

"Hi, Sarina." Unlike her husband, Stella didn't wave or smile, but focussed on me, her brows rising.

"Ben, Stella, this is Amara Grant." Jake wrapped an arm around my waist.

"Amara? Unusual name." The woman's eyes narrowed, but she seemed to catch herself, a tight smile appearing. "It's nice to finally meet you."

"You too." I swallowed hard, fidgeting with my ring as I looked at Jake.

"Well, we should go. We'll drop Sari tomorrow afternoon, Jakob. You'll be home?" Stella reached for Sari, but the little girl turned away, burying her head against her daddy's chest.

"Yeah, we'll be there." Jake kissed his daughter, then set her on her feet, crouching to her level. "You have fun with Nana and Papa, and I'll see you tomorrow, okay? Can you give hugs?"

Sari nodded, but she screwed up her face as she latched onto Jake.

"Aww, thank you. One for Mar?"

I held out my arms, cuddling the little girl and rubbing her back before I tucked her stuffed bunny into her arms. "I love you," I said, signing along as I spoke. "See you tomorrow, okay?"

Ben smiled as I stood, but Stella tilted her head, staring at my left hand as I waved at Sari.

"What is that?" She pointed. "Is that …?"

"Yes, it's an engagement ring." Jake's arm slid around my waist again. "Amara is my fiancée."

Stella stepped back, that look becoming steelier, her lips pursing, arms crossing, and lip curling. "It's so soon. This is not a good idea. Not at all." She scooped Sari into her arms and turned to Jake. "We'll discuss this later, Jakob."

"Stella! It's none of your business." Ben extended his hand. "Congratulations. It's good to see you happy, Jake. Best wishes, my dear." He smiled at me and took the overnight bag Jake held out to him. "Time to head home and let Sari open her presents from Nana and Papa." The man shooed his wife into the blustery afternoon, her hysterical tone carrying into the house until Jake closed the door.

"Well, that went as well as could be expected," Jake said.

"She detested me at first sight. Finally? What was that about?"

"Oh, I don't doubt that Alysa had things to say to her mother. She found a bunch of pictures of us, and she knew we'd lived together. Don't worry about it."

"She plans to make my life hell. I can feel it."

"Ben will rein her in. I'll reassure them that they're always welcome to see their granddaughter, and in the end, that's what matters."

"You seem so certain of everything."

"Just taking things one step at a time."

Yes. One step at a time. Any more than that, and I might freak out, and that absolutely could not happen. Forgiveness was already proving harder to obtain than I ever imagined. Asking for it again would be impossible.

The next morning, Jake sat on the bench by his front door, tying his running shoes. "Are you sure you don't want to come?"

"No." I yawned and stretched. "I'm exhausted. Next time, though."

"Let's go for lunch later." A hopeful smile appeared. "Sari won't be back until mid-afternoon."

"I'll shower." I kissed him and patted his butt. "Enjoy your run."

"Back soon." The picture hanging over the bench rattled as the door closed behind him.

I closed my eyes, savouring the quiet after the bustle of the holiday, relishing the peaceful feeling of being alone in his home. *Our home.* No doubt I'd land here when I moved, if Jake had his way.

This place only had two bedrooms, and barely a thousand square feet of space. As cute as this cozy one story was, I already longed for the open spaces of my condo. That, however, was a discussion for another time. I wouldn't push to uproot Sari if it wasn't necessary, especially during this time of adjustment.

After a long hot shower, I dressed in leggings and a sweatshirt, ready to get to work. Armed with a second coffee, I set out to make this place feel like my home too.

I carried the box of gifts I'd received yesterday into the living room and unwrapped the silver frame—a gift from Dean and Dara—filled with a picture of our new family in front of the fireplace. I positioned it on the mantel beside the picture of Jake with tiny newborn Sari cupped in one hand, moving the more recent Jake and Sari picture to the side table.

The rest of the items I contemplated, then placed the electronic photo frame on the table by the front door, smiling as the pictures appeared. This sweet gift from Marisol contained many of the same pictures that were on the frame tucked inside my own bedside table in Vancouver, with the addition of several taken at Dean and Dara's wedding, along with the ones taken during my last two trips to Halifax.

I tucked the gift certificate for the family photo shoot into my wallet, and then unwrapped the two additions to my stoneware tea set, which was still carefully wrapped and tucked inside my carry-on bag.

Perhaps it was time to unpack it. Bringing it this trip had been an act of hope, or maybe it was a good luck charm for our relationship. Either way, it belonged in my new kitchen.

I'd taken three steps toward the bedroom when someone knocked on the door. "Forgot his keys, I bet." I headed toward the entrance.

The somebody on the other side pounded on the door. "Hang on!" I fumbled with the lock and swung the door open. "You're awfully impat—" My eyes widened.

Stella loomed in the doorway, holding a squirming Sarina.

The red-eyed, tearful girl struggled, pushing against her Nana's chest, little runnels of snot hanging under her nose.

As I reached for Sari, Stella reared back a full step, wrestling with her armful of wriggling toddler. "Where's Jakob?"

"He went for a run. You're early."

Sarina fluttered her feet, motioning wildly.

"Oof, child. Stop kicking me." The woman set her granddaughter free.

Sari scuttled forward, flinging her arms around my calf, leaving a shining trail of mucous across my leggings as she peered at me.

"Aww, Sari. It's okay." Lifting her, I settled her against my shoulder, rubbing the sniffling girl's back in tiny circles. "You can set her bag right there." I jutted my chin toward the bench. "Thanks for dropping her."

Stella stared at the photo frame on the entryway table, then she swivelled her head toward the mantel. "Making yourself right at home, I see. I know who you are." She wagged a finger in my face. "You ruined his marriage."

Gritting my teeth, I said, "Whatever you think, you're wrong."

Stella flung out her arm, waving at the room. "Everything single picture of my daughter is gone. He's erased her, like she never existed," she said, pursing her lips, "and you're the replacement."

I straightened and lifted my chin. "I'm truly sorry for your loss, Stella, but whatever problems they had, it wasn't my fault. Besides, you should want him to find a little happiness after what he's endured. For Sari to have a proper family."

The woman stared at me. "Didn't take you long to move in on him. Well, I wish you luck. He cheated on her, and he'll do the same to you. Once a cheater, always a cheater."

Nausea hit me, my knees trembling.

"That's why she did it, you know. He cheated, and she was devastated. My baby's gone because of him." A fat tear trickled down her cheek. "Now he's taking our granddaughter away. It's only a matter of time."

The doorknob rattled, and Jake entered. "Stella. I thought you were bringing Sari home later this afternoon?" He looked at me, then at the grim-faced woman. "What's going on?"

"I'm telling your fiancée what you have in store for her. Don't think I'll give up my granddaughter easily, Jakob, or that I'll stop making her life better." Stella tugged some glossy brochures from the purse slung over her shoulder and dropped them on the table. "I'll fight you every step of the way."

"Fight what?" He crossed his arms. "Sarina being who she is? Me being happy? Your daughter checked out, Stella. She checked out of our marriage, she checked out of motherhood, and then she checked out of her own life. Like it or not, Sari's my daughter, and you have no right to tell me how to live my life."

"Jake." I touched his arm as Stella looked away, her brows pinched together so tightly it made my heart ache for her. "Please. Don't."

"Just telling it like it is. I'm exhausted by this same fight, over and over." He scrubbed his hands across his face. "Nothing will bring her back. Nothing."

"You won't even consider fixing Sarina's hearing, and you want to cut us out of her life. It's happening, already. You'll let Sari forget her own mother."

"Seriously?" Jake threw his hands up. "I've never refused your visits to Sarina. Not even once. Not even when she comes home in such a state that it takes me hours to settle her down. Make a fucking effort, accept her as she is. Learn to communicate with your granddaughter instead of spouting endless crap."

"My doctor said—"

"That hack knows nothing."

"But the group I'm in—"

"What? The Cochlear Implant advocacy group? Excuse me if I prefer the advice of professionals who deal with deaf children every day, not those vigilantes who can't accept their babies and grandkids. Besides, that's an irreversible procedure, and Sari deserves to have a say, so it'll wait until she's older."

"I love Sarina, and she deserves to hear." Stella sniffled.

Jake's eyes narrowed, but he stood firm, shaking his head. "Implants are not happening."

Stella dabbed her eyes, her mouth twisting. "Alysa's pictures. They're all gone, and Sarina will never know her mother."

"And whose choice was that?"

"It's your fault." The woman drew a shaky breath. "I won't let my granddaughter forget her."

"I promise," Jake said, his voice growing softer, "Sari will know about the woman who gave birth to her, but I have to make space for Amara too." He put his arm around me and his daughter. "Please, let me have this bit of happiness."

Stella glared at us. "I expect to see my granddaughter, and we'll just see about the rest of it." The door slammed behind her.

"Sorry," Jake kissed the top of my head. "You have to deal with grouchy in-laws, and they aren't even yours."

"She's sad." I hugged Sari tighter. "I can't even imagine. The death of a child is the most devastating of losses. I hope I never experience that sort of pain."

CHAPTER 26

I carried a sleepy Sari to her room, the little girl now calm and sucking her thumb.

"Guess lunch is off. Should have known. Stella texted earlier, asking if I was home." Jake took Sari from me and tucked her into her bed. "I told her I was out running. Nice little ambush there, getting you alone."

I shrugged as I headed toward the living room, the joy of sorting my gifts long vanished. This last episode with his ex-mother-in-law told me he hadn't been kidding about the war zone, guerrilla tactics and all. As much as I felt for the woman given her loss, her methods seemed practiced and manipulative.

"What did she say?" Jake asked. "What do I have in store for you?"

I clamped my teeth onto my lower lip, biting hard. It was something I didn't want to believe. I wanted her to be lying.

"Mar? What did she say?"

I sank onto the sofa, staring at the ring on my finger. "She said you cheated on your wife." When I looked up, I wish I hadn't, because then I couldn't deny the truth.

Jake bowed his head, the telltale crease appearing in his forehead. "Yeah, it's true."

I pushed up from the sofa, half-way to the door before I managed to speak. "I need that run."

"Mar, wait. Let me explain."

My vision blurred as I yanked on my running shoes.

"It wasn't a good time, and I made a huge mistake."

I lunged through the door, leaving it ajar as I charged down the front walk, only catching two garbled words from Jake:

"… coat … warning."

Too late. Now at a full run, I dodged slush piles and icy puddles, unable to stop. *Damn. Damn.* Dara knew. She knew, and she hadn't told me, and if she knew, so did Dean. Maybe everyone did. *"Whatever happens next, you can't freak and run."* Did the thing that "happens next" include finding out the man you loved had infidelity as one of his human qualities?

The icy wind stung my cheeks and blew my hair into my eyes as I raced down the street, lengthening my stride at the sight of the trailhead.

Sure, I'd made my fair share of mistakes, but cheating had never been one of them, ill-advised drunk texts aside. *How could he? Why had he? Would he do that to me?* I wanted to stop thinking and just run, to crank up my music. No such luck, with my earbuds and phone sitting on Jake's bedside table.

Finally, the burn of my throat and the fire in my lungs slowed me down, and a cramp lanced my gut. I stumbled toward the bench at the path's edge, supporting myself against the back, my mouth watering as the bitterness of caffeine rose and I regurgitated my breakfast, leaving an oozy brownish mess in the pristine snowscape.

I sucked for air, my vision blurring as I vomited a second time, my legs sinking out from under me as the stark reality hit. The Jake I'd loved would never have broken his vows. *So, who was this Jake; the man existing here and now?* Barely avoiding a mushy landing in the steaming puddle of sick, I planted my bum on the greying weathered bench and scooted across the cold wood to the far end. Shaking, I bent double, then tucked my feet onto the seat and curled my arms around my shins, the light snow settling on my shoulders.

Everyone shamelessly pushed us together, eager to make us a couple once again, even though they knew what he'd done. Was it a trick?

My head swam, scalding tears streaming down my cheeks, releasing the pent-up frustrations of the past forty-eight hours. Inconveniently, along with the lows of the last few days, the highs also made themselves known. Jake's sweet proposal seemed full of promise and hope for our future, his adoption request setting our relationship on all-ahead-full.

It was me who'd said it would be different for us, but would it? I didn't have a clue, but my next decision was the definitive one. Stella's revelation left me in the unenviable position of choosing my future path. Stay? Or hightail it back to Vancouver?

Lifting my chin and absorbing the hush descending on the city, I let the fat flakes floating from the darkening skies settle on my cheeks. Maybe a sign would drift from above and soothe my painful, lingering doubts. I looked left, then right, not truly expecting anyone to appear and impart wisdom. The residents of Halifax had long retreated indoors in anticipation of the coming storm, prepared to huddle in front of roaring fires while flurries blanketed the streets in flawless white.

My bare fingers ached, and I tucked them under my armpits, wishing I'd grabbed my gloves. The breathable mesh of my running shoes had done nothing to protect my feet, leaving my cotton socks damp and my toes frigid. I shivered. Time to force myself up to slog home before hypothermia set in. Maybe it already had. I couldn't make myself move.

An apparition emerged out of the thickening snowfall, morphing into a dark figure, which turned into a man. "Thought I'd never find you." Jake brushed at my sweatshirt and draped his jacket around my shoulders, crouching as he buttoned it with my arms curled inside. "I worried when you didn't answer your phone. There's a blizzard warning."

"I forgot it." I soaked up the remnants of the body heat clinging to his jacket's soft inner lining. "How *did* you find me?"

"This is our old running trail, so I figured it was worth a try." A crease appeared in his forehead as he examined my shoes. "You're soaked." He removed my footwear and my soggy socks, balling them up and tucking them inside my runners. As he lifted my feet and spun me, he sat, cradling my bare toes in his lap and curling over them to remove his boots, methodically transferring his wool socks onto my freezing feet. "Better?"

The circulation was returning to my numb appendages, the burn making me wince as he covered my feet with the bottom of his heavy sweater.

"Sorry, it was stupid to take off like that. Thanks for rescuing me."

"I'm happy you're okay." He pulled out his phone. "Dean went in the opposite direction to search, and Dar's watching Sari," he said, tapping at the screen. "Let me update them, and we'll head home."

I stared at my runners. Squelching down the path all the way to Jake's wouldn't be much fun. "You didn't drive at least part of the way, did you?"

"I wish," he said, "but we figured it would be easier to find you on foot." As he knocked the snow out of my shoes and tied the laces together, he said, "Get ready for piggyback."

"It's a long way to carry me. I'll walk."

"Nah, hop on, and keep those socks dry."

After wiggling my arms into the jacket's sleeves, I stood on the tiny dry spot where I'd been sitting, wrapping my arms over his shoulders and curling my legs around his waist.

Jake hooked his hands under my thighs. "Ready?" He set off at a steady jog.

My faint footprints had been obliterated, the ones Jake had left on his way to me quickly fading under the onslaught of driving snow. The wind whistled through the trees, making me grateful my hands were tucked inside the long sleeves. I pressed my face against his back.

Jake remained silent until we reached the trailhead, then he slowed as we started up the city street, re-adjusting his grip on my legs. "Can we talk about it?" he asked as we trudged toward home.

I brushed my thumb against my ring, gripping him tighter, unable to speak.

"Let's stop for a second." Jake ducked into one of the glass bus shelters along our route, turning so I could stand on the metal seat inside. He faced me, steadying me with his arm looped around my waist. "I'm sorry. I regret it, but I can't change it."

I sucked for air. "How could you let me find out like that? Did you think I never would?"

"One can always hope. Anyway, it's not about us. Why let it affect our relationship?"

"How can it not affect us? It's a breach of trust, you portioning out the bits of your life you want me to know and hiding the rest."

"Yeah, because if I'd told you every detail of my shitty life, you'd have given us a chance? You took off the minute things got real."

"No, I gave myself space. I can't afford to make a rash decision fuelled by hurt and anger, but you assumed the running part."

We stared at each other, that deep crease appearing in his forehead, yet again.

"Why? How did it happen?"

"Why?" He brushed my hair back from my face with a gloved hand. "Dealing with her black moods? Feeling shut out? Loneliness? A million reasons. There were days when I could barely cope. Days when I felt excluded from my own life." He rested his forehead against my chest. "You don't want to hear the gory details."

"Make me understand," I said softy. "I need the entire truth."

Jake's shaky breath tore at my heart. "When Alysa told me she was pregnant, she was practically delirious with excitement, but over time it changed. She got moody."

"Hormones?"

He shrugged. "Maybe, but it was far beyond the normal mood swings. You see how it is with Dean and Dar?"

"Yeah." I smiled, picturing our friends with their constant kissing and cuddling. "They're so cute."

"Yeah, and I'm happy for them." He sighed. "It was never like that for me. She pushed me away. No kissing, no cuddling, no affection. I was there, right up to the moment Sari was born, yet it felt like I missed it all, until I was alone in the NICU with our daughter." He finally looked at me. "Sometimes it's an endless circle in my head, wondering if it was her depression or my cheating that put her over the edge. I'll never know."

"No, Jake. Depression is insidious and difficult to treat, so stop blaming yourself. That'll eat you alive."

"Easy to say, but I fucked up our relationship, then I fucked up my marriage, and now I'm fucking this up with you for the millionth time." Jake slid up the long sleeve covering my left hand, gripping my fingers as he kissed my engagement ring. "It will never happen again, *Mare*. Never with you. Please, please forgive me."

This. This was our pivotal moment. This moment would define our future and our ability to fight for what mattered. Jake had his flaws, but his beautiful soul, and his devotion to those he loved, shone through it all. I closed my eyes, balancing the good and the bad with the dark and the light of my beautiful, imperfect man, letting our happy memories take over.

"Are you leaving me?" he asked.

Leaning in, I cupped his face. "Well, that option sucks. No way to make that work."

A faint smile appeared. "You're choosing option one?"

"Yeah. I forgive you, as you've forgiven me. Time to move on and lay the past to rest." I stroked his cheek with my thumb, knowing to the depths of my being that Jake had already paid too high of a price for each and every mistake. Nothing would be gained from punishing him for eternity, which would double as punishing myself. "Anything else I need to know before we plan our wedding?"

"No, that's the worst of me." He drew me in and kissed me, deep and slow.

"I love you," I whispered against his lips.

No question I loved this man enough to try and try again, his caring and tenderness making me crave him for a lifetime. It was all within reach. All I had to do was stay.

As I settled into my seat for our flight to Vancouver, I took another look out the window, ready to wave goodbye to Halifax, even if only for a short time.

Jake buckled Sari into the seat between us. "No tears," he said, signing along for his daughter's benefit. "We'll be back in a few days."

Sari tipped her head toward me, tapping the thumb of her open hand to her chin and frowning.

I blinked harder. Jake had spent the last few days telling his daughter to call me Mommy and teaching her the proper sign. "These are happy tears," I said, my hands in motion. "Are you excited to see Tía Luci?"

The girl nodded, then pointed to her tiny backpack.

"Two guesses what she wants." Jake handed the bag to her, grinning as Sari pulled out her tablet.

Sari started her game, giggling at the cheeky cartoon characters as she chased them around the screen with tiny fingers.

Jake relaxed into the seat, looking at me over his daughter's head. "Things are going pretty well, huh? New Year's Eve was fun."

"It was amazing." As Sari patted my hand, I peered at the onscreen action and said, "Life will be even better once I sort things out with your sister."

"Don't worry. She was calmer last time we spoke." He drummed his fingers on the armrest. "It's amazing the way you're supporting Dara through her pregnancy. She even wants you in the delivery room."

"She's my best friend. It's exciting, and Dean is all cute and sappy."

"Dara's positively radiant, and the way she looks at Dean … they're closer than ever."

"It's not just about having a baby, though. They fit, one of those annoying couples—"

"Who finish each other's sentences." He reached over his daughter, trailing his fingertips over my cheek. "Maybe we should have a baby."

I whipped my head around, unsure I'd heard him correctly. "What?"

"Not right away, but after the wedding. What do you think?"

"You were so certain about not having another kid."

"What if I've changed my mind? I see that look in your eyes when you're with Dara."

That look? My acting skills needed polishing. I'd done my best to keep my longing well hidden, but of course, Jake had seen it.

"I hate seeing your disappointment and sadness," he said, lowering his voice. "Making you happy is everything, and a family is what you want more than anything. You crave it like oxygen."

"Are you sure it's what you want?"

"Completely. Besides, what kind of selfish ass denies the woman he loves the thing she wants most?"

"Well, when you put it that way …" I linked our fingers. "What made you change your mind?"

"You. I'm not afraid of the future now that you're in it," he said as the plane bumped across the tarmac and turned to the runway, engines revving. "I can picture how it would be, and suddenly, I know our family wouldn't be complete without at least one more child."

Our eyes locked as the jet sped forward, the force planting me firmly in my seat.

"No regrets, *Mare*. Are you ready?"

I smiled. "I am."

We were lifting off, soaring, cutting through the dark clouds to the blue sky far above. Whatever happened next, we would be together, creating our future, surrounded by our closest friends and family. I couldn't wait.

CONTINUE READING WITH LUCIANA'S STORY:
Before You Me & Us, ON SALE SPRING 2021

THANK YOU FOR READING

Thank you for reading. If you enjoyed this book, please consider leaving a review on the retailer where you purchased this ebook, on Goodreads, Bookbub, or recommending this novel to your friends and family. Authors depend on word of mouth and reviews to spread the word on their writing, which allows them to continue bringing you new stories to enjoy.

I always love to hear from readers. I can be contacted at: katesmithauthor.ca

Sign up for my newsletter and hear about new releases, playlists, author interviews, and books I have recently enjoyed.

Follow me on social media:

instagram.com/katesmithauthor/
twitter.com/KateSmithAuthor/
facebook.com/katesmithauthor/
bookbub.co/books/between-you-me-and-us-by-kate-smith